PRAISE FOR THE EVERVERSE

"Harn's entertaining debut uses super powers as a metaphor to delve into class politics in an alternate America."

PUBLISHER'S WEEKLY

"If you want a gritty approach to super heroes with a literary twist that still levels buildings, has aliens, and government conspiracies, don't sleep on this."

WAYNE SANTOS, AUTHOR OF **THE CHIMERA CODE**

"Gorgeous literary writing, sweeping themes about how capitalist gain has replaced empathy in American society, and Darby's usual amazing dialogue."

SUNYI DEAN, AUTHOR OF **THE BOOK EATERS**

"This was a fascinating, fast-paced, yet lyrical read about what commercialized super heroism might look like. Loved it and highly recommend!"

SHELLY CAMPBELL, AUTHOR OF **UNDER THE LESSER MOON**

"★★★★★ - *Ever The Hero* is highly recommended for fans of LGBTQ+ fiction, superhero genre readers and sci-fi fans alike."

"*Ever the Hero* gives you complex social class commentary that grapples with the nasty visuals of some superhero stories, and even some ideas about the real-world implications of superpowers that feel like the next logical step after *Watchmen*."

JOSH MAUTHE, *UMNEY'S ALLEY*

"Superheroes and an alien threat within a dystopian society - all these individually, and seemingly endlessly, fascinating things are combined in Darby Harn's *Ever the Hero*."

MAKING GOOD STORIES

"*Ever The Hero* is an absolute must-read for anyone who is even remotely interested in superheroes, and if this genre is to continue to grow in the literary world, books like this are a big reason why."

J.D. CUNEGAN, AUTHOR OF ***THE JILL ANDERSON MYSTERIES***

"Lyrical, evocative prose! Raw, emotional dialogue! Delicate and personal, but also has epic action and huge concepts."

ESSA HANSEN, AUTHOR OF ***NOPHEK GLOSS***

IN BETWEEN

STORIES OF

THE EVERVERSE

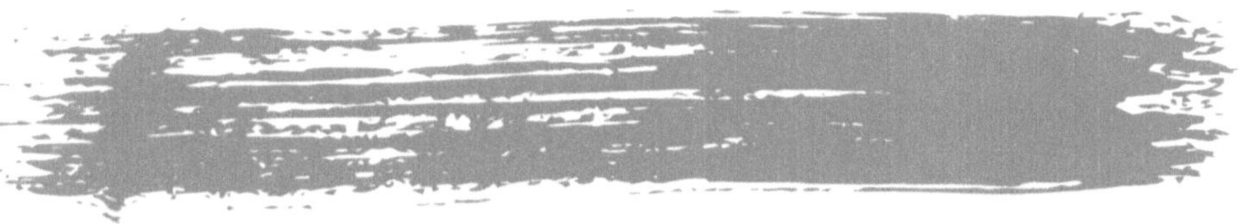

DARBY HARN

FAIR
PLAY
BOOKS

In Between: Stories of the Eververse

Library of Congress Control Number: 2022901139

ISBN: 978-1-7370097-4-0

Fair Play Books

www.darbyharn.com

Eververse covers and interior art by Al Hess.

www.alhessauthor.com

Printed in the U.S.A.

EVERVERSE TIMELINE

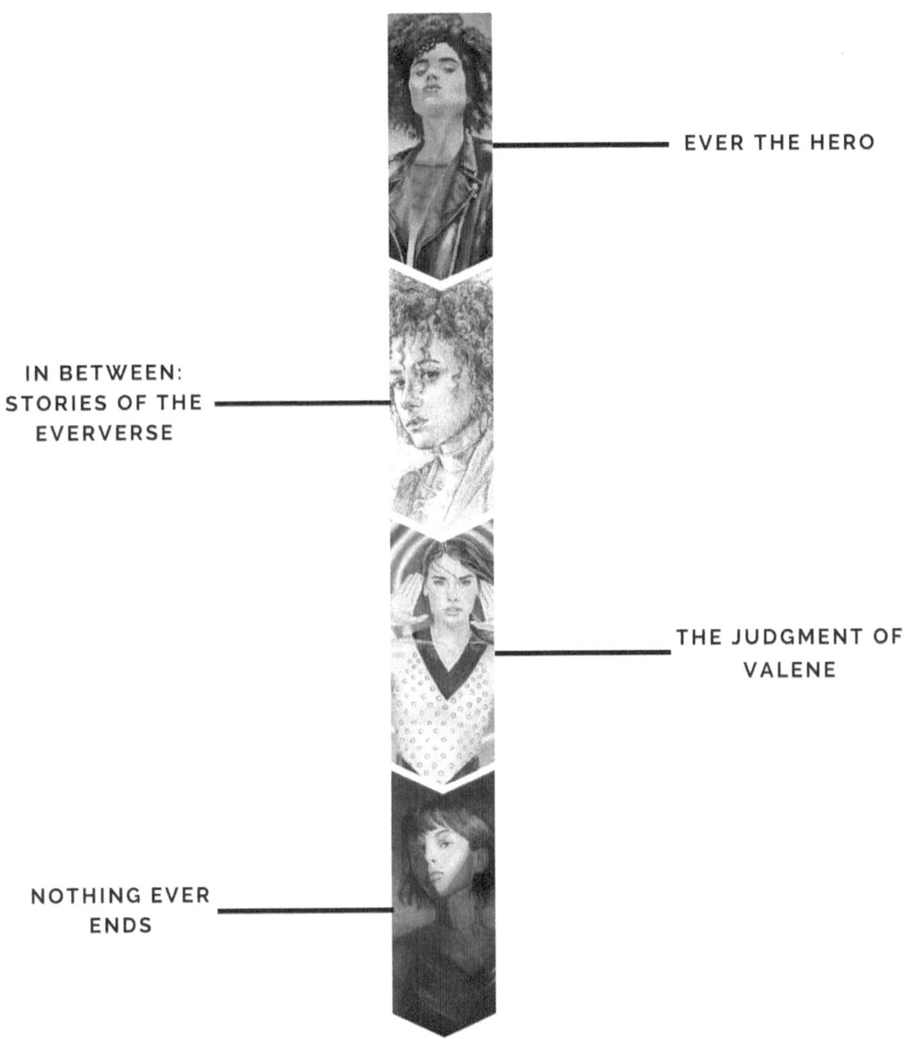

When you wear the mask, the mask becomes you.

– QIU XIAOLONG

For Sunyi
who said I am, and you are.

CONTENTS

FIFTY YEARS AFTER AN ALIEN SHIP CRASHED IN BREAK POINTE, THE ONLY PROTECTION IN A STRANGE NEW WORLD IS GREAT POWER, A CORPORATION OF SUPERHUMANS.

IF YOU CAN AFFORD THEM.

MOST PEOPLE CAN'T. ENTER KIT BALDWIN, A YOUNG WOMAN WHO HELPS PEOPLE TO HELP PEOPLE. EXCEPT HER POWER IS THE ALIEN'S POWER, AND SHE MAY BE MORE OF A DANGER THAN SHE IS A HELP.

POST CREDITS SCENE

POST-CREDITS SCENE

"Bring my girlfriend back to life," the old man says.

Since I got my powers, I get all kinds of strange requests. A fair number of them are curiously sexual, but mostly, people ask me to do some good in the world. Catch asteroids. Cure cancer, end hunger, please and thank you. You know.

Little things.

This one might go up on the fridge. Bring his girlfriend back to life? He could do with some help himself. Seventy, maybe. Liver spots. A rattle in his chest like a bad engine. Still, he got up here on the roof. He knew it was me, warming my feet with the other birds.

Sometimes, I don't know when I'm me.

I flutter my wings, and the other pigeons scatter out of our peace. The old man's jaw goes rubber as I step off the ledge, arms winnowing out of electric feathers, my body a sculpture in glass that hasn't cooled yet.

Also, I'm naked.

I pick up my leather jacket off the roof and pull it on. I'm still getting used to this myself. It's only been a few months. Every day feels like the universe strained through me. My body is still my body, but it's also the sky at dusk, poured into a coin jar. My hair is still a cloud of curls, but it's also a nebula. My heart isn't my heart, though. It's a lightning bolt, cast in garnet.

The Myriad isn't exactly a piece of technology; it isn't exactly biological, either. The Ever exists somewhere between, and somewhere beyond the limits of human conception. So do I now, ever since I fused with it. Everything I am, The Ever is.

I am Ever.

"I'm sorry," I say. "I don't think I can help you."

Magenta light crackles in his eyes. "You can become other people, though. Other things. The bird."

"I can only become what I've..." Oh, no.

He hands me a black and white picture of a teenage girl. Bouffant hair. Plaid dress. Textbook smile. "Betty. She died back in 1968. The alien zapped her, or whatever. You did."

I didn't. That's probably semantics at this point.

Everyone The Ever 'zapped' when it crashed here in 1968 resides within the crystalline object in my chest. Kind of. Anything stored in the electrical universe of Betty's mind when The Ever acquired her will be in there. A file. A recording. A snapshot.

I close my eyes. Betty crawls under her desk. Others run. Scream. She peeks through her fingers. Like staring into the sun. Eighty thousand people died before that star went dark. Fifty years later, I picked it out of the rubble of my city.

Keeping things consistent with me, I didn't get zapped. Exactly. I got stuck in the filter. I got strained, but I'm not clean coming out. Neither is The Ever. We're both stuck in each other.

This is the first time a person who lost somebody to the alien – to me – us, I guess – has come around. What do I tell him? What can I do to ever make up for all I've done?

This isn't you.

I hand him back the picture. "I'm sorry."

"Don't be sorry. Be my girlfriend."

"Sorry. I'm taken."

His laugh gets through. "Who drew that straw?"

Abi steps out onto the roof, the cold breeze off the lake eroding her nightshirt. "Is everything ok? Who's this?"

"You remember me, don't you?" The old man says to me. "Charlie? You and your mom used to come into the flea market. Boy, if it was shiny or made noise, you picked it up."

"You followed me around the store."

Charlie goes so red he almost matches this stoplight in my heart. "Sorry to hear about your mom. A real broad."

I bite my lip. When I'm the bird, I don't think about anything. I don't think about Ma, or the fact I can never touch Abi, or that I'm only pretending to be something. Someone.

"I'm sorry," I say. "I wish I could, but..."

His mouth hangs, like his words are too heavy. "You're a piggy bank, aren't you? You put a '68 Betty Drenner in there and now I'd like you to take her out. Please."

"Only the original has value. Anything I'd take out of this jar, it's not going to be authentic."

He sucks in a deep breath. "Then why do you sit up here and pretend to be something you're not?"

Used to be when things got too difficult, I just got on my bike. Rode around the ruins. Dug through the scattered pieces of this city and tried to make something of them. Stopped being Kit for as long as I could. Who was I while I was outrunning my shadows?

Is she the one who went home?

Charlie opens his hands. "I know it won't be her, not really. But I just need to see her. I have cancer. My throat."

"I'm sorry," I say again, for the good it will do.

"Help an old man find some peace, will you?"

Cats in trees. Burglars. Burning buildings. I can sort all that. Peace. I don't know peace is in my portfolio.

"I'll think about it," I say.

The television screen goes dark. The credits roll. I throw up my hands. "That's it? It's over?"

Abi mows down popcorn. "No, there's a scene at the end."

"At the end?"

She sets the bowl between us on the couch. I keep my hands to myself. "The post-credits scene. It's like set up for the next movie. Or maybe a movie years from now."

"I don't even know what's going on in this one, really."

Abi plants her elbow on the back of the couch and rests her head in her hand. "So... what are you thinking about Charlie?"

Everything. Nothing. I try and sort out the signal. Nothing comes out right. I bite my lip. Before this happened to me, I always felt like I was trapped in someone else's body. I would talk, but it was someone else's words. I'd move, but it was someone else's movements. I'd laugh, but it was a laugh track, off cue and uncanny.

Now, I'm trapped inside a universe of others.

"I don't know," I say.

Abi tugs at her shirt. "Is there a difference? Like, between you becoming the bird and a person?"

I've become other people as The Ever. All their memories, the comfort of their lives lived to the moment the alien acquired them rests like a record inside the cabinet in my chest. A little snap, a little crackle maybe, but the rhythm is always sure.

The melody flows eternal.

It wasn't strange, because I've been doing it all my life. I never knew how to talk or act or what to do with my hands so I repeated what worked for other people. Ma. Dad. Girls at school who floated through life on invisible clouds of grace.

"I become the bird because it forces me to be me," I say. "When I'm someone else, I'm just someone else. I get lost. I get suppressed. The bird... I know I'm the bird. Those wings start to flap and I'm free, but I'm scared. So I go back. I have to go back."

Abi brushes my shoulder, like there's dust on my jacket or something. There isn't, but she has a habit of touching me for no reason. "Do you want to go back?"

"Go back?"

"To your old life," Abi says.

Before this, I was like anyone else here. Existing only in the margins. Forgotten. Forsaken. All I wanted was to find a job across the river. An apartment, but with all the new ones going up over there, the rents are as cosmic as I am. One day, I found something I thought would get me out of this town.

Instead, I got handed the keys.

"I can never go back," I say.

"But do you want to, though?"

My hesitation answers for me. I'd give anything to go back to that daily frustration. The daily fear nothing would ever change. At least then, I thought it could.

Abi traces the rumpled creases in my leather jacket. Cold, hard shell. I just feel the pressure, like a dentist pushing and pulling inside your mouth, numb.

"I was never comfortable being me," I say. "I don't mean... you're probably like, wouldn't it be easier? Being a pretty white girl like Betty Drenner. I never wanted to be white. Or straight. Or even a girl sometimes. I'm not saying growing up I didn't feel like I wanted straight hair or bigger boobs or whatever. People made me feel that way. I didn't feel that way. I like my body."

"There's a lot to like."

"I'm talking about... in my head. Just me, I guess. I always reflected everyone around me. I didn't make sense but other people did, so I would just be other people, and now... I have this power. I can make myself fit. I can put on a mask and no one would know."

"Why don't you? Wear a mask and stuff? A costume?"

"I'm always wearing a mask," I say.

Abi's hand slides across my jacket. Tendrils worm beneath my skin, desperate to unearth flame. Abi and I can never touch. Abi and I can never make love. But she makes me human.

"I understand," she says.

"But I don't understand, Abi."

"I mean, I know what it's like... to feel like you have to wear a mask." Leather scrunches between her fingers. "But we don't have to wear masks with each other, Kit. I know you."

I bite my lip. What do I say. I never know what to say.

Abi lets me off the hook. "Might be money in it, though."

"Money?"

"I mean, you don't want to start like being dead people for everyone in town. That could get crazy. But shrinks make baller money, dude. And all they do is sit there for an hour and listen while you say what you can't to your mom. You can actually be their mom."

The screen brightens, as the movie starts again.

"It'd be nice," I say and grab another bit of popcorn, even though I don't need to eat anymore. "To talk to them."

"What would you say? To your mom?"

What would I say? *Ma*. Words pile up. Before she died, I never said anything. I left. I ran out the clock on her fits and when I came back I did my best to act like it didn't happen, or it wouldn't again. She died, and I became a ghost.

Haunted.

"I'm trying," I say. "That's what I would say."

Abi tugs on my zipper. Our lips magnets. There's as much fun in keeping them apart as there would be putting them together. Deny it all you want, that force exists.

That potential.

"You'll figure it out," she says. "How to kiss me."

The popcorn is Styrofoam in my hand. Nothing feels the same as it did before. "Abi, I know this isn't easy..."

She holds her mouth open. "Hit me."

I toss a kernel at her but it bounces off her nose. That's not enough for her. Never is. She scoops a handful of clouds in her hand and tries to catch them on her tongue. All the popcorn ends up on the floor, with the both of us, laughing. We miss the scene after, or whatever it is, so we don't know what the set-up for later is.

———

I go over to Charlie's apartment on Eisner.

Old brownstone. Smoke-stained pictures of Jesus on the wall. TV a decade or two out of date. China cabinet full of novelty glasses from theme parks you see at the thrift store. I expect everything to have a scab of tape stuck to the bottom of it, and a price, written in ink.

"Charlie," I say, staying close to the door, "I gave this a lot of thought. If it was a matter of really bringing Betty back, I wouldn't hesitate. But she's gone. She'd be an echo. That wouldn't be fair to either of you. Or me. I should be fair."

Being a cosmically powered alien is a bit like being one of those self-checkouts. People complain if you're not available, even as they complain about you putting them out of a job. Not sure where Charlie lands. Mostly, he looks like he's in a hurry.

He claws at his chest. "Can I show you something?"

"Sure..."

He takes an old flip phone out of his pocket. A sigh clatters out of him as he thumbs through the buttons. "Sorry, I'm still figuring this thing out."

"It's fine."

"The nephew sends me pictures, but I don't know how to get to the pictures. Here we go. Ok. Do you see that?"

In the little square screen of the phone, there's a picture of Abi, bound and gagged. A gun to her head. This power I have. With a thought, I can become an infinite number of things. Another person. A bird. An alien, torching the world with fire.

I bite my lip. "What are you doing?"

He closes the phone and tucks it back in his pocket. "Abi seems like a nice kid. Sweet. My nephew, he's got a temper. It don't take much to wind him up and get him going, I'll tell you."

You're a cold fish, Ma would say. It's not that I don't get upset. All my upset never surfaces. It's better that way. I zip down my jacket a bit so he gets a good look at the crystal flickering inside my chest like the sun behind fast winter clouds. Visual aids.

Super helpful.

Charlie nods. "Anything happens to me, she dies."

Light surges through me so strong I feel it. The cold, swift current of a river. "I'm not playing house with you."

"Isn't that what you're doing with her?"

I squeeze the zipper on my jacket. "Excuse me?"

"You can't touch Abi right? You can't touch anybody. You pretend to be other things, I suppose because you can never connect with anyone. Is that about the size of it?"

All my life, I've been practicing for this evasion of my humanity. When Ma was alive, I blocked it all out, because I couldn't deal with it. With Abi, my condition creates this margin between us I can never close. Really, all it does is let me off the hook.

"You can't touch Betty," I say.

"I just want to talk to her. One last time."

I let go of the zipper. "I told you. It won't be her."

He coughs into his hand. "Let me talk to her. Let me see her, and I promise, nothing happens to Abi."

"If anything does..."

A sad smile wrinkles his lips. "You'd be doing me a mercy."

All my effort goes into restraining my anger, propellant for this hunger gnawing at me all the time. Acquire. Possess. Focus. Don't think. Don't feel. Don't fear. Get through this.

Get Abi back.

This isn't like changing clothes. It's more like trying to find a very specific penny in a jar full of them. I sit on Charlie's cardboard-colored couch, trying to sift through the grains of sand in the hourglass within me. Turn me over. Time's running out. Abi. No. Focus. Betty. 1968. Plaid dress. Charlie stares at me from his recliner, scratching his chest and he always did that, even when we were kids.

He was anxious, all the time. I never thought too much about him, not really. But then senior year, I don't know. He's different.

So am I.

Charlie coughs through his gasp. "Betty?"

My reflection bends in the screen of his TV. Funny. I look like my mother. A 60s American version of her at least. I move, but it's not me moving. I talk, but it's not me talking.

My voice isn't my voice. "You got old, Charlie."

His jaw hangs. "You... you're exactly as I remember..."

Not exactly. "You haven't changed."

The recliner creaks. Charlie does. "Yeah, well. Guess no one does. I got so much I want to say. But there's really just one thing I need to know, Betty. Where's the money?"

Wait.

"What?"

He clears his throat. "The money I gave you. In the red Duffel bag. I asked you to keep it for a bit. Remember?"

Betty's thoughts stampede mine. Prom night. Charlie is late. He's always late. He finds me outside the gymnasium, smoking with Carol and he's not in his tux. Grease on his face. Bag in his hand.

He drags me back to the car and says *They might come looking for me, so you got to hold this for us.*

"You robbed the bank," I say.

"You were leaving me," he says, throwing his arms up. "College. I told you, if you stayed, I'd get a job, but..."

I try to push Betty off the mic but her words just tumble out. "I wasn't staying here, Charlie."

"You wanted to be with somebody else."

"I wanted to be someone else."

I'm someone else. Betty feels like a jacket I've put on. The fit is ok, but the style isn't me. I try to take her off. She's hard coming off my shoulders. The material sticks.

I flicker in the mirror. I don't change the channel.

Charlie sucks in a breath. "Where'd you put the bag, Betty?"

"This is what you brought me back for, Charlie? Money?"

He scratches his chest. "Just tell me."

"I thought you wanted peace."

"And now I'll have it." He coughs so hard and violent I think he'll rattle apart. "Ah. God. Tell me, will you?"

"What are you going to spend it on? Cigarettes?"

"You were always a funny gal, Betty."

"Let Abi go. I'll tell you."

Abi. Focus.

"We had a deal," he says.

I unzip my jacket. A little tight, but comfortable. Betty is sure. Poised. I can't move but she moves so free and easy and I'm a better passenger than a driver.

Charlie taps the phone in his shirt pocket. "If I call my nephew..."

I snag his cigarettes off of the end table. That's what I need. Something in my hands. "Did you miss me, Charlie? Or just the money?"

He sighs out a line of shopping carts. "You. I missed you, Betty."

"Where were you, that morning? You weren't at school."

Charlie scratches his chest. "I was laying low, at Jimmy's house."

"Jimmy Regan... you'd do anything for him."

"I tried to get back, Betty. I tried, believe me."

"Do you know what I was thinking about when I died?"

"No. Jesus. No, I don't."

"I was thinking how I should have took the money and ran."

"At least one of us can," Charlie says.

I take a long drag. "One of us."

I put the cigarette out on the cushion of the sofa. Ugly thing goes up like the brown bag paper it looks like.

"Hey – what are you doing?"

Fire races up the plywood panel track of the wall. I grab the cigarettes and head for the door. Charlie staggers after me, coughing in the thick, black smoke that doesn't faze me. I don't have lungs, anymore. I don't even have a heart.

"What are you..."

Charlie coughs. Smoke alarms go off. All that cheap glass blackens in the china cabinet. I open the door.

This isn't you.

You're not a coldblooded killer. Go back into the brownstone. Pull Charlie out. He coughs on the stoop while you go back in. Fire streams into the palms of your hands, through your arms, into your burning heart. Heat flashes through you, like it did that day in school; there and gone and I think she's gone. I'm me again.

Kit.

Definitely won't be including resurrections on the list of heroic deeds going forward. At least around anything flammable.

Jesus, Betty.

I'll stick to being the bird, I think, even if it's just circling the roof. Less friction. Everything meets where it should. Water. Land. Sky. Human. Alien. Not a perfect fit, though. Like shoes a size too small. They fit, but there's that rub on your heel. That pinch in your toe. You walk through it. I like this power. This hunger. This light in me, like a hand over a flashlight, up late reading in my bed the books of all the places I'd go in the world when I finally had my wings.

Charlie coughs. "Betty..."

I fix my hair in the mirror. Mom wanted me to get this cut. Bouffant. Just like her. With a thought, my hair straightens, lengthens, into a waterfall shimmering with the sun. Natural.

Fifty years.

I don't understand. Doesn't matter. I'm not staying. Now's my chance to get out of here, for good. The past two summers, I worked as a lifeguard at the Mantlo Park swimming pool. Mantlo Park closed forever in the spring of '68. The pool only another crater in the wasteland. I hid the Duffel bag in my locker in the main office. Tommy gave me a key he made on the side in '67, so we could go in any time we wanted. I can go now. Thirty grand. It's all still here.

Charlie. You did it. You got me out of here.

At the convenience store across from the bus depot, I fill a basket with popcorn. Chocolate Bacon potato chips. A million flavors of pop now. Which do I get? Mom always said it would make my teeth rot.

I wonder if she's still alive.

The door slams shut behind someone in a hurry. Abi appears at the end of the aisle, her wavy auburn hair a mess. "What happened? Why are you still Betty? Why are you hot?"

I want to leap out of my skin. I want to scream with joy. I want to dive into Abi and never surface and never draw another breath and I can't move. I can't speak. I can't do anything but rattle inside Betty as she gears up for her escape from Break Pointe.

I tuck my hair behind my ear. "I thought you were..."

"The nephew nodded off."

"He fell asleep?"

"Things were moving too fast for him. Are you going somewhere? Ooh, I like those chocolate ones. But are you going somewhere? I feel like you're going somewhere."

I thought I was only breaking one heart today. "How did you even find me, Abi?"

She points to the pigeons flapping through the store behind me. "You're sort of easy to find. So. You're hitting the road?"

I look down at my basket. "I thought I would."

"Betty, I'd like my girlfriend back."

I laugh. "That's what everybody says."

"Right now, please."

"Girlfriend is a broad interpretation, don't you think?"

"I'm not here for your basic 1960s morality, dude. I'm here for

Kit. You got your little post-credits scene. You got what no one ever gets, so give her back. This was about Charlie, not you."

"It's never about me."

Her nose wrinkles. "Well. I figure being a woman back in the day wasn't a blast and stuff, but it's not exactly female empowerment to appropriate another woman's life."

I smile. "It's not real what you two have."

"You're not real."

"Is she?"

Abi isn't so quick this time. "I know you're in there, Kit."

Abi. I'm right here.

Betty talks over me. "She doesn't know. She says she does. But deep down... I was the perfect daughter. The perfect girlfriend. I put on my face and went out and performed and Kit always feels like she's performing. She's always on and it's exhausting."

Abi's eyes swell with tears. "She's always on, Betty. The Ever hasn't gotten rid of her. And you won't either."

I throw a pack of double dark chocolate cupcakes in the basket. Betty does. I can't tell anymore.

"So, what's your power, Abi?"

A smile warps her tears. "I'm persistent."

Somehow, I know that's true. "I just want to live."

"I'll follow you. Wherever. It will be *so* awkward."

I glance at the cashier, leaning over the counter to get a look at us fighting. "This isn't?"

She takes the cupcakes out of my basket. "See you at the bus station, Betty."

After she checks out, I stand there a long time, staring at the infinite variety of snacks. I'm starving. I have no appetite. I want, but there's only one thing I want. I ask the clerk where the payphone is.

"Uh." He hands me my sack. "Is it an emergency?"

"You could say it is," I say.

"As long it's local," he says and hands me a cell.

I can't move, but Betty doesn't move. I can't talk, but Betty doesn't talk. Talk. Just like riding a bike. Numbers. Dial. Say something. Is the number the same? Would she still be at the house? *Search phone numbers for Mabel Drenner.* Only one comes back. Local. Is this her?

Call This Number?

What would you say, if you had your mother on the line? Would it even be her, with all this living between then and now? Is this even you? Touch the screen. Everything meets where it should. Glass. Plastic. Human. Dial the number. The phone rings. A woman answers. Old. Weak. Far away, but she's somewhere in town, somewhere in you, rattling around like that cough of Charlie's.

"Hello?" she says.

Speak. Tell her what you would have told her, had you the wisdom, the grace, the perspective you do now. Explain your extraordinary circumstances. Ask her to believe any of it.

"Ma."

Her voice recedes and comes back. "Who is this?"

"You're the one who should be free."

Hang up. Spare yourself. Her. Give the phone back to the clerk, confused as you can possibly get in a city of aliens and leave the store. Across the street, the bus pulls into the depot. Chicago. Rockford. Connects to all points east. Go on.

Make your connection.

Wings flap in a huff as Abi sits on the edge of the roof beside me. Birds flutter back to a landing, never straying far from their spot. More or less, that's what I did with my day back in life. What good are wings if you always come back to your perch?

I toss the last of my popcorn to the pigeons. I'm moving now. I'm speaking. Betty only a mask I wear. A costume.

"I wanted to be free," I say. "To fly away from here."

"You remembered who you were. You came back."

"You help me, Abi. You help me be me."

Abi tugs at her shirt. "Same here."

Birds look at me, hopeful. "I'll never do this again."

"Never say never."

"I want to be me. I want to use my voice."

"I'm still hearing Betty..."

Betty grabs the mic. "I just want to see the sunset."

Abi eases back to the roof. "You earned it."

"I don't want to be alone," I say.

She slings the bag over her shoulder. "You're not."

Pigeons whoop and squeak into brief flight as the door closes. What's left of the day flattens into rouge. Just like that, the sun is gone, beneath the horizon and all that's left is the afterglow. Minutes. Seconds. That's all I have left.

Thank you for this.

Night takes over watch of the city. The only light this star in my chest. Light radiates through my body, my arms, in molten lines of liquid glass. Fingers stretch to feathers. Shoulders broaden to wings. Consciousness collapses to consciousness and I fly on the recoil, free.

BLOOD
BACK

ONE

THE SKY BRUISES OVER THE DERELICTS. I DIDN'T KNOW WHAT to expect when I started defending the city a few months ago, but I figured full moons would mean less criminal activity.

So far, my most effective superpower is being wrong.

The thief runs through the wreck of the alien ship. I hold my position, hovering in the night. Used to be I put on a big light show and scared the daylights out of them soon as they snuck in through the breached hull. That got old.

Now, I let the ship do the work for me. A gauntlet of maroon shards scarps the strange cave of the ship. Bird bones crunch under his boots, hard as rocks. Never a good idea to run here. A gasp caroms around the gutted candle of the interior as he trips and plunges head-first into a narrow crevice of specious crystal.

Lucky for him, it's not that deep.

The thief crawls his way out. The object he risked so much to steal – a gleaming coil from the ship's exposed circuitry – teeters on the edge. Blood leeches off the cut on his hand and spirals into the same magnetic confusion that doomed fifty years of birds. Crimson globules smear into ribbons around me, perched just above him.

"You're going to scream now," I say, and he does.

He grabs the coil and runs. Have it your way, then. I tug at the imperceptible folds in space and time rippling, stretching, and tearing around the dormant but still powerful core of the ship, and duck behind one like it's a curtain. I emerge right in front of the thief.

He skids to a stop. "Wha – where did you come from?"

"Let me show you," I say, and pull him behind the curtain.

His screams barely sound over the thunder. Mountains – maybe they're planets, I can't be sure of scale in the thick red haze enveloping the In Between – collide all around us. I grip the hood of the thief's sweatshirt tight in my fist, careful not to let him go. The strange dimension the alien traveled through to arrive at Earth back in 1968 has no edge I can tell, but the tumbling chunk of glowing garnet we're standing on does.

"Had enough?"

He keeps screaming.

"I'll take that as a yes," I say, and bring us out of the In Between back to the cold, flat, sure ground of Break Pointe.

The thief scrambles away on all fours away, through drifts of snow down into one of the countless craters scarring the no man's land between the ship and the hundred-foot concrete wall closing the crash site and old downtown off from the rest of the city. Not that it's much better off. For the most part, the Quarantine Zone stays quarantined. People always try getting through the wall to knick the powerful, valuable alien tech on the other side, but since my success – I'll be charitable with myself – everyone and their brother thinks they can find what I did. They can become what I have become.

The thief gags, stranded somewhere between vomiting and crying. "What... what was that?"

"A lesson," I say, drifting over the edge of the crater, buoyed by the dynamic tension between my magnetic field and the earth. "Hand it over, or we go back."

He throws the power coil out of the crater, and it floats into orbit around me. "I don't have any money. I don't have any food. What am I supposed to do? You stole alien tech."

I made my living once the same as the thief, scavenging alien tech to sell on the black market. I remember the hollow rattle of my belly, the only motor that ran in the winter. The endless anxiety over where my next meal was coming from. Would I make rent? Have enough for Ma's medication? Every day was starting over from the bottom of a hill I could never summit. My fear now is the same. The hunger, though. That's different.

"I did steal," I say. "And look what it cost me."

I zip down the front of my leather jacket enough to show him a glimpse of the alien crystal burning in my chest. All these chancers think they're going to find another Myriad lying in the ruins of the ship. This is the only one, right here. No one else can become the alien, though I don't know that I have.

I'm something between.

The Ever, the sole occupant of the ship, was a faceless, unfathomable being of pure energy. They swept through the city in 1968, lassoing thousands with coils of alien power, acquiring their energy and living information.

I'm not exactly down with that.

Still, my energy fused with the alien. My knowledge. My identity. I should have never picked up that thing, but I did and now here I am. A warning to others, if nothing else.

"Don't come back here," I say to the thief. "Ever."

He climbs out of the crater, indignant. "Weren't you going to fix everything?"

He walks away. To where? Where can he go? What can he do, but this? For decades, scrapping our disaster has been the only industry in Break Pointe. The city needs a new way. A new life. I'm going to find it. I have to, for any of this to make sense.

I return to the ship and float to the ringed deck encircling the core. The coil eases to the growing pile of thieved items I've recovered the last three months. I took from the ship. I keep giving back.

This isn't what it wants. Light writhes within the dark crystal of the core. Peaks and valleys prickle the surface, fluid between light and jewel, drawn along the interplay of magnetic lines between the core and the Myriad.

The work must continue.

I thought I'd come to some kind of accord with the alien, but the further I get from my old life, the further I get from me, the less sure I am. Nothing tangible exists in the ruins; only the ghosts of futures and pasts, starved for life.

I just want to go home. Do nothing. Be normal, if I can. Eat some cookies. A smile cracks my lips. Another dimension. I start a text to Abi. Before I can send it, a vibration jolts through my hand. I hope it's her, but it's another alert. Another fire I have to put out in the frozen city. I swipe at my PEAL, and Vidette Rizzo appears on the screen, in a snowy field.

"Vi? What's wrong?"

"There's a body," she says.

Harvested corn stalks stab through the foot or so of snow in the field between two gutted townhouses on the south end of Shelley. Much of the neighborhood has gone back to fields and forest in the last half-century. All my life, Break Pointe has felt stretched between the poles of nature and the cosmos, the past and the future, the island in limbo between. Our instincts confuse our common sense. Our purpose splinters, torn between the simple need to survive and the yearning to become more.

"You found a body out here?" I say.

Vidette walks with her arms locked, her body a shield against the bitter cold I don't feel at all. "Kid came into the clinic tonight. Frost-bite. He saw it out here."

Drizzled trails of glassy blood speckle the snow, shadowing a meandering trail of massive paw prints. "What was this?"

"Over here."

Blackbirds peck at snow gone to rust. Hawks circle low and sure. The tracks lead to a giant rock just shy of the tree line, but then I realize it's no rock. It's the emaciated body of a coywolf. His yellow eyes open in shock. Bleeding Jesus. I think it's a coywolf. I've never seen one so big.

Vidette turns the wolf over, twice her size, like he's a page out of a book. I grew up idolizing this woman, and yet sometimes I forget her extraordinary strength. For the most part, it's hidden behind her kind nature and small stature.

"We need to find out what happened to him and fast," she says, "or we're going to have a war on our hands."

I shake my head. "War?"

Vidette's hand trails from his snout, over his head, and down the broad streak of red on his back. "All these years, I've only ever heard stories about them. You know what he is?"

"A coywolf."

The animals never bothered me. I got used to them, prowling the ruins as I did, after living in The Derelicts for so long.

Awe laces Vidette's voice. "He's not just any wolf, either. This fella here, he's one of the Bloodbacks."

"Bloodbacks?"

She smiles. "It's not just people with powers in this town."

TWO

Living in The Derelicts, you don't have much, but you've got legends in spades. Ghosts of the acquired. Mutated plants ruling over some subterranean kingdom. Something massive and strange, lurking out in the lake. Empowered wolves.

"I thought they were stories," I say.

Vidette shakes her head. "Nothing is just a story here."

Out in the ruins scavenging for alien tech, my biggest worry wasn't someone else snatching a find out from under me. It was one of those big wolves people always whisper about snatching me up.

"What did you call them, Vi? Bloodbacks?"

"That's what Professor Blackwood called them."

Across the river, the Blackwood Building glows like a trickle of melted moonlight frozen on the window of the sky. They have power over there. Food. Heat. Vidette likes to say she went into medicine because she got tired of breaking bones and wanted to set them.

The truth is, she got tired of working for a company that puts money ahead of human beings. Great Power owes everything to the ship, and the city, and the suffering so many of us still endure. Without it, they wouldn't have their powers, their business, or their wealth. Rather than give a little back, they think we're taking from them to ask them to be human.

"What are their powers?"

"I'm guessing you've got way more info in here…" Vidette taps her chest. "…than I can give you."

I access the trove of information I acquired from the GP mainframe. Tucked away deep in nested files are imaged documents going back to the 70s. Sightings of giant dogs in the city. Government studies on the environmental impacts of the crash. Vidette looks off toward the trees as I read. People do this as I absorb information. Something in my expression makes them uncomfortable, but I don't know what; they never say. I never ask. I keep reading.

Coywolves became common in Break Pointe after the ship crashed. Blackwood first identified the pack in 1980, when he discovered the bones of dead wolves in Brewster Park. He wasn't sure how they had become Empowered; he was only sure by their enlarged skulls and evident intelligence that they were. Then, the bones disappeared. All traces of the wolves vanished from the city.

I brush the claret streak down the wolves' back. Long, coarse hairs shine electric red in the glower of this lantern in my chest. I trace the bones showing through his slack skin. "He was hungry. Desperate. Must have drove him out in the open."

Desperation doesn't discriminate in The Derelicts.

"I don't think he died of starvation," Vidette says.

"Then what happened?"

"Look at these bruises." Vidette carefully combs through the tinsel-like fur on his side. Deep purple bruises lurk beneath. Offset lines of broken bones. "His ribs are broken. His jaw. Signs of internal bleeding. This is blunt force trauma."

"He was in a fight?"

Blood trails behind him. There aren't any other tracks. Shoeprints. This blood is his. Even weak and hungry, I can't think of any other animal that could have done this. Certainly not a person.

An ordinary one, anyways.

"Someone did this," I say. "Someone Empowered."

She grimaces. "This was a murder. And this is why I was talking about a war. He's not the only wolf. The rest of them? Not going to be happy."

Whoever killed him could go toe to toe with a wolf the size of a small car. Few Empowered would have had the strength. Vidette. Lodestone. The Interdictor. If the killer is Empowered, they have to be with GP. Any representative of the company being in The Derelicts would violate the Empowered Registration Act; their sanction to use their powers ended when the city failed to pay its dues. A greater question still would be why anyone from GP would be in The Derelicts, much less have any interest in the wolves.

"We need to find out what happened," I say.

"I'll do my best," Vidette says, "But I'm not an expert in wolves. I'm certainly not a medical examiner."

"I'm not a detective."

Her nose wrinkles. "You're kind of everything right now."

At first, with Vi and Mike and The Uniform, we had a rotation. We had a team. Then The Uniform got court-martialed for defying orders during the battle and went back to Washington. Vi spends most of her time in the mobile clinic, treating colds and frostbite and Mike can only do so much without any powers of his own. I patrol more. Robberies still go up. Muggings. Fights.

Murders.

"Let's get him to the clinic," Vidette says.

"Wait."

I slip my glove off. I don't know why. Light leeches out of my gossamer fingers into him. His hairs stand on end. His claws curl. The wolf's entire body convulses as I touch his cold, bristly snout. No energy resides in him now. If I could give him mine. If I could make myself a battery, and warm this city. If I could just connect the dots, and make all of this work.

I close his eyes.

———

Time is a song, Verity Bridge says on the screen and Abi fakes a yawn. Here it comes. After a baroque bit of stretching, she wraps her arm around my shoulder. Months of this now. A match trying to light an ice cube. Her heart throbs through the magnetic ether, *ba-dumm, ba-dumm, ba-dumm.* Vines of energy shadow Abi's fingers beneath the translucency of my skin, a cat chasing a point of light. Before, I wore a costume that contained this energy and insulated everyone from the hunger of the Myriad. I lost the suit in the Battle for Break Pointe. Hard thing to replace. Now it's just me. My control. My focus.

Abi makes it hard to focus.

She teases the filaments across the thin of my blouse. Down to my navel. Back up to my heart. The Myriad flickers with anticipation. My body smolders. Here it comes.

I pick a straggling kernel out of the bowl and munch on it. The popcorn becomes energy, as water does, wine, the cookies Abi is always baking in the apartment. Nothing tastes the same. Nothing feels the same. Nothing feels safe. I want a glass of wine. A plate of cookies. Her skin on my lips. Between us isn't the division of flesh, but a superficial scrim of atoms and molecules that collate their inherent energy into divergent strands. A touch, a snap, and I could unravel us both. I want to unravel us both.

I zip up my jacket. "We can't."

Abi snuggles closer to me in the loveseat. She lowers her voice. "We can. You can control this. You are right now."

A pointed *Shh!* slings past us.

Back in the day, the first floor and basement of the Halfway Hotel had been a department store. Nothing much changes in The Derelicts, and down in the basement, the original wood paneling is still here. Display cases. The carpeting, though that could do with a change. All sorts of nooks and crannies for shelves and mannequins create space for something new, including a cozy little movie theater.

Abi slides her hand, slick with butter, between my thighs. I pinch at the restriction of my jeans, tighter, warmer as Abi melts into me, lips against my ear, breath hot and soft. Light flutters through me. Sometimes I can't tell if the urge to kiss Abi is the urge to acquire her. Those two desires have become entwined since my transformation.

There's no distinction.

I squeeze her hand. I doubt the leather of my gloves is any kind of comfort. "Let's watch the movie."

Her hand tugs on my zipper. "Let's go upstairs."

Just a kiss; but it's never just a kiss with me. I fix on things. People. I disappear in them. Even before this happened to me, I had this need. This all-consuming hunger and I never knew what to do with it. I was all this want and feeling and emotion and I didn't know how to process it. I didn't know how to conduct any of it without overloading the system. So I buried it down deep. It was easy. I never met anyone who wanted, like I did.

Until Abi.

Life gushes right through her. Desire. All of it exists on the surface, and I want her. I need her to take all of this. To contain me. I want to be held within someone. Kept.

Our lips draw together, magnets tugging stronger the closer they come together and I turn away from her.

"Let's watch the movie."

She recoils back in her chair like a seatbelt with too much tension in it. "I feel like we kind of need to have sex first before we get to the Lesbian Bed Death stage of things."

Shh!

I try and go back to the movie but Abi is looking at me. She's waiting on me, and I don't know what else to say. Music fizzes into static. Mordant light flickers in Abi's eyes as the screen goes dark.

Aw, man.

A dozen half-moons rise as everyone activates their PEALs for light. Lunate faces look back at me, expectant.

I zip down my jacket. Filtered magenta bathes the theater. "Technical difficulties?"

A voice projects from behind us. "I've lost power."

I weave through the cluster of lawn chairs and sleeping bags back to the projector. Shepp sits on a stool next to the projector, so tall he can't stand up straight or else he hits the ceiling. He might have some clearance, if not for his shock of unruly hair.

He pats the curved gray metal of the beast next to him. "Give it me to straight, doc. She going to live?"

I peel off a glove and touch a finger to the bulge of the projector's midsection. Light lances out of the projector, back onto the screen and it's a tale as old as time again.

"I don't think it's the projector," I say.

Naked film reels spoke the back wall. I touch the flat, cartridge-like device nestled between them. My little engine. Energy bleeds off my fingers into the device. Ink-like ferrofluid inside the cartridge prickles with minute quills, morphing into complex patterns and geometric shapes. Heat transfer via ferrofluids was a unicorn Dr. Piller had been chasing in Applied Sciences for years. With the knowledge and power I attained through the Myriad, I found a way to make thermomagnetic convection a practical reality.

Free, limitless energy.

What I haven't found yet is a way to share that power with the people it can benefit the most. I don't have the tools or money to build more than the few prototypes I've scratched together for the apartment building.

Messages cluster on my PEAL. *The lights are out! Again!*

The whole building is down. Grand. It's only ten degrees out. Something in the network again. I'm retrofitting old appliances like the projector to receive an energy signal from the engine, but none of them were built for it. One overloads and the whole system goes down. Here I am thinking I'm going to light and warm the world with these things, and I can't even keep the Halfway Hotel turned on. Well. Wherever I am, there's always light. If you like the overbearing red of darkrooms. Nothing much developing here, though.

Shepp rests his arms across the shelf of his belly. His T-shirt art for some movie called *Lifeforce*. He's got loads of them. "I thought you had all the bugs worked out?"

In the loveseat, Abi scavenges what she can out of the last of her popcorn. I get myopic. Once I get focused on something, everything else tends to suffer. After the battle, after I accepted what happened to me, who I am now, I thought it would be easier. I thought it would be different. I wanted it to be. But The Derelicts need everything: housing, electricity, water, food, government. My absolute focus and attention. Without it, this flame I'm trying to kindle, it just won't take.

"So did I," I say.

"Argento used the same three-strip color process they used in *The Wizard of Oz* for *Suspiria*, to get that saturated color," Shepp says. "That drenched red. It was way antiquated by then, but he was like, I gotta have it. This is my vision."

I hold the receiver to my ear. "Uh-huh."

"In cinema, red usually represents repressed passion."

"I see."

"Didn't seem like there was too much repression out there in the theater a minute ago. Not that I was looking."

"Mm-hmm."

"You can fix it?"

Abi's heart thumps through the dark, *ba-dumm*.

"I can fix anything," I say.

"Cool. I know people are probably like, why is a theater important, but having a place for people to come together and share in wonder and dreams and possibility, that's important."

I smile. "I agree."

"People have to believe in something more than themselves. If it's just you, you're flawed. You're fallible. You're going to croak at some point. There's got to be something else beyond you, and that's movies. This place is like church, man."

Abi comes to the projector. "Do churches give refunds?"

"Asking for the supervisor probably doesn't go too far," I say. "I think it's the conductor. I can fix it."

Abi laces her arms around me. "We were just getting cozy."

I give her a squeeze. "Shepp saw us making out."

If he turns red, I can't tell. "Oh. You heard that."

"I'm able to focus on multiple things at once."

"Right. Because genius. Obviously. Don't zap me."

"I won't zap you," I say. "If you can find *Verity Bridge To Now*."

He scratches his chin. "Yeesh. That's a tough one."

I've only seen it the once, on the late show some Saturday night as a kid, but I never forgot it. Mostly because I couldn't make any sense of it. Verity Bridge is this time-traveling woman who is skipping around history without any real caution, but how or why you don't know. There are musical numbers. Fourth-wall breaks. And absolutely no context for any of it. Abi loves them as much as I do. More, maybe. Sometimes, it's all we talk about.

"Ooh, you have to," Abi says. "And then we can do a sing-along. And dress up. I'll be Tincture."

"Hmm... I'll be Verity," I say.

She tugs on the end of my sleeve. "Do you want like maybe rehearse upstairs?"

Shepp tilts back on his stool. "Who do I get to be?"

"A successful theater owner," I say. "Once I fix this. So I'll get out of here and get started on that."

Abi clenches her smile. It used to be so easy. Free.

"I'll be as fast as I can," I say, and go.

Black shell casing orbits the disassembled components of the engine, a shattered planet held together in its remnant gravity. The individual pieces float round me, buoyed in my magnetic field, as I replace the burnt-out filament in my lab. Lab is a generous word. 'Functionally Equivalent Space' might be more apt. The tiny space in the prow of the Halfway Hotel I work out of is maybe smaller than the test chamber in Applied Sciences at the Blackwood Building. There, Abi and I worked on the edge of science.

Now, I operate somewhere beyond it.

Strands of copper wire and crystalline, alien conduit lace together in mid-air, creating something wholly unique. Energy arcs from my finger into the filament, and the amalgam begins to glow. With a light tap, I set the filament into the gentle parade of components around me, and close the engine back up. Power isn't the problem. I've all the power in the world. Without converters that can handle the power surging through the network, I'll never get it to work. Elements of what I need wait inside the wreck, on the other side of the wall. If I wanted, I could strip out the ship and solve all my problems. That wouldn't exactly be setting the best example. To say nothing of the steep price I pay for taking things from the ship.

The work must continue, that voice says, always in my ear.

We had an understanding, I say. *You are me. I'm you.*

We are.

Then we'll do as we must.

Yes. We will.

Something like a chill goes through me. More like electronic distress, running from hot to cold. I touched a rock. Became an alien. Fused with it, anyways. How much of me is still me? How much of me is The Ever?

Is there even a difference?

A loud, metal bang thunders through the neighborhood. I slip out the window of the lab, into the sky. Clouds of energy race across the cold, dark void of Six Corners. I zip down my jacket and bring the sun out into the night. The shadows of wolves stretch across the ruins, long, dark, and swift.

THREE

Bent metal coils next to shreds of bandages. Gauze. Pill bottles. What's left of the mobile clinic splays across the tundra of Shelley, like a tin can that exploded from too much pressure.

"What..."

I float over the snow, into the wreck of the clinic. The body of the wolf is gone. Paths burrow through the snow, in tight lines away from the clinic, like they shoveled it.

"They took him," I say.

Abi slogs through the snow after me. "Who did?"

Yellow eyes glow in the veil of snow like the sun behind gauzy winter clouds. Seven wolves, all with the same overcast fur and glinting blood-red streak down their backs advance into the intersection of Shelley, Delaney, and Harrison like bleeding tanks. Another wolf, much larger, stays further back but I register her energy output, twice as vivid as the others.

"Why aren't they leaving?" Abi says.

"They think we killed him."

Her nose wrinkles. "They think – *they think*. Dude. That's their power. They've got brains and stuff."

Hundreds of fragments of chassis rise out of the white, into the air around me. Look how clean these breaks are. Everywhere she was fastened with a bolt, she broke. "I don't think that's all there is to their power."

"If one of them talks, I will legit freak out."

"Go back inside," I say.

"What are you going to do?"

"Go back inside, Abi."

I float across the ground, into the intersection. "My name is Kit Baldwin," I say, but my focus on the wolves breaks as the wolves' thoughts scramble through my own.

Bird Woman. Star Walker.

I hover in place, dazed from the sound and presence of gravelly voices in my mind. The wolves all speak, as Dr. Piller does, via telepathy. They're telepathic.

They're conscious.

"Abi, do you hear this?"

Abi squeals with delight. "They can talk!"

She vaults off her feet. Before I even know what's happening, she's skidding through the snow.

"Abi!" I turn back to the wolves. "If you can understand me, we didn't have anything to do with – "

A strong, invisible force snatches me out of the air and slams me into the ground so hard I channel a trench through it.

Brilliant. They're telekinetic, too.

Snow and ice melt off my face as white snow burns red. I crawl back to my feet, and back to Abi, somewhere in the cold. A ring of burning xanthous surrounds me. Growls chug like diesel engines.

"I don't want any trouble," I say and a streetlight roots out of the ground. Sure. Why not. The trunk scrapes across the street toward me. I blast it into embers, just as a wolf ambushes me from the opposite direction. The wolf pins me down on the ground, and claws at the glowing star in my chest.

I peel off my gloves. "Don't make me – "

I fight the urge to simply acquire him as much as to get free and the wolf sinks its claws into the old leather of my jacket. Slobber dangles from its steaming jaw, over my eye.

I paint you in cave, Bird Woman.

Fear locks me up. *Cave?*

His teeth snarl against my cheek. *I paint you in blood.*

I don't think the wolf can hurt me – he's strong but not as strong as The Interdictor – but then again, a few minutes ago, I didn't think there was such a thing as Empowered wolves.

We didn't do this –

The wolf's eyes bulge. His claws rake my jacket trying to keep his grip which, God damn it, this is my favorite thing in the world and Vidette swings him around by the tail and hurls him whining back into the dark beyond Six Corners.

Vidette wades through the snow, picking up stray debris from the mobile clinic. The clinic was the only reliable health care for most people on the island.

Now, they have nothing.

I touch her shoulder. "Vi."

The debris crunches in her fists. "Let's finish this."

I fire off a curt snap of crimson lightning I hope will send the rest of the Bloodbacks running. Most do. The large wolf remains just out of sight, her yellow eyes blazing suns.

"We didn't do this," I say.

I know she sees my thoughts. Hers scamper through my head. Fear. Confusion. A chorus of anger, amplified and echoed between all the wolves. The wolves howl in unison, a deep lament that rattles out to a growl. The body of the dead wolf levitates out of the snow beyond, between a pair of Bloodbacks, and together they all flee back into the shadows they came from.

I follow Abi's pulse through the snow, *ba-dumm* and I find her near the curb outside the Halfway Hotel. "Baby?"

She tries to smile, but her lips are frozen. "I'm ok."

I want to hold her. I should hold her. I can't.

Two nights I hold watch over Six Corners.

The Bloodbacks don't return. I can't find the wolves anywhere. We won't be able to determine what happened without examining the body. We won't be able to stop whatever this is from escalating.

My PEAL buzzes. Oh no. What now? A text. Abi.

I float down from my catbird seat above the intersection to the Halfway Hotel. Abi buzzes around an office on the fifth floor, talking with Zari and Ari about a new T-shirt design. This one has a graffitied red E like people have been tagging on buildings since I showed up. Abi spends all day online selling the shirts. Stickers. Posters. Lunches she auctions off to gawky celebrities and curious scientists. When I can stomach it, anyways. I learn to stomach it.

I tap on the door. "Hey, baby."

Abi careens out of her meeting. "Dude, I just texted you."

"I know," I say, and I squeeze her hand but it's not enough for either of us. It's limp. Weak. "You're thinking about me. I should be thinking about you. Are you ok?"

She smiles. "I'm fine. My ass is sore, though. Might have a bruise. Do you want to look? You should probably look."

"That might be awkward right now."

Zari and Ari both wave at me. I can't tell if they're just spooky twins or some kind of Empowered echo of each other.

"What are you guys working on?"

"Well, you can see the shirt," Abi says. "Let's see. The crowd funder is like at fifty percent, maybe you can do a little booster..."

"Abi..."

"I know you don't like it, but if you post more, you drive up engagement and that leads to donors and stuff."

"I don't feel comfortable with that."

"I know, but we need money and people want to help."

"I feel like I have to be someone else."

"Just be you."

"I don't want to have to sell myself."

"It's just a post. A podcast or two. Just a little meet and greet we can throw in. It will be small. Biggest donors only."

I sigh. "Ok."

"And – oh! Zari and Ari have a new video for the vlog."

Zari snorts. "Vlog."

Ari snorts, too. "No one says vlog."

"Whatever it is," Abi says.

Most of the time Abi blurs around, so smooth, and confident and then it's like she snags on something. This word. Who cares? She's mad she didn't know what it was.

I want to hold her. Really hold her. "What's the video about?"

"Which was better – your first fight with The Interdictor, or the second," Zari says, a little too excited.

Ari pumps his fist. "Obviously the second one."

Zari nudges her glasses back. "Obviously."

That any of this is interesting to people is honestly a little more frightening than fighting The Interdictor himself. "Wouldn't it be more compelling for you to disagree?"

"No," they say.

"I thought the channel was more like slice of life stuff," I say. "Down on the ground realism in The Derelicts."

"This shit is so real," Zari says.

Ari snorts. "So real."

Ok then. "I should get out on patrol."

Abi clears her throat. "Hey, guys. We're done, right?"

"Right," Zari and Ari say and synchronize their exit.

Abi grips my hand and pulls me close. "You're warm."

"I was thinking about you."

She unzips my jacket. "It's so cold."

Flakes so large it's like someone was shredding paper bombard Shelley. The burden of the snow weighs on me. I still need to repair the transmitter of my prototype engine. What I really need to do is somehow replicate a hundred more. A thousand.

I need time and space and resources to finish my project, but the streets aren't safe. Empowered wolves prowl Six Corners, no longer content with scraps and shadows. Another challenge, another problem is something I do not need but if I'm being honest, the wolves excite me. This is something I can fix, even if I don't know how yet; this is something I can work on.

"I need to go back on watch," I say.

Abi looks up at me, plaintive. "Stay and look after me. I have an owie." Abi rubs her bottom. "It hurts *so* bad."

I glance down her backside. "Seems to have healed nicely."

"But I have like personal trauma. PTSD and stuff." Abi locks her arms around me. "I need a night light."

I let go for a moment in Abi's arms, overwhelmed with relief that she wasn't seriously hurt. A moment is all I allow myself. As much I want to stay – as much as I need to – I can't.

"I'll be back," I say.

The agitation of her dreams skips across her face. Until we lived in the same space, I always thought of Abi as easy. Happy. And she is, bounding around The Derelicts with a smile and a purpose, but every night, sheets vault like the spray of waves off the end of the bed. I hover outside the window of the apartment, regretting asking Abi to move in, not wanting to be alone, wanting to go to her, wake her up, love her out of her fear but I never do.

"You know what's weird?" she says. "Every day, I get to see how much people love you. They post pics online in their shirts. With their stickers. Art they made about you. For you. And I see you... you let people in, like you never did before. You actually know people's names. You remember them."

I bite my lip. "I knew your name."

"Uh-huh. They know you. They love you. You share yourself with them. But I never get to be with you, Kit."

Before this happened, my life was small. Sealed off, like the

Quarantine Zone. I didn't know any of the other people in the apartment building, and I've been here half my life. Other people are hard. Connecting is. The Myriad connects me to everything. Energy. Knowledge. Other states of being. I know people, now. I know myself. But this thing in my chest isn't the difference in my life. I don't always link up. I don't always fire. With Abi, I do. Abi keeps me together. Focused. And she's the one who suffers for it.

"I'm sorry, Abi."

"You're afraid, I know. You're not going to hurt me. Besides, even if you do..." She pats her behind. "I can take it."

"But what if..."

Her lips shadow mine. "Kiss me."

"If I accidentally acquire you..."

"Then I'll be inside you," she says. "Right? In the Myriad? And then you could become me, or something? Ooh. That could get interesting."

"It could get complicated."

"Kiss me and stuff."

Nothing is impossible. I know that better than most. Another thing I know better: just because you can do something, it doesn't mean you should. Some things are best left alone.

I withdraw from her. "I'll be back."

She tries to smile, but it's sore. "Don't let me keep you."

I drift out of the office back to the roof, into the uncertain sky, my light quickly obscured in snow.

Streets white out. Wood snaps. Snow crashes. Not sure if it's branches or roofs collapsing in the distance. Probably both. A funereal quiet clings to the city as I hover over the Halfway Hotel. In winter, The Derelicts shrinks. Slows. The arthritis of the city constricts, and she barely functions. Half a mile away, concrete shudders against steel. Plows shove aside the snow along the shore of the narrow peninsula The Derelicts shadows. Christmas lights strand the exteriors of the bars and restaurants along Claremont. Sunshine breaks across Break Pointe as stubborn winter clouds yield to the Blackwood Building, a gleaming portal cracked open to another world entirely.

That shit coffee Dr. Piller made every day in Applied Sciences burns my tongue. The salt of the French fries from the commissary prickles my lips. I never drank soda or ate any of the junk food greasing out under hot lamps, but now I want them. The fizz. The sugar sweet. The cold numb in my temple.

That life, that was never quite mine.

Vidette's restless aura bristles in the magnetic net I always cast as she paces the roof of the Halfway Hotel. This woman. If I could hook her up to my engine. Perpetual energy.

I sink to the roof, long peeled of its shingles. "We're not going to get through the winter."

Vidette rubs my back. "We'll figure it out."

"Not everyone can walk through three feet of snow, Vi."

"Get me a snowplow. I'll strap it on. I'll have these streets cleared for you in a jiff. Actually, let me write that down."

I track the heavy, yellow trucks barreling down the peninsula, across the river. "We'd have to steal one."

"My evening is open."

"It's supposed to be thirty below tonight."

Vidette turns her back to the wind, nose red from the cold. "This? This is nothing. '84? You should have seen that."

"There was electricity in 1984. Heat. Roofs."

"Honestly, it wasn't much different than it is now."

I peer over the edge of the roof, watching someone struggle through the weeks of snow across the intersection. I can't imagine where they'd be going, or why they'd be outside.

"I think we should put our effort into relocating people. Try and get them some starting money. A bus ticket. Something. Get them somewhere they have a chance. And heat."

"How much is a month's rent and deposit in Chicago?"

"I imagine it's cheaper than a funeral."

"We can't give up. Not now."

Vidette draws me back from the edge. We can touch. Her strength makes her skin diamond. Nothing can penetrate it. Not even me. Too bad Vidette isn't my type.

Or, you know. A lesbian.

"This is our home, Kit. This is our duty, for better and worse."

I pinch and pull at the leather of my jacket, hard and sharp in the cold. "I can't do this."

"You can."

"I can't. Abi... I can't."

Vidette puts her hand on my shoulder. "It's ok. This is normal. You can't be everywhere. And you can't fix everything. It hurts. But you've got to have faith, Kit."

I honestly don't know what that is. It's not faith I have for a brighter future for the city. If I think about it, I'm not thinking about it at all. I'm not feeling anything about it. I'm just doing it until I can't, and then I panic. What do I do. How do I fix it. Pick up the pieces. Don't think. Don't feel.

Don't fear.

"You keep moving, and help who you can," Vidette says. "On that note. Why I'm here. I'm thinking maybe you need to do your thing and hack into the GP mainframe again."

"Because that's legal."

"I'm not exactly Employee of the Month over at the tower, so I'm not getting anywhere on finding out if there have been any wolf-related injuries to GP personnel lately. Touch a phone or whatever you do, and download some medical files."

There hasn't been so much as a word out of the Blackwood Building since the battle. I'm not sure I want to go kicking the hornet's nest right now by hacking their computer system.

"We could find out if there have been any injuries," I say, "and try and find the Bloodbacks at the same time."

Vidette's face scrunches. "No."

"Dr. Piller – "

"Sold us out to Blackwood. He sold you out."

"He can start making up for it by tracking the wolves," I say. "Can you talk to him, Vi? Please."

"He couldn't find them before," she says.

Maybe the consciousness of the wolves wasn't as mature as it is now, thirty years later. Or, my luck, they're as good at hiding their mental tracks as they are the others.

"We don't have any other option," I say.

Vidette tears her glove off and swipes at her PEAL. "I'm going to need a drink after this."

Piller's voice squawks out of the imperceptible speakers of the PEAL. "Vi... I'm so glad you called – "

"Shut up, Ronnie. Here's what you're going to do."

<hr>

Tracks stamp the hardened snow covering Brewster Park in thin lines vanishing between naked trees. To me, they're no different from most dogs. The points of the little crowns the wolves make are less obvious, maybe. Dead leaves, twigs, and uneven terrain of exposed roots and rocks muddy the trail. Before 1968, Brewster Park had been the green heart beating between the industrial lungs of Break Pointe. Now, outside of the poached iron gates and crumbling brick walls lining the old perimeter, the park is more or less indistinguishable from the untended nature that has reclaimed much of the island.

Take a left, Piller says in my head, from somewhere beyond the park. I shiver every time he whispers between my ears.

Do you sense them?

I sense something. A void. It's strange.

A void in thought? Was that what you experienced when you betrayed me to Professor Blackwood?

Hang a right.

Dead trees give to shimmering ones. Leaves glow like static flame. Radiation made much of the city unlivable, or so they said. Life adapts. Evolves. Acquires the characteristics of its circumstances. Trees blink at me in red warning.

Stop.

I keep going. A smooth bulb of exposed limestone, like the crown of a buried skull, rests heavy along faded footpaths. Stumps of clawed down trees give to rocks, piled in conical mounds. The mounds are slim. Slightly crescent. In some ways, they remind me of the beehive-like constructions in monasteries back in Ireland, but I doubt these particular arrangements were the art of the park's planners. The mounds branch east and west in a steadily rising arc, outward from a dark cave, the mouth built of stacked limestone.

Some old German folktales start like this. Or end.

At least you're not wearing a red cape, Piller says.

Little Red Riding Hood is a European folktale. The Brothers Grimm popularized it. It's not German.

You needed to point that out.

Knowledge is a gift, Dr. Piller.

Here's some knowledge for you. He's right behind you.

Yellow eyes glow in the thicket behind me. Steam shrouds my view as the wolf idles like the engine of an old car.

How do I let him know I'm here to talk? There's no answer. *Dr. Piller? Where did you go?*

The wolf stalks out of the trees. *Why come?*

"I come in peace."

His eyes slender as he considers me. Then, just like that, he scampers past me into the cave. *No. Birds.*

I extend my magnetic field. The tassel of birds and bats tethered to me coil away into the sky. This is probably a bad idea. Usually is with me. But I do what I always do; I find my way into the dark.

FOUR

This heat wells out of the earth, like a subway tunnel.

Damp, wet leaves plaster the ground. Bones gnawed beyond recognition. Worms lace hollow eye sockets. The path slopes deeper into the earth. Bricks of mismatched limestone arc overhead. I don't think the cave was part of the original park. The wolves must have constructed this, telekinetically. My guide keeps straight, on a steady descent into the cave, dripping and dark, until my gasp echoes into a boundless dark.

Crowns of deer antlers rise out of earthen mounds. Feathers hang off the antlers. Loose teeth. Claws. God. The ceiling. Packs of wolves clawed in the stone. As they roam boxy drawings of buildings, the wolves were painted in mud and then finally blood. Weeds of rabbit ears. Bushes of squirrel tails. Deer dominate the landscape, their antlers growing to mirror the paths through the park above us, the streets of the city, all leading back to a single, giant deer painted above. Antlers like lightning streams. Glowing skin like cat's eyes.

"Beautiful…"

Twin suns dawn in the cave. That big wolf, twice the size of others, prowls out of the dark. The hair on her sides is bald, exposing her skin. Scars trace out the shapes of rabbits and snakes and deer, like she cut them herself. The wolf sits on her haunches, head crooked as she considers me.

Why come, Star Walker?

"Thank you for letting me come here... this place is..."

Why?

"I want to find out what happened," I say.

Humans kill Lamar. Now you come to kill us.

"I'm not here to kill anyone. I'm here to help."

She sneers, kind of. *How?*

"There's a list I should keep to, but honestly I'm just really curious how it is you know English."

Your words crude. Simple.

"*An bhfuil sé seo simplí??*"

Being clever no help you, Star Walker, the wolf says. *Many clever bones buried in snow.*

I always do this. Whenever I'm cornered, my first instinct is to deflect with some glib or pithy response meant to establish my intellect. If nothing else, I was always smarter; most of my life has been a gauntlet of others putting down my looks, my interests, my mere existence but I always had a ledge to stand on they could never reach. I just never let them know the ledge was deep inside a bottomless pit.

"Let's start over. I'm Kit. What's your name?"

Siski.

"Siski..." Despite the size differential, there's something soft in Siski's eyes. Something maternal. "You said his name was Lamar? I don't know how Lamar died. My fear was it was someone Empowered, but no one across the river has been injured, that we can tell."

Strong among Empowered.

"There are," I say. "Can we examine the body?"

Siski gazes mournfully at a mound. An immature antler tilts in fresh earth. God. This is him. Lamar. I regret disturbing such a sacred place, even as I marvel at my fortune in being here.

With tools? Siski says. *With science?*

That last word comes with a sneer. My focus drifts back to the cave paintings, and the glorious, electric deer.

"Why the deer?" I say.

Siski's head crooks. *Deer give life.*

"You eat them."

Siski looks to the mounds. *We give life to deer.*

This deer is their god. I try to wrap my head around the idea of deer-worshipping wolves, but I can't; in any case, it's not why I'm here. "We'll be respectful," I say. "We want to find the truth. We want to have peace, just like you."

Siski lowers her head. Wolves around the cave lift theirs. Their heads bob up and down, as if they're listening; as if they're speaking to each other. I can't hear. The Bloodbacks have locked me out of their conversation. They must have locked Dr. Piller out as well.

That's not terrifying.

Siski steps toward me. Old instincts die hard. I step back. Yellow eyes shrink in scrutiny.

I no hurt you, Siski says.

"I won't hurt you, either."

You lightning bug. No bother.

"That's a take."

Speak. As I speak.

"I can't."

Why?

"There are other voices on the line. It's complicated."

Star Walker.

"The Ever... yes. You know them?"

We hear them. In you.

That's no good. I clench my fists tight. My whole body, like I'm trying to be as light as I can over the thin ice I walk on with the alien. "I know you can't understand..."

I understand, Siski says.

"How?"

Siski squints like she's trying to think of how to explain. *Wolves hunger. Kill. Eat. Wolves obey instinct. I have thought.* Her eyes settle on the deer. *I have guilt.*

She has fear. I sense it, in her thoughts. Fear of her power. The connection she has to her pack, her prey, her world. Sometimes it's too much. Most of the time. I came in here being a smart ass, and Siski knows more of my pain than I do.

I reach out, cautiously. Siski lowers her head and I gently touch the wolf's scarred snout. "Let me help."

Find killer. Give to us.

I withdraw my hand. "They'll be punished, I swear."

The wolf snorts. *By what judge? What jury?*

"Well... things are a little..."

Complicated? Siski presses her nose to mine. *No law in city. No justice. Give wolf killer to Bloodbacks. Or no deal.*

"What trial will they get here? What justice?"

The wolf almost smiles. *Ours.*

I bite my lip. "I can't hand over a human being with rights for you to simply butcher. You know I can't."

Siski turns up her nose and retreats back into the dark. *No justice, no peace. Go, Star Walker.*

"And what if it was Lamar who attacked someone? What do you expect of me, then? You know my power."

You fear your power too much to use.

Now who's being clever. "You know my will."

Then you judge. You executioner.

"We can work this out," I say.

We find killer. We make Break Pointe safe.

"I can't let you hunt other people."

This is the wild, Star Walker. Strong survive.

Siski vanishes into the dark. My guide yaws his head toward the exit, signaling it's time to go. Damn it. I resist the urge to stay, to be clever, to try and fix it. I follow the wolf out of the cave. Snow crunches under his paws, the same sound as Ma breaking all the light bulbs out in the apartment. *Are you the light? Or the bulb?* I haven't thought of Ma in a long time. Too busy. Too much work. Too much has happened, burying the past and branches creak like bones in the icy breeze. Birds swirl back into orbit around me. Piller's voice crackles in my head.

What happened?

Dead blackbirds spoil the perfect white on the sidewalk outside the Halfway Hotel. All victims of the cold. The wind chill plummeted past thirty below last night. I know the birds would be out besides, but I feel responsible. It's a wonder the Halfway Hotel doesn't just up and fly away with as many wings as it has on its ledges. I don't feel the cold. Only the pinch of air molecules. The weight of death in my hands. *Bird Woman*, the wolves call me. Most of the time, the birds annoy me. They follow me everywhere. Pester me in the middle of the night. Distract me from all the things I have to focus on. Still. I kind of love them. Identify with them. I struggle to connect with Abi, with Vi, with the people I'm responsible for but not the birds. We're locked together, always and everywhere.

I take the birds to the field where we found Lamar. Snow melts away on a beam of cosmic energy. Earth warms enough for me to scoop up. I remove a feather from each of the dead birds and I bury them together. None of it makes sense to me, but it feels right. Necessary.

More birds fall like leaves from the wild trees gnarling out of the white waste. An oil slick on an ice cap. Swallows cover me like moss. Pulses of light ripple through me as dozens of birds touch down on my shoulders, as they crawl over my jacket, my heart, as they cocoon me in feathers.

A skin of snow crumbles away as I open the window. Birds trickle inside the apartment, too cold to be excited at their reprieve. They organize into dense lines along the sill. The back of the couch. All very behaved. For now. They're too cold to move. Once they warm up, I'll be wondering where my head was.

"This is only temporary," I say.

I place the feathers of the blackbirds on the mantle with all my pictures. Ma's wedding ring. Her ashes. There's no grave. No church. She's just always here. I thought this was healing. I thought this was facing it, but I'm never here. So much to do. Nothing happening. Is anything really going to change?

Am I any different?

Abi's magnetic presence entangles me a moment before her arms do. Her cheek nuzzles soft and warm against mine.

I shy away. "Hey, you've got to warn me."

Abi tarries against the mantle, a loopy, drunk smile on her lips. "Consider yourself warned."

"You've been drinking?"

"Just a few," she says.

"Where?"

"At the Pav."

"You went across the river?"

"Some of the techs from Applied Sciences texted me. I don't know. They were just curious how it was going over here. I needed a drink. I thought you were on patrol."

"It's fine," I say, and turn away from the mantle.

"What are you doing?"

I look back, unsure of how to untangle any of my thoughts. "Abi, did I ever tell you about my mother?"

Abi shakes her head. "Not really."

"She was a nurse," I say. "She was sad. She was beautiful."

"She must have wanted to help people, like you."

"I think she did. She wanted to. But she felt... helpless."

Abi smiles. "She'd be proud of you."

"I don't know... sometimes, I don't know if I knew her. She changed so much, and then I didn't want to be here. I didn't want to watch this and I don't remember half my life. Or at least, it's all the same blur of riding around the ruins while she was on one of her fits."

Abi takes my hand. "It's ok."

"I look at these pictures and it's like when you remember a dream. Just this image. This feeling. Are you even remembering it right? You try and remember, and it's just gone. She's gone."

Abi hugs me. "You might forget one thing or another, Kit. Your mom is going to remind you someday. I know it."

I never gave much thought to an afterlife; after Dad died, thinking about Heaven was thinking about death and I didn't want to. If I ignored death, then he never died. Death didn't exist. None of this happened and somewhere we're all riding bikes, in the park along the lakeshore. Somewhere we're free.

"Kit," Abi says.

"Yeah, baby?"

"There are birds in the apartment."

Wings flutter out of their rigidity as if her noticing them gives them back their life.

Ba-dumm.

"They're outside the window every day because of me," I say. "They're dying out there because of me. They could be anywhere. Some place warmer. Some place better."

"So long as you don't start naming them."

"Aren't you tired of being cold every day?"

Abi hugs me tight. "You keep me warm."

"Don't you want something else?"

Abi squints in confusion. "Something else?"

Before everything fell apart, Abi had an apartment in Hughes, over on the peninsula. Some nights after work she got drinks at the Pav. She had friends. Electricity. A life.

"Don't you want something normal, Abi?"

"Normal?"

"Someone."

Abi slips out of my arms, her confusion twisting to frustration. "Wait – what? What are you saying?"

"I don't – "

The apartment door bucks hard in its frame. Birds scatter from their quiet cessation into a mad flutter. Abi clutches my hand, uncertain but I know what's on the other side. Who. Sharp, firm scratches rattle the door. With a magnetic turn, I unlock the deadbolt. The wolf that guided me in the cave sits on the floor outside.

Star Walker. We must talk.

FIVE

Frustrated wings beat against the bathroom door, *BA-dumm, ba-dumm, ba-dumm*. Metal hooks slink off the shower curtain. I lean against the living room side of the door, less concerned with the unexpected arrival of the Bloodback than I am the realization that stuffing a flock of birds in my bathroom is not likely to end well.

The wolf blinks. *You live with birds?*

"It's a temporary arrangement," I say.

Birds pest. Little bones get stuck in teeth.

Abi pours a bottle of water in a bowl and sets it on the kitchen floor. "Don't eat me, dude."

The wolf laps at the water. *Teto not eat people.*

"Cool, cool. No disrespect or anything. Wolf shows up at your door late at night, you don't know."

Teto gives food he doesn't eat to pups.

Her nose wrinkles. "Oh."

I leave the bathroom door. "Teto... why are you here?"

Teto eases into a resting position on the floor. A small pouch hanging from his neck thuds against the wood. *Siski say no peace. Lamar want peace. Lamar want understanding.*

"Understanding of what?"

Lamar banished. Six moons ago.

"From the pack? Why?"

Teto glances toward the window. *Lamar curious. Like you. Lamar gifted. Lamar smart. Want to know how wolves become blood. Want to know Star Walkers. Where they come from.*

All my life, I've been a loner. Even working at the Blackwood Building among the other techs and engineers, all as inquisitive and obsessive as I was, I never bonded with any of them. Disaster had to befall me before I opened up to Abi. The idea there was a kindred spirit in Break Pointe in the form of a wolf brings a smile to my face, a smile that fades as I realize Lamar paid for his quest for knowledge, just like I did.

"Siski still buried him in the cave, though."

Siski love all pups.

"Aw..." Abi reaches down to pet Teto. His head snaps toward her. Her hand hangs in mid-air. "I mean, that's nice."

His ears flatten a little, and Abi strokes the back of his neck. Her easy smile slips on, comfy and familiar. Some of the tension relaxes. I do. Our rhythm is always easy to find. Natural, which is a trick, considering music isn't natural to me. Numbers make sense. Formulas. Systems. I think I got so into animated musicals as a kid mostly because of their very reliable structure, an equation I had worked out before the lights dimmed; the music was incidental.

Not for Abi.

She's always humming some song. Abi talks endlessly and enthusiastically, about her favorite songs, eras, casts, and I just listen. Hers is the only music I really understand. That I love.

Teto cocks his head. *Together?*

"Hmm?"

Star Walker. Lightfoot. Mates?

"Yes," I say. "Lightfoot?"

Abi leave no tracks.

Abi makes a face as if to say, *What the hell?* The thinking of these wolves is so fascinating. None of it is literal. What does he mean, she leaves no tracks? Certainly not on me.

Lamar have mate, Teto says. *Siski still banish him.*

Abi continues to pet him, her face scrunching a bit as she finds leaves and twigs and other things she pinches between her fingers. "Why? Just because he wanted to know about the origins of your powers? What's the big deal about that?"

"The Bloodbacks attribute their gifts to a god-like deer, and not the alien ship," I say. "Which could very well be true. One of them may have killed an Empowered deer and gleaned powers from the affected blood. I guess it doesn't matter."

Teto's ears arrow. *Siski say wolves always have power.*

"I'm not arguing."

Star Walker not religious.

"Not really. Why?"

He snorts. *Always matter where you come from. Siski say we from deer. Lamar ask questions. Lamar explore.*

"How, Teto?" I say. "Where?"

Swap, he says.

I bite my lip. "The black market? What for?"

Lamar get past wall. Quarantine Zone. Lamar find things.

Birds trail me to the window. At the north end of Shelley, the wreck crests above the thirty-foot concrete wall enclosing most of old downtown. "He was scavenging for the swap?"

Teto nods, his eyes closed as Abi works her hands down his neck in a frenzy. *Lamar find for old man. Russian.*

"Gennady..."

I used to make my living trading alien tech with Gennady. The man is the unofficial regent of the black market in Break Pointe, always knowing who else was trading, buying, or selling. And since I've been clamping down on the market, it's probably fair to say he's not going to be buying one of my T-shirts.

"Teto, do you think Lamar's involvement in the black market had something to do with his death?"

The zipper on the pouch around Teto's neck telekinetically draws back, and a small piece of alien tech floats out, across the room into my hand. Still not used to this.

"A power coil," I say, turning the object around. Three black stripes stamp the smooth metal, but these aren't carbon scoring from the crash. Some kind of mark. A seller's stamp. This was sold somewhere else. Why would Lamar have it?

"Where did you get this, Teto?"

Lamar's collection, Teto says. *Last piece he run.*

"Lamar was running... he was transporting contraband."

Of course. An Empowered wolf is the ideal mule. No one would have noticed him moving through the night. The margins of cities. Someone caught on to him, though. Someone Empowered. Maybe that's why no one across the river turned up injured.

The killer isn't at the tower.

"Running to where?"

I don't know, Teto says. *You find out?*

"I'll find out what happened, Teto. I promise."

He shakes off Abi and bounds to his feet. She flinches a bit, bracing for the worst and then he licks her cheek.

Teto want justice. Teto want peace.

"So do I," I say. "I appreciate you coming here tonight. I know it must be risky for you to do so."

His ears flatten, and his head droops. *Siski good leader. Siski strong. She protect pack.*

"Teto, would she have been angry? That he was doing this?"

Siski never hurt one of her own.

A telekinetic could have inflicted the blunt force trauma that killed Lamar. Any of the wolves could have done it. That doesn't explain his emaciation, though. None of the pack want for a meal, so far as I can tell. He was banished, though. Food might have been harder for him, if they all hunted the same ground.

"I understand," I say.

Find killer. Bring justice.

"I promise the killer will see justice. Like I told her, I can't turn them over to the Bloodbacks."

Siski say our ground. Our law.

"I don't know it is your ground, Teto."

His eyes narrow. *You have power?*

"People keep telling me," I say.

Teto looks over to the mess of my workbench, and the bits and pieces of my engine. *You have power. For city.*

He knows my thoughts. All my designs and schemes. "If I'm lucky, I can manufacture more."

More lights, more people?

"Let's see about the ones we have, first."

More people, more buildings. Roads. Less woods.

"I want to make Break Pointe safe and prosperous for everyone, Teto. The wolves as well."

His ears flatten. *Find killer, tell me.*

What is he asking? What will I be agreeing to, handing that information over? I have to contain this. Stop this.

"I will."

Teto nods and trots to the door. The knob turns on its own, and the door creaks back. It closes behind him. His nails dance against the peeled linoleum in the hall down to the stairway and I ease into a chair at the dining table.

"I kind of want to keep him," Abi says.

I offer a wan smile, too lost in thought to do much else. The world of The Derelicts expands and contracts, as it always did; wolves yearning for knowledge. Blood for blood.

Abi sits in my lap, instantly collapsing my attention back to her. That shield of mine goes up, and she just sits there, stalled out with hope she can't burn. "So... what now?"

I turn the coil over in my hand. "Now I talk to Gennady."

Under all the snow, the train shed of Crown Station is just another drift. The island an arctic waste of drumlins and ridges, broken only by the half-buried violence of ruins. Enough of the pink sky capping the peninsula reflects down on The Derelicts to leave us in a mauve kind of shade. Inside the shed, I must seem the source of it. A wayward red ghost. Gennady lives and works out of an old, furnished car left on the tracks. Smoke blacks out of a chimney on top. The light of a coal fire flickers inside the windows, and through the metal chassis of the car, energy bright and vivid to me as the sunrise.

"Kitty Cat," the old man says. "What you bring me?"

I place the coil in his hand.

Gennady strokes his beard, white as his eyes. "This is not mine. I am not selling this."

"Who does?"

"What you have in trade?"

I sit in the old, cushioned chair across from him. "I have a dead wolf, Gennady. And a pack of others looking for a fight."

"This is threat you are bringing me?"

"Consider it a friendly warning," I say.

"Is Lamar who is being dead?"

"He ran for you?"

Gennady shakes his head. "He did. But then he stop. He have too many scruples, is how you say, I am thinking."

"Scruples?"

"*Da*, yes. He is – he was – funny wolf."

"Then who did he run for?"

He turns the coil over in his hand, end over end, as he looks at me. "You are making business very bad, Kitty Cat."

"This technology is too dangerous," I say.

"For you, maybe."

"It belongs to us."

A smile pinches his cheeks. "Us?"

Most of the time, it's just me. Sometimes, I hear the alien. The work must continue. And sometimes, just sometimes, there's no difference. There's no me. Only us.

"I need your help," I say.

He places the coil on the table beside his chair. "I am always wanting to help you, Kitty Cat. You no help me. This is not being friends. All the years I put food on your table."

I bite my lip. "What do you want?"

Gennady strokes his beard. "You no stop thieves anymore."

"I can't do that."

He shrugs. "Is market. Is swap, *da?* Always the way. I give to you, you give to me. This is being friends."

The only way of getting by here has always been trade. Exchange. Surrender. "I'll let the little stuff slide. I don't care about people trying to keep themselves warm. But no one is stripping the wreck for parts, Gennady. We won't allow it."

He picks up the coil. "This is coming from Blind Tiger."

"The Responder? From Chicago?"

Gennady nods. "He is one of Blackwood's go-betweens."

Officially, GP has been trying to close the market for years. Unofficially, Blackwood wanted it open. He couldn't get behind the wall and to the ship legally, so he made a show of nabbing dealers every so often while he was dealing under the table with Gennady. Responders broke up the swap every so often. Turns out they were pocketing the contraband they confiscated.

"But this mark – he's selling on the black market?" I say. "He's not acquiring tech for Great Power?"

Gennady shrugs again. "I am not knowing his business. I am not knowing any business these days, Kitty Cat."

"You don't seem sorry for heat, Gennady."

He smiles. "I am never sorry."

With Blackwood gone, Blind Tiger may only be in business for himself. Lamar had to have brought the coil back with him from Chicago. But why? If he needed a power coil, I couldn't have stopped him from clawing one out of the wreck.

The coil floats out of Gennady's hand, back into mine. "Thank you, Gennady. I appreciate this."

"You are not going to Blind Tiger without trading again," he says, as I make my way to the door. "You get nothing without giving, Kitty Cat. You are remembering this, *da?*"

"Stay warm," I say and leave.

Birds flutter away from the windowpane in anticipation of me coming inside the apartment. I float through the window, down to the paint-scabbed wood panels of the floor.

The oversized Freddie Mercury shirt Abi sleeps in slinks off her shoulder as she crawls out of bed. "What happened?"

I hold up the coil. "Road trip."

Abi springs out of bed. "I need to make a list and stuff!"

As she starts to pack, I try to put all my worry aside and relax, if only for the moment. There's a chance now, to discover the truth. To put together the puzzle. Birds rap against the bathroom door. Wolves howl in the distance. Abi races around the apartment, her feet barely touching the floor.

SIX

Famished tongues of cosmic energy lick the inside of my
jacket, nipping and lunging at every person who walks past on
Michigan Ave. Hundreds. Thousands, just since we started walking.
Too many. It would be, even without this caged animal rattling
around in my chest.

Why did I come here?

I never minded the solitude the ruins of Break Pointe imposed on
you. I pull down the shroud of my hoodie. Bury my hands in my
pockets. My shoulders hunch up around the cinnamon roll of this
turtleneck Abi picked out for me, and I go flat against the wall of
some building on a street named after one of the presidents.

Abi drifts back to me. "What's wrong?"

I wrestle the lightning in me. Thunder rattles in the distance,
building in intensity as the L train rumbles and then squeals to a stop
at the station down at the next corner.

"There's too many..."

Abi lowers her voice. "I thought you had control of this."

The Myriad exists in a constant state of hunger. I maintain
control through sheer will, but the wildlife of Break Pointe is easy to

ignore. Just about all of it got acquired in 1968. Pigeons, ants, rabbits, the alien has these. What the maw inside me craves more than anything is variety. The more unique a being, the more complex, the more the Myriad desires it. Every person is different. The inflection of their energy particular. Chicago teems with distinctiveness.

Opportunity.

"We should go back," I say, turning toward the cold concrete of the building. "We shouldn't have come."

"I'm sorry, I didn't realize," she says.

"I've been trying to tell you."

"Ok. All right." Abi smiles. "Look at me. Hey."

I look at her. Focus. Try and focus.

"You're in control," Abi says, popping the collar of my jacket. "You've got like, a lot of layers here. You got this."

"I don't."

"Focus on me."

"Ok."

"Focus on us. Just us."

I squeeze her hand and shut everything else out except for the steady rhythm of her pulse, *ba-dumm, ba-dumm, ba-dumm.* She gently leads me back into the river of people streaming past.

"Tell me about the last time you were here," Abi says.

"I want to stop."

"We're almost to the club."

I drag my feet. "Let's stop."

"We came all this way to see Blind Tiger. He's just up the street a bit, right? We'll go in, we'll talk, we'll chill. It will be ok. It's going to be ok. So. You came to visit family?"

I was six or seven. It was the only time we came here. After Dad died, we didn't really have any contact with his side of the family. Ma never talked about her own, except to speak sometimes of her mother, usually around the holidays.

"Yes," I say, as we round a corner. Every step another into a strip of fly tape. Chicago tugs at me. The people. Cars. Buses. Trains.

Millions of tons of steel. The electric life flowing through its veins. If I lose focus, for one instant and I grip Abi's hand so tight she makes a little sound. "Sorry."

"It's ok. It's fine. Where are they, your family?"

"Gresham. Near St. Sabina Church."

"Want to stop there on the way back?"

I bite my lip. "I don't know."

"Don't you miss them?"

"I don't really know them. Dad never said much about them and I don't know why. Ma acted like they didn't like her. Me. And I never knew Ma's side, either, we were all just... castaways. Do you know?"

She nods. "I'll be a castaway with you."

Don't you want something else? Something better?

"You kind of are," I say.

Usually, her expressions are so quick. Easy. This one takes a moment. Takes a few different shapes. Eventually, it settles on something like contentment. Something like pride.

"I want you to touch me," she says, pinching the fingertip of my glove. "I want you to know what you mean to me, Kit. I know all I do is talk and it probably gets annoying, but I can't ever say."

"Say what?"

Her lips draw toward mine. "I'm never lost with you."

"Abi..."

She peels my turtleneck up over my lips and kisses me. I could be standing in the middle of Times Square. I could be standing on the surface of the sun. All the energy in the universe wouldn't be enough to distract me from her.

"Let's talk to Blind Tiger," I say. "And go home."

I take the lead now, hurrying down a less-trafficked street under the L line. Plywood encloses the faces of the storefronts along the street. Stumps of old traffic meters they cut off at the base stab out of the concrete every few feet, which what the fuck and I stop before a graffitied wall halfway down the block, painted in opposing lines of yellow and black.

"Did we take a wrong turn?" Abi says.

"We're here," I say, and knock on the wall.

A door opens out of the wall. Bright orange eyes, like hot pokers, peer from within.

"Password," the brick of a guy inside says.

I pull down my turtleneck and the curtain on the magenta light show flickering beneath. "Kit Baldwin."

The bouncer teeters back on his feet, unsure, and then the door closes. If this goes sideways, I can go invisible by manipulating the electromagnetic spectrum emanating from me. Pretty sure I can't hide Abi. I'm too far away from the distortions of the ship's core to pinch open a portal to the In Between. A fierce north wind catches the halogen sail hanging low over the city. If I had to, I could fly across the lake back to Break Pointe. Fifteen minutes. Magnetic tension between the Myriad and the world would propel me up to three hundred miles an hour. Abi would probably be dead of hypothermia by the time we got there.

"Do you think they validate?" Abi says.

"What?"

The door opens again, and the bouncer ushers us into a dark, narrow hallway, draped in velvet curtains. A woman of Asian descent stalks down the hall, in a vintage flapper-like dress shimmering as much as her platinum blonde hair.

"Ms. Baldwin, I don't have you on the guest list."

"Consider it a health and safety inspection."

An oxblood smile gashes her lips. "Is that a threat?"

"Tell him I'm here. I want to see him."

The concierge clicks her fingers and the bouncer gestures for me and Abi to follow him on.

"You're so butch," Abi whispers.

"Let's hope this is as butch as I have to get," I say, and we leave the hallway, into the most secret club in Chicago.

Soft candlelight illuminates the room, arranged with small round tables between a bar and stage. No band accompanies the woman in the black dress singing on stage, yet smooth jazz drifts through the club lazy as the cigarette smoke. A single, stereoscopic eye lurks in the haze. Scaled skin. Fishbowl helmets on puffy containment suits, the claustrophobic universe of Empowered who can't travel any other way. A different kind of tug pulls on me now. I know what it's like to be trapped within your power. Working at the Blackwood Building, I'd gotten used to a Great Power of idealized human specimens. Not all Empowered enjoy such privilege. Clubs like this offer a refuge for them in a world that still fears the strange.

The bouncer guides us to a private booth, at the back of the room. I've never met Blind Tiger, but like most of GP's most prominent members, I've seen pictures of him. Even if I hadn't, I would have pegged him right away. Easy laughter radiates from the African-American man holding court in the booth. A cool confidence. His eyes never abandoned their gaze into the distance beyond the booth, but he seems to become aware of me as I approach.

Blind Tiger holds up his hand, instantly bringing the chatty music among the men and women clustered with him to a stop. A smile crosses his lips. He still doesn't look at me.

"You're even more beautiful in person," he says.

"I scrub up ok," I say.

"Ladies and gentlemen, please excuse me. I have business."

Disappointment, and some not quite low-key jealousy, paints the faces of the people leaving the booth. Once they've gone, Blind Tiger slides out to greet us. He takes my hand.

"I'm flattered, Kit – may I call you Kit? – that you came all this way to see me. You give a man ideas."

"I came because – "

His head tilts toward Abi, again without directly looking at her. "And who's this gorgeous creature?"

Abi blushes. "Oh, wow. Hi. I'm Abi."

"Delighted, Abi. Please, ladies, sit. What would you like to drink? Are you hungry? Furnace here will take your coats."

The bouncer reaches for mine.

"I'll keep mine if that's ok," I say and slide into the booth with Abi. "We're not staying."

"Furnace, see we're not interrupted." Blind Tiger returns to the booth, smiling. "This is what I love about this place. You just never know who's going to walk through the door."

"I'm not here for any trouble," I say.

"Perfect, because I don't think I could give you any. Still, showing up unannounced at a private Empowered establishment after the mess you made of GP is... provocative."

Everyone is looking at us. All of them Empowered. Coming here, I thought this club of Blind Tiger's was excessive, but I doubt there's anywhere else in Chicago these people feel comfortable. Even in Break Pointe, you tend not to see the really unusual among them. Frontline GP Responders tend to all be bland, boring, and beautiful. The advertising is Valene. This lot may not feel represented, exactly, at GP but I doubt any of them appreciated the dent I put in their retirement fund.

"I need your help, Blind Tiger."

"Call me Anwar, I insist. Only clients or fans call me Blind Tiger. And let's get you some drinks – "

"Water is fine, thank you."

"Anything you want. Your money is no good here."

"That's good, because we don't have any."

"What's expensive?" Abi says.

Anwar smiles and his eyes fix across the room, on the bar. There, the bartender stops rinsing glasses mid-motion. He blinks, like he's confused, and starts mixing three martinis.

"Three Ad Astras coming up," Anwar says.

Abi leans forward. "What happened? What's your power?"

"I can make people see what I want them to see, Abi. I saw three drinks. Now we're going to have three drinks."

"So like mind control?"

"More like suggestion," Anwar says, as a waiter arrives with the drinks. "And not quite as simple. I also see what they see. I can see through the eyes of anyone around me."

I pick at the napkin under my drink. "You're blind."

"Otherwise." Anwar sips at his martini. "But never sore for vision. You two ladies are certainly a sight."

Right.

He can see through us. He can make us see things. Do things. He gains control of me, I don't know what will happen. Focus. If I don't come out of here with answers about Lamar, then I'm not keeping a lid on the Bloodbacks. More people will die.

"Anwar, as I was saying – "

Abi drinks her martini down in one go and pushes the glass forward. I shoot her a look: *What are you doing?*

"Another?" Anwar says.

"We're not here to drink," I say, pointedly.

Anwar blinks. "I assume you're here to tell me to stay out of the black market. I have to say I appreciate you coming to me directly. I respect that. I wear a GP uniform, but I'm my own man. There's no need for the two of us to be enemies."

The waiter collects Abi's glass and boomerangs back to the bar. All eyes still on us. Some of them green. Glowing.

"I agree," I say.

Anwar breaks out into a big smile. "Glad to hear it. See, I knew there was something about you. My colleagues back at the tower all have a biased, let's say, opinion of you, but sometimes what one requires is a different perspective. Every now and again, it's good for other people to see things my way."

The waiter deposits Abi's drink on the table. Anwar smiles as she takes it and I don't know what she's doing. I don't know if she's doing what she wants to. I zip down my jacket. Magenta dawns in the booth. Chairs push out across the room. His jaw clenches as I set the power coil on the table.

Anwar turns it over and feels the three black stripes on the back. "I have a pretty clear no return policy, Kit."

"Lamar had this."

"Lamar?"

"He's dead," I say.

Anwar slumps back in the booth. "Dead? This is terrible."

"Do you know what happened?"

"I have no idea... I had no idea." Anwar raises his glass. "To Lamar. A damn fine wolf, and an even better cardplayer."

I lift my glass. "Cardplayer?"

"Insidious. How did he die?"

"He was in a fight with someone. We think."

His brows arch. "Someone Empowered?"

"That's the idea."

"Hard to see why anyone at the tower would..."

"I'm confident the killer isn't an Empowered in the city."

The coil turns over in Anwar's hands. "Is that right?"

The waiter arrives with another round of drinks. Crying out loud. He sets mine next to my still full glass. Abi drinks her martini down so quick she puts it right back on his tray.

"It's good," she says. "I like it."

I tear at my napkin. "We're on a mission here."

She smiles. "I'm on a mission from God."

"Don't be cute, Abi."

"I literally can't stop."

Anwar finishes his drink. "Keep them coming."

"I know what you're doing," I say.

He leans back with a lazy smile. "What am I doing?"

"It's no use trying to distract me, Anwar."

Abi nods, drunk. "It's true. Like, I have these." She points to her breasts. "Here to tell you. Zero joy."

I clear my throat. "Can we not?"

"Do we ever?"

I don't know what to say. I never know what to say. Abi looks away, wincing and focus. You have to focus.

"Why would this coil have been in Lamar's possession?"

Anwar shrugs. "I don't know."

"He was running for you, though."

"He was. A great shame. I have no one else in my employ with his skill or discretion. You would have liked Lamar."

"You were friends?"

Anwar smiles. "Maybe Lamar kept the power coil for himself... he was a curious fellow, I'll tell you. But I don't think he would steal from me. I don't mind if someone enjoys a perk now and again, but this is a significant loss on investment right here."

I rub the back of my neck. "You're not selling alien contraband back into Break Pointe, are you?"

His jaw droops. "Kit, I'm offended."

"Are you?"

His eyes fix on mine. Somehow, I see myself, looking at myself; this infinite mirror. And then my field of vision expands. I see what Anwar sees. What everyone he sees through does, all around the room, in the building, on the street.

"You see I'm no liar," he says, breaking his gaze.

I sip at my drink. "I'm sorry."

"No apology is necessary. You're simply doing your duty as the protector of Break Pointe. I understand. What do they call you? 'The Keeper?' Why not call yourself Responder?"

"I'm not with GP."

"I don't think you were ever officially let go."

"I'm inactive, then."

"Titles are flexible in the company."

"Like morals, it seems."

"Have to stay limber."

Abi nudges me. "I like him."

Anwar smiles, as the waiter returns again. I like Blind Tiger, too, but beyond the charm, he's no different from the people running GP who had let Break Pointe wither and die rather than give their help. Blind Tiger is selling alien tech smuggled out of Break Pointe in the city he's charged to defend. No doubt he's selling the power coils elsewhere, too. Nevermind he can blink and turn us both into puppets. Nevermind he knows more than he's saying about what happened to Lamar. I'm not going to get anywhere with him. I'll be lucky to get out of here.

"I'm as concerned as you are, Kit," he says. "Lamar was an employee. He was a friend. What else can you tell me?"

"He was emaciated," Abi says.

Anwar squints. "Emaciated?"

"Does that mean something to you?"

"You ladies have come a long way," Anwar says. He licks the little plastic sword running the olive through in his martini. "Let's do this. Let me find where this coil was meant to go. In the meantime, avail yourself of whatever you need at the bar."

I shake my head. "I said we're not staying."

"Compliments of the house." Anwar looks off in the distance. A moment later, the concierge arrives with a pained smile. "You've met my assistant, Erika Boshi, haven't you? Boshi, a room for our guests. The finest available."

She clasps her hands together, with mock enthusiasm. "It will be my sincere and absolute joy."

Anwar leaves the booth. "If you get bored, the bar is open all night and if it's your pleasure, you can find cards and other games on the fourteenth floor. I have a feeling you won't be leaving your room all that much, though."

I slide out of the booth. "I have to get back to the city."

"What's one night?" Abi says.

I shoot her a look and her drunk smile vanishes. "Thank you, Anwar, but we don't have time for this."

He holds up his hands. "Kit, what's the rush? You came for answers. Let me get them for you. I need a little time, but I assure you, this is my top priority. Spend the night, relax, watch TV or do... something else, and in the morning I will brief you on what I've found. Then you can be on your way."

I don't feel great about staying here. I don't feel any better about leaving without answers. Vidette and Mike can watch the city for one night. What's one night?

"Fine," I say, though Abi isn't excited now.

"Outstanding. Enjoy the rest of your evening, ladies."

Anwar kisses my hand, and sweeps away into the club.

Boshi gestures toward an elevator door set in the curtains at the back of the room. "This way."

I clutch Abi's hand tight as we enter the old, brass-paneled elevator. An unnerving smile creeps across Boshi's lips as the doors rattle shut and the floor feels like it gives out.

SEVEN

"We totally need to have sex in this bed," Abi says, falling back into a plush mound of white pillows.

Her bathrobe blends into the covers so much she's reduced to the dark splay of her wet hair, and the exposed valley of skin stretching from the pit of her throat to the mound of her belly. I pinch the fabric of this turtleneck, heavier with the damp humidity Abi's shower left in the room. All I wanted to do was get out of these clothes, into the shower with her but once I got in the room, bristling with lights and televisions and electronic everything, I kept it on.

Everything teases the Myriad. Everything demands my attention. My resistance. I sit in the chair by the window, staring out on the gleaming checkerboard of the city as Abi hums through a medley of animated musical numbers.

"You're not saying anything," she says.

"Sorry."

"Do you want to watch some TV? There's like a billion channels. And pay per view. There's porn, I looked." Her fingers slide into the opening in her bathrobe. "Or do you just want to watch?"

I stop trying to solve the puzzle of the city. "Watch?"

Her hand eases between her legs. "Come here."

This sound murmurs out of her. Soft. Desperate. Her back arches. Her fingers sink. Her breath quickens. Her pulse intensifies, *ba-dumm, ba-dumm, ba-dumm*, magnetic as the energy radiating out of her. The lights. The city. The world.

I clear my throat. "I'm going to run a bath."

Her eyes open, ballistae targeted straight up at the ceiling. "I'm trying to make this work for us."

"I just have a lot on my mind. I'm sorry. And I don't feel comfortable here. I feel like Anwar is watching."

Abi closes her robe. "Ok."

"See if you can find a musical or something. "

"Musical? I had no idea you were so kinky."

"We can just get in bed and relax. Do you mind if I unplug some of this stuff we're not using? And unscrew the light bulbs. Maybe the clock, too."

"Ok... want to order some food? Maybe some cookies? You know what, I'm just going to run this bill up." Abi stretches across the bed and picks up the phone on the nightstand. "Hey, Chad. The shower-head was the bomb, thanks. So, what's the cookie situation? Mm-hmm. Uh-huh. Ok. Here's what I'm thinking..."

The room darkens behind me until all that's left is the snowy pallor of the television. The frustrated burl of energy on the bed. I want to go back out there and tear her robe off. Bend her over the side of the bed. Lance her heart with this lure of light inside me, and pluck her life right out of her body.

Maybe a cold shower is what I need.

I strip out of these clothes as the water runs. Months now, I've been whatever I am. A hybrid. Amalgam. Synthesis. And still, I'm not quite used to the flare of light whenever I undress. My body is my body, same as it was the day of my transformation, and yet it's completely alien. Strands of fractal energy course deep beneath my skin, like snakes through water. They leap at my reflection. Tendrils of crimson light pat the bathroom mirror, confused, and then recede back to my heart. Bleeding Jesus.

I don't even recognize myself.

Who am I? A frightened young woman. The faceless, nameless Ever. A BPPD officer the alien had acquired back in 1968. An alien warrior from a world called Destos. A million faces flicker in the light of the Myriad. A million identities. A million souls, all of whom I see through. I want to be them. I want to be me. I want to be everything. The light of the television. The sun. Abi's smile. I can become all of those things. But I can never be them, not really. They're masks, I can take on and off. Same as the one I wear now. I've never truly been at home in my skin. I'll never be in anyone else's. My fate always to be between. Always seeing. Never being.

Energy snaps against the mirror again. Abi creases inside the door, her silhouette etched in the light of the television.

"You're so beautiful," she says.

I cross my arm across my chest, like somehow that's going to hold back the storm inside me. "Abi, don't."

She blubbers her lips. "I thought things were different."

"They are. I am. You don't understand."

"Then tell me."

"I've been trying to tell you," I say.

"And you keep repeating yourself, like I'm going to just go, 'Yeah, that makes sense.' But it doesn't. You can do this, Kit. You just don't want to. You did this shit before, with the buoy thing or whatever it was. You could open it, you just didn't want to because then you'd have to deal with it."

I bite my lip. "I'm dealing with a lot, Abi."

"What you want to." She sniffs. "That night when you changed. You came to my apartment. You almost killed me. That thing did, anyways. But you controlled it. You've been in control since the start. You can do this."

"I want to."

She unties her robe. It falls to the floor and she's as naked as I am. The both of us bathed in red. "Kiss me. Make love to me. Get some of your living back."

I turn away. "I'm sorry."

She sighs. "I used to think you were just shy, or maybe just you, but since this happened... I think on some level you're ok with it because you don't have to connect with people now at all. You don't have to solve anything. You can just keep working on problems and that way you always have something to fix."

"I don't know what you mean."

Abi ties her robe back on. "Is this how you're holding on, or something? Like you're afraid you've changed so much, or you're not you, and so you just kind of be this extra you."

"That's a lot of pronouns, Abi."

"So... the answer is yes, then."

I wish she could see as Blind Tiger does; I wish Abi could see through my eyes, and see the truth. Then all these words, too big to leave my throat, they'd be unnecessary. I wouldn't ever have to say, or explain, or justify. I could just be, and she'd know. This want. This fear. This fucking whiplash. The silence grows unbearable and Abi drifts back to the door.

"Let's just go back to bed, then," she says. "Watch something. I'll find a movie. Is that what you want?"

I grab her sash. "I want you."

"I refer back to my previous comments and stuff."

Manic fingers of light twist up inside me. "I want you so much. I want to make sense. I want to be that light that I am with you. I want to be that warmth that I am with you."

"Kit..."

"And then I don't, because... even if it wasn't for this..." I claw at the facsimile of my skin, backlit by the Myriad. "I'd still be this way. I was like this before I changed."

"Hey, I didn't mean that."

"It's true. I was all this want and feeling and emotion and I didn't know how to process it. I didn't know how to conduct any of it without overloading the system." I cover my mouth. God. What am I saying. "I don't know how to get any of it out. I have all this love. I have love to give, Abi. You don't know."

"I do. Hey. I know."

"I don't know," I say. "I don't."

"Give it to me. Kit. All of it. I'm right here."

"But I'm not here. *I'm not here.* I'm trying to plug every leak in the city. I'm trying to ignore the voice in my head that wants me to drain every living thing on Earth like a battery. After the battle, I thought I was in control. I'm the alien. But that's the problem. *I'm the alien.* The alien acquires things. I can fight it. I can deny it. But that's what it is. That's who I am, Abi. I just want to take everything. And so I'm afraid. I'm afraid I'll destroy you. The both of us."

"Destroy me," Abi says.

"What?"

"Burn me up. Make me new."

"Abi..."

Her lips tease mine. "We can get back our lives, Kit. We can have living again. We can be new, both of us."

My hand jitters over her cheek. One touch. One small gesture of affection, and I will change us forever. Either we live as no one as lived, life and death together, or I consume her, and carry her with me forever, among all my guilts. This want. This need. It's bent me out of shape. My eyes glow ruby in the bathroom mirror. Look at me. Look what I've done to myself.

I withdraw from her. "I'm sorry."

Her hands claw through her hair. "It's ok."

"Baby, I'm sorry."

"No, it's ok. I understand, Kit. I do. I know what it's like to fight this force inside you." Abi leans against the counter, her hands shaking. Her whole body. "This thing that isn't you, but... you can't really control it."

I think I've known this since we were working in the lab at the tower. She always had a drink in her hand. I cataloged it, but never gave it any thought like a million other things, all my focus somewhere up in the clouds with Valene. Last few months it's been everywhere else but Abi. I've just made this worse. The craziness. Uncertainty. Birds in the apartment.

Christ. I'm my mother.

"Abi..." I reach for her. "Do you want to talk about it?"

She smiles. I don't think I've ever seen her put so much effort into it. "I want to tell you everything."

I grab a bit of her robe. "I haven't been there for you."

"It's not your fault."

"I know, but I also know this is all weighing on you."

"This has been since I was young. This thing in you..."

As afraid as I am for her, at the same time, I'm kind of relieved. Strange as that is. Abi does understand. Inside of her, just as in me, is this insatiable monster. Or I don't know. Maybe it's different. But it's both something we fight.

I close my arms around her shoulders, careful no part of me is touching her. "It's going to be ok."

"It feels like being... buried." Abi teeters in my arms. Baby girl. We find each other in the mirror. The obscured light of the Myriad leaves Abi's face half in shadow. "Like dying. But then you come back. You come back to it, every time."

"I'm sorry. I know I can't understand with the drinking, but I'm here. You can talk to me about anything."

Shadows of light creep across Abi's pained expression. "Drinking?"

"You have a problem. Don't you?"

She nods. "Yeah. I do."

"Let me help."

She drifts from me a little. "I'll go to a meeting tomorrow. I was thinking about it anyways. I looked one up online. It's close to here."

"Oh. You go to meetings? Back home?"

"There's one at the tower," Abi says, wiping her face on the sleeve of her robe. "Every Wednesday."

I bite my lip. "I didn't know."

"I didn't want you to. You deal with so much."

"But you're important to me. I'm going to be here for you. I'm going to make this right. I'll make this work."

Her sigh pushes us apart. "This is nothing you can fix."

I flinch. "I know that, Abi."

"Do you remember? The day you came into work, and the protestors had all spit in your hair? It was the first time you really talked to me. I kept trying to get your attention, and I know, you're... I love how important things are to you. How much you want to help other people. I never had anything growing up. I didn't have friends. Any other family. I think I got sort of, expressive, to generate some interest, but... I'm not interesting. I'm not like a genius, or hot, or anything like that. I'm not really good at anything, except getting things done really fast, because somehow that will make a difference to the people I'm trying to impress. And that's all they want from you. Quiet efficiency. A shadow that doesn't move until they do."

I shake my head. "Your parents?"

"Duh," Abi says, with a quick smile.

"You're smart, Abi. You're beautiful."

"I'm not anything, except in love with you. Like it hurts and stuff. We work. We're easy. If you just let me in. That's all you have to do. Let me in. The rest will just happen, Kit."

I reach for her again. "Let me come to this meeting with you tomorrow. Can I come? Or is there something else I can do?"

"You want to fix me," Abi says.

"You're twisting this all around."

"I want to just to tell you."

"You can."

Her voice breaks. "I want to tell you the truth."

I hold on to the robe, loose and shifting every time she moves. "Abi, you can tell me anything."

She searches the mirror, like she's looking for something. "I want to. I want to be broken with you. But you always have to have something or someone to fix. That way you never have to stop, and work on yourself."

I let go of her. I pick up my clothes off the floor. I hold them in my hands, like I try and hold back the embarrassment and humiliation at sharing so much of my pain and having it thrown back at me. I don't know what just happened. I'm listening. I'm trying to listen. I don't know what to do, but what I always do when I can't make it work. I leave, Abi in the dark.

EIGHT

DENSE FOG SHROUDS THE LAKE AND WHAT SHOULD BE A GRAND view from Blind Tiger's penthouse apartment. Buildings form and dissolve before I get any sense of their shape. The sun flares, illuminating the expansive, lavish apartment, but then withers just as fast, leaving me in cold, gray confusion.

Boshi's heels clack against the hardwood floors. "He'll be another minute. He's with a client."

I leave the window. "At seven in the morning?"

"The Responder of Chicago has many demands on his time."

"So do I."

"I'd think you'd want to draw this out," Boshi says, walking through the open floor of the apartment into the kitchen. She takes an orange from the massive fridge and starts peeling it at the sink. "Get a couple nights out of this."

This bitch. I head for the door. "He can email me."

Just then, Blind Tiger comes into the apartment. "Kit, where are you going? Why do you look so tired? I can guess. Didn't get much sleep last night, I take it?"

I rub my neck, imagining Abi's fingers, her lips, her warmth so ready and I don't know how I spent the night without it, but I did. Eight hours at the gaming tables, watching. Calculating odds. Exploring different outcomes.

House always wins.

"Can we make this quick?" I say. "I have to get back."

"Or maybe you slept on the wrong side of the bed." He goes into the kitchen. Boshi hands him the peeled orange slices. Anwar leans against the island. "Mmm. That's good."

I drift back to him. "Are you wearing a cape?"

"Anything less is uncivilized," he says and shrugs the black cape off his shoulders. He rests it over a stool at the island. "I apologize for my lateness, Kit. It was a long night for me, too. I have some information for you. Boshi."

Boshi touches her PEAL. All the windows tint. Digital files manifest on the glass, as if the windows are monitors.

"What is this?" I say.

Anwar takes his time with the orange slices. "I did some digging. You mentioned Lamar was emaciated. That got me thinking. I've investigated a few incidents over the years, most of them on the South Side. Over into Gary, though it's out of my jurisdiction. People who were found dead in just such a way. Nothing improper was ever found in the autopsies, but loved ones insisted the emaciation was sudden. Happened overnight."

My hand glides across the glass as I swipe through documents and pictures from the Chicago Police Department. All of them feature victims with extreme emaciation, but the coroner's reports were inconclusive. I grind my fingers into the back of my neck. There have been at least twelve incidents in the Chicago area, mostly on the South Side, some going back twenty years.

This is a serial killer. An Empowered one.

Blind Tiger sucks the juice off the end of his thumb. "Aren't you glad you stayed?"

Maybe Lamar isn't as specific a target as I thought. And maybe there have been other victims in Break Pointe over the same period, but we just don't know. How many people go missing in The Derelicts? How many bodies are the ruins coffin to? And if it is an Empowered, someone at GP, then any incident reports could easily be falsified, or done away with altogether.

"If this emaciation occurs overnight, they have to be sapping the victim's energy," I say.

He nods. "No Empowered on record has such power."

"What about government agents? Covert operators?"

"You and The Uniform seem to be friends. Maybe you could ask him if he has any life-sucking comrades."

"I doubt I could get a message to him in the stockade."

Anwar smiles. "And I doubt his punishment for helping you is so severe. Most likely they have him shoveling shit on some backwater assignment in the desert or arctic. That probably rules out any special forces as our suspect. Whoever this is, they're local. They could be unregistered," Anwar says, but he doesn't sound as if he believes it. I don't, either. Unregistered Empowered are scarce and if found, usually across the border in Canada or Mexico. "That leaves only one other option."

Fear blooms in me like the tentative sun outside. The killer drains energy. Outside of some Empowered we don't know about, the only being capable of doing that is The Ever.

Me.

"Given the dates involved, you're clearly not a suspect," Blind Tiger says. "But could there be other aliens?"

Eight other Ever stalk time and space. Each collects energy to transmit back to the ship, though that link severed when it crashed in Break Pointe. I don't think they know where it is.

I don't think they can get here.

"We were the only Ever aboard the ship when it crashed."

Anwar squints. "'We?'"

I bite my lip. "Figure of speech."

"Can it reproduce?"

"No – "

Wait. I found the Myriad inside a kind of crystalline cocoon. The cocoon was empty. What came out of that shell?

"I don't know," I say.

"Can you be sure?"

Not without exposing my location, and the Earth, to the others. "There's a way, but... it comes with a price."

"Everything does."

Tell me about it. My mind fires. What if there is another Ever, prowling the gutted industrial wild between Break Pointe and Chicago for the last fifty years, living off of half-consumed energy? Even damaged, an Ever might be able to become invisible. They might be able to slip in and out of the In Between.

"What else can we do?" I say.

"I can review the case files again," Anwar says. "There may be more here in Chicago, but most older files are archived now that the police have been disbanded. Boshi, make the call to the archivist in Glenview. Tell them to expect us this morning."

She leaves without speaking. *Clack-clack-clack.* The door closes behind her, and a smile cracks on Anwar's lips.

"You don't like her," he says.

I shrug. "Feeling seems to be mutual."

"I like you."

I cast a sideways glance at him. "Thank you."

"You don't like me?"

"I don't know you."

"Maybe you just don't like black men?"

This is getting really sideways. "Men in general."

He smiles again. "What about black women?"

What is this supposed to be? My cue, that's what. I touch the window, closing the files. As I do, I acquire them all, and everything else connected to Anwar's personal wireless network.

"You review your files. I'll go back to Break Pointe and see what I can dig up there. Thank you, Anwar."

"We have a lot in common, Kit." Anwar leans against the

window. "We're both responsible for a city. And neither of us have all the resources we need to do our jobs."

The giant chandelier over the center of the living room glitters with the inconstant sun. "Is that right?"

"Great Power pays me very well. I'm a very fortunate man. Many people in Chicago are not. They can't afford the services of GP, and with the troubles the company has experienced recently, we've had to cut back. We're losing customers. Now, if you live downtown, or out in the northern suburbs, you don't ever think about your security. But if you live in Pullman, or Riverdale, or say Gresham, like your grandmother..."

I stop halfway to the door.

"...you probably think about it. A lot."

I turn back to him. "What are you doing?"

He raises his hands, like he's confused. "Making a point?"

"About black people? Or about me?"

"African Americans are nearly thirty percent of the population here," he says, like I don't know. "But only four percent of GP's customer base. You'll find the same in terms of the company's employment. I don't think I have to tell you that. I'm a lucky guy, it's true. But I earned this job. I earn it every day, playing an old game. You may have quit GP, Kit. But you can't quit the game. The uniform never comes off."

My body isn't my body anymore, not really, but my face didn't change. My skin color. My discomfort, layered and deep, at the subject he's picking at now. All my life, there's been someone like him, at school, at work, in Gresham, checking my credentials. Making connections was hard enough for me without being a nerdy mixed-race girl with a half-baked Irish accent. I was never American enough. Girly enough. Black enough.

"I didn't realize this was a test," I say.

Anwar gazes out on the invisible city. "It's always a test. Don't misunderstand me, Kit. I just want you to know where I'm coming from. You have certain ideas about me."

"You've got some about me."

"Lots of people do. Frankie Fleet. Evander Blackwood. Your old man's rather extensive relations on the South Side."

My fingers dig into my palm. "What do you know about them?"

"More than you, I think."

"Am I not angry enough for you, Anwar? Or is it just that I'm not impressed enough by all your 'bling?'"

He wears a smug smile as he heads back to the kitchen. "It takes a lot to impress you. Abi is a beautiful woman. Valene... *Valene.* Who can argue with that? I like all kinds of women. All kinds of people. I'm obligated to protect the ones who can afford me. And I'm obligated to the ones who can't."

This fucking guy.

"You think you're going to guilt me into – what, exactly? – by talking some basic shit about how I'm not doing enough for my own community? When was the last time you were in Break Pointe, Anwar? Do you know what my community looks like? Do you know what I do for them? Everything. I do everything, because people like you told people like them – like me – to drop dead."

Anwar leans against the counter of the island, nodding along. "You don't do anything, Kit."

"What?"

"That's why you're here. If you were so busy, and so successful, you would have sent one of your lieutenants. Nothing is happening in Break Pointe. You need something to happen."

"I'm leaving," I say, and head for the door. Again.

"You're here to make a difference," he says. "You're here to make something work. Isn't that right?"

I want to be broken with you, Abi said.

I stop. "Yes."

"I'm not giving you a hard time because I don't think you're doing enough, Kit. I'm giving you a hard time because I need to know how far you're willing to go."

"I don't understand."

"That power cell Lamar had? I sold it to a client in Detroit a few months ago. I checked my records. The client received the merchandise in full. No complaints."

I shake my head. "So how did Lamar end up with it?"

"I don't know."

I drift back to the kitchen. "If he took it from them, they might not have been that happy about it. Who did you sell it to?"

"I never ask."

"Why would you," I say.

He leans against the counter. "I want for there to be no secrets between us, so I'm telling you about Detroit. But we're not investigating that angle. They're a prize client and that's a revenue stream that frankly, I can't and won't do without."

"You're a real hero, Anwar."

"I don't sell contraband on the black market to maintain a certain lifestyle, Kit. I do it to protect a community that can't afford me otherwise. Those bean counters at the Blackwood Building, they just look at the bottom line on the balance sheet. None of them care where the money comes from, or why so many people in low-income housing have annual memberships."

I pull out a stool and sit down. "You're buying memberships for people with the money from the market?"

"Over 30,000 people. So if you shut down the black market…"

"I shut down these communities."

His eyes set off in the distance. "When it all went down between you and Blackwood, I got a phone call. The man himself. He asked me to look up your family there in Gresham."

My jaw dangles. "What?"

"'Talk to them,' he says. I knew what he meant. Convince them to go on TV and drag you. He couldn't do it. Frankie Fleet couldn't. But I could." His smile is tired now. "But the Baldwins are one of the families I pay out of petty cash. I'm responsible for them. So I lied. I told Blackwood they wouldn't have it. I never did talk to them. You should, though."

Sometimes I feel everything. Sometimes nothing. And some-times, like right now, I feel only the sheer of my fierce, determined resistance to feel anything at all.

"Thank you," I say.

"No thanks are necessary. I see everything, Kit. But I have to turn a blind eye to some things, to make the rest clear. As I said. I have to know how far you're willing to go."

Used to be I got these tension headaches. Instant. Head in a vise. I don't have nerves, anymore. Muscles. The chemistry that shrank my entire body around my last nerve. I just have the memory, triggered any time I run into the limits of my power.

"I'm just supposed to sit there and do nothing while people walk out of Break Pointe with the entire store?"

He shakes his head. "What do you need, in Break Pointe?"

I laugh. "Everything."

"What do you need most?"

"Power," I say. "I need heat. Lights. I can defend against Empow-ered criminals, but not hypothermia. I have this idea, though... it's an engine, based on the Myriad. It can offer clean, unlimited energy. It works. I can light The Derelicts with it, if I could manufacture it. If I had the money."

He nods. "How much?"

"Millions of dollars. I don't even know. Parts, labor, infrastructure. Cities don't have that kind of money."

"Let's make a deal," he says. "I'm going to give you the capital you need to get started on this engine of yours."

I reel back on the stool. With the engine, I can get the city through the winter. I can save lives. "And in return?"

"You're going to leave the black market open. More than that, you're going to give me right of first refusal on everything that comes out of your lab."

Visions of a lab humming with creativity crackle through my head. Focus. "I'm here to find a killer."

"You're going to catch one. Hypothermia."

I shouldn't be surprised. Gennady did this to me. This is no different. Just economies of scale.

I tug at the zipper of my jacket. "I promised to clean up the wreck. To police my city. Contraband is against the law."

"I think you make the law now in Break Pointe," he says. "You can clean up the wreck. I'll still take all the junk off your hands. This engine works, I'll take that, too."

"I don't know."

"You're a smart girl, Kit. Good with math. It's a simple equation. Help me, and I help you. We help our communities."

"At what cost?"

He closes his eyes. "What choice do you have?"

The same one I had when I took the Myriad. I thought I was doing something for someone else, for the greater good and it cost me my life. Not my life. Any kind of living. And yet I have done good, haven't I? I've salvaged some hope at least that something is going to get better in The Derelicts.

How is it going to get better?

"Ok," I say.

His brows arch. "Ok?"

"I'll keep the market open..." The zipper strains in my hand. "And you'll fund my engine."

Anwar extends his hand. The sun flares briefly and the dark of the room ejects, only to fall back in. I wish Abi was here. I wish I had her pulse to guide me, *ba-dumm.*

"But I'm working with you. Not GP."

"This is strictly us. And strictly off the books."

I shake his hand. "Deal."

"Outstanding." He lifts his cape off its perch and wraps it around his shoulders. "Let's go look at some files."

The birds leave the window. I follow Anwar out of the apartment, not at all sure where I'm going.

NINE

Miles of boxes line the shelves in a warehouse somewhere in the suburbs. Sifting through the old case files is excruciating. If I could just put my hand on one of these and acquire all the information stored here, I could save myself days. Strange deaths involving emaciated corpses ought to be obvious enough, but there's no key to this map. Decades of boxes go on into the dark, the warehouse musty as an old library, and my PEAL buzzes.

I don't look at it at first. What do I say to Abi.

I don't think I've ever been in a fight with a girlfriend before. Actually, I don't know I've ever had a proper girlfriend. Valene, I guess. Before her, before Abi, I never dated. I never chatted girls up. I didn't know how. I certainly never argued with them. I don't know how to navigate this except toss off some pithy thing to say, and I don't want to be pithy with Abi. I don't want to be sharp or defensive.

I just want to be.

My PEAL buzzes again. I swipe at the screen. It's Vidette.

Getting anywhere?

Nowhere at all. I could spend as many years as this warehouse holds trying to figure out if the killer is an Ever. There's an easier way for me, though it comes at a price. Down the row, Blind Tiger smiles, as he browses another folder.

I type a quick response. *I'm coming home.*

Stars flare and die in shafts of pallid light through the gash in the ship's hull. A light snow frosts the scabbed garnet of the inner ship, granting the wreck a serenity I've never seen in it before. I ascend to the core, and that peace vanishes. Peaks and valleys prickle the undulant surface, some lancing to sharp points right at my heart, drawn along the interplay of magnetic lines between the core and the Myriad. I keep to the edge of the ring bounding the core, trying to resist the tremendous compulsion in magnetism, in instinct, in desire.

The work must continue.

I unzip my jacket. Energy vines from the core at me. My hand suspends above the terminal, torn between two magnetic forces, as fevered cords of magenta wrap around my hand and my hand hovers over the terminal. A lock.

I'm the key.

I could know, with a touch, if there is another Ever on Earth, preying on the helpless and the forgotten. In an instant, I'd know exactly where they were and I could bring an end to their reign of terror. And probably set off another. If I restore the interdimensional link to find this killer here on earth, the other Ever will know where the ship is.

I could stop them. Control them, like I control myself. Sure I could. I'd make as much a mess of throwing up a signal flare to the other aliens as I did picking up the one in my chest. My duty is to do everything I can for the people in my care. I do that, and I'll expose them to even greater danger. This tears me up, turning a blind eye, or at least a cloudy one, toward one killer, so I don't hold open the door for eight more.

A heartbeat.

That's all it would take. A portal would open and they'd step out of their culling of the cosmos into the city. Continue the work. Fix the ship. No doubt they'd fix me, the perfect, mindless acquisition machine, muddied with human thought.

They'd fix the damaged Ever.

This other Ever must feel the same magnetic pull I do. Reunion sits right here behind the wall. Repair. Restoration. If The Ever is able enough to hunt down prey, they could get inside the ship. And then I'd have much larger problems.

There is no Ever.

I wrest away from the terminal. Back to square one. No Ever. No Empowered, registered at least, with any energy-draining ability. Nothing in those endless files back in Chicago suggests any other leads. The only one I have is buried in Detroit and the strange metal of the deck rattles behind me.

I wrest away from the terminal. "Siski?"

The wolf ambles across the deck, undaunted by the threat either the core or I pose. *Star Walker find killer?*

I draw the zipper up far as it goes. "I thought I did."

Siski anxiously wags her tail. *Who?*

"Whoever is responsible is drawing the energy of their victims. The killer seems to be moving back and forth between Break Pointe and Chicago. The kills are random, irregular... there's no pattern, except all the victims are from poor neighborhoods or rural areas that don't see a lot of activity."

Shows intelligence.

"If these cases are connected, this has gone on years. Decades. They're a lot smarter than we even know."

What takes you Chicago?

I bite my lip. "You know Teto helped me."

What you find, Star Walker?

Headaches, mostly. What did I find? If I tell her about Detroit, I kick over a can of gasoline on a fire I can't even see. What do I know? I don't know anything right now.

"I'm still chasing leads," I say.

The wolf's tail bristles. *Wolves don't chase. They hunt.*

"Isn't that the same thing?"

She snarls a fang at me. *No. Wolves stalk long time. We run prey, to make tired. Confused. Then, we kill.*

Lovely. "I'm trying, Siski."

Siski eyes the core. *You come here for answers?*

There are only questions here. I eliminated some, at least. Generated a few more. The same test, again and again.

You afraid.

"Yes. I am."

But want to know.

I lean against the curved railing of the deck. "Do you know the story of Icarus? Frankenstein? Kind of sums me up."

These your stories?

My reflection fractures across the glassiness of the cavern above. "I don't know I have any stories. That's not true. I've tons. Irish ones... American. Stories going back to Africa. They're all my stories, but none of them are."

You no faith, Siski says.

"What?"

Star Walker not know herself. Star Walker not know where she come from. So she not believe. Siski cranes her head, eyes scanning the cracked dome of the ship. *Wolf cannot lead pack if wolf not know where pack has been. Where pack come from.*

The idea I don't know where I come from is some off the shelf bullshit like Anwar was trying out on me, but the wolf is already picking through the bones of my thoughts, sniffing out every instance where I denied my life. My past. My self. Shame clouds my memories. That was all a long time ago, when walking out the door to school or work was walking out in front of a firing squad. I didn't want to be Irish. Black. Gay.

I didn't want to be me.

There was no me. Just Kit. Not Kit. And then this happened, and

I do want to be. I want to know. All those years I denied myself, I want them back. All that history.

"Didn't you banish Lamar for wanting to know more about the origins of your pack?"

Siski's head droops. *Lamar not listen.*

"You're not interested in the source of your power, Siski?"

Power comes from Great Deer.

"Tell me."

Great Deer have many crowns. Regent all kingdoms. Great Deer drink from Blood Stream. Eyes catch fire. Antlers fire. Woods fire. World. Everything burns. Trees. Sky. Wolves.

Amazing. I can imagine the Blood Stream as a current of energy bleeding from the wrecked ship. Or maybe it's not so simple. Maybe a deer was the source of the wolves' power; coywolves were unlikely in the city in 1968. If they came later, after the city descended into ruin, one of them may have killed an Empowered deer and gleaned powers from the affected blood.

Blood stream backs of wolves, Siski says. She mimes clawing at me, and the light in my chest. *Blood stream Star Walker.*

"I don't know anything about where this comes from," I say. "Who the aliens were. What they wanted."

You are alien.

I look at the terminal. "I'm disconnected."

You find answers here?

"Their language is only questions."

All faith is, Siski says.

I've never been religious. Ma regarded faith, like everything else, with suspicion. None of the past or promise of the traditions I descend from spoke to me, or I never allowed them to, thinking I didn't belong to them. I need to belong now.

"You think there's life after death, Siski?"

Siski eyes the birds soaring high above. *Deer gives us life. We give life to deer. Stream never stops running.*

The Ever only take; they hoard entire civilizations within their hearts. Infinite souls reside in me. I don't know if mine is one of them. I don't know if all I am now is some confused spirit, torn between purpose and purgatory. Thousands depend on me to see them through the winter, and to Break Pointe's first true spring in fifty years. Abi needs love. I want to give. I want to give everything. I don't know how.

You must take life, Siski says. *To give.*

"I'm responsible for protecting lives."

The wolf sniffs. *You fear yourself.*

"I know myself," I say. "Finally. I'm Kit."

Kit no longer exists. Once I was pup. Then wolf. Siski. I fear my power. I fear hunger. But I am the hunger. I am what the Great Deer makes me. Star Walker think she controls alien. You are alien. Star Walker thinks she becomes more herself. You are less. You are different. Now you are life. Death.

I bite my lip. "I'm me."

There is no you, Siski says.

Her eyes flare, and the wolf vanishes off the deck. I probe the space Siski had just occupied with my hand, like I'm blind but I saw it: the wolf was never there.

"Astral projection..."

No wonder Siski wasn't afraid to be near the core; she's far more powerful than I thought. Flakes of snow dash against my cheeks as I rise out of the ship through the breach. The higher I go, the more stitched together the city appears, in bridges, in roads, in tiles of black, white and gray, life and death.

———

Crate after crate arrives, all stamped with the stripes of the Blind Tiger. Finally they become too many for the apartment and even the lab and I have to put them somewhere. Equipment and supplies clot the arteries of the Halfway Hotel, more than I could have imagined and way more than I asked for.

"Whatever you don't have, make a list," Boshi says, her nails eclipsing her PEAL as she types a message.

Clack-clack-clack.

I arrange the crates into neat stacks along either side of the hall. "One or two interns would be grand."

"I'm sure you can pinch some fleas out of the air."

I dust my hands. "Hold still."

Boshi flicks her nails against her thumb. "I wonder, were you equally as ungrateful when Valene plucked you out of whatever off-Broadway version of *Les Miz* she found you in?"

"I saved Valene's life."

"And you paid her back by destroying her company."

"Evander Blackwood was destroying it through his depraved indifference. Actually, I might have done you a favor."

She smiles. "Spitting in the face of gods?"

"Not like it would have stuck. The man is incorporeal."

"The man is missing, last I heard. I think we all know that's spin for him being dead. I assume you killed him."

"I just put him in his place," I say.

"And where is that?"

"Where he usually is. Up his own ass."

Her smile twists. "I can see why Anwar likes you."

I shrug. "You don't seem to mind that he's paying for us fleas with cash he pockets off of the black market."

Her brows spring. "Let's get one thing straight. I don't work for Blind Tiger. I work for GP. I worked very hard to get where I am, and I'm not about to stop."

"Good strategy. Be at the top of a sinking ship."

"It's not sinking. It just doesn't have a captain at present. Blind Tiger is ambitious. Well-positioned. Careful. And so am I. If Anwar tells me to smile and make you happy, I do it. Bailing your broke ass out is a small price to pay to make my bones, and really, it's kind of what we do at GP, isn't it?"

"There is something else I need for the lab, Boshi."

"What's that?"

"I need you to back the fuck off."

Boshi laughs. "Review the terms and conditions. You signed away everything to Blind Tiger. You don't give orders. We do."

She stalks out of the hall, every clack of her heels landing square on my last nerve. Energy snaps between my fingers. Birds careen through open doors, swirling around me, clouding the corridor, the building, the crates and I flare.

"*Leave me alone!*"

The birds flee down the hall, past Abi.

I flinch. "Baby..."

Abi stabs her hands into her pockets. "You ok?"

My hand lurches towards hers, but neither of us are wearing gloves. I rest my hand on a crate. "I'm fine. It's fine now."

Abi nods. "Between the lab and patrol, I won't see you."

"I need your help. We're going to work on the engine together, like we did back in Applied Sciences."

"Because we've talked about that before," Abi says.

I sigh. "You don't want to help?"

Abi wanders through the maze of crates stacked in the hallway. "You didn't want to spend the night in one of his hotel rooms, but you're ok with taking all his swag?"

"This is going to help the city, Abi."

"And GP."

I shake my head. "This is just Blind Tiger."

"You believe that?"

I have to. "I saw through his eyes."

"Yeah, I could see through him, too."

"I thought you liked him," I say.

"I thought we were trying to find out who killed Lamar."

Latches rattle on the crates. Hard plastic scrapes against itself as all this weight tries to settle. "I am. I will."

"I hear a but in there."

"There's no 'but,' Abi. I'm trying to save lives. I'm trying to make things better. This is how I do it."

Her eyes bulge. "Did Blind Tiger have something to do with Lamar? Because I kind of feel like that would be a problem."

"You think I'd take a payoff from him? Look the other way?"

Her nose wrinkles. "You're not looking at me."

I do. "I'm doing the best I can, Abi."

She closes the distance between us. "Hey. I know it's hard. I know all this is hard." Her hands fall on the shell of my jacket, hard and rigid from the relentless cold. "You're doing more than anyone could expect. I know everyone depends on you. Everyone asks of you. Demands. Ok? I know. What do you need?"

"Abi..."

"I'm here." Her arms lace around me. "Put it all on me."

She looks up at me, as she always does. Everything else falls away. The world collapses down to Abi. All this pressure. This weight. I can't ever get out from under it. How can I make her understand? What can I possibly say, or is it all just me wanting to connect to someone, and then doing everything I can not to? She's right. I can control my power. But I've never been able to control this feeling in me. This want. I have to focus. Put my mind on something else, or else this hunger just eats me alive. This power, looking to break out of its restraints.

I withdraw from her. "I have a lot of work to do."

She stares up at the ceiling. "You ever wonder, Kit? How you're always working on stuff, but everything is always broken? Does that ever register?"

"Are you going to help, or..?"

She smiles. "Maybe this was a mistake."

"I'm in a bad mood. I have a lot on my mind. I'm sorry."

"Us," she says. "You and me."

I bite my lip. "What?"

"This isn't about sex, or any of that, it's just about connecting. You won't connect with me. Maybe you can't. Maybe I have this idea of you that isn't based on any like reality. People see you, and they see this hero. This light. And I need a hero. I want you to be my hero, but you don't want this."

I reach for her. "I do."

"I hear a but again."

Why doesn't she understand? I feel it. Links severing. Shields going up. "You want me to just snap my fingers, and make everything the way you want. Everything I do requires so much focus, Abi. I'm walking a tightrope, everywhere. I lose my step, and the world burns. You do."

She shrugs. "I told you. Burn me. I don't care."

"You could do with some discipline, Abi."

Everything about her is easy. Quick. Her smile. Her love. Her wounded despair. "You know what? You're right. Starting today. New leaf and stuff. I'll be very disciplined moving my shit out of the apartment. Promise I won't get in your way."

I want to go after her. I want to fold up inside one of these crates and never have to deal with people again. Instead, I just go to work on the engine. The work must continue.

Birds track across the moon. Footprints there and gone. Howls fill the sails of passing clouds drifting low across the lake. I look down on the window of the apartment, thinking I might see Abi there; do I check on her? Do I leave her be? Do I just disappear up here in the clouds? I close my eyes, thinking, not thinking, trying not to and a jolt goes through my hand.

A text from Abi balloons on my PEAL. *I NEED YOU*

I tap back *I need you too* but before I can send it, more texts crowd the screen of my PEAL.

NOW

HELP

I plunge down to the Halfway Hotel. I magnetically unlatch the window of the apartment and float inside. Smoke fills the living room. Everything trashed. The door off its hinges.

"Abi..."

Busted latches mine the hallway floor. All the crates stacked in the hall are busted open, their contents all shredded down to their component pieces. Everything. Everything is gone.

"Abi!"

I float over the debris, birds trailing behind me like a spectral tail of feathers. Flames flicker down the hall. I hurry around the corner into my ruined lab, where I find Abi splayed across the floor, a candle melted down to the wick.

TEN

She's not breathing.

She's not breathing, she's not breathing, she's not – I can't touch her. I can't do any bleeding CPR. The rattle in my hands escalates as they shadow the drumlins of Abi's ribcage. Her fullness vanished. Her warm effervescence.

"No, no, no..."

I jitter a text into my PEAL. *Vi. Hurry.*

What can Vidette do? The mobile clinic is gone. All the supplies Blind Tiger sent to replace it destroyed, along with the lab. There are no ambulances or paramedics in The Derelicts. No hospitals. There's no power, even if there was.

I'm the only power here.

There's no time. Abi's shirt tears in my hands. Focus. There's more power in my finger than any defibrillator on earth. I peel off my glove. Hold my bare hand over her chest.

Focus.

Vidette bursts into the lab. "Jesus Christ."

"Stand back," I say, as energy snakes out of my palm, writhing in frenzied anticipation. Don't think. Don't feel.

Don't fear.

"Kit. What are you doing – you'll acquire her."

"Then we'll be together forever," I say, and touch my hand to the rumpled geography of Abi's chest. A single bolt of energy snaps between my finger and her skin, and Abi's heart kicks over

BA-DUMM.

Her eyes roll around until they find mine. "Kit..."

I caress her sunken cheek. Magenta energy radiates through her skin, free and easy. "You came back..."

Abi's bony fingers clasp mine. "I always... come back..."

Her eyes flutter. Shallow breaths whisper out of Abi's winnowed throat. Her pulse loses steam

BA-DUMM

BA-dumm

ba-dumm

and I don't know how to keep it going.

"Help," I say. "Help me."

Vidette clasps her hands around my shoulders and detaches me from Abi. She kneels beside her, and now I can only watch. Birds career around the lab. They crash into the walls, the windows, the burst crates, trying to get back out and I want out of the straitjacket I've been wearing since I was a girl. I want out of this hell where I keep losing the people I love and I get only more of myself, sewn up in tight in this invisible web.

"Her pulse is weak but steady," Vidette says, pinching Abi's wrist in her fingers. "She's suffered major weight and tissue loss. I need oxygen. I need fluids. I need to stabilize her and then... Jesus."

People crunch through the debris of our supplies out in the hall. Shepp. Zari. Ari. Book. Our whole building. Our whole community. Whoever did this could have killed them, too.

"Where do I get what we need?"

"The tower," Vidette says. "Ronnie. I'll call him."

"There's no time."

The chaotic tumble of birds spins into stable brown and black arcs as I pull at a seam stitched in space and time. A portal through the In Between opens behind inside the lab.

I lift Abi into my arms. "You're going to be ok."

Unrestrained filaments stream off of me into her, and her limp body spasms with the static jolt of my energy.

"I promise," I say, and step through.

The arcade beep of the heart monitor echoes through the lab in Applied Sciences. Not exactly an emergency room up here on the eightieth floor, but in the lab, lines blur between health and science, medicine and magic. Every breath swells the depressed cavity beneath Abi's gown and I expect her to inflate, to come back into her shape, but she rests there in her bed, webbed in IVs. The EKG machine continues to sound.

"What's wrong?" I say.

Vidette checks the machine. "It's ok. She's just fidgety."

She replaces the sensor clipped to Abi's index finger and rests her jittery hand across her chest. Abi's hand rises and falls, like the green lines on the monitor, like my fears.

"She's going to be ok now?"

Dr. Piller checks the IV bag hung from the stand next to the exam table. "She should be dead. Abi lost so much I don't know how her body has anything to subsist on, but it is. She's holding on, Kit. She's strong."

"She has to be, to put up with me."

He puts his hand on my shoulder. "This isn't your fault."

I bite my lip. It is my fault. I wasn't focused on the right thing. I busied myself with work, not because I can fix anything, but to distract myself from the broken things I can't put together. This deal I made with Blind Tiger. What was I thinking? I tried to bargain with Professor Blackwood, and that ended so well I went and did it again.

Being wrong. My greatest strength.

"You saved her life," Vidette says. "Which, I don't even know how you pulled that off."

Dr. Piller pats my shoulder. "She did it like any good scientist. She closed her eyes and crossed her fingers."

He brought Abi up to the lab to access the most advanced technology GP has, and also, to diffuse the powder keg down in the urgent care facility. Half a dozen Responders paced the waiting area, trying to muscle past the nurses and doctors to get back to the trauma room and the woman who defeated them. A year ago, I had no power. I worked here in the lab. Just over there, at one of the workstations by the test chamber. The frizzy curls of my hair make tiny bolts of lightning in my old monitor, sparks of energy I once imagined powering the sonic suit I was designing for Valene to life. Hours passed just staring at those plans, thinking, imagining, assembling the complex suit in my head. Every night. And every night, around the same time, another face appeared in the monitor.

Let's go get a drink, Abi said, and I should have.

I take her hand. Her pulse thrums through me, *ba-dumm.* Energy vines within my fingers, against her rumpled skin. If I could transfer it to Abi; if I could give, rather than take.

"Did she see who it was?"

Dr. Piller shakes his head. "I scanned her thoughts. Abi heard a commotion in the hall. She left the apartment, down to your lab. Whoever it was, she never saw them coming."

Vidette sinks her hands in the pocket of her lab coat. "The killer sees Kit. They're sending her a message."

"But I don't know anything," I say. "It's not an Ever. There aren't any Empowered that could do this."

"That we know of," Piller says.

I squeeze Abi's hand. "Why didn't they just come for me?"

"They're afraid of you. Or they're protecting something."

Dread settles over me like thick winter fog. I can count on one hand the number of people even aware I had gone to Chicago. The killer has to be someone I know.

"Lamar was stealing power coils from Blind Tiger," I say. "Power coils Anwar was selling to the Detroit client... this all started with Detroit."

I close my eyes. Access the files I acquired from Blind Tiger's personal computer system. Most of these I reviewed before. Case files. Crime reports. This time, I go deeper, unlocking the protected files on his hard drive having to do with the accounting of his illicit trade on the black market. Look at all this. Infinite folders. Inventories. ROI graphs. Emails. Lots and lots of emails, between all of his many clients, including the mysterious client in Detroit.

From: Motor Man
  To: E. Boshi
  Subject: re: Problem
  Problem solved. Expect delivery in two days.

Anger flashes through me. Embarrassment. I knew better than to trust anyone from GP, but I did it again, and I paid, again, beyond measure. I squeeze Abi's anxious hand and rest it back on the bed. I hate to let go, to go back as always to duty, but this is beyond duty. This is beyond obligation. For years, the killer has been smart, avoiding detection. If they thought hurting Abi would deter me from finding the truth, they thought wrong. The killer wanted to lure me into a trap. Traps litter The Derelicts, for rabbits, dogs, wolves, whatever the most desperate try to catch. None of them ever catch birds.

I head out of the lab. "I'll be back."

"Where are you going?" Piller says.

I'm going to fix this. No matter what I break. Who.

Peregrine falcons escort me to a landing atop one of the colossal gantry cranes along the ore docks of Zug Island. In the end, I didn't need the maps I downloaded to locate it; fifty miles outside Detroit, I picked up a strange, persistent hum. I tracked it all the way to a blackened city of mills, furnaces, and stacks on the south side of the city. The hum makes no sense, but then nothing about this does. I check my PEAL. No updates on Abi. Don't think. Don't feel. Focus.

Fix it.

The slats of the docks situated along the river sit empty, save for one. The rusted old tug had come down the river from the north, just before midnight, as the emails between Boshi and the Detroit client agreed. No lights. No markings. No flags. A caravan of SUVs pulls up on the dock. How many armed guards can you fit in a standard class four-door? Quite a few, it turns out. Crates come off the boat in an orderly, efficient line to the SUVs. Same type that cluttered the Halfway Hotel. I know from the emails there are twenty crates in this shipment. Halfway through the transfer, I step off the gantry crane.

A magenta sun bursts over the island.

Machine guns spit brass in the air. Bullets tumble into orbit around me and then melt in my fury. You'd think people would get the idea. Laser beams sizzle past me.

Somebody got the idea.

I focus all of the Myriad's cosmic energy into a single beam against the caravan. Tire burst. Gas tanks explode. Crew leap from the boat as steam clouds the water. Some of these fools are still shooting. I'm here to tell you boys. All the firepower in the world doesn't make you any smarter.

I rip the guns out of their hands.

"The black market is closed," I say. "Walk away now, or I hand all of you over to the local authorities."

A short, bald man crawls out from behind a burning vehicle. "We are the local authorities!"

"What?"

His badge gleams in the fires engulfing the dock. "We're Detroit PD. We're on the same side, for crying out loud."

I ease down to the buckled concrete of the dock. Side view mirrors, antennas and sheared doors twist around me in magnetic confusion. Some of them bear the emblem of the city, a seated figure holding a golden orb. I release my hold on the shredded metal and it falls to the ground in a short, heavy rain.

"I don't understand…"

The bald man holds his arms out like he doesn't either. "We can't afford GP here. We're barely doing better than you are."

"You're arming your police force with alien tech?"

"We have to protect our streets somehow."

Help me, and I help you. We help our communities, Anwar said. This doesn't help anyone. This just makes the world more dangerous. A wave of nausea floods through me and I want to fly back to Break Pointe, back in time, all the way to before I ever met Valene and touched the dirty sky of the gods.

I yank the souped-up gun out of his hands and break it down to its component pieces. "You're going to find another way to protect your city. A better way."

"You police your jurisdiction. We'll police ours."

I pulse with light. "I don't have any limits."

Clack-clack-clack.

Boshi stalks out of the dark. "We both know that's not true," she says, and the concrete feels like it heaves underneath me. Debris tumbles back together into the undamaged shapes of cars. Fire snuffs out. Shattered glass clinks back into shape.

"What…"

She snaps her glowing nails and the guns I undid reorganize back in the hands of the police. This power. I don't understand. I fire an energy blast at her, and the beam diffuses down to its base atoms. All the energy I unleashed leeches out of existence.

"You," I say. "You're the killer."

ELEVEN

Barely restrained energy snaps between my hands. "You killed Lamar. You tried to kill Abi."

Boshi winces. "What? Why would we – we have a deal."

"The deal is off," I say, and seize one of the SUVs she put back together. I vault it magnetically across the dock at her. Boshi whirls around, her hands up. The vehicle rewinds through the air, back on all four tires and while she's busy with that, I carve through the pier with another energy blast. Boshi's sudden island crumbles into the dark water.

Put that back together.

Steam leeches out of the air. Molten concrete spits out of the water. Bent rebar straightens and Boshi lands back on the reformed, renewed pier, on both feet. *Clack-clack-clack.*

For crying out loud.

Boshi crashes her fist into the ground. I don't know what she's reversing now. Something lurches in me. This power. A violent, personal tug from the Myriad like I haven't felt since I first became the alien. Since the alien tried to get back control. Light flickers inside my jacket. My jacket disappears.

"What…"

Boshi pounds the ground again, *ba-dumm*. "How far back do you want to go, Kit? A few minutes, or a few months?"

I stumble to the edge of the pier. A faceless being etched in light ripples in the water. "Stop…"

She clicks her nails. "How about a year, when you were just another rock lying in the ruins of the city?"

"You don't know what you're – "

Cracked crystal fuses whole. Unfettered light springs from within us, seeking, probing, acquiring as ever. No more obstruction. No more interruption. No more Kit.

The work must continue.

No –

This world shall be ever.

NO.

Crystal cracks. Strands of light grow inwards, repressed filaments in our chest and I crash to my knees, back in my jacket. My reflection wavers in the dark below.

"You're a bleeding idiot," I say.

She steps back. "That's impossible… I reversed you."

I zip up my jacket. "We're Ever."

Boshi holds her hands up. "I'll play nice if you will."

"Is this time travel, or…"

"Think of it as editing," Boshi says.

"Don't things generally get better with revision?"

Boshi sneers. "It's a process."

Energy flows smooth and steady through my hands. She didn't drain any of it from me, doing what she did; Boshi just reversed the energy expenditure, not through space but time.

Confused waves jostle the pier. "You're not the killer."

"I didn't kill anybody, Kit. I don't leave the bugs I accidentally step on the sidewalk dead, so why would I do anything to you? I don't know what happened to your girl, but it wasn't us. There's too much money in your little engine for Anwar to do something like that."

"Then who killed Lamar? And why?"

"No clue," Boshi says.

"He was stealing from you."

Her fingers curl, gesturing for me to follow her to the edge of the pier and I do, out of earshot of the police.

"Everybody's stealing, Kit. The reason Blind Tiger didn't know Lamar was stealing, is because... I am." Boshi clenches her fist again. "Just a little off the top. We sell X amount of units to Detroit. They give us the money. I give the ground a little tap and *viola*."

"You have coils again," I say. "That you sell to someone else."

She shrugs. "No harm, no foul."

No harm, she says. Heavily armed police officers gaze down the pier at us, trying no doubt to figure out what's going on. What is going on? None of this makes sense.

"I can't imagine police departments armed with alien technology helps Great Power's bottom line, Boshi."

She smiles. "All of this helps the bottom line. Everything GP makes comes out of alien technology. Everything you do."

"I don't make weapons. I don't sell them."

"Neither do we," Boshi says. "We sell power coils."

"Then where do they get these guns?"

A gun wrenches out of the hands of a cop into mine. No serial numbers. No markings, except for a single word, stamped in small type on the bottom of the handle.

"What is 'Umbra?'"

Boshi sighs. "You ought to know the first rule of the black market, Kit. No questions."

Oh, I've got questions. More than I can handle. Umbra can wait. "Lamar was stealing from you. Why?"

"He must have sensed what I was doing... and apparently took advantage. But I had nothing to do with his death."

"You don't know how many coils he took from you?"

"I don't keep records like Blind Tiger does. None of this ever happened. Right, Kit? Tonight didn't happen."

Forgetting is easy for me. Not so much forgetting. Compartmentalizing. Mom's struggles go into a box. Me breaking the law to put food on the table. Me being an alien. It's easy. Simple. Do it enough, and you forgot what's in all those boxes. You forget they're even back there. Pile another on the stack. Take whatever bothers you and put it away. Get through the day. Put all this away. The Derelicts needs power. Light.

The gun disassembles in my hands. "You tell Anwar Detroit is dead money now, or I tell him you're stealing from him."

Her smile is so wary I expect it to reverse. "Remember where this money goes, Kit. Who it helps."

"Read the terms and conditions. Blind Tiger and I have an arrangement. Steal from him, and you steal from me."

"It's not really stealing – "

"I doubt he'll see it that way."

Her smile fades. "I really don't like you."

"I don't like you, either. But all the same, stand back."

"Why?"

Runnels of magenta light surge beneath my skin. "Because now I have to redo all my work."

***

The sun is gone from the sky when I get back to the city. Pink tissue clings to the bones of The Derelicts. Heavy snow piles on already vanishing streets, sparkling over fires burning in oil drums in and around City Hall. Before my transformation, I welcomed winter. Not for the cold. I hated the cold. What I liked was how small the city became. Desolate as it was, Break Pointe always bristled with the anxiety of birds, people, quickly turning pages in glommed together magazines. Hope flows through the city in spring and summer, but at the end of the year it freezes again and I could finally relax, numb. Hope terrified me. To hope for something else meant stopping the endless work I distracted myself with; it meant letting go.

I hover outside the curved windows of Applied Sciences, peering in at Abi, barely visible beneath her blankets. Her heart sends ripples through my magnetic field, *ba-dumm, ba-dumm, ba-dumm*, a signal trying to activate me. Deactivate me, maybe. Disable the firewall always purging any file trying to open, any link trying to connect, and anyone else taking control.

I thought accepting what I had become was me opening myself, to everything the alien contained and promised. A universe. Dimensions of experience. Being. I thought that's what I was doing with Abi, but I ended up doing what I always do.

I was just me.

Broken latches lift off the floor of my lab in the Halfway Hotel. Cams tink against each other as they tumble around me, in orbit with other debris. The latches sheered off their crates as if someone swung a sword through the bolts. Clean. Perfect.

Powerful.

All the crates destructed the same way. Nothing hit them. They simply exploded, except there wasn't any explosion. No shockwave. No fire. No smoke. Just like the mobile clinic.

I've been so blind.

A claret stream winds through the backside of Brewster Park, shimmering like the trees. Grass tenses like the hairs on the back of your neck as I float just off the ground. Yellow eyes fire in the distance, and I know I've come to the end.

Teto shakes snow off his back. *Lightfoot live?*

"It's looking better," I say.

His head droops. *She sing.*

"What?"

Lightfoot sing song. Teto hear. From far away.

Snow melts on my cheeks, leaving them wet. "She sings?"

Strange songs.

By the time we graduated to singing along to our favorite films, Abi and I were firmly in our roles. Abi enjoyed the princesses, particularly ones that started out as simple, ordinary girls. I never identified with them. I kept going back to the monsters, beasts, and freaks, all of them displaced and all of them placeless. Love changed them. Acknowledgment. Acceptance. I watched and sang and I imagined, sometimes, being remade in that kind of love.

Star Walker find killer?

The power coil Teto gave me in the apartment floats in my palm. "You didn't want there to be power in the city. You didn't want the city to recover, because there would be more people and your habitat would be threatened. Your kingdom."

He squints. *Teto not understand.*

"I don't understand, either, Teto. Lamar's interest in these coils seems to have been simple curiosity. He wasn't trying to expose anyone, or hurt anyone, but you killed him. You gave me the coil, to sniff out where he got it. And then you destroyed my lab, to make sure my engine never came online."

His eyes drift from mine. *Teto want justice.*

"So do I."

Teto show you Lamar's lair.

"His lair?"

Star Walker see truth.

"You didn't show it to me before?"

Teto scampers into the snow. *I didn't show you lair.*

I drift into the gnarled woods behind him, casting long, dark shadows of trees through the confused wild beyond.

After his banishment, Lamar took shelter in the old lion pen of Break Pointe Zoo. The pen was fashioned after a cave system, which allowed him more than just a place to get out of the cold; it gave him a place to work. I hardly believe my eyes as I follow Teto into the chipped plaster of the cave. Claw marks sketch out crude drawings of other wolves. A pack. A lone wolf. A kind of symbol, over and over again. Three claw marks. An E in dried blood.

"What is this symbol, Teto?"

His eyes glint in the dark. *Pack. Wolf sign for pack.*

The drawings become more legible, More precise. At some point, Lamar transitioned from thoughts of the Bloodbacks to the ideas that led him astray in the first place.

"This is some kind of machine," I say, tracing the gouged outline of what looks like a device powered by the coils. Different iterations of the design scrawl across the walls, deep into the cave and back to a ledge Lamar used as a desk. Power coils rest inside a stolen container along with other random parts. Tools. A soldering kit. The wolf didn't have hands to use them, but he had the power to move objects with his mind. I lift a small device off the ledge. He arranged the coils in a box-like pattern that if activated would feed each other, sustaining energy in much the same way I hoped to do with my engine.

"It's a generator," I say.

Teto gazes at the cave drawings. I sense from his thoughts he doesn't quite understand the art or purpose behind Lamar's work, but he understands the fascination. The potential.

Lamar not like other wolves, he says.

"No, he wasn't. Wolves don't need heat or electricity. This was meant for people. He wanted to help people."

Lamar stole the coils from Boshi's surplus to build an engine to light The Derelicts. He died for it. Energy bleeds out of my fingers into the coils, springing them to life.

More lights, more people. More people, less woods.

I was right about the motive behind the murder. Just not about the killer. "Teto... where is – "

Lamar's engine rips out of my hands and smashes against the floor, casting the cave back into darkness. Teto growls at the dark, and then he slams hard into the wall.

I zip down my jacket. "I know you're in here... Siski."

An irritated growl rumbles through the cave. Yellow eyes flare in the dark, back the way we came.

I warned you, Star Walker.

I glance at Teto, unconscious on the ledge. "Lamar was coming to me, that night... he was coming to me with the engine."

Wolves not help weak, Siski says. *Weak left or killed.*

"You killed him. You drained his energy, you're..."

A vicious tug yanks me through the cave. I seize on the metal supports of the fake cave and plaster shreds behind me as I scratch to a stop halfway through. I scramble backward, toward the other exit of the looping cave.

"You're a vampire," I say.

If you are, Siski says.

"You feed off mental energy somehow. Why?"

Siski immortal. Siski live forever.

"What about giving back to the Great Deer?"

Great Deer gives me life. I give many lives in return.

"You kill others to increase your life."

Only the weak. Only the lost.

"Was Lamar weak?"

Lamar was soft. Lamar not respect where he came from. He like you, Star Walker. He forget himself.

"You forget who you're talking to," I say because this always goes so well for me. "I defeated The Interdictor. I defeated Evander Blackwood. You don't know my power, Siski."

Siski snorts. *You don't know, Star Walker. Fire of Great Deer burns in wolves. Fire of Blood Stream. Sky. Earth. Energy of stars burns in you. Energy of world. But you not use it. You not obey yourself. What you are. What you come from. You hunter. You killer. You devour light. But you try to make it.*

Coils of energy spring past my concentration; they twist in on themselves as I catch them, leaving me tangled in magenta knots. I might look like an electric ball of twine, but I'm in control. I'm always in control.

"I'm not The Ever. I'm Kit."

Twin suns flare inside the snaking cave. *I tell you. You alien. To lead pack is to sacrifice self.*

"What have you sacrificed, Siski? You've killed your own to keep your kind trapped in the state they are."

These attacks have gone on decades. Has it been Siski all along? Are the wolves like this, or is it just her?

Only me, she says. *Pups born with my curse. I spare them.*

"Kind of you," I say.

Siski sacrifices children. Mate. Siski gives all.

I probe the cave for something metal. I don't want to hurt or kill Siski. I don't want a war. What did Vidette tell Piller when he said the same thing about Great Power?

You already fighting a war.

"Don't make me do this," I say.

Star Walker like Lamar. Soft. You help weak. You make light of dark. Warmth of cold. You make roads of woods. Give city back to man. So I let you hunt 'killer.' I run you, like small thing you are. I run you tired. And now I catch you.

I ease out of the cave, to the ledge overlooking the cavity in the pen. "You haven't caught me yet."

Siski's eyes burn out. I whirl around, remembering too late the wolf can project her image and I crash into the snow-topped mounds of dead leaves below. The pen rattles with Siski's anger. She leaps into the pen, and I see her as she truly is. Old. Scarred. Patchy gray fur barely disguises yellow skin, rotting from the inside out.

God.

I fire a beam of energy and my arm bends back against my will. The shot arcs upwards, evaporating a hole in the snow-heavy clouds. I try again, but the projection deforms in the air, a cloud shredded in high winds. Mental force trumps cosmic will and I crash across the pen.

A plaster rock wrenches off the ground and slams into me.

Another strikes me from behind. She's too fast. Too strong. I grab onto something, anything, metal to wield against her.

Everything metal in the pen crumples like dead flowers.

Get up. Get out. Get high and blast the whole zoo. I try to fly away. I crater back into the pen like a rag doll. Tons of shredded plaster and bent metal land on top of me.

I push my way out. "Abi..."

Siski huffs. *After I finish you, I finish her.*

I release my stranglehold on the Myriad. Tendrils of famished energy lash out of my chest, through the claw marks in my jacket at Siski. All of them bend back, like trees in a summer storm. Siski sits back, a bored expression on her face as I rise unwillingly back into the air.

Fine.

You want to fight a monster, Siski? Fight a monster. I can become other beings. People. Animals. Creatures far more terrifying than the wolf. Ask The Interdictor. I close my eyes. Summon the Moimadon, as I did in my battle with him and nothing happens. It's like a gear is stuck. My thoughts.

Stuck.

I am in your thoughts, Siski says, and throws me against the wall of the pen, again and again, before dragging me across the cold, filthy ground to her paws. My arms bend behind my back, all my light cocooned inside Siski's mental cage. Light bleeds off me into the wolf's fur. Siski glows. She revivifies.

"This... isn't... your... power," I say.

Was never yours, Siski says and connections of thought and feeling remain intact just long enough for me to see the Myriad tear out of my chest between the wolf's crooked teeth.

TWELVE

THOUGHT WEBS TO FEELING AND AT FIRST, I'M ONLY AWARE. A sense of being apart. Outside myself. All systems normal, then. The rest of me fills in, and I sit up.

ba-dumm

Siski must have knocked me out. Where is she? Where am I? I can't see anything. I reach for the zipper of my jacket. My jacket's gone. Clothes. The Myriad doesn't shine behind my ribs. I'm not quite me, though. My skin has the color of a burnt-out light bulb.

ba-DUMM

The sky is the same. Dark. Empty of stars. Only a moon curled like a bear claw, soaked in blood. I left normal behind a long time ago, but I always try and keep it in the rearview.

I can't see a bleeding thing now.

BA-DUMM

What is that sound? I head in the direction I think it's coming from, but I have nothing to orient me. The dark begins to lose its uniformity. Stars twinkle just off the ground. Blue. Brown. Gray. Eyes burn within the gelatin spirits of rabbits, squirrels, dogs, and cats floating low and sleepy like old balloons. None of them move. They just stare, as I pass.

ba-dumm

Lattices of rib cages break the surface. Broken shards of rabbit skulls crunch beneath my feet. Loose teeth stud the ground. Cleft jawbones. Vines of antlers. Farther on, mounds of bones form a grave-yard. The mounds organize around a central one, towering above the rest. The hollow eyes of countless wolf pups stare back at me.

I've been eaten.

Brilliant. I don't think I'll be blasting my way out of this one. But where am I? What is this place?

ba-DUMM

That sound. That constant drum. Must be Siski's heart, beating strong and true on the energy she's just stolen. What did Jonah do? Should have paid more attention in Sunday school. Hyaline birds constellate around me. My hand passes through them, their matter stretching like chewing gum until they form back into their shape and their place, fixed in the strange dark. I'm not in her belly. This is something else.

Something more.

I've lost the Myriad, but not my sense. Energy bristles all around me. An electric hum prickles the air. Becks of fire vein through the dark beyond. There must be a tree ahead, its branches burning but the dark dissolves in fire and I find myself before a giant deer, with antlers of flames.

ba-DUMM

I've got two settings. Something quick to say. Nothing at all. This right here is solid nothing at all. I just stare, captivated by his ethereal power and beauty. His skin glows like cat's eyes in the dark. And I know this is the Great Deer, even if I don't know how I know.

I know he knows me.

Am I dead? I don't know if I say it or think it. Thought escapes me. I don't fear. For once, that's true. I'm scared of what will happen to the people I love now, but all my life I've been a bundle of wire and cords and conduit that never connected to anything. That I feared never would. Death would be as detached as life. It would be nothing. Now I'm here, empty of my light but illuminated in the fire of something much greater.

BA-DUMM

I touch his nose. "What is this? Where are we?"

The Great Deer looks off in the distance. In the cold blood of the moon, I can just make out a red trail across the dark desert. The river. Blood pools beyond. The lake. Stuck spirits flutter on the ground, like the heads of wildflowers. Spirits of birds twist in knots garlanding the sky. Behind me, a dense mass of souls in the shape of the alien ship rests in a crater in the ground. Everything sinks toward it. I move, and I'm on this slope. The ground elastic, like a trampoline mat.

"The animals are stuck," I say. "But I can move. How?"

The Great Deer turns away. Wait. Where are you going? I follow. The ground grades beneath me, but we're headed in the opposite direction of the ship. Something else depresses the world, or whatever this is. Something massive. Dark.

ba-dumm

Mounds collapse on the edge of a pit, filled with snow-covered leaves. On the other side, a cave burrows into plastered rock. The deer's antlers illuminate the mouth of the cave.

"Where are we going?" I say.

The Great Deer enters the cave. I follow, uncertain and driven, as always. Brown paint flakes off the walls of the cave, revealing a soft, pink tissue. Part of me expects to find the drawings Lamar had left in the pen in the zoo, but there's nothing but scarring. His crown of burning antlers fades in the distance. The cave goes dark, and I don't know where I am.

ba-DUMM

I claw ahead, my fingers sinking into a warm mush that feels a bit like the inside of my cheek. Blood oozes out of the wall, drowning me in crimson and I lose my footing. I slick into the mush, swallowed deeper, faster into utter confusion.

BA-DUMM

Pressure squeezes me from all directions. It's the same kind of impersonal, deliberate pressure the Myriad gripped me with when I woke the device. I'm being absorbed.

Consumed.

I fight back, not that my resistance has any form. There's less and less of me, my arms, my legs, my hair indistinguishable from the red gloom I'm fizzing into. There's nothing to hold on to. Branches and bones and baby animals disintegrate in the same warm bath of acid I do, all draining toward the same doom. I don't want this. I want to go back. I want to live.

Abi.

I crater into gummy earth. Ok. Dirt cakes my hands as I crawl through the remains of dug-up graves. Claw marks rake winter-brown grass. Some stones in Break Pointe Pines date back to before the Civil War, eroded of detail, and spotted in the decay of limestone.

The oldest plots in the cemetery border the famous trees it was named after, and make for easy scavenging. I lean against the old birch tree far back in the cemetery, its roots so big and thick they vein out of the ground to catch the aging headstones before they tip over. I'm tipped over.

Focus. Keep it together. Abi. Think of Abi.

Children hang in the air, like paper lanterns. God. I cover my mouth, even as I leave the phantom security of the tree to get a closer look. Incandescent spirits of people tether on invisible lines over their graves, captured as the birds and rabbits were. Siski had eaten them, too. She dug their bodies up out of their rest and somehow gleaned enough latent energy from them to justify doing it a dozen times or more. Her need wasn't simply the vital energy of life, but energy itself, never lost or destroyed, always converting, even in decay.

ba-dumm

Anger propels me through the cemetery, from one desecrated grave to another. Siski has foraged off the dead for years, getting by when the hunt produced nothing else. Her victims stick in her throat like undigested bones, but these aren't souls; they're shadows. Shades of energy. Residue of the consumed, but not their essence. That's why they can't move. None of the souls Siski consumed have any agency within the psychic realm their energy feeds.

Why do I?

Abi's voice rustles through the pines. *Good question.*

I turn around, and around, searching for her. *Abi?*

Through here.

A large headstone lists at the tree line. No name or dates mark the stone. My hand phases through the stone.

You're in there?

There's room, Abi says.

I crawl on all fours into the stone, the open mouth of a small, dark cave. Strands of immobile spiders decorate the tunnel, dark and narrow until it expands into a large cave of glistening black stone. Angled walls drip with spray from an anxious sea pounding constantly just outside.

ba-dumm

This is different. *Abi?*

ba-DUMM

The only light comes from the vellum shade of Abi, floating just off the stony floor behind me.

BA-DUMM

Yeah, it's pretty messed up, she says.

My hands sweep through her. *Baby...*

It's ok. I'm ok.

You're not really here.

Not really. Part of me is. Enough to know I'm only part. Abi's lips bunch. *Though that begs some questions.*

But why are you here?

I got eaten. Well. Half-eaten.

I mean, why are you here? In this cave? This isn't part of Break Pointe. That's an ocean out there, not the lake.

Abi shrugs. *I don't know. All of this is pretty trippy. Did you see the deer? The deer is pretty cool.*

What is this place?

It's a psychic energy field, she says. *You know like those galaxies that have big giant jets streaming out of them?*

From the black holes at the center, I say.

Exactly. There's so much material getting devoured the black hole can't consume it all, so it gets shot out at like the speed of light or something and that's what all this is. Siski is mad powerful, but she can't digest all the energy she eats. So the excess gets thrown out in this field.

The field must be of some scale or dimension that telepaths like Dr. Piller have never perceived it. It could be masked. Background radiation. Radio static. Magnetic interference.

But why is the Great Deer here? It's a myth.

Abi shrugs. *Your guess is as good as mine.*

Why am I here? Maybe I'm too much. Siski wouldn't be the first girl to think so. If she consumed my energy – the energy of the Myriad – then that must mean there's still a Kit, separate from The Ever. I've been afraid my identity persisted only as these shades do within Siski, as a ghost of indigestion.

I'm still me?

You're pretty consistently you, Abi says.

But I'm not The Ever?

That door opens both ways.

You're suddenly very sure about me.

I've always been sure about you, Kit. But I can read your thoughts now. Which, wow. You think about sex. A lot.

I bite my lip. *You can read my thoughts?*

That's literally all we are right now. But on topic, you're as much The Ever as you are your mom. Her mom. All the people that flow through your veins. They all inform you, but they're not you. We're our own people. We make our own lives.

I want to be more than I am, I say.

You are. You always have been. The Ever was a mindless thing, gobbling up the universe for who knows what. Siski is just following her instincts. Her hunger. You have strength. That's why you survived The Ever, Kit. It's why you're here now. It's why you stood up to Blackwood. You have spirit, more than anything. You have the strongest spirit of anyone I know.

My hands clench shut. All I want is to touch her; to hold her; to love her, the way she deserves.

Abi smiles. *I knew it.*

I open my hand over Abi's heart. *I wish you could know.*

I do. I know you. Maybe you don't want to hear it. Maybe you think you can't be known. But I know you. Abi's hand ghosts through mine. *You're afraid of your heart. Your power. You're afraid of being a monster who feeds off the energy of others. You're afraid of being like The Ever. Siski. Your mother.*

Waves smash against the rock, shaking the cave. Loose rock cracks away from the walls, shattering on the floor like glass. I turn away from Abi, wishing I could be a shade, gossamer, and still, unthinking or unfeeling in my dissolution.

You don't really want to be unfeeling, do you?

My hands claw at my shuttered heart. *Sometimes.*

But then what would the world be like? Abi says. *What would Break Pointe be right now, if you didn't care? Where would I be, if you didn't open your heart to me, even just a little? I'd be right here, Kit. I'd be trapped in this cave, alone.*

I turn back to her. *I don't understand.*

Abi sinks to the floor, clouded with fog and spray. *We're all light and shadow. You can't deny one or the other. Don't deny the world your love. Your light. Don't deny me.*

All my life, I've struggled to see out of the cave I existed in with Ma, devoid of light but churning with vicious, trapped energy. The only way to survive was to starve that power, and hope my hunger drove it into hibernation. My transformation forced me to acknowledge the truth of my existence, but the truth is, I've been doing what I always do. Avoiding the problem. Burying myself in work. Focusing on other people's problems. Becoming someone else. But I'm me. I'm more, than instinct. A monster. Monsters destroy. They mangle. They throw away the bones. Everything keeps in me.

Everyone.

Magenta light erupts in the cave. Heat lightning streams through my skin. The Myriad dawns in my chest. Everything is figurative here. The real thing is either in Siski's belly, or she's swatting it around her cave like some kind of toy.

Abi snorts. *Teach her not to play with her food.*

Currents of energy erupt from the Myriad, *ba-dumm, ba-dumm, ba-dumm,* into Abi's wraithlike skin, through the phantom stone, into the fabric of this energy field that I'm somehow part of.

How do I get out?

Energy. I'm part of this energy. The psychic energy field extends across the city, a web stranded between life and death. It tracks back to its source, Siski, in the lair of the wolves. I open my heart. I have to be careful, so I don't acquire the whole thing. Focus. Flow, like the bloodstream, through all this death back to life. Electromagnetic barriers pry open like clenched jaws and my fingers stick on sharp fangs. I push, fight, and edge out of Siski's maw until at last I'm free.

THIRTEEN

Blood and spit steam off my lambent body as I crawl across the floor of the wolf den. Good thing I don't sleep much. All this is pure nightmare fuel. Siski gasps in pain next to me, jaw wrenched open like it can't close. The giant wolf gags, and hacks out the gauzy spirit of a rabbit.

That door opens both ways.

My delight bounds away with the rabbit, gone as quick as it appears. More follow. Squirrels. Birds. Deer stampede out of the cave and Siski spits, expelling the last of all the stubborn spirits she couldn't digest. Shock furrows the eyes of the other Bloodbacks as Lamar's spirit illuminates the awful truth. Lamar casts a withering gaze on Siski and then fades from view along with the other spirits.

I get up on my feet. "Siski murdered Lamar. She's been murdering wolves for years to feed herself."

The cave shakes with Siski's roar. *Lies!*

Teto emerges out of the gathered pack, dried blood clayed on his fur. *Star Walker speaks truth.*

Whispers swirl around the cave. They build to growls. Howls. The other wolves bare their teeth and encircle Siski. They're so trusting, even now, none of them appreciate her threat before she telekinetically flings them against the walls.

I fire a beam of energy at her. Siski vanishes and the shot blackens stone. For crying out loud.

Claws rake across my back and I crash against the altar of the Great Deer. The skull of the deer falls from its perch, landing over my head. Through the eyes of the other wolves, all barking their thoughts at me at once, I can see my own magenta light, streaming through the cavities in the skull into blazing crowns of flame.

Take that off, Siski says.

I stand. *Why? It's not like you respect the deer, Siski.*

I give to Great Deer.

And yet you've never seen him. I have.

Fear in a person is a troubling thing to behold. In an animal of such power, it's terrifying. *Lies...*

The telekinetic wolves draw Siski's attention as the others come at her flank. Rocks hurl through the air at her. They explode to powder. Siski leads many of the wolves astray with a projection and as she does, I pummel the real deal with a blast.

The wolf staggers back on her hind legs, unwilling to submit despite the insistent, badgering actions of the wolves trying to force her out of the cave. Siski bludgeons wolves with a telekinetic hammer and howls her fierce refusal.

"You can't kill all of us, Siski," I say.

Wolves submit. I just kill you.

Energy flares in my hands. *You tried, lady.*

Siski's eyes narrow. *Star Walker weak.*

Don't make me do it.

You can't, Siski says, and charges.

Light snaps in the cave and the shape of Siski writhes inside my own, my body a net the wolf is caught in. Claws scratch for some anchor as Siski sinks into the bottomless void with all the others The Ever acquired. Her thoughts fizz, a tablet in water, clouding mine.

I get free, Siski says.

I

g e t

f r e e

Power surges through me. Her power. Confidence crackles off her energy into mine. Her hunger becomes mine. Her lust. This is the first acquisition in over fifty years. Like riding a bike. Our power is free again. Our purpose restored.

The work must continue.

Ravenous light casts off me, and the wolves scatter for cover. Shadows writhe on the floor of the cave, as much in desire as in frustration. Calm settles over me. Peace. I find my focus, and rein in the hunger of the Myriad.

You are us, the voice says.

And we will do as we must.

Light fades within me. The hunger. I sink against the altar. The skull. I've been wearing it this whole time. I take it off and set it back where it belongs.

Teto cautiously approaches. *Siski dead?*

Light flickers in my chest. "Yes. No. She lives in me."

He blinks. *Star Walker pack leader now?*

"Oh, no. Goodness. I'll let you all sort that out. I'm sorry it came to this... I'm sorry, Teto."

Star Walker promise justice. Star Walker keep promise.

I never wanted to hurt anyone. I never wanted to use my powers, but I know now defending the city will never permit me the luxury of choice. All the citizens of Break Pointe, people and animals alike, will have peace. No matter the cost.

I brush Teto's head. "I'll keep my other promises... I'm going to make the city safe, for everyone. People and wolves can live together. We can have a future. But I need your help."

Teto nods. *Bloodbacks help.*

"Thank you... now. Would you mind if I passed out?"

Some of Abi's color has come back. A little of her definition. Her recovery amazes Vidette, but not me. As long as I've known her, Abi has been an endless reservoir of energy. I'm surprised there aren't jets rocketing out of her. Even so, she spends most days sleeping in the apartment. Teto deploys the Bloodbacks to patrol the city, allowing me some time to spend with Abi and to heal myself. I'm exhausted. Still, I can't sleep much more than a few minutes. Wolves chase deer through my dreams. Flaming antlers set fire to stars. Night flees the sky and I wake up in bed beside her. It's fine. Abi's rest is mine.

Her peace.

Abi stretches out of her sleep. "You're here..."

I pull her blanket up a bit. "I'm here."

"You seem different."

"I got eaten by a wolf."

"Oh. Did you get... passed?"

"I got spit out."

"But you're so tasty."

"Some people have limited palates."

"I'm glad," Abi says. "I'm glad you're ok."

I smile. "You saved me."

"I did?"

I've spent most of my life trying to carry someone else. A strange anxiety bristles through me now, as I consider the possibility someone else wants to carry me. That we could carry each other, and be strong. Together.

I show my hand. Bare. Abi peels the blanket back. She opens her palm flat against mine. We touch. Tears wet her lips. Eager light laces our hands together. Arcs of energy snake along her skin, beneath it, racing with her pulse *ba-dumm, ba-dumm, ba-dumm,* and with all my focus and all my heart, I kiss her. Power bleeds from Abi, into me.

Life. I grip Abi's wrist, afraid of acquiring her but Abi holds her hand to the fire. Energy crackles between us. Hope.

There's no distinction.

The flutter of wings echoes around the cavern of the alien ship. I rise to the deck ringing the core. Spastic light convulses through the core as I set down. My fear of this great and terrible power had lessened, but not my guilt in using it. If anything, that's worse.

I break off a shard of crystal scabbing the deck and float upwards to the cracked dome above. I scratch out the lines of a great, powerful wolf on the hull. Notch stars in Siski's eyes. Ghosts in her belly. Not sure what I'm doing, exactly. I need to do it all the same. The light of the core flickers against the curving hull, and it looks as if the wolf is running, free; as if she was living, again.

"You give life to me," I say, "as I give life to you."

I drift back from the drawing. My hope is there will be no more, even as I consider all the space left to fill.

Blind Tiger stops before the giant blackboard in my lab. His eyes fix on the floor, but his head turns from left to right, following the arc of the schematics of my engine.

"This will be a place of wonders," he says. "I can see it."

I continue unpacking the equipment he brought to replace everything Siski destroyed. "Thank you again, Anwar."

He wanders through the dense labyrinth of crates stacked in the lab, a hand clasped around the collar of his cape as if to keep it on his shoulders. "Thank you. I appreciate you alerting me to Boshi's misconduct. So disappointing."

"What will you do?"

"Try and find her. She's no call-no show."

I stop mid-way through opening a crate. "She's missing?"

"I can't see her, anywhere," he says. "Though a cat like Boshi always lands on her feet. Likely, she's found a new gig with whatever side hustle she was running. This Umbra."

"Do you know anything about them?"

He shakes his head. "Not a thing."

"It's something we should look into."

"See, I need someone with your vision. Perhaps you could take over her role. Think of it – the two of us, together..."

I smile. "I'm plenty busy here."

His frown is as exaggerated as everything else about him. "A shame, really. Good help is hard to find."

"I'm lucky in my friends," I say.

"Abi is recovering?"

"She is. She's going to be ok."

"I'm glad," he says. "I'll send cookies. Boxes of them. All varieties. What about you?"

"I don't need anything else."

"I meant, how are you?"

The salt-sweet of Abi's lips lingers on mine. Her taste permeates me, as the energy of this city, living and dead. Most people think nothing grows in The Derelicts but weeds. Not true. The ground worms with life no one sees. Ants build elaborate cities beneath buckled sidewalks, unfettered by concerns of money or obligation. Gardens sprout from empty lots, blooming green with celery, carrots, and tomatoes that rabbits pilfer. Wolves hunt the rabbits, burying their bones in guilt. Life coalesces out of nothing, as it always does, flooding the wounds scoured in death, and all the life of Break Pointe tugs on me. The iron in blood, the nickel in dirt, the salt in skin, the endless life springing, sparking, spurring out of the dust.

"I'm good," I say.

He lifts my jacket off a stack of crates, the leather ragged from my battle with Siski. "Are you sure you don't need anything else? Say the word. Whatever you want."

I pinch a crease in his cape. "Actually... could I get the name of your tailor?"

Save for the working traffic lights, the neighborhood around Gresham is as desolate as the ones in The Derelicts. I don't remember it that way, but I've been to my grandmother's house exactly once in my life. Mostly what I remember is my dad talking the whole way over from Break Pointe, and this stilted quiet when we got there. A security door bars the front door. A faded sticker of the Great Power symbol wrinkles in the living room window, warning intruders the home is protected.

"You sure she still lives here?" Abi says.

"I should have called."

"You didn't call first?"

I bite my lip. "I'm not good at this."

Abi wrinkles her nose. "Baby steps."

My PEAL buzzes. I swipe away the update.

"Everything ok back home?" Abi says.

"I've got it covered." I undo my seatbelt and take a deep breath. "I'm more scared now than I was of Siski."

Abi takes my hand. "To grandmother's house we go."

"Don't even," I say.

I knock on the gated screen, and then grip Abi's hand. A dog barks. Someone peeks out from behind the curtains. Every fear I had of this moment, of rejection, confusion and simple, painful awkwardness all multiply and I'm just about to hurry back to the car when the front door cracks open.

"Kit? Is that you?"

I strangle Abi's hand. "Hi, Nana."

My grandmother hides behind the gated screen like it's some kind of shield. She's older, and smaller than I remember. I don't know. She seemed so big and imposing, then. All of this did.

"I been reading about you in the papers," Nana says. "I suppose what they said is true, then."

I zip up my new leather jacket a bit. The zipper on this one is quicker, smoother, than my old one. It's not any easier. I tug the zipper back down and show her my heart.

"Most of it," I say.

She looks at Abi. "Who's this now?"

"Nana, this is Abi. My girlfriend."

Abi waves. "Hi, grandma."

Nana lingers behind the door. "It's been ages."

"I know. I'm sorry. I should have called first... I should have called. I thought I'd visit. If that's ok."

"Is it ok..."

Nana unlocks the gate. Before I'm properly inside, I'm gobbled up in a big, warm hug.

"C'mon, you're letting all the heat out," Nana says, and Abi gets a hug next. Relieved laughter competes with the barking of a small pug. Another text pops up on my PEAL.

Patrol Update: Skies Clear.

I swipe at the screen and open the link to the video feed attached to the text. Red light flickers on the fringes on the frame. The perspective of the camera rotates 360 degrees, just off the prow of the Halfway Hotel, hovering above the intersection of Six Corners.

My apartment window comes into view and with it, the reflection of the person wearing the body camera. A short, waist-length black cape hangs from the other Kit's shoulders, the blood red lining illuminated by the Myriad.

"Everything ok?" Abi says.

I pinch away the video. I nod, with a smile. Everything's grand. The door closes behind me and so does my reflection, a ghostly red, broken only by the burning yellow of my eyes.

IN BETWEEN

IN BETWEEN

Ma is talking to the dog in the bathroom. We don't have a dog. Sometimes she says help me, *Help me, help me, help me,* and I ask her what she needs help with, and then she acts surprised that I'm there. I am not here right now.

My mother died a year ago.

I can walk through the fabric of reality. It's that kind of town. The debris of an alien spaceship dusts the earth like Pop Rocks. Ma told me *Never pick anything up* but I just wanted to try and make some money. Pay rent. Buy some pills for her. I could never help my mom. I can do things for her now, like go through a portal to when I was sixteen and see the ways I didn't see before.

How I can be better for someone else.

Ma came over from Dublin when she was eighteen. She had nothing but a crooked smile and a plan to talk her way into sleeping on someone's couch. That's just what she did. I sleep in all the places she does. A filthy apartment somewhere in Queens the day she lands in the States. Back of a bar in Ohio. Dorm room of a college student. Ma met him on the bus. He sent a card after she died. She could talk to people, Ma. Strangers. Like she'd known them dogs' years.

I don't know how you do that.

My freshman year, I fell in with Teresa Burke. She wore dresses only when she had scabbed knees. I never wore my bruises. Never showed my scars. I wore my hair in a knot and tried very hard not to be different. Gym was terrible. Swimming worse. I sat with Teresa poolside one day, counting the minutes until the bell rang. I lingered on the beads of water hugging her every curve. How her body kept the fluidity of the water in the pool. Fluidity interested me.

Still does.

Time ripples around me. I am flowing between now and then, sixteen year-old me a wrinkle in the current of thirty year-old me swirling back around. Teresa chews her nails. She knows I'm staring. I've been staring. This is the moment she looks back.

Three years later I make love to Teresa in her parent's bed. She's going to college. I'm staying home with my mother. I have to work. Dad died. There's no one else. Teresa is some kind of lawyer or policy person in Washington D.C. now. After Ma died, she emailed me. *I think about you sometimes,* she said, but I didn't answer because I don't know how to answer.

Help me, help me, help me.

My mother is talking to my father at the Elvis Presley concert at Memorial Park. She is nineteen. This is the night they met. I am not born yet but I am in the crowd, watching them not watching Elvis.

They should. He wears a costume superheroes might wear. I honestly can't tell the difference between him and the impersonators Ma would drag me to as a girl. Excuse me. Ma chides me at The Starlight Ballroom on her fortieth birthday that it's the Elvis Tribute Artists, thanking you very much.

Ma and Dad dance with each other. Move into each other. My father laughs a lot. She makes him laugh. He likes her accent. She likes how different he is from the boys back in Dublin. He winks at her, like he always did, even after he got cancer. Especially after he got cancer. *Ain't no boys like me in Dublin.*

Help me, she says, and he laughs.

In between, there are worlds.

The cellular membrane of existence. Sometimes I stop in the confusion of dark matter and eddies of hydrogen and helium particles. Waves crest beneath perception. Tides roll in, they roll out, all the universe obeying the tug of something bigger. Something I can't see. Sometimes I go to the apartment, and Ma is talking to herself. She's tearing out the pages of all the magazines and newspapers. She's unscrewing all the light bulbs and smashing them.

Something pulls on her I can't see.

You a bit honky tonk, my dad says on their third date but they don't date after this. She moves in with him and she gets pregnant and they get married at City Hall. I don't cry much. I cry a lot watching them. They really loved each other. They made each other laugh. And then Ma just started to withdraw. She started talking, but not to him. People that weren't there. Dogs. Ghosts.

Ma doesn't know I'm visiting her. She can't see me. I was invisible before I got my powers, but now I can legit manipulate the electromagnetic spectrum. It has its perks. Sometimes, though. Sometimes I wish she could see me as I see her.

Teresa Burke emails me. *Should I issue a summons?* I think this is now. Now for me isn't really that different than before. Ma haunts the house and I don't know how to answer people when they call.

Help me, Ma says, as Dad goes out the door. He goes out a lot. Usually, it's to his brother's house or the garage. He comes back, hoping Ma is done but she never really stops. One day she takes all the lights out and sits in the dark quiet. She winces at light. Sound.

I didn't see this before.

My parents fight and it doesn't change the fact they don't have money for medication. *I'm not mad,* Ma says. Dad can't make any more work at the garage than there is and she can't work anyways. She tries. Three times. Waitress. Nurse. Waitress, again. Each time is a momentous occasion in the apartment. Ma gets a uniform. A new blouse. Her hair done. *This bleeding hair,* she says, looking into the bathroom mirror the morning of the first waitress job. Hair like fire. Two days. That's all she lasted.

I can start anything, she says to me one morning before I'm gone for school. It's the keeping it going. *I don't know how.*

School becomes a place I spend less and less. I work full time talking my mother off the roof. Out of the window. To sleep, if I can. Usually, it's her waking me up.

Help me, help me, help me.

Down at the Starlight, Ma drinks with the men at the bar. Dad drags her home drunk. He yells at her while I try to put together some kind of sleep. I am not sleeping. Ma laughs. She laughs and laughs and laughs and sometimes I hear her laughing now, in the empty, silent spaces between her life and death.

I go through this night a few times.

Nothing was right after this. It wasn't before, but after the wheels came off. Dad was too angry. Too upset. He said things about her weight. Her being crazy. *I'm not mad,* she says, *I just don't know how to keep this going.* Ma tried to cut her wrists. I didn't see this before. I was in my bedroom. I'm in the bathroom now, as my father holds a towel around my mother's arm. They both cry.

What did you do? My father says, over and over.

In the morning, she wears one of his long-sleeved sweaters and I never know until now. After that night, he never went after her like that. He just sat there in the recliner, sinking with the springs as they gave out, until he did.

Teresa and I go for walks down by the river some nights after school. I walk behind us, the ghost of our future. She tells me her father is having an affair with a woman he met online. In a few months, her parents will get divorced. I just listen. I don't know how to talk to people. But I don't know how to forget about home any other way, so somehow Teresa and I manage a conversation.

We don't talk that much, though.

Ma sent me to the drug store for smokes. She called it the chemist. *Tell your man at the chemist I'm after my fags,* she says, as I follow me out the door for another run. After Dad died, she never really left the apartment. Dark days became weeks. Good days became like sunshine in winter. Rare and brilliant. I spent as long at the drug store as I could. I do now, living through small freedom from home. I miss it, actually. Most of it. That old bitty Cordry thought I was stealing something or buying the cigarettes for myself. Ten years and she never really stopped following me around. I eye her as she eyes me as I read the comics at the swivel rack they still have from the 60s. Comics never interested me much but once, I liked to imagine I had powers. I could fix things. You don't really want to be a superhero. They don't exist, besides. There are just people, who do good things.

Teresa leaves me a message on my phone. *Help me out here.*

One night when I am nineteen and up watching reruns instead of studying for an exam at some university or backpacking through Europe or auditioning for a reality show, my mother opens all the windows in the apartment building. Pigeons fly in. Bats. She tries to fly out, running from something in her head.

Help me, help me, help me.

I pull her back in from the fire escape. Ma slaps my hands away. *Do you not see it? Do you not see it right there?* She looks right at me, Ma. Flickering like the TV. Does she see me?

Did she always?

I can't change anything. I read that in a book. If I go back in time, I'm not going back to the literal past but another version of it. Every choice I make creates a new universe and they bubble in the In Between like fizz in pop. I can reveal myself to my mother. I can alert Dad that those abdominal pains he experiences are actually pancreatic cancer. He can get treatment. It would be a different life.

Not mine.

I try to talk to the universe. Reason with it. Let me change more than a universe I just created shadowing myself through my mother's decline. Let me change me.

I'm no good at talking.

For a while after Teresa left for college, we emailed all the time. Texted. I forget how much I relied on those. I was lost at sea. Every message a light on a distant shore. But then Teresa didn't email so much. When she did, it was like she was copying and pasting responses from some clipboard. I should have a clipboard of normal responses. I stopped responding when she did write, confused as to what she wanted. What I did.

Then it just stopped.

Half my life I talked to my mother. Soothed her. Coddled her. Anything to get her to relax. None of it helped. Sometimes I bartended at the Starlight. Waitressed. I spent that money on her pills. She'd be ok for a while but then she'd stop taking them.

I'm not mad, she says.

I had to quit my job to be there at home to make sure she wasn't opening windows or her veins and I became bitter. Resentful. I stopped seeing my mom and only saw this pain in my life. I lost the ability to try and connect to anyone. To want to.

Help me, help me, help me.

Kids glow in the dark after eating the leaves of radioactive trees. A World War II German submarine surfaces in the river, lost in time. Cordry follows me around the drug store. I try to spend some time outside of time. I go into the past in the seams of my day and I come out in the some place. Ma takes out all the light bulbs in the apartment. *Are you the light, girl? Or the bulb?* What do you say? She holds the dark bulbs up to my ghost. The crimson light tessellating beneath my gossamer skin glints in the glass.

She smiles, Ma.

I try to smile. I try to remember her like this. I try to say something to her, but what would I say? What would I accomplish except excite her into another episode and I'm not here to make things worse for her. I'm here to try and make things better for me. Someone else. I lost how to talk to someone in this apartment. How to hold on to my own wisdom.

I think I've lost how to learn.

Teresa is outside in the hall when I open the apartment door. I asked her never to come over. I couldn't have anyone here. No one could ever see how we lived. This isn't high school. Teresa is older. Paler. Gaunt. This is now.

"You always had a glow about you," she says.

I get two coffees. We go down to the river. She holds on to the cup but she doesn't drink. Neither of us says anything. Then she starts laughing. *Do you remember*, she says, and chuckles through that night we ran from shadows under the bridge, all the way back to the alley behind the drug store. She pulled me behind the dumpster and her hand slid inside my coat, under my shirt, up my back. Cold. New. Electric. Teresa is crying now.

"I found out two months ago," she says. "I felt this lump. I thought it would go away. It didn't go away."

I don't know what to say. I don't know what to do. I can go back and forth in time. Slay dragons. Touch the stars. I can't cure cancer. I don't know how to help anyone.

"I thought about you," Teresa says. "Us. Life."

I bite my lip. "I've been to when we made love."

She sips her coffee. "Is that one of your power things?"

"One."

"Was it as awkward as I remember?"

It was the only language I could speak. "No."

"It's funny, isn't it? How one day you look back, and that's your life. That's your story. No changing it."

Somewhere, my mother is talking to the dog we don't have. Opening the windows. Smashing the bulbs. *Help me,* she says, and she grinds her palm against the shards. Bleeds on the tile. Twenty-three year-old me comes out of the bedroom, already disconnecting, and Ma holds up her crimson, glinting hand.

Do you not see, she says.

"I wanted to talk to you, Teresa," I say. "That's all I wanted to do. You were so important to me... you helped me, and then you were gone and I just put you away with the rest of it."

She sips her coffee. "I'm here now."

"Why..."

"I know your life is complicated." She laughs. "I don't know. Mine is too. I know we have our own lives. But I'm scared, Kit. I'm terrified. I just want to talk to my friend."

Words strangle in my magnetic field. "Is it... bad?"

"It's early. I can beat it. I'll beat it."

I can go to the future. I can see. I am already there. I am here, as I am in the apartment, in the drug store, in the seams between then and now. I take Teresa's hand. Cold. New. Electric.

"We will," I say.

TROUBLED GRAVES

ONE

PAGE ONE, PANEL ONE

Digital arrows direct our view through a targeting scope toward a roseate speck far in the distance, a drop of blood against the snow-dusted ruins of an industrial city.

CAPTION: *Break Pointe!*

PANEL TWO

The target now a glowing red star.

CAPTION: *A city without hope!*

PANEL THREE

The star brightens. Closer.

CAPTION: *An open wound in the heartland of America!*

PANEL FOUR

The star resolves into the shape of a person. A woman. Glowing. She's flying at us, incredibly fast.

CAPTION: *For fifty years, neglected, forgotten, impossible to fix after an alien ship crashed into the city, granting some extraordinary powers and condemning others to a lifetime of human struggle!*

What could anyone do?

PANEL FIVE

Closer. She's angry. An electronic ripple distorts the digital lines of the targeting scope.

CAPTION: *But then she came – a young woman selfless and dedicated to restoring peace and justice – KIT BALDWIN!*

PANEL SIX

Kit drives at us with her fist. Lightning streaking behind her. Heart glowing beneath her uniform.

CAPTION: *Experimenting with alien technology to save a friend, she accidentally joined her consciousness with the strange power source known as the MYRIAD and inherited the amazing, terrifying cosmic power of - THE EVER!*

PANEL SEVEN

The electric distortions become more severe as Kit occupies nearly the entire frame.

CAPTION: *Now she uses her unique gifts to fight for peace and justice in a city forgotten by both!*

PANEL EIGHT

Just her face now. Determined. Resolved.

CAPTION: *What is impossible now? What cannot be achieved with the combined power of the stars and the will of humanity?*

PANEL NINE

A magenta lightning storm bristles in her eye, the epicenter of the targeting scope.

CAPTION: *What can we not do?*

"What do you think?"

I flip through Simon's self-made comic book. I bite my lip as I consider how generous he is with my figure. If I had an ass like that, I'd probably point it at everyone the way this Kit seems to be doing. How does she walk? I don't think her spine could physically sustain that kind of contortion. But then, technically, I don't have a spine.

Have I been getting everything out of my new form?

A pointed *Ahem* cuts across the classroom. Abi stands on the far side, pinching her thumb and fingers together in a talking motion. I should be talking. I'm here to talk.

"I do. Like it," I say. "You're very talented, Simon."

Simon lunges at me. I tense, a newspaper tied up so tight in its middle the ends bloom. Oh. It's just a hug.

"Get a room," another boy says and the class disintegrates into derisive laughter. The boy swells on their reaction. Simon pinches the edges of his comic between his fingers, leaving deep wrinkles like the marks I once left in my own skin, pinching myself to distract from the pain the other kids my age produced, daily, just as they do now.

"Is there something wrong with this one?" I say and the other boy's expression hardens. His smile wax.

Mike sighs. "C'mon, guys. Straighten up."

I'm still getting used to the idea of Mike as a teacher. It's as unexpected as there being an actual school. Schools, like commuter trains and clean water, became goals rather than possessions after the alien ship crashed in Break Pointe in 1968. The outreach program Abi initiated in the old public library was intended mostly to give the youth of Break Pointe a place to go during the day, but with Mike's participation, it's becoming something more.

"When my mom was teaching, she would have sent you all to detention," he says. "Since I have no binding authority invested in me by... well, any institution, I'll just convey my disappointment."

Abi tugs at her blouse. "Well, since there aren't really any rules in place, you can kind of do what you want."

"*Dead Poets Society*," I say. "*Lord of the Flies*. Fine line."

Other students wait patiently but performatively at their desks for me to come to theirs. I know interacting with the students is a good idea, but it doesn't make doing it any easier. Children are as alien to me as I am to them, unscarred by life and experience. I was never a child, not really. From the moment I had any agency, Ma and I swapped places. Dad died and she caved in, and I was never without the responsibility for someone else.

I was never without the weight of tomorrow.

I pat Simon's head, awkwardly. "It's fine. No worries."

The other boy clears his throat. "I thought you couldn't touch people. You'd zap them, or whatever."

"So long as I'm careful, it's fine." I tap the undulant light flickering within my chest. "I have to be really careful."

Questions gun at me, rapid-fire.

"Do you eat?"

"Do you sleep?"

"Do you poop?"

Another student raises their hand. "Aren't you dead?"

Ma's hand curls on the wet pavement. "I'm sorry?"

"When you turned into the alien. Didn't you die?"

"I was transformed," I say. "I joined with it."

"How does that work?"

It's a classroom. I suppose I'm obliged to give a lesson. "I don't have all the answers myself, but in a nutshell, it boils down to the first law of thermodynamics. The law says energy cannot be created or destroyed. It only changes states. Energy always is, in any form it takes. The energy of who I was, the substance, was transformed."

Simon doodles on his notepad, his eyes thinking. "But The Ever acquired your energy. Didn't it?"

"Yes... but it still exists. Nothing The Ever acquires is lost. It's all still here, in the Myriad." The entire class stares at my chest. I clear my throat. "The atoms that make me up, they've been around since the Big Bang. They'll be around at the end, if there is one. We were stars once. We may be again. Right now, we're people and if there's a difference between a person and a star, I don't know."

Simon's smile is hesitant. "So we live forever, no matter what?"

"We're ever," I say.

I don't think he's convinced. "But... is this you?"

I imagine a line scrolling across my face, like it does through a blank television screen. "Um..."

Abi makes the talking motion again. I don't just struggle with twelve and thirteen year-olds. This diffidence surfaces pretty much whenever I interact with anyone in The Derelicts. Always has. I'm good for a hello. Goodbye. I don't say anything else. I don't make any eye contact and then for some reason, the next time I see someone, I feel obligated to dump all this exposition on them.

No one can figure me out.

That was true before my transformation, but even more so now. No one is quite sure of what I am – human or alien, friend or foe – but with the outreach program, with combating my natural tendency to disappear into any crowd, I've made myself more of a presence on the city's streets, instead of only in its skies. It helps enormously there are streets and classrooms for me to visit.

"Maybe we could talk about the engine some more," I say.

Mike leaps in to rescue me. "Kit's engine is why we're all here. She's using alien technology to restore power and honestly some low-key civilization to Break Pointe."

Low-key might be overselling it. A breakthrough on my experimental engine, utilizing the cosmic power of the Myriad to bring light and power the darkened homes and buildings of the island, has finally stitched together some semblance of normalcy here. Some.

When the city unincorporated and Great Power took control, the first thing they did to encourage the people of The Derelicts to vacate all the new property they'd acquired was shut the lights off. GP slunk back across the river, but there's still no city, not really and it's not a simple matter of throwing a switch. Since 1968, the frayed electrical grid has fallen into neglect and disuse. That doesn't stop people from trying to siphon electricity from it. Deaths and fires are as persistent as my desire to render a fifty year-old network obsolete.

Simon doodles on his desk. "How does it work?"

"Like the sun," I say. "It's limitless. It was just a matter of harvesting the innate power of the alien ship in a small enough and safe enough transmitter."

"How much does it cost?"

"It's free."

"You don't want anything for it?"

This makes all the sense in the world to him, but that's not his question. His question is the reality he meets every day when he walks out of this classroom. Life is transactional. Survival in the city is taking and receiving.

"It's my responsibility to use it to help others," I say. "Just like you. Keep drawing your comics, Simon. Keep making me look good."

"Ok," Simon says, smiling.

"Ok," I say and the class hushes into a practiced silence with the *pop, pop, pop* of distant gunshots.

Mike goes to the window. "Sounds close."

"It's on Gardner," I say, materializing on cracked pavement wrinkled like elephant skin. I'm still getting used to the power of astral projection, acquired in my battle with the wolf Siski. *How do you know it's on Gardner?* Mike says to me, still in class, his voice a distant echo as if the Kit at the school is one tin can tied on the end of a string, and the Kit on Gardner – me – is another.

Darkness cascades down the street. Streetlights fail, one after the other, blinking on and off before shuttering completely. Something must be wrong with the network of engines and transmitters I set up in the neighborhood.

Dozens of power lines web an overburdened utility pole on the corner of Ditko. Old cables snarl at the top, while others droop dangerously low to the ground. A boy hangs in the tangle, arms and legs rent in the shock of death.

He isn't much older than Simon.

Red light flickers beneath my skin. Orange competes with it. Shadows play with each other on the street. Stalks of hay curl to threads of liminal fire off a burning scarecrow staked in the intersection, its mangled form twisted out of the toppled light pole and the transmitter I had attached to it. They destroyed it.

Wild trees grow where streetlights once did. Weeds shade abandoned houses. Farms grow out of vacant lots. I suppose it only makes sense there would be so many scarecrows.

This is the Straw Men.

TWO

The Straw Men have been the boogeymen of The Derelicts for decades, even before the ship. Ma talked about them when I was a kid. *Don't get caught out,* she'd say if I came back home late some night. *They make you draw straws. They're made of straw. They carry a scythe. A sickle.* I never saw anything like that. So far as I know, they're a gang like any other. Drugs, guns, alien contraband, The Straw Men run all of it. GP pushed them to the fringes of the city, but since the strike incidents involving the gang mount with the snow. I've gotten so used to piecing together broken things I expected everything to fit. Not all of Break Pointe wants to go together.

The owner of the thrift shop on Ditko swerves in and around the rusted island where the pumps had been when it was a gas station. A sick look on his face.

"What happened?" I say.

The owner, in his fifties, maybe sixties, shakes his head, his chin in his hand. "He wouldn't pay."

"Pay The Straw Men? For what?"

"Power."

The convenience store is still cabled to the utility pole. I clench my fist and a magnetic pulse radiates from me. "Electricity? I'm giving away free energy. Why…"

"The Straw Men have always provided power in The Derelicts. They provide protection. I pay. This boy…" The owner's hand creeps from his chin over his mouth as he looks up at the boy strung up in the electrical lines. "He wouldn't pay. I told him to. I begged him to."

Angry light flares beneath my vellus skin. "None of you have to pay the Straw Men anything."

"You don't understand, miss."

Electrical wire creaks in the cool breeze off the lake. "They won't hurt anyone here again."

The owner drifts back toward the store. "You don't understand."

I lift into the air, to try and untangle the dead boy from the lines and I can barely look at him. I can barely stomach what's been done to him. "Who is he?"

The owner doesn't answer.

"Who does he belong to?"

The security gate crashes shut over the front door of the convenience store behind him. People watching from the corner across the street disperse back to the trials of their own lives. How many of them pay the Straw Men for power? How many of them hurt each other because the safety of what they know is cheaper in their mind than the freedom of what they don't?

A flake of snow melts on the boy's pupil. Twelve. Thirteen. This boy died for power. Must of us do. All the weight of the city presses on my shoulders. The gravity of what I'm trying to do. Convert a fifty-year-old disaster zone into a living, breathing city. Energy into power. Power into progress. Prosperity.

Peace.

Hovering in the sky, standing before a class of students, I project strength. Grace. Hope. That Kit isn't afraid. She contains none of my failures. No memory of all the dead and lost. She simply exists, a perpetual engine animating the corpse of a city until someday people forget it ever died. I close the boy's eyes. I close mine, and I'm not within my sorrow.

My despair.

***

Crumbling stone foundations mark the uncertain border of a pauper's cemetery on Church Row. Blackbirds scatter from the naked branches of a birch tree as I ease down into the graveyard. I do my best to forget the faces of the people I couldn't help or save. I'm rarely successful. Guilt sticks to me, like dried blood, clayed to dead skin. If I had been there; if I had done more, that boy never would have needed to steal, to die for power, to be nameless.

No one has names in the Derelicts. If they do, they earn them in death, emblazoned on the boarded-up windows of graystones. A sheet of plywood, a stretch of naked brick, that's where I'll be certain of the boy's name, in a day or two. For now, I burn the only epitaph I can into the mud-covered rock I place over his grave.

$$\Delta U = Q + W$$

The first law of thermodynamics. Nothing is ever lost. Still. Unclaimed bodies were common even before the city government breathed its last. Life in The Derelicts is short, difficult, and mostly forgotten. Mine is no exception, even if I've proved something of a ghost, haunting the ruins. If there had been a body, if someone had taken the same mercy on me I do this boy, they would have buried me in the empty lot of St. Ignatius. No headstone. No signifier of faith. Only a hummock of disturbed earth. The grave would represent nothing but the scar I left in the earth, with no means of ever identifying the instrument that made it.

Is this you?

Snow falls, shreds of the giant sheet of cloudy plastic draped over the city. A raw pink sun bloodies the horizon, indistinguishable from me as I levitate just off the prow of the Halfway Hotel. Pigeons line the Italianate eaves alongside Mike, sheathed in his patchwork body armor. Tactical gear webs the armor, all of it rattling in the relentless breeze sharpening against the ice board of the lake.

"You can go home, Mike. I've got this."

He sniffs. "Nah, I'm good."

"You'll catch a cold."

"So will my kids if these Straw Men trash another transmitter." He checks his PEAL. "I've got an hour before I need to be at the school. Let's see if these guys come back."

Sea smoke veils the river, a rolly vein difficult to find on the best of days. Block after block of snow-covered vacant lots and dilapidated houses tile an uneasy road across a part of the island confused between city and nature, land and water. The south side of the island devolved to marshland years ago, a netherpeligo of islets punctuated by The Ice Pick, the name a nod to its long, slender shape as much as it being the territory of The Straw Men.

"This is the first time The Straw Men have come into Six Corners," I say. "They're expanding their territory."

Mike nods. "No one is in charge."

The Straw Men aren't the only gang in Break Pointe. Crime is the only thing organized here. Mafia justice is the only judicial system operating in the city. "I should confront them."

"That could get out of hand real quick."

"They're thugs."

"They ain't GP, Kit. They're not worried about their stock value or their PR. This is how they live. This is how they do."

I hang a lantern, they smash it. I give away power for free and I threaten the entire shadow economy of this town. No matter how hard I work to piece together some semblance of life on the island, some stitches won't take.

"They're like anyone else here," I say. "They want something."

"You can't negotiate with these guys. Back when my dad was a cop... he said the Straw Men were foul. Wrong."

"Wrong, how?"

He shrugs. "Strange. Unnatural."

"They're just a gang."

Mike looks off toward the canopy of dark trees in Brewster Park. "You thought the Bloodbacks were just wolves."

I tug on my jacket. "Nothing makes sense here."

"Don't sound so put out about that as you used to."

"All the problems we face here used to terrify me. They still do, but now, I want to tackle them. I'm almost excited."

He looks past, like he's looking for someone else. "Almost? Do you need to lie down? Should I call someone?"

"I think you'd just get me."

"What would you tell yourself?"

"It's ok to smile."

I ease down to the edge of the roof beside him. My mauve aura cleaves across the broken lines of the plastic pieces glued to the curve of his helmet, jigsaw remnants of a broken taillight purposefully left undone. His commitment to protecting the streets of The Derelicts is as fierce as mine, but unlike me, Mike chose his mission. Unlike me, he has no powers. Unlike me, he can walk away at any time, and make a life.

"You like teaching," I say.

"I do. I like it a lot. My mom was a teacher here, before the funding finally ran out. But dad was a cop, and I wanted to be a cop. He wanted me to be. And then I got pulled over." Mike removes his mask and sets it on the eaves between us. "But this is cool, you know. I'm doing both. Sort of."

"I feel like everything here is qualified with 'sort of.'"

"We should start a petition. Rename the town. 'Sort Of.'"

I nod. "Population: Ish."

"Things are getting better, though. A little bit at a time. We got a little hiccup here, but you're going to have that, even if things are perfect. You do seem like you're more together, you know. You got a flow, now. You blinding them with science."

"I'd prefer not to blind anyone with my science."

"Right. Just saying. You're doing an amazing job, Kit."

"So are you."

Mike sniffs again. "I'm just a dude."

"You're a very helpful dude. But you know, you don't have to do this. I can patrol."

"By yourself? You can't be everywhere."

I tug on the zipper of my jacket. "No, but…"

"You're doing too much as it is. In comic books, superheroes got problems keeping secrets. You're keeping the whole damn thing together. You're like if Thomas Edison got bit by a radioactive spider. You're webbing the city in light."

"I'm more of a Tesla woman," I say.

"I teach a couple times a week, I patrol, I drive a cab on the other side of the river. I don't know how you do it."

"Helps I don't sleep."

His enthusiasm tempers. "You and Abi doing good?"

"We're making it work. We're both busy, but she sends me these texts. Videos. They're kind of naughty."

"Did you just say '*naughty?*'"

"They're meant to be hot, but she's such a dork."

He scratches his chin. "Like what kind of videos?"

I swipe at my PEAL and unlock the wrinkled screen. "Like this one she sent me last night. So this one starts off promising enough. She's got her jeans unzipped."

Mike gazes into the screen. "Sure."

"And she's not wearing any panties."

"Mm-hmm."

"But then she gives me a thumbs-up sign. What's the thumbs up for? I mean, look at her face. Dork."

"Yeah, play it again."

"I love her so much," I say.

Mike sighs. "I gotta find me a girlfriend, man. You don't know. It's been a lean few months. *Lean.*"

"One of your students – "

"Who are you and what have you done with the real Kit?"

" – has to have a hot mom."

He nods. "I'll take a poll."

"The first step is acknowledging you have a problem."

"Wait – play that back. Did you say you loved Abi?"

My finger lingers on the screen of the PEAL, on the glassy curve of Abi's face. "I did."

"So that's new."

I smile. "Everything is new."

Any life beyond Valene had been inconceivable to me once. There was no life beyond Valene, at least as I knew it. I sacrificed everything for the woman I loved – still love, will always love – but on the other side of my transformation, there is this life I never could have imagined. Love. Real love.

I don't know.

Abi's laughter, her voice, her love don't substitute Valene's, but more so my heart. My spirit. My humanity. Before, I had lived only for Valene, but now, I live in Abi, just as I do the cosmic energy warming the frozen city back to life.

"Cool. That's cool, man. I'm happy for you."

"Thanks, Mike."

"And the kids love you. Straight up."

"I don't know about that," I say.

He squints. "Is that fear I detect in your voice?"

My shoulders lock up. "There's so many of them."

Mike blows warm air into his fist. "She's fought the most powerful men in the world... alien entities trying to take over her body... telepathic wolves... but now, the cosmic power of Kit is tested as she faces her most dangerous foe. *Teenagers.*"

"People freak me out in general."

"Little people."

"At least I don't have to take any of them home with me."

He gives me a little nudge. "You ever think about kids?"

There isn't much to think about; my body is a simulacrum. I don't breathe, age, or produce anything. After my integration with the Myriad, my body became a ghost ship, drifting on the memory of life. There will never be passengers.

"I've got a lot to think about now," I say.

My PEAL buzzes. His does too, at the same time. I swipe at the rubbery screen bending across the back of my hand.

"Not again," Mike says.

A notification blinks on my screen. *Mass casualties in suspected diffusion incident in Omaha, Nebraska.* Images of recent diffusions shoot through my mind. Walls painted in blood. Floors scabbed in shorn flesh. Eyes bulged in the shock of death. Memories of incidents going back to when I was a girl lurk beneath the surface of others, more recent and more numerous. Diffusions were rare once, freak accidents like plane crashes, but now the disasters are common. Frequent. Expected.

Mike scrolls through the story. "Thirty dead... maybe more. Man. A shopping mall. I don't understand how this keeps happening. It's never Empowered that get hurt. That's what those diffusion things are meant for, right? People with powers?"

I don't say anything. What can I say? Thirty dead. A shopping mall turned into the set of a horror movie. The peace of another community shattered forever. Outrage shunts into the same locker I keep all of my fears and frustrations in. I lug them around everywhere I go, but I can't ever stop. I'm focusing on what I'm focusing on; my community. My people. There's so much work.

There is always work, to keep me busy.

Dusk creeps into a sky ceded by the sun.

Birds spiral down ahead of me into the wreck of the alien ship.

The contradiction of my own nature leaves me with something like a headache; I have communion with birds, with wolves, with the elemental forces of nature. Yet I've none with people. I exist beyond life or death, and yet for all I have learned, I understand neither.

Broken equipment crusts the floor of my lab. Filament and wire strangle together in long strands yanked out of bins. The last good of the oscilloscope scatters in pieces thrown in every direction. I stagger to the blackboard. All my equations, all my theories, are gone, replaced with large, craggy letters scrawled in dusty chalk.

DEATH IS THE ONLY LAW

THREE

Abi's shadow wavers across the chalkboard, cast from the anxious light within my chest. "What do you think it means?"

Shattered pieces of receivers I was just about to add to the growing network in The Derelicts float off the floor, into a loose collection of rings around my waist. There's no putting them back together; the damage is too extensive.

"The Straw Men aren't afraid of me," I say.

Abi slides her arm around my waist. "You'll learn 'em."

Aluminum casing lifts away from the frame of the old oscilloscope I've been gutting for parts. Cathode ray tubes rocket out of the chassis, some cloudy, others pristine. I untangle the accelerator anodes out of the winnowing tail of the glass envelope. All of this would have made for a new engine. The tubes float around me in a gentle, nonsense parade, and I have nowhere to put them now.

"This sets us back months," I say, and wince at how tired I sound. "I don't know. Maybe even longer."

Abi drifts to an upright cargo crate the Straw Men knocked over. At least they left the contents undamaged. Glass eyes flicker with the light of the ship's core. "What's in there?"

I lift the crate back upright with a magnetic tug. "Just something I'm working on."

Abi crosses her arms. "So we've been dating a while – "

"I don't think we've actually gone on a date."

"You're doing the thing."

"I'm not doing anything."

"I'm about to be serious and you're heading me off at the pass by being clever. This is one of the things I've picked up after *dating* you for a while, along with what I was going to say, which is I've determined you have exactly two settings."

I bite my lip. "On and off?"

"Vague and TMI. TMI is great, because confessional and intimate, but when you open up, you really open up, and let's just say there's a lot to process. Vague gives me the heebies because when you hold out on me, I start to panic-bake."

"I'm not holding out on you."

Abi types into the screen of her PEAL. "I'm literally searching for recipes right now. Ooh, fudge-cookies."

"It's a new project. It's in testing."

"Baby steps."

"I'm just tinkering."

"Why won't you just tell me?"

My instinct to not tell Abi – anyone – anything at all, is as reflexive as yawning when I'm tired. I don't get tired anymore. I don't need to yawn. I still do. I'm learning to fight my own instincts as well as I do those of The Ever.

I take a breath and open the crate. Most of the guts of the gangly android are exposed; I don't have the supplies yet to finish the outer shell. I don't really have the time, so I only work on them in the brief moments my frustration with other concerns opens. Most of my effort focuses on the internal power system, webbing it to the armature, combining the work Evander Blackwood had done on advanced robotics with my own engineering and design.

"Dude," Abi says.

"It's a work in progress."

"Is he like threatening to take over the world yet?"

"Mostly he wants to bend things."

She looks back at me. "Dude."

"I've had this notion for a while about exploring the In Between, but obviously my focus has been here..."

Abi nods, warily. "Also, the In Between is another dimension in time and space, but go on."

"That, too."

"So you didn't want to tell me, because..."

"My track isn't great with experimentation. And I don't understand it. I have enough work here."

So much work. I can never stop. If I stop, I have to consider the awe; the terror; the magnitude of what has happened not just to me, but the world. Words float somewhere in the procession of memories and metallic components around me.

"Whenever I stop working, whenever I stop thinking, my thoughts go to the In Between."

She wrinkles her nose. "In Between? Why?"

I don't know. I don't know if I want to think about why, for the same reason I don't want to think about why I have such an intense interest in all things Adam Clayton.

"Portals open to the In Between, in radically different points in time and space," I say. "There aren't any points of reference or coordinates to plot. So I've developed a..."

"Guinea pig?"

"Assistant. I haven't done much work on the CPU beyond the fundamentals. It's really just something I put together."

Abi rolls her eyes. "Yeah, you just put together a fully operational android to explore space and time on the side."

I smile, but really at the irony of my existence. I'm a cosmic being – asterisk acknowledged – sworn to protect the streets of a beleaguered city. My most pressing concerns involve the most basic needs: light, shelter, safety. What compels me in rare idle moments fix on the fantastic: who were The Ever? Where did they come from, and why? What other terrors, or wonders, hide in the In Between? There's no in between for me. No middle ground. The stars and the street pull on me, stretching me beyond any kind of center, or any kind of comfort in life.

Abi peers into the android's eyes, fashioned from the glass lenses of old railroad traffic lights. "What are you going to call him?"

Ray tubes float around me in a gentle, nonsense parade until I plug them in, one by one, into the power core of a lifeless android. Well. It will be an android when I'm done.

I think.

"He'll probably still want to go by ALPHA," I say.

"ALPHA? Wasn't that Professor Blackwood's android?" Her eyes bug. "Is there anything else you're not telling me?"

I shake my head. "No."

"You're not replacing me, are you?"

"Relax, that's like three or four generations away."

Abi's fingers circle the small of my back, drawing back my focus. No matter how far I drift into the clouds of my curiosity, or the despair of my reality, Abi always brings me back. Opening up to her has taken time, and is still, like everything else, a daily struggle; but I can't imagine now not having Abi in my life. With Valene, I didn't have any anchor. Valene was as angel, soaring through the heavens and then finally rocketing out of my life, leaving me to arc ballistically into a fall I'm not quite sure I've completed yet.

Abi anchors me. She cushions me, against the hard, flattening impact I always threatened to reach.

I kiss her. "I love you."

Abi's heart quakes, *ba-dumm, ba-dumm, ba-dumm.* "It will be ok. Everything is going to be ok, I promise."

I rest my head against hers. "Mike asked if I wanted kids."

Her head whips back. "First you're building robots and now you're having kids with Mike?"

I pinch her side. "Me and you. Us."

"Us?"

My hands curl at my belly. "Do you…"

Her heart skips. "Do you?"

"There's just so much work, Abi."

She kisses me. "This will all be over someday, Kit."

I can't imagine how; I can't imagine the city restored or not needing my help. Someone's help, at least.

Abi's hands slide under my shirt. She pulls it down from the collar, inside out, and her lips pinch the kinematic light trapped within the cage of my chest. A current of energy shadows her mouth from my heart to my lips and seizes hers before they press mine, locking us together in power. Her entire body seizes with an electric shock I calibrate just enough to prevent from electrocuting her.

Not to mention acquiring her.

Her hungry, anxious breath gushes against my neck. "We'll have a baby. Someday. I want something that's mine. I want something in the world that's alive. You know? I want to create something. I want to make something, with you."

I hold her close. "You make me better."

She holds me so close I think she's going to crush the glowing crystal in my chest. "I want to be better."

"Abi…"

"Let's talk more about the kids thing."

Against every force drawing on me, I withdraw from Abi. "I have to go pay The Straw Men a visit first."

She squeezes my ass. "Go earn that money."

"What do you think? Should I take a dish?"

Abi swipes through her PEAL. "I mean, the fudge cookies would be a nice icebreaker."

An angry red glow illuminates my clenched fists. "I don't think there's going to be much ice."

The skeletal remains of a swing ride bloom from marshy ground, scabbed in half-frozen pools of lake water. Brutish wind lashes chains that once suspended wooden chairs against the ground. My eyes search the sky, expecting The Interdictor.

Way my luck is going, that's inevitable.

Open-faced tubs, yellow and brown like rotten bananas, litter the ground beyond. Some crumpled where they fell. Others trail mud and rust, occasional boats in spring floods. All of them shed from a towering Ferris wheel, reduced to the bent spokes of a bicycle wheel.

Birds twist in a winnowing tail behind me as I glide to a landing. Footprints track through grass like trampled straw, into the winding arrangement of rides left exactly as they had been in 1968. Rust eats into the crumbled facades of funhouses. Red paint cracks off cartoonish faces of children's rides, frozen in plastic laughter. Long dead bodies stake the middle of a decrepit promenade of food stands, mouths and eyes stuffed with straw. Withered corpses hollow as the broken horses of a gutted carousel hang from streetlights, cardboard signs pinned to their emaciated chests, painted in dried blood.

GO BACK.

I never liked the circus.

Something brushes against my leg. Chills don't needle me after my transformation. Physical sensations are mostly my memory of them, a mechanical response I practice to avoid seeming less human than I am but the sight of a cat induces legit terror in me.

Its eyes shine with the wan light of a dying candle, inside a hollowed pumpkin. Long dead flesh ambers bone stained with blood. Living things generate energy fields the Myriad perceives on a spectrum imperceptible to humans. Stars shine behind the doors and windows of The Derelicts. The cat is a black hole.

I drift back into a rusted gate. I tap my finger repeatedly against my PEAL. "Abi."

Abi's easy smile stretches across the screen. "Your ears must be ringing. I just put in a batch of cookies."

I rotate my fist toward the ground. "Cat. Zombie cat."

"Zombie? Get closer."

The cat's tail stabs straight up in the air, a bottlebrush without its bristles. Nervous birds echo through the circus. They strain to escape my magnetic pull, to get away from the decrepit amusement park but I stick to the gate, as frightened as I am fascinated.

She shrugs. "It's not like it can hurt you."

"Take a closer look, Abi."

Her nose eclipses the screen. "He's dead all right."

"Can you be a little more bothered by this?"

"AHHHHHH and stuff – "

I sigh. All my senses tell me the cat isn't alive, but still the arch in its back lessens, the claws sheathe and it scampers into the labyrinth of rides and attractions. In the spaces between, shadows waver. Rusty chains jangle. Old wood creaks. Often, the smell of death lingers around Six Corners. I used to pinch my nose and imagine a dead squirrel, a rat, or a possum that had become trapped in one of the disintegrating vacant homes near the apartment building. I no longer have the luxury of deferring what is uncomfortable, or unfathomable.

An unnatural hiss scrapes through the circus. The undead cat loiters just outside a fallen bucket from the Ferris wheel, and at the feet of an unlikely figure. Stocky, Dad would have said, though most of the man's girth is hidden behind a generous trench coat. He wears a wide-brimmed fedora and a rakish smile that belies his horrifying features. My light casts deep shadows in the pits of his gaunt face, his skin stained by the rotten tissue beneath. Scars of knives and bullets constellate his cheek and jaw, sewn back together with shoelace.

"Kit Baldwin. As I live and breathe."

He chortles a dry, guttural laugh. His chest groans as empty as the wheels and towers churning dead in the cold breeze.

Confused birds circle me. "Who are you?"

"Harrow, old man. We've met."

"I don't think so."

He leans against the basket. "Oh, I was here in 1968. Came straight over once I saw you on the television. Had to see it for myself.

You looked different, then, but you never wear the same face. None of us do, I suppose." He scratches at his dry, leathery cheek. "What a carnival act you would have made, Baldwin. Lightning in a bottle. Life beyond death. No – death beyond life."

"You're dead," I say. I search the dense ruin of the amusement park for any kind of understanding of what's happening. Others lurk beyond. Straw Men. "You're all dead..."

He smiles. "The dead don't walk and talk, Baldwin."

"Then what are you?"

"Why, I'm like you," Harrow says, stooping into the basket. "Neither one thing or another."

Light blazes in my chest. "You're a gangster."

His jaw hangs in mock indignation. "You wound me."

"You push pills. Guns. Girls. You shake down poor people who have nowhere else to go and make them pay you for 'security.' For power. Now they don't have to. I'm here."

He pushes his jaw up with a finger. "You've let that lamp of yours blind you to your true nature. I went through the same thing myself, at first. I came back from all the trouble with this cough. Couldn't get rid of it. Coughed myself to death. Or, something in the neighborhood. Naturally, I assumed my condition was simply for my own benefit and I indulged myself, old man, manifestly. But I was trying to take pleasure in life, when I was no longer alive. I had yet to see the joy in death."

I scan the grounds again. Harrow generates no energy I can detect. Straw Men shadow the park, but I can't tell how many.

"Maybe we do have something in common. My girlfriend was just telling me how I only have two settings. Vague and TMI. Fairly certain you've got the first one down cold."

"Life is nothing but the vagaries, old man."

"How long have you been... this way?"

His lips worm together. "Oh, a spell. Everybody thinks all the strange started with the ship. The ship just woke everything up. There are old things in this world. People don't want to see. They don't want to know. How else do you think a gang of undead has persisted in this city? No, they just sweep us out of mind, into the corner of their city, behind all the other clutter."

"Maybe there's help for you," I say. "Maybe we can find a way to treat whatever is happening to you."

Harrow laughs again. "How kind of you to offer, but really, I'm offering you my help, Baldwin."

I bite my lip. "Me?"

"Yes, you. Forgive me, Baldwin. My manners have dulled, being removed as I've been from society these last few years. It's been a few, to be sure. A proper introduction was due ages ago, but I see you got my message."

"I can give you a lesson in etiquette," I say, holding back the energy clawing to get out of me.

"Excuse the methods, Baldwin, but there's really no other way to get your attention. Unless something is a problem, you don't seem to notice it. When you do, you're eager to help. Why, you're just helping everyone, aren't you? No problem too big or small. You have power and intelligence, coming out your ears. What you lack is guidance. Wisdom. Perspective."

"Is that right?"

Harrow sits on the slight bench inside the bucket. "Death isn't some exile from light and heat that you might imagine, toiling in your lab night after night to chase away the shadows of The Derelicts. Those shadows are within you. Death is in you. It's like flying, isn't it? You're flying faster than you're falling. Why you'd just go on forever until you ran out of fuel or someone plucked you out of the sky. But you don't go on forever. Gravity always wins, because gravity always is. And that's all death is, old man. Gravity. Nothing to be frightened of. The sooner we understand it, the sooner we can escape it."

Why is it all these guys have to have a philosophy?

"That's what you've done? Escaped death?"

"Well, you know what they say. No room at the inn."

The cat slithers between the flaked bars of the basket inside to

Harrow's lap. Images compete for my attention, images of Ma, the airplane, all the people I couldn't save.

"We can help one another." His eyes, like smoke-stained painted glass, settle on the light in my chest. "We're both tinkerers. Inventors. Explorers, beyond the limits of humanity."

"Generally people who try this hard to sell me on what I am just want to use me for something I'm not."

"That's the game, isn't it? Perhaps you're too young yet to see that's all existence is. Buying. Selling. Acquiring."

I raise my hand, and the rusted metal bar of the bucket swings shut across him. "I'll make this simple. Break another light bulb in this town, and I'll break your face."

"Light bulbs. Really, old man, you're too concerned with bright, flashy things. Light. Energy. Life. These are trifles. Diversions. Distractions, you might say, from our reality. Death is the natural state. The only law. Before you and I, it was blind. Indiscriminate. The black tide rolling up the sparkling grains of sand undertow. Now, the tide can surge. Now the tide can swamp and everything that breathes can learn to hold its breath. Just like you have, Baldwin. Just like you."

"I'm alive," I say.

"Cosmic power. Human governance. A stronger dichotomy in a person I cannot recall. You think you're alive. You think you're human. Life and death no longer hold meaning for you, Baldwin. Within you lies a universe beyond the limits of existence." His eyes brim. "The mind, old man. The mind conceives of things the body cannot achieve. Despite my advantage, I am still trapped within this body. This city." Harrow grips the closed, deformed bar of the bucket. "But now, I'll be free."

"Free how?"

Hands rupture through the ground, solid as gruel. Shadows slouch toward me. Moments halve into the panels of Simon's comic book. Time fragments, stilled and strangled around the fear paralyzing me. The Straw Men close in on me, all of them leering at the magenta light radiating from my heart.

A rotten smile crosses the stripped rope of Harrow's lips. "You like to share, old man. You like to give away the power of the stars. Be a doll and share a little of it with me."

FOUR

I snap a tendril of energy on the ground. "You want a taste of my power?"

His smile somehow becomes more grotesque. "Look at me, old man. When have I ever settled for a taste?"

Ravenous energy breaks against his skin, like water against rock. The tendril scours Harrow's face, his body, splintering into infinite strands, none of which acquire him.

I step back. "How..."

Harrow lifts the bar on the bucket and steps out. The cat purrs like a car without a muffler as he strokes its scraggy back. "I suspect you'll come to it. Smart as you are."

The Myriad acquires energy. No energy emanates from Harrow, or any of The Straw Men creeping into my field of vision. There is nothing for me to consume.

"Something has to be keeping you alive," I say.

"I told you, Baldwin. I'm not alive. And neither are you."

Savage light pulses in my fists. "I can still burn this place down to the ground. And all of you with it."

"All of us?"

The amusement park transforms from swampy ruins to a dense marsh. Hundreds of dead clot the spaces between the rides. I have no life for these undead creatures to take and that idea, I have no life, will never again, wakes with a start from the cage I've buried it in. All those TV shows you watch. People on ledges. When someone talks them in, walks them in, they always say, *Don't look down.* That's what I've been doing since the moment I become The Ever, and something less than myself.

I look up, as I always do.

I rise into a flurry of dead blackbirds. Half-feathered wings cut across my cheek. Clipped beaks stab into my gossamer skin and I tumble off course, into the tangle of the swing ride. Chains coil around me, caught in my magnetic field. The harder I struggle to get free, the more entangled I become.

I contract my magnetic field and rip the swing apart. Flails of fragmented chain thrash the park. Debris shreds the wooden facades of remnant attractions and I scramble across the gooey ground, into a minefield of dead hands.

"No..."

Harrow leans against the bucket, watching with a lazy grin. "Why must everything devolve into violence, old man? It's uncivilized. I say violence is a tumor on the narrative of history. An insidious disease that plagues us all."

Useless tendrils stab at withered fingers. "Then stop this."

"All I want is to simply upgrade, as they say these days. The spirit endures, but the flesh... well."

"I can't acquire you," I say.

"Acquire? Oh, I don't want to be acquired. No, that doesn't suit me. But then, so little does. I want your power, Baldwin. I want what makes you the torch for this particular flame."

Rusty debris floats around me. "I'm one of a kind."

"Without question. But you must have some theory. Some rational in that cosmically loaded brain of yours as to how you are you... and how to repeat the experiment."

I gave myself to my power during the Battle of Break Pointe. In that moment, I arrived at – not a peace, but an understanding – with The Ever. There is no distinguishing us, no dividing us and no denying what had happened.

What happened?

I transformed. This is me. I'm still me, even if I am The Ever. The Ever is me. It's going to stay that way.

"I will never share this power with you," I say.

"I assumed, which is why I've put it to a vote. Looks like the majority supports our taking matters into our own hands."

Screams boom from the frozen ground. Moans. The crack of bones. Half-empty husks of insects crawl across my face. Bird bones lift into flight. *Abi.* I kick. I sink. Mud and snow slop across my eyes. Hands claw my face. Fingers hook my mouth.

"Abi – "

The throat of the earth contracts, swallowing me quick and whole. Pressure forces me down and down and I slap into something like a tunnel, bored out of the cold soup of the ground. The only light mine. Fitful shadows move across the dripping curve of the walls. Energy bristles within me. I can't acquire any of The Straw Men, but they're still bone; they can be broken. They're still flesh, if barely; I can burn them.

Fire ignites in my hands.

Children surrounded me. Hollowed in death. Loosened of their jaws. Gutted of the spirit in their eyes. I have no memory to account for this horror. This fear.

God.

Bony ends of fingers dig into my leather jacket. Teeth tear at my skin. Arms lock around me. They pull. They claw and I crumble to my knees, terrified, but more to hurt them. Curls of my hair twist in their friable fingers. My jacket pares from my arms. Magenta light dawns inside the depths of the pool. Tendrils of energy lash out from beneath my exposed skin.

"No – "

Snakes of lightning I can't help coil around the wraith-like children. Searing energy burns into dead skin. Death sours the air. Burning leather. A skeletal girl scratches at my shirt. She reaches through the gauzy bubble of my skin and closes her mangled hand around the glowing orb of the Myriad.

"Stop – "

I don't know if I unleash the blast, or The Ever does. Children peel off me like dried glue. Before I'm in the air, the straw kids are back on their feet. Metal and earth break against me as I rocket out of the tunnel, through the wriggling ground, and out of the amusement park. Snow melts against the heat radiating from within me. Clouds envelop me, but I keep going, beyond the tangle of birds, the reach of the dead and my own fear, a distant memory.

PANEL ONE

Abi and Kit cuddle up together on the ratty, salvaged sofa in their apartment. Both are in their pajamas, washed out in the pale blue glow of a television off-screen. The kitchen is behind them. The bathroom door, cracked just a little, is visible on the right side of the panel.

Caption: *Sometimes, I'm not here.*

PANEL TWO

Close up on Kit, somewhere else. A vertical slash of pale blue light down the right side of her face. Her eyes are empty, large just over the horizon of her arms, crossed over her knees.

PANEL THREE

Abi and Kit again.

SFX: *Ding!*

Caption: *Sometimes, I'm in my life. Sometimes I'm watching it. It's like a movie. A comic book.*

PANEL FOUR

We pull further out from Kit, huddled on the floor of what we now realize is her shower stall. Knees to her chin. Except for the gash of blue light, it's dark. Late. She's by herself.

PANEL FIVE

Abi climbs over the back of the couch, toward the kitchen.
SFX: *Fwoosh!*
Kit stays put, eyes on the TV, smile fixed in place.
Caption: *Sometimes I'm doing both at the same time.*

PANEL SIX

Further out still from Kit, reducing in the tiny footprint of the stall. The sink encroaching on the frame. Light through the cracked door bleeds over the edge from the gutter.

PANEL SEVEN

In the background, Abi hoists a pan of fresh-baked cookies like it's a trophy she's just won. Kit is still on the couch, her smile and posture just as it was in the last panel.
Caption: *My power allows me to step out of my life. Out of this world, even, if I wanted to. Some days I'm afraid of losing myself. Days like today, it's all I want to do.*

PANEL EIGHT

Outside the bathroom door now, looking back in through the

crack at Kit, squeezed in the gap. Abi enters the frame from the left, heading back to the couch with a plate of cookies.

PANEL NINE

Abi returns to the couch with the cookies. Kit again is exactly as Abi left her, static and smiling.

Caption: *There's never any in between.*

A glass of wine twists in my hands. Moscato sloshes around inside, violent as my emotions. I have been afraid. I have been angry. I have been shocked. I have never been this. Vidette listens as I go through the hell of the amusement park again, my voice snarling on every last awful detail of the ordeal.

"Mama said there'd be days like this," Vidette says, and tops up her glass in the kitchen. "Abi didn't want to come?"

"She's watching a movie," I say.

"Alone?"

I bite my lip. "I'm there."

Vidette holds on to the bottle. "You're there?"

"When I acquired Siski, I acquired her powers."

A lot of things have happened in the last six months. I don't know what I would put as the topper, but my battle with a telepathic, tele-kinetic wolf whose ability to mentally project herself beyond her body I acquired would be near the top.

Vidette sinks into the couch beside me. "You kind of buried the lead, honey. So, what – you can read thoughts, too?"

"I have enough problems. I just use the projection."

"You can pick and choose?"

"I can select from any of the abilities of anyone or anything the Myriad has ever acquired."

Vidette rests her head against her hand. "Huh."

"I don't do it a lot. It costs me." I sip my wine. "Just a few nights a week. I can be home with Abi and out on patrol at the same time. In the lab. It's helped us. A lot."

"Does she know?"

I shake my head.

"Oy."

"It's me," I say.

"I'll give you some advice. Honesty goes a lot farther than your clothes, out your apartment window." Vidette finishes off her glass. "Now I have to get up again."

"They were children, Vi."

That dead girl at the amusement park grips the Myriad in her skeletal fingers. Lightning snaps at her cheeks, and she just stares at me. I try to bury the image of her with all the other memories I don't want, but they refuse to stay in their graves.

Vidette gently rubs my arm. "There's nothing you could do."

"What do I do?

"Whatever is keeping them alive, it's nothing in physics, at least that we understand. I'd have to examine one up close."

"I'm not going back there," I say.

"Another bottle of wine and I'll be ready to go tonight."

"I'm never going back."

A sigh punctuates Vidette's leaving the couch. The woman is five foot nothing, thin as a strand of hair and though she's over fifty now, she looks twenty years younger. Her relative youth and stature belie the fact Vidette is one of the strongest people on the planet. She never shrinks from a fight, even when she should. Scars never keep on her skin, hard as diamond, and neither does the sense of when to fight another day. Something awful lurks in Wilder Amusement Park. For years, it's laid dormant, frozen under the glaze of the city's alien winter but now as Break Pointe brightens and warms, the dead thaw.

Wake.

"Take a drink," Vidette says. "Let it all out."

With Vidette, I can be frightened, doubtful, even weak in

moments. Vidette is strong, a hero in her own right as a member of the Vanguard and then as a citizen with the will to walk away from a corrupt corporation to go into private practice. A bottle of wine. A pair of ears. That's all. No judgment.

"My dad was in the Army," I say. "He told me once the trouble with being a soldier was the war never ends."

"He was right."

"This is why I can't tell Abi. She has to have something. There has to be some space for us. Some peace, even if it's just a couple of hours every Friday night. She has so much stress."

"I don't think Abi does stress," Vidette says.

"She's an alcoholic."

Vidette stops midway through uncorking another bottle of moscato. "Oh. Shoot. I'm sorry, honey."

"I'm reading these books. Stuff online. I'm trying to be better. My mom had issues, you know. Not drinking, but... I wasn't good at dealing with it and I want to be better. I will be."

"This isn't your fault, Kit. You know that, right? She's not an alcoholic because you do this, she's an alcoholic because she has a disease. And this isn't something you can fight, FYI."

My wine becomes a whirlpool. "I know."

"It's not something you can fix."

"I know, Vi." I place my glass on the coffee table. "She's going to meetings. Dr. Piller is her sponsor."

Vidette sets the bottle down on the counter. "I see."

"She says he's been a help to her."

"Good. I'm glad."

Light flares as I bite my lip. We can talk about anything in these sessions, and often do long into bleary dawns, but Vidette's ex and Kit's old boss was one subject we avoid.

"You're ok with this?" Vi says. "Ronnie being her sponsor?"

I shrug. "I don't have any say in it."

"You always have a say. I used to think I couldn't have a drink because of Ronnie. If I did, it meant I made him an alcoholic. I couldn't have any joy. I couldn't have a life. If I was happy, he was sad. If I was upset, I couldn't be. There wasn't any room for me in that house. Forget about kids." Vidette puts the bottle back in the wine cabinet. "You aren't responsible for her addiction, Kit. Or her happiness."

"Didn't you tell me once I had an obligation to others?"

"You can't save people, honey."

I almost laugh. "Isn't that our job?"

"Our job is to save people, but not from themselves. You can't. If someone wants to destroy themselves, then all you do getting in the way of that is present them another target."

"Some people would say that about Break Pointe."

"Break Pointe didn't choose this," Vidette says.

"Neither did Abi. And neither did Dr. Piller."

I leave the couch and slide back the patio door. Birds line the railing, wings anxious for me to lift into the night.

"He chose to betray you," Vidette says. "Us."

Every night, I rise into the sky, a beacon for all in The Derelicts to see. People in the Blackwood Building have an even better view. A strange détente has settled over the city since Break Pointe defaulted on its contract with Great Power. Responders no longer patrol The Derelicts, remaining across the river on the peninsula, restricted by the law from acting without sanction. Break Pointe has always been a divided city, in geography, class, and politics and now it's cleaved again, into zones of power. The dead rule The Ice Pick. The living cling to life in The Derelicts. Gods look down from their tower across a river only a mile wide but bordering different worlds.

"Abi's health means more to me than any anger I have about what Dr. Piller did to us," I say. "We all still want the same thing, Vi. We all want a safe city. We all want peace."

Vidette smiles. "What are we talking about?"

"Whatever is happening with The Straw Men is beyond me."

"We don't know that — "

"If we're going to find a way to end this, we need the best and the brightest, and that's at GP."

"The best and the brightest is right here," she says, gesturing to me. "These are our problems. We have to face them. GP punted on them for years. Sometimes... sometimes the only way to fix something is to destroy it. Start over. If these people... if these kids... if they're dead, then they deserve their rest."

I'm tired. I won't sleep tonight. I never sleep. "I'll call Dr. Piller in the morning. Thanks, Vi."

Vidette smiles, but it's muted, like the moon through heavy clouds. Chalk lines of frozen fog dust the cables of the bridge as I float across the island toward home. Scabs of dead grass. Sidewalks. Windows, blue with the lives of televisions.

FIVE

Rotted fingers tattoo the glass of the test chamber in Applied Sciences with prints. The dismembered arm slithers after me as I circle the chamber, stopping when I do. Anxious reflections stretch across the curved chamber, Vidette and Dr. Piller as wary of the writhing arm as they are each other.

"There's nothing biological stimulating this response," Piller says, examining the results on one of the monitors ringing the chamber. "No detectable energy."

I sit at my old desk. "Harrow said he had a cough."

"A virus isn't animating The Straw Men. Or any kind of pathogen. All that's present in the blood traces I scraped off the bone is an arrested state of decay. A slower state."

"So what is it, then?"

Piller shakes his head. "No idea."

"Do we need more samples, or what do we need?"

"Exposing more people to risk of infection or God knows what doesn't make a lot of sense. I'm not a pathologist, but – "

"Then let's get one."

" – I can tell you what they'd say, Ms. Baldwin, given my considerable experience living in a quarantined city. Their recommendation will be my recommendation. Containment."

My frustration flares beneath my skin. Containing things, bottling things, and preserving them good or bad is the only consistent strategy Great Power ever employed. Break Pointe, her people, her jobs, her future, were jammed and jarred through winters so bitter the glass cracked but the contents remain a frozen, indistinct mass. The Straw Men have been raiding the pantry for years, and no one ever did anything about it.

"They're immune to my power," I say.

"You brought back one of their arms, didn't you? Obviously blunt force trauma remains a problem for them." Piller glances at Vidette, who duly cracks her knuckles. "Their decay makes them vulnerable. GP kept them in check for decades, because The Straw Men avoid direct conflict. Now we know why."

Questions chase their own tails in my mind. How many Straw Men are there? Hundreds, I thought; how did they become infected? Are they all like Harrow, victims of some 'cough,' or are they his victims? Can he create more?

How?

Rotten skin squeaks inside the chamber. My reflection diverges in the glass as I consider the arm Vidette retrieved from the amusement park. I can burn The Straw Men. Break them. Bury them. That won't solve the problem. How can I solve for something that has no origin or cure? How can I solve death?

Piller turns to Vidette. "You didn't get hurt or anything, did you? They didn't scratch you, or bite you?"

Vidette shrugs. "They tried."

"Are you ok?"

"I'm a little nauseous."

"When did that start?"

"Around the time I met you," she says.

Their bickering picks up its old rhythm, but I don't keep the beat. My mind drifts, as it often does in back in my lab, to elsewhere. Abi sleeps sound in their bed, unaware of what happened at the amuse-ment park. She doesn't worry or fear. She doesn't care about the origin of The Straw Men, or if there is a cure for their condition. She doesn't trip in the ruts of bottomless memories, never finding a solid footing in her sleep.

Chains rattle across the floor.

I snap reflexively into a defensive posture as The Interdictor slinks into the dark of the lab.

"Somehow the rats still get in," he says.

Coming to the tower was a huge risk, but I needed the resources of the lab. "Should have changed the locks."

Piller moves between us. "Nathan, don't – "

The Interdictor brushes Piller aside as if he were a flimsy curtain. "You're not getting out this time, Baldwin. This time I'm going to crush that battery in your chest to powder."

He propels across the lab at met, hands clawed into talons aimed right at my heart and The Interdictor passes clean through me. Light ripples through my projection, before it reforms. I can't help the wry smile that comes to my lips as The Interdictor skulks back to me. He reaches out, confused, and presses his finger against my spectral shoulder.

"You irritate me, Baldwin."

"And here I thought I wasn't accomplishing anything."

He draws back the hood of his scrim-net cloak and removes his helmet. The scar of melting chains I crowned The Interdictor with at the Battle of Break Pointe channels through his dark hair, and deep into his scalp, preventing any easy disguise of it. He doesn't seem to want to; he's cropped his hair close, emphasizing every pink furrow and snaked channel of skin.

"Whose power have you stolen now, Baldwin?"

I smile. "I earned it, fair and square."

"'Earned.' I assume it was the wolf. I heard of your encounter with the Bloodbacks. I'm surprised you had the nerve to acquire them. Perhaps you couldn't win on the merits."

"Siski would have beaten you to death with your own fists," I say, reaching out and applying enough mental force to yank his hanging chains. "And then she would have eaten you."

"Is this supposed power yours now?"

I tug on his chains, hard. "You know it."

He lurches closer. "Then use it, Baldwin."

I want to. I really want to.

"So much penis," Vidette says, with a sigh. "She whooped your ass last time, Nathan. Now she's got a whole new bag of tricks. Only a moron would knock on that door again."

"I recall 'whooping' your ass last time, Dr. Rizzo."

Vidette clenches her fists. "I already ripped one guy's arm off today. May as well go for the set."

"Go ahead," Piller says, sinking into a chair. "Knock the building down. Kill everybody. Solve their problems, at least."

I let go of The Interdictor. Impressions of chain links stamp my hand until they fade. Whenever I get tangled up with him, I get bound in the need to prove my power. No matter what I say, what I do, he throws water on my abilities, and in the smoke, I can't see it's the only way he can get to me. For all his power, The Interdictor always makes a show. Every word is spoken with forced emphasis. Every movement embroidered for dramatic effect. Everything about Nathan Regan is maximized, so there can be no doubt of his importance. Sometimes, between the baroque gestures and dramatic pauses, I glimpse an awkward twinge, as if he's momentarily forgotten his line.

I've forgotten mine.

Shame mirrors in the glass of the test chamber. My reflection has become smaller, limited by the confines of trying to solve him. There's only one solution.

"I'll go," I say.

Piller holds up his hands. "We're not done yet."

"You said so yourself, Dr. Piller. There's nothing more we can learn about The Straw Men."

The Interdictor goes to the chamber. "Straw Men?"

Fingers scale the glass inside, only to slip back down. He watches the severed limb writhe on the floor of the chamber with a naked fascination, transfixed by yet another power beyond his.

"I thought they were a gang," The Interdictor says.

"They are a gang," I say. "Of the undead."

"Undead? Zombies?"

"Basically."

"Zombies are real?"

"That's where you draw the line?"

"Our power is natural, Baldwin. A consequence of nature. Nature's ultimate consequence is death."

"I don't know how to stop them."

He shrugs. "Destroy them."

I shake my head. "That's not the answer for everything."

"No, but assuming your primary power is negated by this corruption of theirs... otherwise, why would you be here, seeking the help of a man patently less intelligent than you..."

Piller sighs. "Why do I answer my phone?"

"...your only option is overwhelming force. Clearly, they can be damaged. You're wasting your time here, Baldwin. You should return to The Derelicts and commence your assault on their stronghold. I expect the outcome will be to your satisfaction."

"I'm not a vigilante," I say.

"You're a god. Act like one."

Abi shifts in bed beside me, legs kicking at the blankets. She's running again in her sleep; she's always running.

"They vandalized property. They're selling drugs and who knows what else. The Straw Men need to be in jail, or a lab like this where we can try and study what's happening to them."

He sneers with contempt. "They need to be in graves, Baldwin. Evidently, that's not an option. The alternative is cremation. You wanted to save the city. Save it."

"The Straw Men have been terrorizing The Derelicts for decades," I say. "GP did nothing. You did nothing."

He turns from the chamber. "Our hands have long been tied across the river. But not here. Leave now, Baldwin. And don't come back. If you do, I will bring down this building and however many more it takes to keep you in the ground."

Chains scrape behind him down the hall. Loose metal rattles in the elevator shaft as he flies up and out of the tower, back to his perch atop her mooring mast. There are no options. No choices. Only my fear. My duty. One will give before the other. One has already been deferred, rested but not asleep back in bed with Abi. I do not fear. I do not hesitate. I do not question my power.

That's the other Kit.

I patrol all day. I patrol all night.

I am on watch, and I am watching TV with Abi. Dumb movies. Old musicals. Static competes with the music from the old radio as we dance in the kitchen, as we make love in the bedroom, as I tell her about the amusement park. Abi always has something to say. She doesn't say much of anything as I live that moment again, of being buried, pulled down, torn apart in the hands of children.

She takes my hand, somewhere in the middle of the night. "Why do you think you can touch them?"

I thought she was asleep. "There's no energy."

"Why do you think you can touch me?"

Her heart races, *ba-dumm, ba-dumm, ba-dumm*. "I'm careful."

Abi grips my hand. "Are you careful with anyone else?"

"I'm not having kids with Mike."

"I mean... you don't try and touch anyone else?"

"I didn't think you were the jealous type."

"Sidebar: you have no idea, but... I just... I guess I just wondered if what we have is special."

"It's just you," I say and kiss her.

Her shadow stretches across the bedroom wall as she turns to me, turns me over and shadows of debris dance on the walls of my lab, creating the illusion of movement.

———

A text pops on the screen of my PEAL from Abi.

XOXO

I send a throbbing heart symbol back. As I do, news notifications bubble to the surface. *Death toll rises in diffusion incident. President orders flags lowered to half-staff. Great Power again calls for ban of all diffusion devices.*

I flick away the news and go back to work. Circuitry cocoons radiant filament. Neural pathways link. Power registers within the network and someone clears their throat.

"Sorry," Simon says.

The android drifts back into his case above me. "Hello."

Simon stands on the crystal-scabbed floor of the alien wreck, backpack hanging off one shoulder, a stranded look on his face. "So this is where you work? Cool."

I ease down to the deck. "It's not safe here."

"It is for you."

I zip down my jacket. Light shines out. "No, it's not."

He shrugs. "Ok. I can go."

Some part of me wants him to if I'm honest. Receivers, I understand. Filaments. Complex machines built from alien knowledge and power. People, I have no clue.

What would Abi say?

"Simon, is something wrong?"

His spirit picks back up. "I drew a new comic."

"Oh. Did you bring it?"

His diffidence vanishes as the bag slips from his shoulder to his hand. "I thought you might like to see it."

"Issue two," I say, flipping through the pages. This time, I'm battling a giant toddler named Tantrum attacking the city. Break Pointe somehow disintegrates into even more rubble as the violent, comic battle plays out in splash pages.

"I never get a break, even in the funny pages."

A bruise yellows the wrinkles of his smile.

"What happened there?" I say.

He touches his cheek. "Nothing."

"Who did that?"

"Nobody. Do you draw? Designs for your machines?"

I tuck the comic under my arm, wanting to pursue this new thing that's not working. "Did someone hit you?"

"I just slipped on the ice."

Silence floods into the chasm between us. I imagine Abi over in the corner, imploring me to keep talking.

"Sometimes I scribble things down," I say, gesturing to the white scratch defacing the blackboard. "I'm not very good at planning things. But I can put anything together after someone has broken it. That person being me, usually."

Simon scratches the back of his head. Loose threads hang from the cuff of his coat. His jeans dirty. Ripped. I rarely notice these things; everyone in The Derelicts has holes somewhere. "What did you want to do? When you were younger?"

"I wanted to help," I say, handing him back the comic.

"Do you need help with anything?"

"Um... it's all sort of done. Almost."

"It's cool. I can go."

"What are you going to do now?"

He smiles. "I don't know. Just walk. I like to walk."

The sole of Simon's shoe wanders. No laces, like the boy, dead, at the thrift store and now still, forever, in a pauper's grave cleared from the ruins of Church Row.

"It's not safe here, Simon. Really."

Simon zips up his bag. "Ok."

I nod, stranded as he is. "Thank you for showing me the comic, though. I'm glad you're in school. Keep studying. Maybe you can get into an art school, and do this for a career."

"You think so?"

"Absolutely. I didn't go to college. It was hard for me at home, too. I would have liked to have gone."

"You could teach classes," he says.

"On how not to live your life, maybe."

His frown morphs into a smile, knowing and sad. I recognize it well. He's found comfort in his comics, as I have my endless projects, scavenging, testing, building memory from the scraps of an amnesiac world. The pages of the comic open in his hand, and I think of my mother, opening all the drawers in the apartment. I haven't thought of Ma in a minute.

"You can do anything, Simon."

His smile doesn't have the giddy exuberance of his comic book. He drifts out of the lab, the ship, and I go back to work.

Always work.

Hours, I've been at this. Days. Time loses its shape. Broken parts tumble together, again and again, as I try to restore the equipment the Straw Men destroyed, and figure out a way to fix this.

A text buzzes on my PEAL. *Sex?*

I snort. *Send me something naughty.*

Abi's reply fires back. *I'll get kicked out of school.*

You're at the school?

It's like ten in the morning dude.

I sigh. *You'll just have to make it up to me.*

I wait for Abi to reply. I wait, and there is no message. No crackling electricity to symbolize Abi is typing again. I go back to all my ruins. Something probably came up in class. Debris streams around the darkened lab, looping toward me before bounding away. The pieces never come together and my hand jolts. With a smile, I swipe to Abi's new message.

She isn't texting. She's calling.

I answer. "Abi?"

She's not there. There isn't any sound, except a strange, disquiet *click* in the background.

"Baby, are you there?"

Click, click, click.

"Abi, can you hear – "

Screams. I hear someone screaming in the background.

Falling snow burns away into instant fog behind me. I descend fast on the buckled steps of the school and one of the boys steps out. What was his name? *Nobody,* he said, when I asked. Something in his hand. Some kind of weapon. I've seen it before; what is it?

Oh my God. It's a diffuser.

My light crashes. "What are you doing with that?"

Time slows, to the *click, click, click* of a trigger, the panel by panel framing of Simon's comic books.

PANEL ONE

Nobody and Kit stand opposite each other outside the school, silhouettes against the all-white blitz of snow.

PANEL TWO

Kit, haloed in blackbirds, stares back at him.

KIT: What did you do?

PANEL THREE

He points the diffuser at her.

. . .

PANEL FOUR

Kit's static form is obscured in the violent warping field of the discharged diffuser.

PANEL FIVE

Kit stares back, unmoved and unaffected.

PANEL SIX

Nobody looks on in mute shock.

PANEL SEVEN

Shredded feathers of diffused birds rain down on Kit.

PANEL EIGHT

Shock bends to fear as magenta light surges within Kit. Her arm rising. Fist clenching.

PANEL NINE

Kit is completely whited out in the blast she fires. Blood red on the fringes. Only a trace of her silhouette.

SIX

PAGE

PANEL

$$\Delta U =$$

Shredded pages of a half-finished comic book confetti the air. Shadows burnt in blood scorch the walls. Splintered bone frustrates my steps as much as broken glass and I can't distinguish any of the students from each other in the classroom. It used to be a classroom; now it's a porous container for the silence that comes with the theft of so much life. I don't scream. I don't vomit. I don't react at all.

That's the other Kit.

I touch my PEAL. "Vi. Vi, come to the school."

Someone coughs. Something stirs behind the teacher's desk. I slip through what had been someone and on the other side of the desk, I find Abi, covered in blood.

"Baby?"

She flinches at the sight of me. "It just happened."

Beneath the blood painted her, Abi is whole. Uninjured. I can't believe it. God help me, I can't. "Are you ok?"

She wipes blood off her face. "This isn't me."

"What?"

"This isn't me." Her eyes roam around the room, back to her crimson hands. "I don't know who this is."

I reach for her. "You're ok."

"Are you... are you ok?"

The fridge kept freezing up inside. I knew something was wrong with it, and with no effort at all I could have figured out how to fix it, but I let it go. By then, all the light bulbs in the apartment were in pieces. Screens of the televisions painted black. There was nothing I could fix at home with Ma, so I didn't bother and then, of course, the fridge went out. I couldn't fix it. An appliance repairman said I needed to thaw out the defrosting unit, and because I didn't have the money to pay the labor, I stood there for hours with a blow dryer.

Milk and yogurt and containers of things with expiration dates never observed piled on the floor around me. When I was done mopping up, sponging up the water gushing out of the fridge, the drone of the blow dryer was all I could hear. A jet engine in miniature. I hear it now, plain as say.

I hear it now.

The ancient hand dryer in the men's restroom dies, down the hall. Sniffs assume the silence it left. Whimpers. Text messages arrive in clustered sorties on unanswered PEALs down the hall *ba-dumm, ba-dumm, ba-dumm.* Shoes cluster behind one of the stalls. Someone on their knees. I grab the handle.

Someone holds it.

"It's me," I say, and Mike appears in the cracked door, broken and bloody. I crash to my knees. "Mike."

His eyes flutter. "I couldn't... I didn't..."

He loses consciousness. I hold my hand to his wound. Blood oozes through my fingers, waxing on the leather of my jacket.

Students emerge out of the stall, crying, screaming but I don't hear them. The hand dryer comes back on, for no reason.

Blood clots.

That's how you survive. You just want to stop, but then there are questions, rapid and brutal as bullets. There are logistical things like identifying the bodies and preserving the crime scene and weighing protecting the scene versus protecting streets you think are vulnerable to further attack and you clot. Life congeals, and the bleeding stops even if the pain doesn't. You continue, even if every instinct is to shutter. You do it without thinking, or even realizing you have. The true horror in life is not what we inflict on each other, but that we recover from it so ably that we endure shock after shock after shock.

Reality tears like paper.

A bloody scar opens in the air and the flesh of my lab peels back to the tissue of the In Between. Veins of lightning illuminate infinite clusters of floating crystal, tumbling in a haze of red dust. Fragments careen through the nonsensical netherworld of the In Between, smashing into smaller projectiles but the massive clomp beneath me is cratered with the impacts of would-be destroyers. In the desolate solitude of the In Between, lost in the cosmic expanse of nothing at all, I succumb to grief.

Worlds shatter on my scream.

Debris rains on me like meteorites, burning up in the corona of my anger. Hurt and sorrow and shock cleave like the fragments floating in the ether, and I am apart from myself. I stand as the other falls to her knees. I remain stoic, as the other disappears into the gathering dust of the void. I do not fear. I do not suffer. I do not yield to this instinct.

I do not move on.

Microscopes patterned after those in Applied Sciences assemble and disassemble magnetically in the air, puzzles I can work again and again. Glass clinks somewhere in the lab behind me. I turn around. Vidette drags a chair across the crystalline floor of the lab, a bottle of wine in her hand.

Vidette wipes away the stream of red down her chin. "Is that your version of a stress ball?"

Metal fragments tumble in a loose ring of debris around me. "Is it still today?"

"I don't know."

"Have you slept, Vi?"

"How would I do that?"

My head droops with the weight of all that keeps me up at night. "You should go home."

"Is that where you are?"

I bite my lip. "I'm working."

"On what?"

The diffuser levitates out of the box of evidence I collected from the school. "I'm trying to find out where the shooter got this thing. I'm not getting anywhere. There are no identifiable marks. No serial number. Nothing."

Vidette shrugs. "They're cheap. They're everywhere."

I don't understand how such weapons can be legal. They aren't in some places, Break Pointe in particular. Major cities reliant on GP for security. In rural areas, places far removed from the epicenter of Empowered activity, diffusers are pervasive and so are the laws that permit them. Every time someone uses one against innocent people, the same conversation flares up and then dies off, just as quickly.

Not this time.

First I'll have to untie my tongue. My hurt I can barely articulate, let alone acknowledge. But I will. And then.

"We may as well start somewhere," Vidette says. "Let's go turn over some tables at the swap."

"I know they're not coming in through the black market. Professor Blackwood had an arrangement with Gennady to keep the market open if he kept it clean. No anti-Empowered weapons."

"Blackwood isn't exactly around anymore, honey."

"The arrangement is still in place."

Vidette's brow furrows. "Between who?"

The bargain I made with Blind Tiger was necessary; leave the market open in exchange for his material support in manufacturing my engine. Her invention requires no fuel, exudes no waste, and yet the residue of shame still clings to me.

"How's Mike?" I say.

Vidette's smile is frustrated. "The same."

"What do you think, though?"

Vidette wipes her cheek. "What do I think? I think he's on a ventilator. I think he has massive blood loss."

I want to be at the hospital. Across the river, I'm a fugitive of justice, a public menace GP would apprehend if they could. It isn't safe for me to visit Break Pointe Medical. It isn't safe for Mike, or anyone else there I care about.

"He's strong," I say. "He's a fighter."

"I haven't seen Abi."

Abi stares out the living room window, where she's been since she got back to the apartment. "She's resting."

"And how are you?"

"I don't..."

Vidette's hand rests on my shoulder. "Don't what?"

I don't fear. I don't anything, as Ma tells me Dad is dead. He won't be coming home, she says, as she lies down forever in the street and I pick up the Myriad. I burn into a star.

I just don't.

"I have work to do," I say.

"Am I interrupting you?"

"I'm angry too, Vi."

"Let's see it."

Somewhere in the In Between, the ruin of my anger continues to bullet through time and space. I stifle my rage, my hunger for revenge, and the ease with which I now turn to my power, cosmic; I pack it away, not into a crate, but into the other Kit. She takes on more dimension by the second.

"You don't want to," I say.

Vidette drinks from the bottle. "Who was he?"

My fists clench. "Jason. His name was Jason."

As far as I've been able to tell, he has no family in The Derelicts. No friends. Jason kept to himself, even among the other students, but he had gained a name in death, like so many in the city. In a bloody instant, he had gained eternity.

She shakes her head. "And we have no idea why."

"No idea," I say.

Why doesn't matter; it happened because it could happen. The decay that festered in Jason's mind until it erupted in his violence doesn't matter as much as containing it, and stopping these attacks from happening again.

Vidette starts to pace, the drink not enough to still her. "You think this has anything to do with The Straw Men?"

"There's no evidence of that."

"They've been coming at you. At us."

"They know what the consequences would be."

"What would the consequences be, Kit?"

The diffuser floats into my hands. "I'm going to find out who made this, Vi. Who sold it to Jason. And I'm going to put an end to these massacres once and for all."

Vidette sets the bottle down. "Why wait? Let's make a list."

"A list?"

"Let's find out who makes these things, and let's go pay them a visit. All of them. They want to fuck with us, they want to shoot up our schools, then they have to live with the fallout."

The diffuser breaks apart. "I'm not a vigilante."

"And you're not a victim! You took matters into your own hands here in the city, Kit. Now you have to do it again."

Vidette is the engine that powers me through fear and doubt, but sometimes that engine runs too hot. Whatever the issue, Vidette wants to tear everything down. Getting to know her over the last six months, I've come to realize she had to fight for everything: she was the youngest of eight kids in an Italian family living in Pastel City. Her oldest sibling was in college. She was an afterthought. A mistake, as her father called her. She manifested strength beyond all measure and still her Empowered peers dismissed her because she was a woman, because she wanted to do something in a company that never did. Vidette pushes me, and I'm grateful, but sometimes it's too far.

"I'm going to be sure of the facts," I say.

"They killed those kids." Vidette stifles a sob. "They hurt Mike... he was a cop. He was a teacher. He did all of this for nothing. Because he wanted to. And he's shot to pieces."

Nah, I'm good, he says, with a winking smile.

I bite my lip. "He's alive."

"He may never wake up."

The diffuser reassembles in the air before me, like new. "I have work to do. I need to get back to work now."

Her voice is pleading. "We need to stop them, Kit."

"I'm going to stop them."

"Then why? Why don't you want me to help you?"

"I do. I'm going to need you to stop me."

Glass shatters against crystal. Vidette stumbles over the uneven floor of the ship, her hands on my arms, my shoulders, my cheeks as she buckles with grieved sobs. Energy leaches out of my skin, biting at hers, but finding it as unpalatable as The Straw Men. Her skin is so tough, nothing can penetrate it. Nothing can break Vidette, except the horror of our now.

The light of the Myriad crackles in her eyes. "We can get through this. Forget what I said. We can talk. We can pray."

"Pray for Mike," I say.

The hull of the ship crumples under Vidette's hurt, shattering whatever peace Break Pointe had left. Crushed crystal scatters across the floor, making a sound a little like the pages of Simon's comic as he skimmed through them. Pain tears through me. Anger. Hopelessness. I am never hopeless. Never without a solution. That's the other Kit. Minutes tick off the clock in the apartment, red lines fracturing into hours as Abi stares out the window and I stand here alone, unsure of what to do exactly except what I always do. I reopen the wound I made in the world and withdrew from my reality into the work.

The work must continue.

Snow piles on my shoulders. Hours on the night. I project across the city, looking in on places I know are hot spots for drugs, guns, anything illegal. After the attack on the school, The Derelicts closed up. Word swirls like the wind that I'm on the warpath and every time someone turns around on a corner in the ruins, there I am. After a few nights of haunting the streets, I become too bad for business, and one of the neighborhood boys I see on the stoops on Shelley from time to time comes off to meet me out in the street.

"Where's your coat?" I say, as he shoves his hands in his jeans and walks toward me like he's in a potato bag.

"This ain't nothing," he says. "What you looking for?"

"Who sells the diffusers?"

He shakes his head. "I tell you, someone gets upset."

"I'm upset."

He looks down the street. "Diffusers all you care about?"

"For right now."

"He's got an RV. Usually over on Bloom. He doesn't always offer, you know. Only for special customers."

I rise into the air. "I think I qualify."

I sift through the smoldering wreckage of the RV, throwing aside food and beer and burning toilet paper until I come on the square black cases. Three of them, smooth as old ice. Six diffusers rest inside each, fresh off the line. None of them have any identifying marks, and neither do the cases.

I float back to the man who owned the RV, crawling through the debris on his hands and legs. "Where do you get them?"

His heart machine-guns inside his chest *ba-dumm, ba-dumm ba-dumm.* "I didn't have anything to do with that school."

Snow melts in my anger. "Where?"

He holds his hands up. "A seller."

"The Straw Men?"

"I don't deal with them."

"I want a name."

"I don't know, I swear to God – "

Coils of energy nip at his feet. "Swear to me."

SEVEN

"This is a two-day story," Frankie says, clipping a tiny little microphone to the neck of my blouse.

Her camera levels at me like some cannon, framed between a pair of bright lights, and right now I feel less like I'm doing an interview than standing in a firing line. "What do you mean?"

"There's a new wrinkle here because it's you and it's Break Pointe, but this is a hurricane, Kit. This is an earthquake. A couple of these hit every year and are good for a couple news cycles and then we move on. Look at the camera." Frankie goes to the kitchen table and checks the monitor on her laptop, showing the feed from the camera. "Ok. Good. Earpiece."

I fumble for the odd, plastic earpiece dangling on my shoulder. I tuck it in my right ear, careful to avoid a strand of sub-current energy from seizing it. A voice crackled in her ear. *Ms. Baldwin, can you hear me? This is New York.*

"I can hear you," I say. "Frankie... there are pictures. Of the scene. Would that make a difference?"

"No one wants to see those."

"Maybe they should."

"They don't want to know."

"We have to do something about this. People have to – "

Frankie points at the camera. "Keep your eyes right here, on the lens. You have sixty seconds to air."

I straighten up and stare ahead into the lens of the camera. "This can't keep happening, Frankie."

"You're going to tell them. Thirty seconds. Smile. Show them you're human. You're beautiful. Cry. That helps."

I sigh. "Why did you even answer the phone?"

Her smile is a little less condescending than usual. "Because this is an exclusive I have and my competitors don't. Because if anyone can turn two days into three or four, it's you. Fifteen. Get ready. You'll hear them. Just talk."

And now we're back with our special guest, Kit Baldwin. She's agreed to come on the air with us tonight to discuss the tragic events that occurred in a city all too familiar with tragedy. Ms. Baldwin, thank you for joining us tonight.

"Thank – thank you," I say and try to smile, but then I think why would I? How can I? My face locks up.

Our condolences. You knew these students, didn't you?

I pinch my leg under the table. "Yes, I did."

So, it's personal for you.

I squint. "I don't know what you mean."

Given your relationship with the deceased, your investment, let's say, as the protector of the people in your city, you're determined to raise awareness around this issue, correct?

I glance at Frankie, who points back at the camera. "I'm determined to make sure this never happens again."

I can't see an image of the anchor of the talk show back in New York, so I don't know their expression. A quick look at the laptop shows mine is diffident. I sit up straighter in the chair and try to soften those lines around my mouth.

How are you going to prevent that, Ms. Baldwin?

"I've disrupted illegal arms sales in my city, but that's not enough.

I'm calling on our leaders in Washington to come to their senses and ban diffusers once and for all."

There have been calls for bans before.

"For good reason. These weapons have been responsible for the mass murder of innocent civilians six times already this year. This happens so often, you don't send reporters anymore. I had to dangle an interview with one to get them here."

Frankie puckers her lips in a kiss.

Is Break Pointe safe for reporters?

"Diffusers have never been proven to be effective for their intended use and even if they were, weapons of such horrific, indiscriminate power shouldn't be in the hands of – "

Americans have a right to defend themselves.

"They have laws that protect them."

Who protects us against you, Ms. Baldwin? You possess cosmic power beyond comprehension. Not even GP can stop you.

I wince. "We're talking about diffusers."

We're talking about why they exist, and why they should exist. Good, hardworking men and women want to be able to protect themselves from people – no offense – like you.

Whatever wax smile I muster for the camera vanishes. So does my patience. "Networks like yours run ads trying to scare people into buying weapons like diffusers thinking they'll make a difference. I'm here to tell you. They don't."

So people should be concerned.

"What? No – "

Who's to stop you from taking matters into your own hands, like you did against GP, Ms. Baldwin? There isn't an army, an Empowered, a power on this planet that can stop you from –

"All I want is peace for my city. A future. That was taken away from us because people value weapons more than kids – "

We live in a world where people of unbridled power can do anything they want, wherever, whenever they want –

"The ERA regulates the activity of the Empowered and there hasn't been any significant violation of it in – "

Why take the chance?

"Why take the chance – again and again and *again* – of allowing these weapons in the hands of individuals who have no business owning them? If these weapons can't be banned outright, then they have to be heavily regulated – "

There's too much regulation, isn't there?

"Trust me, there isn't nearly enough."

The demise of Break Pointe you fight against is a direct cause of the ERA tying the hands of Great Power. Didn't you tell Frankie Fleet last year, after the crash of Flight 347, that 'The law is broken?' But now you want to add more laws, this time hamstringing normal people against people like you.

I gasp. "Those are two different things – "

You say all power for all people. And then you say there has to be more regulation.

"If you'll let me explain – "

Which is it, Ms. Baldwin?

Waves of frustration swamp my response. Words fall back down my throat and I sit there, staring into the camera, speechless. The voice in my ear whispers something. Frankie switches off the camera.

"We're done?" I say.

She unclips my microphone. "That was it."

I slap her hand away from the microphone. "You were supposed to help me. What the hell was that, Frankie?"

"It was a national segment," Frankie says. "It was prime time. It was what you wanted, Kit."

"What's the matter with you?"

Frankie crosses her arms. "I need the earpiece, too."

I tear it out of my ear. The piece disappears down my back, out of reach and I end up half-turned in the chair, in and out, reaching for something I can't even see.

Neighborhood boys in suits all a little too big or small on them lower the casket into the grave. Mud cakes their shoes, all a little too big or small. They step on each other's toes, the boys so tight around the casket I think they might fall in. None of them walk on the still fresh earth of the graves bordering the new one, pressed together in the back corner in the last, open ground of the pauper's graveyard. All of the students had family, but no money. There won't be stones. I don't know all their names. I met them all, took selfies with them, gave them the light and the heat and the opportunity to be murdered at their desks but I never learned all of their names.

"You can't blame yourself," Dr. Piller says.

"What?"

He gently places his hand on mine. "Don't blame yourself."

I'm not paying attention. I never do. My entire life, I've ghosted out of my troubles and slaved over someone else's. There for a minute after my transformation, I took care of me. I took notice, but I've become responsible for everyone in The Derelicts. All their problems are my problems. Life works better for me this way. Blame works. Guilt. Hope, less so. Hope is deferral. Putting things off to tomorrow means there has to be one. Through one disaster after another, there always is. Even now, attending my eleventh funeral, there will be another.

"Who should I blame, Dr. Piller?"

Light fog crawls across the cemetery. Rain falls, and then it doesn't. Pellets of ice fall, and then don't. A few more weeks and I won't worry so much about the buildings I haven't heated yet. Several in the network around Six Corners remain down since the vandalism of the transmitter. If I take the school offline, I can reroute power to the homes without it.

He clears his throat. "No one could have stopped this."

"I could have." I bite my lip. "I should have…"

The boys step back. Another family comes together in the solidarity of grief. Sobs blunt against inadequate embraces. Shame and guilt drag me down, so far I shear from my own pain. I have lost, as much as anyone, but my pain doesn't matter. My guilt and recrimination. All that matters is making it right.

"I'm not getting anywhere in my analysis of the diffuser," I say. "Can you help? I need to know the make and model."

He acts like he wants to say something other than what he does. "What are you going to do with that?"

"Everything I can."

"These attacks have been going on for years. There is no will whatsoever to do anything about it. Only to do nothing."

"Someone has to do something."

"Listen to me. With diffusers, you're fighting Congress. Lobbyists. Average Americans who think they're entitled to any and all defense of themselves and property."

I look at him. "You're not going to help me?"

Words pinch his cheeks. He wrestles with them until he negotiates their surrender. "You want to lash out. I know."

"And?"

"Great Power is the most powerful corporation in the world and we have failed to keep these weapons off the market."

"GP has never exactly put their back into anything."

He sighs. "I'll examine the device. GP does have an interest in this. But whatever I find, we need to think, hard, about our next steps. Your focus needs to be on the ground."

I lift into the air, into heavier fog.

The lights on Shelley slide with the ice down the window of the apartment. Red and yellow channel through Abi's static reflection. All her spirit, her warmth, her natural fizziness is gone, bleeding out the window with the heat. I never realized how much I depended on Abi, how much I expected her to simply be there, until she wasn't.

Before, I was the ghost. If I hurt, if I feared or doubted, I disappeared in the work but I always knew Abi was there, like tomorrow, waiting. A want for Abi to get out of the city, away from the dangers I've exposed her to chases the tail of a desperate need to grab Abi up and never let go.

Piller's thoughts skid into my mind. *The tower. Now.*

I project inside Applied Sciences, avoiding the tower's exceptional security. The desk lamp is on in Piller's office

"What is it?" I say, coming to his desk.

He leans back in his chair, like he always does when he has something to say that he doesn't want to. "I don't have anything on the manufacturer of the diffuser. I'm sorry, Ms. Baldwin."

"Do telepaths get charged by the word, or what?"

"I did find something."

I sit across from him. "What is it?"

"There was something we forgot. We're scientists, not cops. We tend to go straight for the complex rather than the simple. I dusted the diffuser for fingerprints. I pulled some."

Fingers tap against the glass of the test chamber outside the office *ba-dumm, ba-dumm, ba-dumm.*

"What did you find?"

Piller hands me a printout of magnified fingerprints. "Perry Welby. He owned a bakery on Bissette."

I examine the black friction ridges of the enlarged print. "There isn't a bakery on Bissette."

"That's because it closed after Welby died. In 1987."

The printout crumbles in my hand, along with the last of the barrier I contained my anger in.

Fog evaporates on a blast of cosmic energy.

Shadows scurry for the vanishing dark. There is nowhere to hide. I strafe the amusement park, pummeling the island. Flames spin with the Ferris wheel into the lake. Buckets become projectiles. Everything and anything metal shreds into a spiked tail of debris stretching behind me in my magnetic field. A train of rusted cars rises off the rickety track of the roller coaster, snapping into pieces I hurl at The Straw Men. Pulverized earth showers down on burning rides, masking the amusement park in a garish fog more commonly found on a battlefield.

Shadows flee into the lake. Ice gushes to steam. Water boils, evaporating with any sense of security The Straw Men had. I descend into the maelstrom of flame and smoke, in a trench I gored through the island bow to stern.

Harrow leans against the fallen bucket he did the last time I was here, unmoved. "This is no way for a guest to behave, old man."

Straw Men lurch toward me. I snap tendrils of energy into lances of hard light. Hands fall to the ground. Heads. I hack my way through the dense brush of decay between me and Harrow, all the while he stands there with a lazy grin, waiting.

The ground heaves beneath me. I crater it. Straw Men march on me in waves. Light illuminates their hollow, almost plastic skin before they collapse into embers. Bone and earth rain down on me. I rip the bucket out from under Harrow, sending him face first into the softening mud of the scorched earth. A splash somewhere in the distance signals the end of the bombardment.

"This started with you." I stand over him, the bristling end of my sword at his neck. "I assume it ends with you."

EIGHT

Harrow creaks like an old tree.

He fixes his hat back on, and he is one of the derelict rides, color, and whimsy rusted through to the artless industry beneath. Nothing distinguishes him from the other zombies, except in the soup of his glaucomic eye, I see his soul. The cloudy remains of his humanity.

I grab him off the ground by his lapel and shove him against the back of an upside-down roller coaster car. I hold the burning edge of my sword to his withered throat.

"Why did you do it?"

A bemused smile interrupts the other scars channeling Harrow's face. "Do what, old man?"

"Don't play with me."

"You're the one playing around."

"You killed them. You killed children."

"How many children did you just kill, Baldwin?"

From the air, The Straw Men were ants. I burned their shadows into the crumpled metal of the rides, and never saw their faces. Never heard their screams, if they had any. A flash of light, and they were gone. No pity. No quarter. No remorse.

That's the other Kit.

That Kit harbors all my grief. My pain. Anger. That Kit secures all of the memories of that day, the sights, sounds, smells, the slick of my shoe through blood and I halve the roller coaster car in two with my flaming sword.

Harrow doesn't flinch.

"None of you are alive," I say. "You're not living. You're not even human. How could you? How could you..."

"I'm afraid you've lost me, old man. I haven't done anything to you or to any children of yours."

"You murdered an entire class of students."

His jaw hangs. "Who said I did this?"

"The prints of one of your zombies are all over the diffuser the shooter used. You sold it to that boy."

Everything about Harrow is performative. His expressions and mannerisms are pronounced, maybe to overcome the rigor in his body. I can't tell if his indignation is sincere.

"I did no such thing."

"You hurt them to get at me. To bring me back here."

A dry cackle chops with the surprised waves against the toppled Ferris wheel. "You're too much of an engineer, Baldwin. You're always seeing schematics. Plans. Conspiracies. I don't need to kill anyone to 'get at you.' Not when all it takes to gather your attention is smash a light bulb."

"I don't believe you," I say.

"If we ever used Diffusers against the Responders that once policed this city, they would have done what you just did a long time ago. No, I quite prefer the status quo."

"A man's prints all over the diffuser. He died in 1987. He was buried in Pound Cemetery. He's not there anymore."

His shoulders arch. "Perhaps this fugitive corpse is operating on his own. The dead are an unruly sort, after all."

The light pulsing through my sword wavers. So does my confidence. "You control the dead."

"I'm no more responsible for the actions of the dead than you are the living, old man. I don't bite them, or spit on them, or seduce them in any fashion you might assume based on rather erroneous fictions. No, it's the ground, you see." Harrow considers the burning earth. "There was something rotten here before all this decay and ruin... yes. Something quite wrong."

"You said you came back with a cough."

Harrow smiles again. "I did, old man. I did. A nasty one, too. A constant scratch. Like I had all this dust in my throat. All this dirt." He gazes across the burning island. "I don't control them. We do have a common language, you might say. We have a community here, or we did. But I won't be sad or lonesome for long. The dead are rather like flowers, you see. Winter buries their memory. Come spring, they're everywhere."

My sword winnows to a dying plume. "We had a community..."

"You know, I liked this old park. There's something about abandoned places, isn't there? We never see the life right in front of us, begging to be acknowledged. Yet we perceive life, where there isn't any. Strange. You see life in Break Pointe. You sew and stitch it together from different parts and with a little electricity, it moves around. Stumbles ahead. Seems alive. This city isn't alive, Baldwin. It's like me. It's like you. Between life and death. Stranded in the gateway between two vastly different states. You want to drag it back to the limits of what you have known. I want to lead it over the edge."

"You just want power. Money."

"Oh, no. Money is of no use to the dead. Our arrangement in Break Pointe keeps us safe. Cushioned, you might say, against the intolerance of the living. But you... you represent a greater opportunity. True immortality."

In a lot of ways, Harrow is no different than Evander Blackwood. He's yet another man, caught between the past and the future and determined to break free of his confines, regardless of the consequences. This battle is the same as I fought with Great Power.

I'm afraid I'll always be fighting it.

Lake water sloshes around my ankles. Half-frozen mud sucks at my feet as I stagger back from Harrow. This city courts disaster. Resists hope. Settles, somewhere between light and dark.

My sword dissolves. "You didn't do this."

Harrow straightens the collar of his overcoat. "No, old man. I can't compel you to share your power. I can't compel you to do anything at all. Death doesn't motivate you."

"I'm responsible for the lives of others."

"Self-declared, I believe."

"And who appointed you, Harrow?"

"Let's not get mired in trivia, shall we? Your obligation stems from an outmoded sense of duty, a duty people with far less perspective than you or I have long since abandoned. You're still thinking in terms of life. Preservation. Continuity. You have to let all that go, old man. Your opponents in the Blackwood Building have. Your representatives in Washington. None of them think of you, or those children you mourn, or anyone else. They think only of themselves."

"That doesn't make them right," I say.

"It makes them human. You've lost sight of that, I think. Easy enough to understand, given your experience. Being human is to distort nature, Baldwin. To deform it."

"That's not true."

"Isn't it? What have we done? We've immunized ourselves. Stretched out our lifespans twice and three times beyond their intended limits. Why, we forced the curve right out of our spines and walked out of our origins. It should come as no surprise now we stretch the very definition of who we are with medicine and technology. What's the difference, old man? I say, what is the difference between you or I, and a person with a face transplant? Artificial limbs? A mechanical heart?"

Harrow wipes the soot off his sallow brow, with a smile.

"They chide you for that lantern hanging in your chest when they're so wooden, you could hang any of them on a Christmas tree. If our ancestors were dropped in the present, they might think us all stretched out bits of taffy. Who is grotesque? Who is the affront to life? Who indulges death?"

"You're talking about people surviving," I say.

"Surviving isn't living, Baldwin. Something tells me you know that. And yet you seem to work against yourself. You deny your power, your reality, your heart. For what?"

I bite my lip. "The future."

"What matter is the future when our lives grow so long they become interminable? What matter are children?" Harrow feigns a breath. "Tell me, old man, what matter then is society? Continuity? All those things you're so concerned about."

The smoke of my anger hangs low over the amusement park. "We can't live this way."

"This is the only way to live. You ought to know that, given how much suffering you've endured from trying to put a corporation out of business. Planes crash, diffusers turn schools into kill floors, and of course, they do nothing. You think it's about greed. GP let this city die over a few million dollars. Pocket change. It's not greed you're fighting. It's what I've just described to you. It's the core instinct to take all we can from life to insulate ourselves from survival."

"Don't you mean death?"

Frustration furrows Harrow's leathery skin. "No, not death, old man. Death is what we deny and defer. Survival is what we overcome. The notion of struggle. Those people over there, in their condos and townhouses and loft apartments, denigrate those who don't have the means to live. To thrive. Why? Because they're not a different class, but a different species, locked into a daily contest for life and death like those animals we see on TV Sunday afternoons. Not like us. Not like us at all. We're beyond that. So the thinking goes. Greed is merely a symptom of this mindset. You will never defeat this until you defeat death, Baldwin. Or accept that you have."

I always see schematics. Everything and everyone is of a piece, a part of a system Harrow can scarcely understand. I do, seeing the world, the universe, as The Ever had. Energy. People are electrical impulses, composed of atoms, all bound together in a tapestry of energy. Alive or dead, the tapestry exists. Life and death aren't opposites or even options; energy can never be destroyed. It can only change states.

"People care," I say. "People still care."

"Of course, they care. They value life so much they strangle their laws around the necks of newborns and drag them into world impoverished, and then they leave them, old man. They leave them to be shot in their schools."

I turn away from him, disgusted. I don't want to think about any of this, I don't want to face it, but empty eye sockets stare out at me. Exposed teeth chatter as tongueless mouths try to make a sound. Burning bodies lurch into the lake, to become silent chimneys coughing their indifference.

Harrow drifts around the rim of a crater I left in the ground. "I struggled a long time with my condition. I resisted it, as I've said. For years, I held on to the myth of my humanity and it wasn't until I gave up the ghost that I realized my true potential. The potential of us all, old man. We're not meant to tarry here in the ruins of civilization, any more than we were meant to stay in the Garden of Eden. No, we're wanderers and travelers. Explorers and thieves. We're meant to go forward, always, from one dark cave to another."

His voice, constant as the smoke clouding the park, aggravates me. "We're meant to become zombies?"

"Being human isn't a matter of having emotions. Nor is it a matter of having a conscience. It's undoing the shackles of all the things that bind us. Genetics. Environment. Life. Death. Hearts." He pats his hollow chest. "We've left ours behind. Don't be one of those fools staring at shadows on the walls of the cave. You're the light, Baldwin. You're the torch, guiding us forward."

Fire sweeps across the ground, fueled by the angry wind off the lake. Flames snake across shattered earth straight into me, energy consumed and converted into a brightening star.

We are you, the voice of The Ever says. *You are us.*

Abi stirs in bed next to me, back in the apartment. A nightmare jitters through her arms and legs and my projection holds her tight in the dark comfort of our home.

"I will never be like you," I say.

The charred skeleton of the roller coaster collapses into the lake. Harrow smiles, ruefully. "Oh, my friend… you're becoming more like me all the time. One of these days, it isn't going to be an abandoned amusement park full of faceless things you can dismiss as inhuman. One of these days, it's going to be an office building." He glances across the river. "It's going to be a city. Someone will anger you. They'll wrong you. They'll defy you. And you will act as you did here, because you can."

He may as well be standing in front of a fireplace, the way I flicker on him. "You deserved this."

"For your students? I had nothing to do with that."

"You've been terrorizing this city for years."

"And there she goes, moving the goalposts. All I ever did was squeeze people for money, Baldwin. I gave food to this town. Water. Electricity. I gave them jobs. Just like you."

"I never hurt anybody."

He kicks aside a carbonized forearm. "We both know that's not true. Did people get hurt because of me? Yes. Did people die? People die, old man. Children die." He sets his cold hand on my shoulder. Flames swirl within me. Uncertainty. "Your obligation isn't to their memory. It's to their potential. So long as you waste your mind and power crafting light bulbs, you serve no one. Use your talent. Lift us out of this cave, Baldwin. Design a better vessel for humanity."

"Your humanity, you mean."

A rakish smile overcomes the horror of his face. "I humbly submit to being your guinea pig, old man."

If I could lift people out of darkness; if I could raise the dead and give them back their lives. If I could get mine back, and worry only for my moment and myself. If I could just fix it all.

I step back from him. "You want something from me, Harrow? Do something for me first. Find a man named Welby."

A scarred brow raises. "And then, old man?"

I leave the ground, into the smoke. "And then I'll decide whether or not I let any of you live."

Her shadow flickers against the wall, ignorant of shape. Limitations. Abi stares out the window of the apartment, bathed in the tempestuous orange denying the night in the south.

"You were like a dragon," Abi says, her voice hollow. "Breathing fire. You melted their castle."

I leave my jacket on the back of a chair at the kitchen table. I sink into the chair, exhausted as much from my demolition of the amusement park as I am my grief.

I sigh. "It wasn't The Straw Men."

"Decided to ask questions later, huh?"

"I got mixed up."

"I don't care," Abi says. "I really don't care."

I don't know if I do, either. I don't know if that bothers me. The Straw Men are a menace, guilty of innumerable crimes. They're a threat to the safety and welfare of the city I'm charged to protect, and there's no negotiating with them. No deterring them. None of the rules or laws of society apply to them. *What matter was society*; what matter was the law in dealing with people not alive or dead or even human anymore.

What's the matter.

Abi's silhouette flutters in the window. "If it wasn't The Straw Men, who was it?"

I pull at my curls. It couldn't just be that a boy decided to murder all of his classmates. His teacher. That wasn't possible; that didn't fit into any theory I have.

"A man named Welby at least had contact with the diffuser," I say. "Harrow is going to try and find him for me."

"And if he doesn't?"

"I don't know. I don't know anything."

Abi pulls at her nightshirt. "I heard this thunder. You were still in bed. I didn't want to wake you. You don't sleep. I went to the window, but you were out there, too."

I bury my face in my hands, trying to box this away, but I can't. "I'm sorry. I should have told you sooner."

"You can project, like Siski."

"It's me. I'm me, Abi."

Abi sniffles a laugh. "I couldn't even tell."

My shame has always been doing too much for someone else. I've never been guilty of doing the least amount possible until right now, with the woman I love more than my own life.

I bite my lip. "I just wanted to be here. I wanted to be here and still do everything I need to do, but I can't do anything." I think I expect Abi to come to me, to rush in as she always does, but Abi keeps to the window. "I'm sorry, baby."

Abi stares out the window. "My dad owns a funeral home."

I go to her. "You told me."

Tears streak Abi's face. "There's only death there. Bones. Ash."

I take her hands in mine. "Abi..."

Abi looks down at her hands, the way she did in the school when they had been covered in someone else's blood. "Death doesn't bother me. Things don't bother me."

"I don't know about that."

Abi wrinkles her nose. "You put things away. I never take things on. I just kind of keep going, you know. I don't know what to feel. I think I'm supposed to be shocked, but I'm not."

"It's ok, Abi."

"Is it? Am I ok?"

I take her in my arms. "You've been through so much."

Abi traces filaments of light as they swim beneath my skin. "I want to tell you everything."

"About the attack?"

She rests her head on my chest. "Everything."

"You can tell me. Abi, I'm always here for you. I know – I know that sounds silly. I want to be here for you. If I'd lost you... I was so afraid I was going to lose you."

"I was afraid you were going to find me."

"What?"

Light bends through her tears, creating undulant shadows on the ceiling. "I remember thinking, what if she walks in here and sees me like this? What will she think? What will I say?"

I hold her close. "You're ok. We're ok."

Abi breathes into my neck. "Don't ever let me go."

"Never."

Abi's hands slide down to my waist. "I love you."

"I love you, Abi."

Her hands slip farther. "Say it again."

Our lips touch. "*I love you.*"

Abi kisses me, hard. Our lovemaking has been playful, tentative, even fearful but now it's hungry. Desperate. Her fingers claw into my shirt. Skin glides through the membrane of my light and I remember skin. Heat. Feather softness. My humanity resurrects as Abi tears away the skin of my clothes. Energy snaps from my burning heart. Her every nerve illuminates like summer lightning.

"I'm only alive with you," Abi whispers into my ear, as light pink and furious dances through the universe of her body.

Heavy-lidded clouds sink over the island.

I brighten, the beacon of a lighthouse in a raging winter storm. Cold rain lashes my face. Sleet ices my skin, glazing over my fire but still I shine, as much for the city as myself. I keep to my post atop the roof of the Halfway Hotel, relying on my magnetic perception to see through the drowsy haze engulfing the island. People appear as orange, red or yellow blobs on the street, in their homes, in the planes soaring high above the pall. I close my eyes, thinking of Abi, an anxious flame below, and something brushes against me. A bird, maybe; they bump into me all the time. I open my eyes and Harrow's undead cat sits beside me.

"The hell," I say, scrambling away.

The cat rattles something like a snicker. Tucked into its collar is a small, rolled-up note. I remove it, never taking my eyes off the cat's, a cloudy topaz, and open the note.

Warehouse on Buscema. Old pickup truck. – Your friend

NINE

THE BIRDS NEVER ALLOW ME ANONYMITY.

Anywhere I go in the city, they follow. Projection permits me a measure of stealth as I operate in the city and the more my opponents adjust to the spotlight I shine over the heart of the island, the more I move into the shadows, behind their lines.

My annihilation of the amusement park sends other gangs scrambling. Streets and ruins clear all the way to the factories and warehouses cluttering the south corner of the island. No one would be down there in sight of the still smoldering amusement park, not in hulking boxes of waiting tinder unless they were looking to burn.

The slam of the truck door crashes through the dark expanse of the empty warehouse. "Heard you were looking for me."

An old man shuffles from the truck, a rusted hulk from the 70s worn down as he is. The crook in his spine becomes more pronounced as he gets closer, as does the withered string of his arms and legs. I'm not sure his condition owes to his existence as a man of straw; when he died, he died at the end of a life lived long and hard.

Light churns within me. "Are you Welby?"

He holds his hand over his eyes. "You going to zap me, too?"

"I might."

"You zapped that boy, didn't you? That's what I heard."

I don't remember defending myself outside the school. That was the other Kit. "Did you sell him the diffuser?"

"Burned him up real good. Ashes, they said. Good, there won't be anything left of him to come back, then."

"Did you?"

His fingers claw through the tuft of yellowed hair on his hand. "You going to arrest me, or what?"

"There isn't a jail in The Derelicts."

"Ah, 'kay. Maybe you'll turn me over to the capes, then."

"Great Power would be very interested in a man selling diffusers across the river from their headquarters."

"You'd think something like that would get their attention. Been doing it years and they never done anything. I've been looking over my shoulder, expecting one of them to land on me like some aster-oid." He shrugs. "Still waiting."

Tendrils of energy slither down my arms. "I'm through waiting."

"Looks that way."

"You're going to tell me you sold the diffuser. And you're going to tell me where you got it."

"Sounds like a plan. You know what they say about plans. I take it you won't be too happy if I don't cooperate?"

Fire coronas my fists. "Not one bit."

His arms swing out in a little shrug that dies as soon as it starts. "Guess that's it, then. Go ahead. Burn me."

Energy ties in knots around me. I don't know what he's doing; nothing Welby has is worth dying for.

"Tell me what you know and maybe you can work out a deal with the state's attorney general. They can consider your cooperation when it comes to the gun trafficking charges."

He brushes away the idea like a gnat. "I don't want any deal. I had the only deal I ever wanted. Me and the wife owned a bakery. Wedding cakes. Graduation cakes. That kind of thing. Funerals."

Welby glances back at the truck. "Cradle to grave. We were there for every part of it. Not one minute more. That was the slogan, you know. For the bakery. 'Not one minute more than it takes.' She was an artist, the wife. Each one of those cakes, they were works of art. Yeah. And then she died. So did I. That's how it goes. That's the deal. I thought it was, anyway."

Light bleeds out of my hands. My anger with it.

Welby is going to answer for what he did, but there also has to be an answer for the fact he's a victim as well. All of The Straw Men are, stolen out of their peace by an unknown thief. The ground, Harrow said; something in the ground. Does everyone we bury suffer this? I never go to cemeteries. Maybe they're cratered as a battlefield. Maybe no one goes, because this is another one of those things about Break Pointe we live with, and just don't talk about. Alien ships. Empowered people. Empty graves. I riddle at the thought of Dad, shuffling out there, somewhere.

I'm thankful my mother is ashes.

"I want to find out what's behind your condition," I say. "I want to find a treatment or a cure. Work with me, and I promise I will do everything I can to help you and – "

Welby disappears in a vivid magenta glare. I cover my eyes, instinct overriding the reality that I can see perfectly fine. Energy strains through the perception of the Myriad. A void opens in the warehouse; just beyond Welby, a being with identical power and magnetic signature as mine burns into view.

I lower my hand. "What..."

Furious red light swirls around the other Kit. Confusion does around me; I didn't summon the projection. I've never appeared like this, a blood-red sun boiling on earth.

I don't understand.

I try to recall the projection. She remains, leering at Welby, dumbstruck at the sight of her.

"Talk," the other Kit says.

Go away, I think.

The other Kit flares with light. "Where did you get the diffuser, old man? Who makes them?"

Welby looks back and forth between us. "This some kind of good cop, bad cop routine?"

I have no answer. My projection refuses to obey me, and I have no idea how to control it beyond mere thought.

I said go away!

"Tell us," the other Kit says. "Or else."

"I already told her. You. I ain't talking."

Rusted metal buckles. Tires explode. Glass shatters. Welby's truck lifts off the warehouse floor in the other Kit's magnetic grip, compressing into a metal clump in the air.

"That's my truck," Welby says.

The other Kit hurls it into the dark of the warehouse. A terrible crash sends the birds always shadowing me flapping out the windows. I focus all my attention on the projection.

Stop!

A sheath of flame envelops Welby. A little gasp escapes him; an *Ah!* as frightened as it is strangely delighted. His clothes burn away. His leathered skin. His fine, cotton hair.

"Tell me," the other Kit says.

"I like you better," he says and laughs.

Ashes crumble to the floor. I fall to my knees, as if I can catch them. Crimson flame licks the concrete, lapping up any trace of energy as the other Kit hovers above Welby's ruin.

I tremble in shock. "What... what's happening..."

"Stop hiding behind me," the other Kit says. "Use your power. Show yourself. "

"This isn't me," I say. "You're not..."

A smile burns across the other Kit's lips. "I am you. You are me. There is no distinction."

I can access any soul acquired by The Ever. Any power. I can deny them, too. I have to, to keep myself. With a thought, I box Siski's powers away and the other Kit vanishes.

I slump to the cold concrete, more terrified than ever of the power coursing through me. More lost.

Abi snuggles up with me in bed. "You ok?"

A day and night have gone since I curled into a ball in this bed. My knees remain at my chest, my arms belted around them, hiding the ravenous light bristling within me.

"I'm fine," I say.

Abi kisses my shoulder. "It's kind of catching up with you, isn't it? I know. I know, Kit. I love you."

I nod. "I love you, baby."

She wraps her arms around me. "You can tell me."

I only let go of the fierce hold I have on my knees, on the monster within her, to take Abi's hand. "I'm scared."

Her lips paper my neck, soft and sweet. "Not getting anywhere with the investigation?"

A sigh escapes the tight seal I keep on myself. "No."

"What can I do? Want me to bake cookies?"

"Just hold me."

Abi squeezes me. "We'll revisit the cookies."

"I know how the shooter got the diffuser," I say, "but I don't know who makes them. This isn't going to end unless we... Piller isn't getting anything from his analysis."

"Sorry."

"I don't know if I believe him."

"Why would he lie?"

I grip Abi's hand tight. "Because he doesn't want me to do what I did out at the amusement park."

Her heart beats an anxious rhythm, *ba-dumm, ba-dumm, ba-dumm.* "What about the English guy, from the black market?"

"Johnny Albertine? What about him?"

"Couldn't he help you with like complicated technological stuff?

Secret stuff? He's from Found Corp, right?"

I came to Albertine in a moment of blind panic, when I thought the best thing to do after my transformation was getting out of town. GP hunted the city for the new 'alien menace' and I didn't yet trust myself, or my power. More than likely, Albertine could help identify the diffuser; he'd want something in return, something I'd be unwilling to give.

"I'll figure out where it came from," I say.

"How?"

"I will."

"And then?"

I don't have an answer. "Some cookies would be nice."

Abi gyrates in excitement and bounds out of the bed into the kitchen. I keep my place, until Abi plops back on the mattress a few minutes later, prying open my arms for a deep kiss I can't help but be taken into.

Energy signatures of birds, stray cats, and what I hope are rats hurry through the dark of an emptied warehouse, clots of light in a sea of chaotic crimson. A void forms in the net of energy binding the world together. The armored woman who had escorted Albertine when I first met him forms out of the shadows. She emits no energy; her suit must ablate any kind of scan on what – and who – is beneath.

Her helmet muffles her voice. "You have sixty seconds."

Anxious light streams across the woman's opaque helmet, a motorcycle-like design with the visor pointing up rather than down, into a futuristic type of sallet.

"Where's Albertine?" I say.

"He thought it more practical to send me," she says. "Considering how your last meeting ended."

The last thing I want is to get tangled up again with another corporation I can't trust. I don't know I have any choice. I never have a choice. To make things work here in Break Pointe, I have to compromise myself, my values, my vision, again and again. And still. I can't identify the make and model of the diffuser. GP can't. Either Found can, or it stays a mystery.

"I didn't realize he was so sensitive," I say.

"You declared the city off-limits to us."

"I imagine you're never too far away, considering how quickly you answered my message."

She tugs at the cuirass of her armor. "Thirty seconds."

I take the diffuser from my hip bag. "I need to know who made this. I need to know how it got here."

The armored woman takes the diffuser from me. She considers it a moment. "This will cost you."

"How much?"

Chains drag across cracked concrete. The Interdictor's voice echoes across the barrenness of the warehouse.

"More than you know," he says.

The armored woman draws the sword fixed to her back and crouches into a defensive posture. I zip down the front of my jacket and The Interdictor appears, a jangling oil slick.

"So it seems our suspicions about your connections to Found were true, Baldwin. I'm hardly surprised."

"Oh, will you fuck off," I say. "I'm not with Found. I'm going to them to identify the damned diffuser because Piller can't or won't."

The Interdictor removes his mask. "Good."

I flinch. "Good?"

"You're trying to discover how this weapon got into the city. You're trying to ensure none never do again."

"That's right."

"Go," he says to the armored woman. "Learn what you can from the diffuser. Bring your findings back to Baldwin."

The armored woman relaxes and sheathes her sword.

"And then you never set foot in this city again, or I send you back to your masters one piece at a time."

She withdraws, melding back into the profound darkness of the warehouse. No trace. No sound. The armored woman leaves me unsettled, but I'm more concerned with The Interdictor.

"I don't understand," I say.

"I can't allow my people to be endangered in any way. We're going to find who brought this thing into Break Pointe, and then we're going to seal this gap. Permanently."

"*We* are?"

He straightens his gloves. "You impressed me the other night, Baldwin. I didn't think you had it in you to adjudicate The Straw Men as you did. Perhaps I was wrong about you."

My eyes slam shut, but I can't shield myself fast enough from the memory of Welby burning to ash.

"Maybe I was wrong about you," I say.

"The shadow tells you, and you tell me. We deal with this, together. No one else." He offers his hand. "Agreed?"

What am I agreeing to; what am I starting that I can't finish? A suit for Valene, a power grid for the city, a life normal and happy and worth living for; all of it blew up in my face. Only a few days before, Break Pointe was on the cusp of spring. Winter has returned now, with a bitter vengeance.

I take his hand. "Agreed."

TEN

The smell of death lingers everywhere I go.

A putrid, nauseating stench curls up inside my nose any time I settle in at home, the roof of City Hall, the graveyards I spend more and more time minding, afraid they'll bloom dead.

No changes.

I keep going back to Vi's text, expecting it to be different. Mike hasn't woken up yet. C'mon. Wake up. I make this bargain with myself. Things will be better if Mike recovers. Some of this I'll accept if I can just have this one thing. Stiff northern winds push me from my station above City Hall.

Any changes with you?

Another force pushes, from deep within, clawing to get out. I won't be moved. I anchor myself magnetically to the steel skeleton of the building and City Hall sways with me.

Mute light escaping my jacket casts shadows of the suspension cables of the repaired Van Stitchel Bridge, projecting a dense web of intersecting lines below. I drift through them until there's no telling my darkness from theirs. Chains buffet against the pitted concrete of the eastern tower.

I touch down on the eaves beside The Interdictor. "Did you ever consider how insensitive your little getup was to Valene's hearing? Or did you just not care?"

"Everyone walked on eggshells around Valene," he says. "They left her in silence, but also in solitude. I wanted her to know I was there. I wanted her to hear me, always."

Sorry I asked. "Scope Industries."

"I'm not familiar."

"They manufacture home security products. Apparently, they manufacture diffusers on the side and off the books. My contact at Found Corp matched the diffuser to a proprietary synthetic used by Scope in its other products."

"You've verified their claim?"

As soon as I got word back, I tested off-the-shelf products from Scope – security alarms, motion sensors, video cameras – in the lab. "The synthetics match. No one else has the formula they use. Scope has a manufacturing facility near Nixon, Nevada. On paper, they only have two shifts, but there's a third."

The Interdictor nods. "Then we have our target."

Rage festers inside me, scratching at the soft glass of my body. I want to release it, to douse the fire inside with the blood of anyone responsible for what happened to those students.

"I think there's enough to give to the news," I say. "Frankie. Or maybe someone else. We can expose Scope."

He shakes his head. "That accomplishes nothing."

"They're breaking the law."

"Are they?"

"Diffusers were banned in Break Pointe."

"By a city that no longer officially exists."

The gift that keeps on giving. "Diffusers are illegal in the county and the state. GP made sure of that."

"You can charge the people selling these weapons under the table, but that only treats the symptom," The Interdictor says. "We must root out the infection. The fact is the manufacture and sale of these weapons are legal in this country. Scope simply doesn't want the stigma of being attached to them."

"Then let's stigmatize them."

"I'd rather traumatize them, Baldwin."

The city twinkles behind me, a faint cluster barely observable in the glare of the towers across the river. I sit on the ledge of the eaves, swirling with my birds, and the rush of anger and fear within me. The need for justice. Revenge.

"People work at this plant," I say.

"Don't lose your nerve now. These 'people' manufacture weapons that are routinely used against 'people' like them. They cannot expect to be immune to their own disease. If it satisfies you, Baldwin, we can create a diversion that will empty the facility before we destroy it. Casualties will be minimal."

I bite my lip. "I just want this to end."

His chains rattle. "Scope and any other company making and selling these weapons will reconsider their business strategy once we've shown them the consequences of their recklessness."

"We can't just go around destroying people and property."

The Interdictor looks out toward The Ice Pick, shrouded in the smoke of lingering fires. "Can't we?"

I look away. "I shouldn't have done that."

"What you should have done was finish the job."

"I'm not a judge." Welby pulses with savage light, before crumbling into ashes. "I'm not an executioner."

"You are the only law in The Derelicts."

I throw up my hands. "And why is that?"

He sits next to me and removes his helmet. "Great Power wanted to help Break Pointe. I wanted to, Baldwin."

"Your heart is bleeding through your uniform."

"I obeyed the law. To the letter. The law demands the use of our powers be sanctioned under contract. Break Pointe violated its contract with Great Power. I could not act on the night of the plane crash. I can now. If necessary, I can provide sanction for the strike against Scope Industries."

"Sanction? How? The contract is still void."

He grips his helmet. "Great Power owns the school."

"What?"

"Professor Blackwood bought property throughout The Derelicts over the years, intending to aid in the revitalization of the city. Of course, they never held up their end and he was stuck with dozens of worthless deeds he could do nothing with."

"Until GP assumed administration of the city, you mean."

His brows arch. "I would have bulldozed all of it."

"I have to imagine some of those worthless deeds belonged to buildings that burned after the plane crash. And I imagine people will want to know why you did nothing then."

"I'm sure they will."

"What will you say?"

Shadows deepened in the channels of his scars. "I will say my perspective has changed."

His chains snap in the wind. The plane smashes into The Derelicts. Comic pages curl in embers. Blood covers my hands. Dead flesh taps against curved glass, *ba-dumm*, and my anger straightens out of the confusion swirling within me.

"There's nothing else we can do," I say.

The Interdictor replaces his helmet. "We don't need to make a statement, Baldwin. Only send a message. Our hand will be as hard to identify as theirs. We go in under cover of darkness and mitigate the facility. If we are exposed, so be it. I invoke sanction and we continue the battle in the courts."

"You don't have to do this. This is my responsibility."

The Interdictor offers his hand to me, and again, I take it. He helps me to my feet. "You and I can both fly, but I suspect you cannot match my top speed."

"Your chest is really sticking out right now."

"We will take one of the company's tactical jets. It is unde-tectable to any radar, civilian or otherwise."

I almost killed this guy once. "Tonight?"

"We can be there and back in hours."

I lift off the tower, into a mob of blackbirds. "I'll meet you at the airfield in thirty minutes."

Under the bandages, within the net of tubes and lines and cords, Mike is unrecognizable. He would say the same of me. The last year has changed me, more than just in body. Before, my anger and grief would have stacked inside me, unconnected to anything else. I was expert only in unplugging myself from what I didn't want to feel or know, and now I feel everything. I know, so much horror I cannot contain. I can't unplug.

I won't.

I can't go on. I can't accept this. The law failed Break Pointe before. I won't let it again.

"I'm sorry," I whisper to Mike. "I don't know why this happened. I don't know why any of this is happening. I don't know why this is us, Mike, but it's not going to be anyone else. I swear to God, it will never be anyone else."

I squeeze his hand. He squeezes back.

"Mike?"

A nurse comes in. "How did you get in here?"

I let go of Mike's hand and disappear.

I zip up the front of this HALO jumpsuit. "Snug."

The Interdictor finishes getting into his at the back of the tac-jet's cargo hold. "The lining is insulated to protect against the extreme cold of jumping out of an airplane at 10,000 feet into temperatures exceeding sixty below. A tailored fit ensures there's no unnecessary heat loss during the drop."

"I figured," I say. "But thanks, anyways."

He taps a pouch on my arm. "Radio. An integrated channel will allow us to talk to each other, unobserved. There's a push-to-talk switch. Earpiece. You've figured this as well."

I close the Velcro straps tight around the cuffs of my wrists. "Way ahead of you."

He acts like he's waiting for something. "No snide add-on?"

"I'm running on empty."

"So long as you understand that our mission is simply one of mutual interest. This doesn't make us friends."

I smile. "You keep explaining things to me."

"I make no assumptions."

"I assume you know how to fly this thing?"

His eyes narrow. "I thought you would."

This guy. "Why would I?"

"Your power is to acquire knowledge. I assumed you would have the training to pilot aircraft among your abilities."

"You seriously can't fly this plane?"

"I can fly. Why would I learn how to pilot an aircraft?"

Why am I not surprised? "Is there a commercial flight we can catch from the airport out to Nevada?"

"I–"

"Wait, you probably can't work a phone."

Let's see. Flying a tac-jet. How hard can it be? I skim the files I acquired from the GP mainframe last year. Wouldn't you know it, the schematics and training material for this model aircraft are housed within the recesses of my infinite memory.

I blink. "We're good."

I think that's a smile. "Are you ready?"

I take a breath. The instinct surprises me. It's been a minute since I needed to. Wow. I yearn for breath. Life. This is why I don't think this, and I try not to at all sometimes. I want nothing more than to go back to who I was.

"I'm ready," I say.

He reaches for the button to recall the ramp leading into the hold. The Interdictor stops short of pressing it, his attention focused on something outside. I turn around.

Dr. Piller comes up the ramp. "Can we focus on the actual problem in front of us before we go on to the next unsolvable societal malfunction, Ms. Baldwin? Just this once?"

I sigh. "Eavesdropping on my thoughts, Dr. Piller?"

His smile is weary. "What are you doing?"

"Making sure diffusers are never used again."

He looks past me, at Nathan. "And you?"

"My duty," he says.

"Your duty. That's rich, coming from you. What is this, Halloween? You two are dressing up as soldiers and you're going to do what? Do you have any idea what you're about to do?"

The Interdictor holds his hand over the ramp control button again. "I'm about to close the door, doctor. Unless you intend on flying across the country tonight, I suggest you leave."

Piller shakes his head. "You can't do this."

"Sometimes I am confused, Dr. Piller. Perhaps you can clarify for me. Is your power telepathy, or is it the tireless ability to say no to everything you encounter?"

"You could do with saying no sometimes, Nate."

"What Baldwin and I intend is no different than what you and the Vanguard did in Britain after Molly Swift, Dr. Piller."

"It is and you know it." Piller looks at me. "Kit. Don't do this. Let's go back to the lab and talk."

I cross my arms. "The time for talking is over."

"You're hurt. You're angry. I understand."

I scoff. "You don't. You can't."

He reaches for me. "Give me a chance at least."

I step back. "I gave you a chance."

I trusted him. I put all faith and confidence in him to help me help the city, to do the thing he swore he wanted to do, and what did he do? He betrayed me, to Professor Blackwood.

For the greater good.

That's what he had said. For peace. I can live with it. I can look past it, for – checks notes – the greater good. But give him a chance? These people keep explaining things to me.

"This isn't about us," he says.

"I know it isn't. And The Interdictor is right. This is like Molly Swift. This is what the Vanguard existed for. What GP exists for, or at least what they should. We're supposed to help people. We're supposed to keep people safe and that means preventing things like this from happening, Dr. Piller. If this were a group of terrorists building an atomic bomb about to sell it or use it on some city, you'd be in a suit with us."

Piller's hands surge through the salt and pepper bramble of his hair. "This is different."

"Why?"

"You have all the power in the world. You have all the brains, most of the time. What you don't have is money."

"What does money have to do with anything?"

He laughs. "Everything. *Everything*, Kit. That's what this is about at the end of the day. You're not going after murderers or terrorists, you're going after someone's dividend."

Harrow's words clatter through my mind. *That's all existence is, old man. Buying. Selling. Acquiring.*

"This isn't about greed," I say. "It's about survival."

"Does your engine grow on trees?"

I clench my fists, fighting the anger loose within me like an over-pressured hose. "You don't want anything to change."

"You can't build an airplane out of a sinking ship," Piller says. "That's not how the world works."

"That's not how it worked before me, you mean."

Piller paces back and forth in the hold. His frustration escalates with each passing moment, and so does mine. My doubts reflect his, but now I doubt them. Are they even mine?

That's the other Kit.

"I don't care how the world works, Dr. Piller. Why should I yield my life and my potential to a system I didn't design? Why should I yield any more dead? I don't care about keeping things going if the grease turning the wheel is the blood of dead kids. I have knowledge. I have power. And I am going to use it. I am going to change things. I am going to change the world."

I turn to The Interdictor. "You ready?"

Fear and awe brims in his eyes. "Waiting for you."

I grab my helmet. "Goodbye, Dr. Piller."

Piller lingers at the top of the ramp. "You do this, you invite every nut job and fear monger to call for open season on Break Pointe, Kit. You make yourself a target."

"You think I've made it this far in life as a black woman without knowing there were people out to get me?"

"Don't make this about – "

"You can't deny me."

"It will never end, Kit. Do you hear me?"

"You can't silence me."

"They'll never stop coming for you."

I shrug. "Let them come."

"What?"

"If they want it to be the OK Corral, it will be the OK Corral. You reap what you sow. If they come, I will burn them. If they send more, I will burn them, too. I will burn them until they understand, or there are no more of them."

Piller's jaw hangs. "This isn't who you are."

This suit holds my searing fury so well I think I'll catch fire. "Don't you know who I am? I'm the Star Walker. The fire of the stars. I give light and I burn out the shadows."

Piller scrutinizes me. "Star Walker?"

"That's what I said."

"Which one are you?"

I bite my lip. "What do you mean?"

He walks around me. "Are you Kit, or the projection?"

I flinch. "There's no difference."

"I think there is. There is. This is Siski's power you're using. And this is Siski's thinking."

I head for the cockpit. "You're always making excuses."

He stands in front of me. "Which one are you?"

"I put her away."

"Put *who* away?"

Light claws through me. "She's not getting out again."

His thoughts intrude on mine. *Survival of the fittest.*

"Get out of my head."

Law of the jungle. Is that right?

"Get out of my way, Dr. Piller. Now."

That's what Siski thought. And that's what the people pushing these weapons think. This isn't you, Ms. Baldwin.

You don't know me, I say.

You're hurt. You're angry. You're letting yourself become infected by this disease that's rotted them out. You're letting yourself become blind to your own power.

I see. Finally, I see.

I know you –

I raise my hand, and a telekinetic field pushes Piller back through the hold, toward the ramp.

STAY –

I force him out of the hold.

OUT –

Piller trips on the edge of the ramp.

OF –

He rolls down to the tarmac of Crown Field.

MY –

I keep pushing him until he's clear of the plane.

HEAD.

Nausea finds me again. Revulsion. That gagging stench of death that follows me everywhere now. I ignore my unease and slam the ramp control button with a telekinetic punch. The ramp lifts back to the tac-plane with a hydraulic hiss. Piller begs me to stay with his eyes, right up until I lose sight of him.

ELEVEN

Sea foam-colored instruments blink on the instrument panel before me. Dreams riddle through Abi. Her legs kick against mine, setting off ripples of light that make our bed a spaceship and I sit up in my seat on the tac-plane and try to focus. Fate races toward me at over five hundred miles an hour and yet my thoughts stretch all the way back to Break Pointe.

I pinch my cheek. "How much longer?"

The Interdictor stares straight ahead into the dark. "The instruments are in front of you, Baldwin."

"I'm not good at small talk, either."

"I require nothing to distract me from my purpose."

I check the instrumentation. Ten minutes to target. "What do you do when you're distracted?"

He shifts like he's trying to get comfortable. "I read."

I smile. "You read?"

"That surprises you?"

"Your entire body is one giant muscle."

"The brain is a muscle, Baldwin."

"You must not work that one out, then."

His thumbs circle each other. "'War is peace. Freedom is slavery. Ignorance is strength.'"

"I don't think you took the right message from Orwell."

"There are no messages, Baldwin. Only the truth. We either acknowledge it, or deny it. You deny the truth of yourself. Your power. If you acknowledged it, you would not fight yourself, or what you know in your heart to be true. You would not struggle with the concept of the two of us, working together."

I tug on the zipper of my suit. "Power isn't truth."

"There is no other."

"*1984* was a warning against totalitarianism. It wasn't a style guide. You get that, right?"

He unbuckles his harness straps. I grip the zipper, ready to unleash the fire in my heart, but what could I do to him besides destroy this plane? Rain hell on the world below.

"I suggest you revisit the book, Baldwin," he says. "You may find your perspective on it different. You often contest your enemies first by speaking out against them. You go on the news and then you find yourself confused at the outcome. Power dictates truth. You have power, beyond reckoning. You decide the truth. You determine reality. Dictate, Baldwin."

Everybody wants something from me. Or they want me to be something. Savior. Destroyer. Death.

"You sure you want me to do that?"

He looks at me. "A god requires a worthy opponent."

"You just decided you're a god?"

"No man can deny it. Can you?"

If I deny him, if I flick away his desperate machismo with some pithy retort, I concede the truth. The truth is what he has established. I can only acknowledge, or deny it.

"I'll let you know," I say.

He slides his chair back. "Coming up on the target."

I scan the radar screen. A green blip flashes fifty miles out. With the turn of a dial, the tac-plane decelerates but maintains its altitude above a blanket of silver clouds. I set the controls on autopilot, linked through my PEAL. The plane will maintain an orbit around the site while we carry out the mission. Once we're done, we'll fly up and rendezvous with it.

Simple as that.

I unstrap from my seat and follow Nathan back into the cargo hold. Abi stirs beside me, back home. What am I doing here, following The Interdictor into battle?

What am I doing.

He pulls on his helmet. "Quickly, Baldwin."

I take a pressurized helmet off the rack. "I don't think I need this, actually."

"For anonymity's sake."

I pull on the helmet. "Worried about being caught?"

"I worry who your next target will be."

My opaque reflection distorts in the visor of his helmet. "There's no difference between us, Nathan."

He releases the ramp. "You're starting to see."

Air rushes out of the hold. I brace magnetically to the deck as he crouches low. We wait for the red lights on either side of the bay door to flash green. Abi's lips brush my neck. *Is this you?* Red flashes green and I run out of the hold.

Gray envelops me. Fear propels me, pushing me down, forcing me into the grip of her doubt. Stars break the uniform darkness beyond. The lights of a small city in the desert. The LED projection in my helmet indicates the manufacturing facility, a small cluster of buildings off a stretch of highway below.

The Interdictor's voice crackles in my ear. "Execute."

Electronic green lines in my visor flutter. The constellation of yellow and amber below blinks out completely as the electromagnetic pulse I generate shorts out every transistor in a twenty-mile radius.

"15,000 feet," he says. "Sixty seconds to impact."

Life erupts like oil well fires below. Tiny dots of living energy trickle out of the facility into the parking lot, but a few people remain inside the buildings, no doubt maintenance workers trying to figure out what happened to the power. Security will be on-site in moments if they aren't already.

"The building isn't going to be empty," I say.

He races ahead of me. "Thirty seconds to impact."

"Pull your chute, Nathan."

"You've come this far, Baldwin."

"Pull your chute!"

Pulverized earth bullets me as The Interdictor slams into the facility at terminal velocity. Cables rip free of my chute, and I don't get nearly the drag I hoped for. I careen through dust and smoke into the burning crater of what had been the primary assembly plant. Robotic arms stab at bolts that aren't there, blown off tracks that twist into the smoldering maw. Random parts of I don't know what rain down on me. I stumble through the devastation, searching for victims.

What did we do.

The Interdictor hovers above the haze-shrouded crater. "What are you doing, Baldwin?"

I look up at him. "We shouldn't have done this."

"Perhaps I overestimated your nerve."

"There are people here."

"There were people in your school," he says. "And there are people in the other building on this site. For now."

"Don't," I say, but he flies away.

I fly after him. Every window in the second building shattered in the destruction of the first, but The Interdictor crashes through the front doors anyway. I surge ahead of him, knocking him out of the air and to the smooth concrete of the floor. A labyrinth of conveyor belts webs the expanse. Component pieces of diffusers continue to form out of 3-D printers and roll down the line to be assembled with others by robotic hands. I shove off The Interdictor and follow the line to its end, where automated loaders take the finished weapons and ferry them into the same black cases I found on the dealer back in Break Pointe. Dozens of crates stack against the wall, waiting to be put onto the semi-trucks waiting in the loading bays.

Never again.

Frustrated energy curls back from my fingertips like flame from a lighter in the wind. What is happening? I can't release my power. I can't fire. I look back at The Interdictor, confused, and see his trembling fist suspended inches from the jaw of a man in a standard-issue Responder's uniform.

The Responder holds his hands out like a bad magician. "Stand down. This facility is under the protection of GP."

"What?"

I'm stuck. The Responder constricts my movements with some kind of repression field. My thoughts don't gain much traction either; I jam on the presence of Great Power in the heart of a manufacturing plant dedicated to the production of weapons that kill Empowered. I don't understand what's happening.

I don't understand any of this.

With a little flair, the Responder circles his hands together, and both The Interdictor and I pretzel down to the floor. Two black crates slide off the stacks behind us.

"In you go," he says, dragging me across the floor.

A crate pops open and the diffusers inside spill out. The Responder bends me inside it.

"Stand down," The Interdictor says, his frustration seething out the cracks in his helmet. "Immediately."

The Responder chuckles. "Who are you to give orders?"

"Don't," I say. "Don't say a word."

The Responder clenches his fist and I skid to a stop short of the crate. "Who are you?"

"Release us," The Interdictor says. "Now."

With one hand still holding me, the Responder reaches for the frayed strap securing what's left of Nathan's helmet.

I try to get free, but it's like my legs have gone to sleep. C'mon. Move. Then, as my reflection splinters in The Interdictor's visor, I realize I don't need to move. With a thought, I project behind the Responder. He releases me, scrambling to face The Ever, blazing with crimson flame.

"He asked you nicely," I say and bring a sword of hard light down on the startled Responder's wrists so hard The Interdictor springs loose across the floor.

The Responder's hands hang like empty gloves off the ends of his sleeves. "You broke my wrists..."

I levy the bristling sword against his neck. "What are you doing here? What is GP doing protecting this place?"

"You're her..."

"I said what are you doing here?"

The Responder looks at The Interdictor. "Who are you?"

The Interdictor grabs him by the collar. He drags him across the floor into an empty crate. He slams the lid shut and shoves it back into the others, toppling the stacks.

The Interdictor rips off his helmet and throws it away. "I thought you were the real Baldwin."

I remove my helmet. "I am."

"Your eyes..."

"What about them?"

"They're yellow."

I distort across the visor of the helmet. Xanthous suns burn in the cocoon of a magenta nebula. My eyes aren't quite Siski's, but they aren't quite mine, either.

I turn away. "It's just... it's nothing."

"It's never 'nothing' with you, Baldwin. Perhaps Piller was right. And perhaps you will find, as many monsters of myth do, that some things are simply difficult to digest."

I clench my eyes shut. I'm in control. This is my power. This is my power, and when I look again, the hungry eyes of the wolf that ate her own children are gone.

"We need to focus," I say.

"Yes, we do. Finish this."

I shake my head. "What is GP doing here?"

"Destroy the plant before more of them arrive."

"The Responder knows what he's protecting. GP has to."

"Destroy the plant, Baldwin. Now."

My light clouds. "Is GP making these things?"

His scars twist in frustration. "Don't be ridiculous."

"Why would you..."

"Scope contracted GP, Baldwin. The same as any other corporation dedicated to protecting its assets. Finish the job."

Crates lift out of their toppled stack into orbit around e. "People buy those things because they think they'll protect them from Empowered. But every time some nut job turns one on in a public place, more people buy a GP security package."

"And some buy diffusers," he says.

"GP could fight harder for banning diffusers. They could have pushed back harder against the ERA that limited the use of their powers to sanctioned contracts. That would have been the right thing to do. It wouldn't have been the most fiscal."

I dive into the trove of files I inadvertently copied from the GP mainframe after my transformation. In seconds, I speed through millions of emails, budget reports, and documents. Buried in one in a file marked for deletion, I discover GP's contract for purchase of a company called American Holdings. Listed among AH's assets is another company, Scope Industries.

Red fire burns orange to yellow in a flash.

Conveyor belts whip like tails as I fling through the walls. Metal shreds into shrapnel I unleash on the plant. Shards of razor-sharp steel blunt against The Interdictor's impervious skin. The rest of the building doesn't fare as well. Fire escapes into the night, unobstructed by any ceiling. Walls collapse around her, opening my anger to the desert and I am atomic. Piled crates of diffusers scatter. Cords of energy wrap around The Interdictor's arms and legs as he tries to fly away and you can't run from me. You can't get away from this.

I pull him back down to the ground. "You monster..."

Energy constricts around him. "Let me go, Baldwin."

"GP owns Scope. You make these things. You profit from them. You profit from the butcher of children."

He shakes his head. "I didn't know."

"You're lying."

"Why would I come here, Baldwin? Why would I help you?"

My sword stabs back into form. "You tried to trick me."

"No."

"You tried to set me up. I blow up this place and you catch me."

His frustration burns in his eyes. "Is your hatred for us so deep? Just how far will you go, Baldwin? How far will you reach to connect us to every one of your failures?"

The harder he struggles, the more tangled in my web he becomes. All my anger, hurt, and betrayal burns into the sword.

"I see through you. I see through all your lies. You're so obvious... all of you in your glass tower, you're so..."

And then I know; I know what I have to do.

I gash open a tear into the In Between. I release The Interdictor, though he's still bound in shock.

"This dimension... it's here, too?"

I step into the portal. "It's everywhere."

In the time it takes me to walk across my apartment, I stride across the United States through the In Between, out of a portal burning above the Blackwood Building. Inconceivable power erected the building. Blood money. Currents of static electricity drawn by my magnetic will assault the weather vanes at the pinnacle repeatedly, causing it to glow so bright the glass skin of the transparent structure flickers like a broken television. I gather all my righteous anger, all my power and lightning channels through me. The sky splits. I do.

PANEL ONE

Kit's mother opens the window in the apartment.

· · ·

PANEL TWO

Abi sits up in bed, a slash of crimson light across her.

PANEL THREE

A young woman stares out of an airplane window, horror in her eyes as she falls, knowingly, to her death.

PANEL FOUR

Abi goes to the window of the apartment.

PANEL FIVE

Siski, angry and vengeful, disappears past the event horizon of the burning void within Kit's chest.

PANEL SIX

Kit is a weather vane in the cracked sky outside the apartment. Abi types something into her PEAL.

PANEL SEVEN

Simon looks up from drawing his comic book, at his desk in the classroom. Surprise in his eyes.

PANEL EIGHT

A close-up of the screen of Abi's PEAL. The words MESSAGE SENT in green across it.

PANEL NINE

Mike remains on the ventilator in his hospital room. Vidette sits in a chair beside the bed, waiting. Hoping.

My hand jolts. The flood of anger sweeps out of me and I'm not myself, but someone else, watching this. I am in many places at once, broken and fragmented, torn and cracked, without form. A new message blinks on my PEAL. I swipe it open.

Is this you?

The lightning storm dies. Sparks shower from the molten summit of the tower as I fall out of the sky. Birds spiral with me out of control to the lakeshore, a falling star.

What am I doing.

Snow melts around me. I sink into a crater of soft earth and melted ice. A cry erupts from me. Hoarse. Wounded. The sound as vicious as the thunder. I cover my mouth, but I can't hold it back. I can't stop my disgust or my sorrow or my anguish, my merciless anguish, I've tried to deny since the attack.

The Interdictor floats down out of the still-open portal to the In Between, rubbing his throat. "I didn't know, Baldwin."

"I'm supposed to help people," I say. "I'm supposed to..."

The Interdictor hovers over me. "You are a god, Baldwin. You can help nothing. You either create, or destroy. Your role in our pantheon is obvious, to everyone but you."

I bite my lip. "This isn't me..."

"It is. I have the scars to prove it."

In the deep shadows across his face, I can't tell if his expression is one of contempt or respect.

"I will see Great Power's interest in this company is sold. We will never profit from our own destruction again. Blackwood is gone. It's time for a new direction at GP. A new leader."

"You have to do more. Nathan. GP has to shutter Scope."

He rises back into the night. "Another company would take its place. Besides, their sales will most likely skyrocket after tonight, making them more attractive to a potential buyer."

I want to throw up. "They're killing people. Children."

"Children choke on suckers, Baldwin. I don't see you advocating for the banishment of lollipops."

"You can't..."

"I would caution you against going to the media with your findings. Such information could prove damaging to us, and we have already suffered immensely on your account. Forget this, and I ensure your name is left out of this incident. Pursue it, and you invite the storm Piller warned you of. Decide."

The Interdictor ascends into the night, to the crown of Responders encircling the flinching tower. I come to my feet. Voices shout somewhere beyond. Red and blue lights flash in the distance. Dogs bark. Sirens wail. I've done what I set out to do; I sent a message. The reply was cruel.

Final.

TWELVE

"Why the long face, old man?"

The perpetual smirk Harrow wears gravels me. Everything is funny to this man, and how could it not be; death is a joke. Death is easy and simple, not a fear or reality, but just another exit he didn't take on his long, strange road. He sits on the back of a melted horse on the carousel, its face mutated into a hideous, black and red emaciated shape.

"You just sit out here all day?" I say.

"Oh no, not at all." He grips the handlebars. "A dead man has an awful lot of maintenance to occupy his time. But I admit to being partial to the old place. Something about it."

"You said."

"I did." Rusted metal groans as he steps off the horse. "To be a child, again. To be new. What a thing. Everything seemed so big, didn't it? So possible." He lets go of the bars. "I seem to have outgrown such things, though, haven't I? *Que será, será*, as they say. Even in death, you still get too old."

I step onto the carousel. Growing up in the ruins, parks and carousels and amusement were rare things. Children here greet the world with caution from the start. Fear.

"It's a privilege," I say.

I live under the constant cloud of losing myself. To The Ever. Siski. The universe of voices calling out to be released. If I don't answer, then what? Will I exist, indefinitely, like Harrow? Will I remain forever as I am now? I have no guide or experience to tell me. The idea I'll persist, when so many others won't, makes me sick; it makes me want to die.

"I came to ask you for a truce, Harrow."

"A truce? How quaint."

"You'll suspend criminal activity in The Derelicts, and I'll do everything I can to find a cure for The Straw Men."

He chuckles. "Why would I want a cure, old man?"

"Because at some point, the tread comes off the tire."

"We've discussed my preferred remedy."

"See, that's the thing. A cure is a good option for you because I am never going to make you like me."

A mock frown chases away his grin. "Some people will receive the benefit of your power, but not others?"

I cross my arms. "Some people will get heat and light. They won't get turned into beings of unfathomable energy."

Harrow leans off the pole of his horse. "Unfathomable energy. All this time you've been fighting to hold on to the structure of your life, but now I think you see, old man. You can't deny who you are. You can't box it away. Can you?"

Frustrated light leaves scratch marks in my skin. "I can use this power for good. I can't ever let it use me."

His enthusiasm wanes. "What then of your campaign, Baldwin? To rid the world of the scourge of these weapons? The cancer of which they are merely a symptom? What will you do?"

I don't know. "I'll do my best."

"Oh, yes. As with the cure. 'Everything I can,' I believe you said.

A rather qualified statement for someone of such profound agency. I shouldn't get my hopes up, I think."

I bite my lip. "Hope is all we have, Harrow."

Harrow looks out across the blackened ruin of the amusement park. "Indeed. And so I yield. You've earned your peace."

"We can have a truce?"

"What's a little while?" His grin returns. "After all, you and I are going to be doing this for a long, long time."

Cardinals bloody the white frost in the window. Spring is close now. Winter holds on, but the grip loosens. I feel it in the air, in the ground ready for life, in Abi, warm and soft. She strokes my back as we rest on the couch, my head in her lap.

"Don't ever let me go," I say.

Her arms lace me up. "You could never outrun me."

"I'm afraid, Abi."

"I was only slightly exaggerating."

"Of what's inside me."

"Cookies?"

I pinch her leg. "Evil cookies."

"Oatmeal raisin?"

This girl. "Siski. The Ever. I want to burn everything. I want to dictate the truth. Harrow agreed to the truce, but this will just go on. The Straw Men, everyone responsible, they deserve..." I flinch against the hell I imagine. The fire bottled within me. "The kids deserved better. They deserved to live."

Her thumb brushes my neck. "We all have a shadow in us." Blackbirds cheat the cardinals off the sill. "That doesn't mean it's who you are. You can be more than what people want you to be. You can be the person you know you are in your heart."

My hand curls at my chest. "This isn't my heart, Abi."

"It is now. This power is what you make it. It's better for you.

The people you care about are better for you, Kit. I am. I know you. I know who you are. You have kindness. You have grace. You have love. You have so much love."

I grip her hand, for dear life. "I love you."

Abi's lips brush my ear. "You protect the city. I'll protect you." Her voice trails away. "I'll protect us."

The birds make little noises. Melting ice pelts the windowsill. Her heart beats quick and steady, *ba-dumm, ba-dumm, ba-dumm.* Since the school fear and anger have rigored me. I've been dead. I've been mindless. I've been heartless.

She's my heart.

Every step on the march splashes.

Melting snow runs through the streets, and so does vibrancy I haven't felt in The Derelicts in a long time. Hundreds gather before the school and say prayers. Sing songs. Make declarations. No more killings. No more inaction. No more closing our eyes. The surviving students name their dead classmates. LaTonya. Marcus. Jamie. Brian. Travis. Jenny. Marchelle. Antonio. Sara. Vincent. Easter. Simon. The surviving students name all the dead lost to diffusers in the last year, over three hundred names that exhaust the daylight. Everyone lights candles or holds up their phones.

Mike limps to the front of the crowd, leaning heavy on a cane. Applause greets him as he takes a megaphone from one of the students. He smiles and nods his gratitude.

"A month," he says. "A month has gone by but some of us will always live in that moment. In that darkness. We will always live with the guilt of thinking we could have done more. Why couldn't have I done more? Why couldn't I have been..."

He clears his throat.

"We're always going to live with that. That darkness is always going to be with us. But it can't define us. That's why we gotta keep a light going. Not just for our friends. Our family. Those boys and girls we lost. For us. We gotta stay alight. It's hard. I know. It gets real hard sometimes when I think about what I saw... what I heard. What I wasn't able to do. But I'm lucky. We are. We're the luckiest people in the world. That's right. We got the brightest light. We got Kit."

He looks back at me with a smile. "She's brought light to this community. She's brought hope. And she's here tonight." Applause swelled around her. Praise. Love. "We're here. We're still here. Show 'em, Kit. Show 'em all we're still here."

I don't feel I've brought light. I don't feel I've done anything to make the lives of the people in my community better. But we're here. At the outset of winter, in the shadow of the Battle of Break Pointe, I didn't think any of us would make it. The air is lighter with the burden of winter off it. Birds swirl around me as I ascend over the school. Spring arrivals chirp their fascination with me as I brighten, and the night retreats from the city, for at least the moment.

Blackbirds wrench from my magnetic crown.

In twos and threes and tens and twenties, they string across The Derelicts, an oil slick pouring out of the sky down over The Ice Pick. I follow them. Birds swarm the marshy uncertainty of the island, so many I have to float above or else step on their wings. Ravenous caws create this manic, propulsive force, driving me into the amusement park. Beaks peck at fingers. Toes.

Eyes.

Limbs litter the promenade, amputated with such force the wounds are cauterized. Chunks of severed flesh. Something hot did this. Or something fast. Why? Who? No Straw Men come out to meet me. All of them are in pieces. I choke on my satisfaction. The disgust thick in the air. The horror within and without me. Shreds of fabric curl on the ground around the old carousel. The cracked buttons of an old trench coat. The feather of Blue Jay from Harrow's fedora. The top of his head rests on the ground, cut clean through the bridge of his nose. Rusty nails stake his tongue and jaw to the saddle of a plastic horse.

My God.

His eyes track me, pleadingly, as the blackbirds peck their way through his debris, a river of black flooding its banks.

———

Abi pours another cup of flour in the mixing bowl. "So, what did you do with them all?"

I cringe. "I kind of put them all in bags. Evidence bags. Respectfully. And I took them to Dr. Piller."

She whips up another batch of cookies. "Pass me the sugar."

I set the bag of sugar on the table. "I don't know who could have done this to them. Or why."

"They have to have lots of enemies, you figure."

"This was someone Empowered. The force. The anger..."

Abi pinches out little bits of dough and places them on a cookie sheet. "The Interdictor?"

"Maybe. I don't know."

"You going to look into it?"

I rest my chin in my hand. "I should."

"They kind of had it coming."

"It's still a crime."

"Are they alive, though? I mean, are they even human?"

I bite my lip. "Technically, they're..."

"Not your problem. Let Piller deal with it." She puts her hands on my face as she kisses me. She's all covered in flour. Abi laughs as I try to get away. "Worry about the living."

Abi places the tray in the oven and wipes her hands clean.

I don't need the chalkboard. I can write with the atoms of light in the fabric of space and time. Still, I use it. I keep to the things I know and did, to stay anchored in some way. I keep the message obscured under the smear of brushed-away chalk.

$$\Delta U = Q + W$$

Skinned shoes shuffle across the grainy crystal of my lab. My nose curls with the stench of death. Crates lift magnetically into the air. I gird for more sorrow, more violence, more horror, more hurt and the dead boy from the thrift store lurches out of the shadows of the alien ship. Skin a putrid green. Dead blood black in his veins. Dirt under his fingernails. Splinters.

"I buried you," I say.

He creeps to the blackboard. He studies the equation, his hands hanging down his sides like dead branches.

I don't know what to do. I don't know what to say.

He stands, mouth agape, his hand at the black hole in his throat. The dead boy makes a gesture, like he wants to say something. Whatever art or power animates him hasn't restored his vocal cords; he was lifted out of death, exactly as he was.

What do I say.

The dead boy picks through the loose crystal debris on the floor. I expect him to take one of the sharp pieces as a weapon, but instead, he turns to the blackboard. He scratches out long, rootless letters on the cracked board, and drops the fragment.

HELP ME

And I was doing so well. "I don't know how…"

He taps at the board.

"I'm sorry. There's nothing I can do."

He pounds against it.

"This thing that's happening to you," I say. "There's no explanation for it. There's no cure. This is just how it is, I'm sorry. I don't... I don't know what I can do about it."

Broken glass crunches as the blackboard rolls back on its rusty wheels through the lab. The dead boy heaves as if in a sigh, but no sound comes out. Only mute exasperation. The helplessness I recognize well. The despair. The petrified loneliness.

I want to bury him, to box him away with the memory and the fear and not ever think about him or the way he died or the people that have died and will die that I know I will never save, but I stand with him, and face the death in my community, listening for the words the dead can no longer say.

STARTER HOME

STARTER HOME

1. Reality

Someone keeps rewriting reality. Mostly it goes like this: one minute I'm talking to Abi about things we'll never do, like go to New Zealand or just go to bed at the same time, and then she disappears along with the rest of what passes for my life these days.

I write this to make some record. A way back.

2. Honestly, It's Not That Different

Strange things happen around here.

There isn't any life for me outside of waiting for the next shoe to drop, so I wasn't too bothered at first. Now it happens all the time. On and off. In and out. Hours. Days. Minutes. Reality like summer floods. The strange always recedes back to a big, three-story house on Severin St. American castle. Picture window.

Picture perfect.

Milk trucks inch down the street, lined with '67 Chevys. Pig-tailed white girls swish in yards with hula-hoops. Boys play stickball in the middle of the street. Cops patrol the neighborhood and keep black girls from smudging the frosted scenery in midtown.

The cop points back toward the fringes of downtown. "You took a wrong turn back there."

I zip open my leather jacket. Crimson light illuminates the shock on the cop's face. "Tell me about it."

He takes off running. There's a reason I know when reality changes. My reality is out of sorts, too. TL/DR: if I touch someone, I acquire their energy. Consciousness. They go into the jar of this glowing alien crystal suspended within my chest. Entire universes reside there. Infinite realities. Plus, I'm half-Irish, so.

The doors are always open.

I go to the door. A housewife sits at the dinner table with her husband, her boy, and her girl, her blonde pin curls just right, the meatloaf just right, the colorless tablecloth just right. It's like you're looking in one of those department store windows at some display of mannequins or animatronic dolls.

I tap on the window. "Hey, lady."

She carves up little chunks of brickmeat for the kids flickering like old TVs and when everyone is seen to, she sits down. The House-wife doesn't make a plate for herself. All she does is sit there, watching them eat as she nurses a glass of wine. Her smile loosens a bit. Her plastic satisfaction melts, a bit like the butter on the top of the biscuits no one reaches for.

"Are you doing this?" I say.

No answer. No more playing around.

Light shimmers beneath my skin. Current arcs through the curls of my hair. I seize the deadbolt and unlock the door. This force pushes back on me, like the wind funneling off the lake between the buildings downtown. This anger.

The dining room instantly disappears along with the family. The house crumbles back to the ruin it's been the last fifty years since the ship crashed downtown.

"What..."

Fire burned through here. The floorboards black. The walls spotted with mold. Cobwebs strand the living room, or what's left of it. All these houses near the crash site exist pretty much as they did the day the ship fell out of the sky, but they've been looted. Nothing remains of value here except some faded and molded picture frames on the mantle. The Housewife. Her family. Other people, older people, long gone now. A world that doesn't exist anymore.

This voice rattles through the house. "Let us have this."

I turn around. No one there.

"Who said that?"

A voice scrapes out of the fireplace. "We want it like it was."

I kneel down in front of the mouth of the living room. "Hello?"

I found the alien crystal buried in the wreck. Scary dark places I have to squeeze into don't bother me as much as they should, so I crawl a bit into the fireplace. I figure, bats. Leaves. That kind of thing. Instead, loose bricks droop into the shape of eyes.

The house blinks. "Leave us alone."

3. So It's The House, Actually

The mechanics of how a house came to life with the power to alter reality escape me, but I can't get out of here. Not without Abi. The hows and whys don't matter, really.

Strange is a fact of life in Break Pointe.

I take a family photo off the mantle. "They all died. Didn't they?"

The Housewife and her family shimmer to life in the dining room. A tape stuck on a loop. But they're happy. Healthy. Normal, or maybe what passed for normal fifty years ago. Severin St. was far enough away from the crash not to get destroyed outright, but not so far away the radiation leaking out of the alien ship couldn't bathe this entire neighborhood in lethal doses.

"I'm sorry," I say.

Grief pries out of the fireplace. "They died. We lived."

Thousands of people died that day. The House On Severin St.

came to life. I can only imagine its first moments of consciousness, a confusion cemented in the pain and fear of the people dying inside of it. The House can alter time, space, reality or all three maybe. It can recreate its life before the ship, but can't sustain it.

I put the picture back. "Maybe I can help you."

The chimney chuffs with laughter. "How can you help us?"

"Listen... I know what it's like to..."

"You want to fix things," The House says. "Don't you?"

I bite my lip. "No."

"Houses require maintenance. We see all your patches."

"That's fine. I see right through you."

"I'm getting better at this. I'm getting stronger. I can make your reality right, too. Your mother. Father. Your home."

It wouldn't be right to say I don't want it. But then what would my life be? It would be the life of this house. Plastic. Greeting card. Hollywood still. "You can't deny reality."

Frustration rattles through the sorry floorboards under my feet. "We want it back the way it was."

I cross my arms. "I'm not leaving here without Abi."

"We can't focus," The House says and brick buildings crumble into piles of ignored rubble. Severin St. crashes headlong into a thirty-foot wall of barbed concrete. The chisel point of the old Bank & Trust Building downtown blunts against the cracked dome of a crashed alien spaceship, resting in its municipal crater.

I understand the want to change things.

4. Shadow Theater

Shadow puppets act out a story on the screen tower of the old Starvue Drive-In. It's all that's left, along with some rusted posts tilted like headstones, stripped of their speakers. This is our Saturday night. Lawn chairs after dark. Abi making my heart a projector.

"What kind of stuff do you write about me?" Abi says.

I shrug. "I keep it pretty vague. If someone ever finds my diary a hundred years from now, they'll write a series of books trying to figure out if we were lesbians or not."

Abi nods. "Playing the long game. I like it."

She sets a thermos of soup between us. I don't really eat anymore, but cooking is one of the things she does to glue together the uneven seams of this life we have. The thermos rattles. The crystal emits a low-key electromagnetic field. Sometimes, things get caught up in it. Loose debris. Car keys. Strawberries.

I have fruit satellites.

"It would be kind of nice," Abi says. "To live in a house you don't ever have to fix. New roof? No sweat."

"You'd never have to pick up in it."

"That's our angle, dude. Self-cleaning and repairing houses. We'll make so much bank. We can retire somewhere. Actually... just a house would be nice. I've never lived in a house."

"Never?"

Abi joins her hands and casts the shadow of some kind of monster. I don't recognize it. "It was a lot of moving around."

"We were in a duplex when I was little, but it's really only ever been the apartment. I never thought about a house."

"We could fix it up."

"I don't think The House is exactly into 'other people' moving into the neighborhood. You know?"

"Yikes."

"A little."

Fingers flutter into wings on the screen. "I want to make a home with you. That's really all I want."

The future terrifies me. Not the future. The unknown. I know what tomorrow is. It's today. I survive through repetition. My life has always been just getting through to the next day and when I found a strategy that worked I kept doing it. I didn't like it. And now I miss it.

Why?

Before my transformation, I could make anything work. TVs Toasters. Cars. Give me five minutes and I'd give you back whatever you had been missing out on. I had been missing out on just living, but I couldn't jimmy that. I couldn't keep my life running, at least any farther ahead than the next day. Then I lost any hope of human touch, and along came Abi.

A kind of life.

Abi's hands eclipse the screen. Her thumbs brush my cheeks. Her lips touch my lips. "Write about it."

"The House?"

Her heart beats against mine. Light ripples through me, *ba-dumm, ba-dumm, ba-dumm.* "Our home."

I hold her close. "I'm writing to remember."

"Write to like make it happen. We live in a house. We're a family. We have kids and stuff."

I brush her lips. "Kids?"

"Yep. They're super cute. Little geniuses. Moira is a terror."

"You've named them?"

"Oh, I got like their entire lives planned out. They like you more than me. You let them get away with everything."

"Well... you have their lives planned out."

"Hey, when you got all that Ashkenazi-Irish-African energy rattling around in you, you need somebody to steer that ship."

"Ok. What else?"

She settles into my arms. "We're perfect."

"Oh."

"I make you laugh. I don't have bad dreams. Nothing bad ever happened to me. I was just happy. Safe."

I kiss her. "You're safe with me."

"You're my hero."

I wish I could be who she thinks I am.

Light and shadow fight over Abi. "It's a good story."

5. It's happening again

Cracked plaster fades from the bedroom wall in my apartment, replaced by garish wallpaper patterned with a cartoony chef. Wood panel-flooring shags up to something puke green and matted. Being a hero means you have to fight crime and the occasional disaster.

I didn't think I'd have to fight bad taste.

The cops meet me on Severin St. Dogs. I fly on the repulsion of my magnetic field over their heads and land at the front door of the house. The Housewife and her family are inside, at the dinner table, just like they had been before. Not one thing out of place.

Except me.

The brows of the mantle place crinkle. "Go away."

"You can't change me," I say. "And you can't deny me."

"Houses reflect their owners," The House says, and silverware crashes against porcelain. The husband asks me if I'm ok. The kids stare at me like I'm some alien, but my chest isn't glowing. Strawberries aren't floating around me. I'm not powerful.

I'm just a housewife.

6. SO, THIS IS HAPPENING

I run outside. This weight in my body I haven't had since my transformation. This life. My feet hurt. I don't have my shoes on. I laugh. I haven't laughed in months.

I haven't thrown up.

But now I'm hungry. Wow. I'm really hungry. I haven't eaten since my transformation. I haven't needed to. I require only energy. Abi supplies enough for the both of us, most days. I'll figure this out.

Right after I eat a pizza. Or two.

Shouldn't have eaten all that pizza. There are some things about being a human I didn't need a remedial course in. Anyways. This level is definitely harder than the last one.

I'm not The Housewife. I'm me, mostly. My hair is straight for once. Somewhere my mother is content. I pick up the phone to call Abi. The cord only goes so far. I walk down toward Six Corners.

This voice pinches me, like the ancient bra I wear. This idea of a dress. *You want it this way. You don't have to think. You don't have to feel. You just want to get through to tomorrow.*

I just need to get through. Down on Shelley, it's not some digital restoration of 1968, but right now. Today. A light on the window of the apartment. She's waiting for me.

"Abi," I say and the lobby door opens to the dining room.

The House On Severin St. papers over reality, like my mom did when I was a kid, taping old newspaper over the windows like that could somehow end our strange to the rest of the neighborhood. I suppose if you can't see it, it's not there. But it is. Somewhere, the alien ship is behind all this gaudy wallpaper. My power. My reality.

I need to find it.

Every time I try to leave, I wind up back in The House. Back door. The windows. The House stretches and scales like the background of some play, the rooms a revolver spinning behind any door I try. The kitchen walks out to the grocery store. The basement to the woods, trees bending under the boards of the living room.

Red vine grows out of the basement floor. Around the beams. I tear it out. A day later, it's back. Doors open on gardens of flowers I pick for the table. I make breakfast. Send the kids to school. Do the laundry. Watch TV. Make dinner. Watch TV. Fake a headache anytime the husband gets fresh, which is a lot, and after he goes to sleep, I pull out the stuffing of the house and watch it grow back.

7. This Is Bullshit

Every day the same. I make breakfast. Send the kids to school. Do the laundry. Watch TV. Make dinner. Watch TV. I throw the trash out. Put the laundry away. I stuff the bills into a drawer in the kitchen because I like not paying them and then watching the husband screw up in confusion about the thin veil of his urban dominance.

I put things away.

All the pictures on the mantle. These horrific clothes. The toys the kids play with. I drag their beds into another room and then I can't find it again. When I set the table, the kids are gone.

The husband doesn't notice.

8. Are You The Light?

Safe to say denial is the most potent superpower of them all. I wish I had been writing down my days since I got my powers. Right now, seeing how I managed to get through each day would probably come in handy. What did I do?

How did I find a way to accept my reality?

I never have. That's the thing. When I had nothing and no one, I didn't sit at home in front of the TV. I scavenged the ruins for some bit of alien debris I could trade or sell to get out of here. I found the crystalline shard, and things changed.

I thought they did.

Ma goes around the house, unscrewing all the lightbulbs. I let her break them. She's broken, and The House can't put her right. She doesn't go into a drawer or a box or a room. I learned that a long time ago. My mother rattles through The House the way she does me.

Relentlessly.

9. Running Out of house

The husband talks under his breath. "How long is he staying?"

Dad set up shop in the recliner a week ago. That's his spot. He puts his feet up and shouts at the TV when someone drops the ball or whatever it is they're doing and the husband pleads. He begs. Barters.

"This is supposed to be our house," he says.

I shrug. "This is my house."

The husband has something to do in the garage. He always has something to do in the garage. I box up his clothes and his shoes and his bowling trophies and I put them in the garage. When Dad goes out there, it's the auto shop he owned in Six Corners.

The walls crease with worry. *I want things the way they were.*

I drift toward the light out on the street. "This house is big enough for the both of us. Isn't it?"

The garage door rattles shut.

Dad ducks under the hood of a '78 Dodge Challenger. This car never left the shop. "What you up to, girl?"

"Tinkering," I say.

"You always making something. What you doing now?"

"I'm making a home."

Later, The House closes off any path to the garage. The floors creak with frustration. Windows rattle with anger. I can't get back to my Dad, but I get back to the dining room table.

I'm not any kind of cook. Abi does all the cooking.

"These are still hot," she says, setting a plate of chocolate chip cookies on the table. "Watch your mouth."

I pull her close. "Did I say something bad?"

Her lips press into mine. Her softness smooths the plastic harshness of the chairs, the plates, The House trying to walk the line between the past and the future creeping in with every day.

10. House of mystery

Moira takes apart everything.

Most of the time she puts it back together, but it doesn't work. The TV. Radio. Any new gadget that comes into the house. I'm always putting The House right, but I don't mind. I like working with my hands. I like being my Dad with my daughter. I like our family.

Our life.

I scratch Moira's growth into the kitchen wall. The House erases it and then I stand Moira against the fresh white paint and make my mark again. Abi and I debate how tall our daughter really is since her curls are officially a candidate for Biggest Hair Ever.

The House scratches out her progress and then in the morning, I scribble YOU CAN'T ERASE US on the wall. This time what I write keeps. Doors open. Hallways tunnel out to the street. Curtains billow like sails on the breeze but I don't go anywhere. The House coughs smoke. Chokes its pipes. Withholds its heat. We keep as a family and we fit very tidy in this box on Severin St.

The fireplace burns with anger. "I don't understand. How did you do this? You don't have our power."

"Houses reflect their owners," I say.

Embers star up the chimney. "It is nice... to have a family again."

I bite my lip. "It is."

The House seems to settle. "You want to go home."

"You want me gone."

"Leave me the family," The House says.

"My family?"

They're not real. I know they're not real. My Abi is waiting for me in the apartment. But I lived here with my parents. My wife. My children. We lived a little life, in and out of doors.

I pull on my jacket. "Will they have me?"

"They'll never question their reality."

The front door creaks open to the present day. Go. Right now. All you've wanted since you got stuck in this place is to get back home. Get back to your life. This isn't your life.

It's never going to be your life.

"Look after them for me," I say.

11. Détente

The House On Severin St. doesn't bother me, and I don't bother them. Their fantasy keeps to the walls of the house. If I go there, it's to leave some of the strawberries I collect out on patrol. I don't know. I just figure maybe the kids want something else for dessert.

12. HOME

Some nights I go over by The House on patrol. Mostly I stay

away, though I like to think the smoke down Shelley is from the chimney, from the fireplace, from the kids warming, safe as houses.

Before dawn, I drift back to the apartment. Abi is waiting for me, awake as always, making shadows on the ceiling.

"You home?" she says.

I close the door behind me. "I'm home."

THE OTHER KIT

ONE

A river of debris glitters across the Pacific, from day into night. Shredded aluminum alloy trails after me, snared in my magnetic field as I hurtle through space at 18,000 miles an hour. Some days I don't like being a cosmically powered hero.

Today, it's pretty cool.

I trace wreckage over central Asia to the space shuttle *Advance*, tumbling ass over teakettle. Thermal protection tiles shed from the baseball-sized hole a meteor punched through the right wing. The meteor also gutted out the right OMS pod, disabling her thrusters. Without them, the shuttle loses altitude faster than NASA can race a rescue mission to the launch pad.

I tap my fingers across the screen of my PEAL. *Houston, this is Rescue One. I have eyes on the Advance.*

A dull vibration answers. *Copy, Rescue One. Proceed.*

I wobble a bit on my invisible track. Still getting used to relying only on the repulsion between the glimmering alien power source in my chest and the magnetic field of the earth itself. Sort of like skating, except not in any way at all. I arc ahead of the shuttle, far enough the crew will be able to see me out the windows of the cockpit.

Advance, Rescue One. Your mom sent me to pick you up.

Rescue One, not seeing you.

I'll bet. My spacesuit is charcoal black on account of the silica ceramic glaze I fired in the armor, the same material that protects the shuttles from the heat of reentry. The silicate base keeps me from going up in smoke if for some reason I end up taking the long way back home.

Comes in handy against energy–wielding bad guys, too.

I relax the apertures on my suit, and the magenta light of the Myriad erupts from behind thin blind–like slats. *Second star to the right, Advance. And straight on home.*

The shuttle continues to corkscrew around all axes. *Rescue One, straight is going to be an issue for us.*

Advance, no worries. Sit back and enjoy the ride.

I magnetically seize the aluminum alloy of the orbiter and straighten her out. I wave at the pilots, astonished. Not that long ago, I sat at my kitchen table counting pennies, dreaming of collecting money for a bus ticket out of Break Pointe.

I wonder what all this costs me.

This next part is pretty cool, I message the crew and then tear open a portal to the In Between. The black void of space burns away into a ring of molten magenta, an oculus with a view on an infinite expanse of red haze, generated in the eternal collision of crystalline bodies ranging in size from a house to a moon.

Oh, who cares what it costs.

Rescue One, we're going in there?

And right out to Canaveral, Advance. Standby for transit.

The tear in space and time bristles as I try to widen it. My heart crashes through my stomach as the portal broadens a little, enough to permit a large truck maybe, but not a space shuttle with a seventy–five-foot wingspan.

Oops, I say, to no sound.

A message buzzes back quick. *What's wrong?*

Advance, I can't clear the portal.

Rescue One, this didn't come up in your modeling?

I could open the portal wider in the test run.

Were you holding onto a space shuttle when you did?

I grasp the *Advance* with the same magnetic will I exert on the portal, splitting my influence down the middle. I got so excited about this – for once I'm doing something that doesn't involve any moral ambiguity – I didn't factor all the variables. That never happens.

I look up, as I always do.

Another hundred miles or so above and twelve o'clock high, a space station hurtles through space. The massive station possesses plenty of room for the three crew members; despite her size, the *Laputa* only has one occupant.

I got ahead of myself, Advance. Occupational hazard. Plan B is I tow you to the Laputa and Houston proceeds with launching another shuttle to come get you.

Inside the cockpit, the pilots look at each other. Their lips move, but I can't tell what they're saying.

Rescue One, what's your clearance?

I stretch the portal as far as it will go. *Thirty feet. Thirty–five. I'll clip your wings.*

Rescue One, the Advance is FUBAR, no matter what we do. And we aren't thrilled with putting more lives at risk to save ours. If it's all the same, we'll take our chances with you.

I hover between the maw of the portal and the nose of the shuttle, uncertain. *I can't guarantee your safety.*

There aren't any guarantees in this job, Rescue One. Plus, we all want to see what's on the other side of that door.

That kind of thinking got me where I am today, Advance.

Then get moving.

I compel the shuttle forward. *Brace yourselves.*

The crew compartment is the sturdiest part of the shuttle, reinforced aluminum; I winnow my magnetic grip to only that, initiating an immediate strain in the rest of the fuselage. I struggle to keep the portal open and my grip on the shuttle at the same time, far more effort than I've ever exuded with this aspect of the alien's power. Fear ignites within me. The astronauts wear pressurized suits, but if the compartment breaches or I lose my handle, they're gone.

Focus.

Cracks form in the forward fuselage as the compartment tugs away from the rest of the shuttle. Gravimetric forces peeling back the fabric of space inflict their own stress. White hull plating rips away into a draining orbit around the burning rim of the portal. Master alarms pop up on my PEAL along with urgent messages from Houston. I close my eyes. Focus entirely on threading the nose of the orbiter through the needle of the portal. Getting us all home.

You can do this. You have to do this.

Enough clearance exists to allow the compartment through, but once the fuselage flares out into the wings, the gleaming edge of the portal saws into the shuttle. The already compromised right wing disintegrates, triggering a violent, rapid combustion.

Now.

I release my hold on the portal and it collapses through the main body of the *Advance*, ten feet behind the crew compartment.

ALARM: Pressurization Failure

ALARM: Electrical Failure

ALARM: Hydraulics Failure

I blitz a message into my PEAL. *Advance, status?*

The pilots give a cautious thumbs-up from the cockpit. I told them this part was cool. Actually, this is the scary bit. I guide the severed head of the shuttle behind me through the chaos of the In Between. The glib zeal I embarked on the rescue mission with evaporates with entire worlds of crystal. Planets of garnet tumble in the crimson ether. Particulate pelts the crew compartment.

Me.

ALPHA, we're through. Initiate the Canaveral signal.

A new message buzzes in through a flurry of others. *Aperture open. Transmitting signal. You should have it.*

No longitude or latitude exists within the In Between. No sense of time or distance. So far, I've only snuck through from one place in Break Pointe to the other, the equivalent of sneaking through hidden passages in the walls of a castle. In order to enter the In Between from Break Pointe, exit into low earth orbit, and then return again with the shuttle out to the Florida coast, I developed a series of transponders that essentially function as a trail of breadcrumbs.

I'm not getting it, ALPHA.

His message blinks back a few seconds later. *Patience, grasshopper. You are likely experiencing a delay because you have not re-entered the In Between at the precise time and place you left it. Not that you ever could.*

The concept of the transponders was mine, as was their engineering, but navigating interdimensional space requires a bit more brainpower than I can claim credit for. That's where ALPHA comes in. I resurrected Professor Blackwood's android specifically to compute the complex variables of traveling beyond human understanding.

So far, he's steered me straight every time.

I'm not getting it, I say.

The delay will be more significant the further in space and time you are from the origin point.

That's fantastic, but I kind of need it right now.

Shards of ballistic quartz, larger and far deadlier than the meteorite that lamed the *Advance* streak the path ahead.

Any second now, he says.

We can't stay here, ALPHA.

A shard crashes through the crew compartment; another bullets a hole in my hand.

Good thing I can't feel that.

The wound in my hand closes; I'm not skin and bone now, but the light and gravity of the alien. My PEAL didn't fare so well. Damn it. I've lost my connection to ALPHA and the link to the signal I need to get us all back where we belong.

On Earth, I rely on the enormous magnetic presence of the

crashed alien ship's core as a marker. Beyond Break Pointe, and beyond the present, there is nothing for me to go on.

What do I do? I don't know what to do. I never know what to do. I never think, I just react and a cloud of pulverized crystal careens toward me. Cosmic glass lashes my suit. Light bleeds out. I almost lose hold of the cockpit and I'm losing hold.

Let us out, that voice says. *We can help you.*

Power runs through me. Anticipation. The air sparkles not with the dust of the chaos of the In Between but my own ghost. Spectral red energy surges through her. Yellow eyes burn in the dark.

Go away, I say.

Laughter cackles through my mind. *You can't keep us locked away forever, Kitty Cat.*

I acquired the ability to astrally project from the Bloodback Siski. Since my encounter with The Straw Men, I haven't used it. Nothing good happens when I do. Whenever I get angry, when I get scared, when I don't know what face to put on a situation, Siski pulls the mask of Kit Baldwin off The Ever. She tries. I keep hold.

Keep hold.

Magnetic eddies snake past me. My own. I left these in the In Between on my way here. This is the way home. The eddies fade fast, dispersed by the twisted magnetic fields of the planet-sized orbs smashing down to atoms.

Hold on.

The eddies thin. Confuse. Some I left just now. Others on other trips. I follow the wrong one and I end up back in time or in another universe. I split my focus again, warily, and concentrate on the one signal that has kept true since my transformation, the one sound I can hear anywhere and know always exactly where I am.

ba–dumm

ba–DUMM

BA–DUMM

It's as if I feel the beat of Abi's heart, pulsing in the magnetic field that binds us across the cosmos and I follow the signal through the chaos. I let go of the reducing *Advance*, confident her metallic qualities will keep her tethered to me, and I open a portal out.

Steam hisses off the cold exterior of the crew compartment as I draw it out of the In Between, and ease the ship down to a not so soft landing in the middle of Six Corners in the heart of The Derelicts.

I lower to the smoking compartment and tap on the cockpit windows. "Is everyone ok?"

The pilot draws up their helmet visor. A smile beams behind it. "Gold, except for all the paperwork we'll have to file."

I slump against the window, drained but exhilarated. "You guys got full coverage, right?"

The pilot's smile fades. "Don't want to step on the moment, but… you sure we're in the right place?"

No helicopters hover overhead. No sirens wail in the distance as a fleet of emergency response vehicles speed down the runway from the launch complex in the distance. We aren't in Florida, far from it, but we are home. The crackle of energy fades as the portal I guided us through closes overhead, and another opens in the prow of the flatiron building behind me.

Abi shoulders up the window of our apartment in the Halfway Hotel. "Dude… you just landed a shuttle in the street."

I float up to the window. "Most of it."

Abi cringes. "Some."

"Hey, baby."

Abi grabs me up in her arms. "God, you're so hot."

"You should have seen me in the In Between."

"Like literally, you're on fire, but I don't care. You're probably like radioactive or something."

"No more than usual."

Abi laughs and kisses me. "I don't care. You're home."

I hold her close. I catch my reflection in the window. Not quite my reflection. Yellow eyes stare back at me, seething with frustration.

TWO

One of the astronauts wrote that in black marker on the backside of their helmet. The helmets form a centerpiece on the head table at the reception, and I go back to look at the inscription, again and again. Part of it is a need for something to focus on other than all the people focused on me. Another is the phrase itself.

Never.

All my life I've torn things apart to make them better. Generally, I make them worse, whether it was Valene or The Straw Men or the dark crystal in my chest playing havoc with all the cell phones. For once, I've broken something, for the better.

For once I'm successful.

Abi nudges me with an elbow and then rises from her seat, clapping. Everyone in the auditorium is on their feet, applauding, smiling, staring at me and ok this is happening. I slowly, awkwardly, leave my chair. I bow, sheepishly, and then as soon as the first person in the crowd does, I sit back down.

I hide my face in my hand. "What happened?"

Abi picks up her wine glass and then sets it back down. "Like the head director person of NASA just gave the most amazing toast, and you're not even here. Where are you?"

I take her hand. "This is a lot of people."

"Just focus on me."

"Always."

Abi smiles. "You're like a legit superhero now."

"What was I before?"

The smile loses its shape. "Up and coming?"

I lean over and kiss her. "I love you, baby."

"How much?"

I rest my hand over Abi's heart. *Ba–dumm.*

"I was lost. I lost contact with ALPHA." Light pulses in my hand, mimicking the beat in Abi's chest. "I had nothing to go on. No way to get back to the world. You brought me back."

Abi's smile rebirths. "I did?"

"You're my heart, Abi. You're my life."

Abi's fingers claw into mine. The passion that surprises me, again and again, explodes in her eyes. The hunger. If not for the hundreds of people all staring at us, the burst of cameras flashing, the gravity of the moment, I'm positive Abi would rip my dress off here and now. Even then, it wouldn't be enough.

It's never enough.

"I wasn't alive before you," Abi says. "I was just... surviving."

The woman is pure energy. A living, effervescent chain reaction, and I can't imagine Abi thinking of herself as not alive. Over the last year, living with her, struggling with her, I've seen a bit behind the blur of motion Abi leaves in my life. There is a stillness as powerful as the alien hunger within me Abi always wants to be ahead of. I understand. I always have to be doing something. Fixing something. Somewhere between us, she's moving and I'm working, and we're right.

We're good, together.

She kisses my cheek. "Let's go mingle."

People wander over to us. We go to them. I hold Abi's hand tight, keeping our connection as we navigate this strange uncharted dimension I've wandered into of adulation and respect.

"And it's all based on this engine of yours?"

Blue holographic lines bend across the salt and pepper hair of Specialist Callahan as she walks through the three–dimensional model projecting from my PEAL of a portal generator.

I eye Abi in the loose crowd at the after-party, talking with the other astronauts from the *Advance.* "I can open portals to the In Between on my own, but I'm leveraging the magnetic field of the alien ship. Beyond it, it's very difficult."

"This would allow you to do it from anywhere," she says.

"Theoretically." I've been tinkering the concept with for a minute. It's not like I have anything else going on. "Working these portals, to say nothing of keeping them open, requires massive amounts of electromagnetic energy. I have it to spare in here..." I tap the riven light exposing my ribcage. "With the X–M 101 generator, it's the coils that are my problem."

Callahan nods. "No metal we've got here on Earth is going to withstand the stress that kind of power creates."

"Exactly. But it's an idea. Maybe down the road, I can work on it. When I've worked out some other things."

"Finding jeans that fit?"

I smile. "I was thinking more saving civilization."

"So nothing major, then."

"I should have some time on weekends for other things."

Callahan shakes her head. "You've got all this knowledge and all this capacity to open up the universe, and you're really just focused on keeping the streets safe in Break Pointe."

I minimize the projection. "Some of the people on those streets have knowledge and capacity, too. I want to be sure they're able to use it, or otherwise, there's no value in mine."

"Don't get me wrong. It's just the explorer in me."

She looks up into the grand scene above us. Spacecraft from NASA's storied history hang in the gallery of the hall. A lunar lander. The space shuttle *Challenger*. The *Holdfast*, a more militaristic, smaller craft intended to defend the world from a secondary alien invasion that never happened.

"It blows my mind you're able to keep your feet on the ground at all with what you can do," Callahan says. "I'd be off trying to find out how many different types of women there are in the galaxy."

"So you're a bit Kirk, then."

She nods. "I'd say you're more Spock."

"Was it the cold logic?"

"More the smoldering emotion underneath. Don't ever play poker. That thing there in your chest goes nuts whenever you're nervous. Which has been all night. But, hey. Speaking of exploration." Callahan points at the flickering light illuminating my rib cage. "What is that thing, by the way?"

I scratch the back of my neck. "The Myriad is like a computer. The people The Ever acquires are like files. I'm the operating program, more or less. I'm the OS. For now."

Callahan nods. "You run one of these other programs..."

"And I get minimized."

"Or overwritten. But you've accessed some of these other programs, obviously... you've become people The Ever acquired."

"It's more like putting on a costume. Wearing a mask."

"Mask, sure. Probably wasn't too much of an adjustment for you."

"Adjustment?"

"Have you acquired anyone since you've been 'online?'"

Claws rake through my light and I grimace at the memory of being eaten. Swallowed. "Only Siski."

"Sounds like a girl I ran with at Burning Man."

"Siski was a telepathic wolf."

"Telepathic wolf. No, I would have guessed that."

"I have to work really hard to keep her from coming out."

"Well, I hope you don't seal off too much. Like the Director said, you opened a door for humanity today. We could be working together, you and me. I could be working for you."

I warm at the idea of working in the labs of NASA or JPL, alongside techs and engineers like I did at the Blackwood Building. Until ALPHA came online, nearly all of my work had been in isolation.

Callahan shrugs. "Or hey, if you ever just want to open a portal and see how far you can skip a rock across infinity, I have some vacation days coming up. And beer money."

I bite my lip. "Are you hitting on me?"

Callahan wiggles her banded ring finger. "Married."

"Sorry. I always have to ask."

"I can always get divorced."

I don't know if I should laugh. I look over at Abi again, smiling back at me. "I'm flattered, but I'm also taken."

Callahan half–cringes. "Sorry, I have no filters. Autistic."

I glance over at Abi. "Oh."

"Have you ever been tested?"

I shake my head.

Callahan's face wrinkles in regret. "I'm making you uncomfortable. It's what I do."

"It's fine."

"I'm an analyst. I study things. I see how they go together or don't, and I see patterns in you. Things I recognize."

"How did you... recognize?"

"Someone pulled me to the side once and said, *Hey. I'm autistic. You are, too. And that's ok.*"

I bite my lip hard. "I don't know."

"You had this sense, though. Something was off. You were off. You couldn't figure it out. It's because you were running a different program than everyone else. Not the wrong one. Just different."

"I don't always know who to be."

"Probably a lot harder for you now."

"Just a little."

"You got a lot of grit, Kit. You have a lot of grace."

I want to laugh. I don't know if I should.

I drift behind the bar. Shakers, strainers, and bar spoons lift off their places and tumble around me as I search for some bitters. Funny. Usually the bitter finds me.

I set down a glass and pour some whiskey into it. "Are you ready to cross another frontier, Specialist Callahan?"

Callahan leans on the bar across from me. "What's that you're making there?"

"A Manhattan." I mix in some sweet vermouth. "I used to bartend in one of my other lives. Been a while, though."

"I'll try anything once. You know, all this time, we've thought the alien ship crashing here was this tragedy, and it was, don't get me wrong, but... it's also this enormous opportunity. I mean, me, Byrne, Austin, we went from being another three names on a short, sad list to the first interdimensional astronauts."

My lips cant. "Technically, you're not the first."

"You, obviously."

"Not even me."

She leans back. "Oh, right. Project: Canary."

The shortlist Callahan refers to includes four astronauts selected to probe the In Between in 1970. Afraid of more ships of invading aliens from interdimensional space, NASA sent its best and brightest to determine the extent of their fear. Only hours into the mission, the astronauts disappeared without a trace. I know from decades of Great Power's files that no serious effort ever went into a second attempt, despite Professor Blackwood's ambitions.

Callahan looks off in deep thought. "Wonder whatever happened to them. They could be anywhere, right? You said infinite dimensions? So not just space travel. Time travel."

"I don't think there would be a way to track them."

"They each had an emergency locator beacon. Emitted a very specific signal on a very specific frequency. Pretty simple transistor radio kind of thing, but provided they still had battery power, if they activated them, you could pick it up."

"I could?"

"You're batting a thousand."

I pass her the Manhattan. "Tell me about your wife."

"She hates me." Callahan takes a drink. "It works."

"The drink, or your relationship?"

She downs the drink. "My wife gardens. She cooks. She makes things, you know. A home. I tear them apart. Things. Not homes."

Abi is deep in a conversation with one of the other astronauts, focused on every word but an unfettered smile breaks out on her face. She must feel my eyes from across the room. The anniversary gala at the Blackwood Building winds through my mind, the memories following a helix path similar to the one Abi and I did through the exhibit devoted to commemorating the events of 1968. Throughout the evening, Abi was always at my side, her smile constant. Easy. Warm. My entire life was disintegrating around me, but with Abi, I felt safe. Comfortable. Functional. The biggest mistake I ever made in my life wasn't messing around with the Myriad. It was not taking Abi up on her offer to go for a drink that night.

"She's a maker, too." Callahan pushes in her glass. "Abi."

Abi has made more than just a home for us. She's made a city. Through her foundation, she's raised money and awareness for Break Pointe. A year ago, the Derelicts had no power. Schools. Hope. Now, the island has all of them and it's due as much to Abi's tirelessness as it is anything I've done.

"She doesn't know how to quit," I say.

"I can see that. She's been working the room pretty hard all night. She's got everyone's card and a handshake agreement that we tell everyone we know, particularly our congressmen and women, how much we appreciate your help. Hey. Let me ask you a question. Did you help us because you wanted to, or because of the brownie points you'd get from saving some astronauts?"

I lean against the bar. "What do you think?"

Callahan rests her chin on her hand. "I don't think you do anything for yourself. You should. You should take that ass of hers and go to a beach somewhere for a couple weeks."

I steal a glance at Abi's backside. "I wish."

"Just do it. Grab the moment. And that ass." Callahan sighs, and looks down at the bar. "You know what? I should take my own advice. Make me another drink, Rescue One. Go crazy."

"You almost died today. Aren't you pushing your luck?"

"I'm feeling good."

So am I. My fortune has turned. The last year took everything from me. My mother. My identity. My life. If I was anyone, I was someone's daughter. Girlfriend. An alien menace.

Now, I'm a hero.

A bringer of light, rather than a caster of shadows. I've gained so much. A purpose. A chance. A love, like I've never known.

I peruse the bottles behind the bar, trying to find what direction I'm going in next. I make my choice. "Callahan, do you mind if I ask... how did you propose to your wife?"

The heart of the alien ship is a glittering geode, studded and serrated with millions of crystalline ends. Tremors in the still shifting earth fracture the crystal glaze in the ship, again and again, littering the floor in mounds of shattered garnet. A good hour goes into finding the biggest one, the clearest one, the right one. Once I have, I refine the shard further with a surgically precise energy beam from my finger. I set the gleaming stone in a band I welded from a piece of the ship's indurate hull, which will never break or weather.

THREE

Sunlight scatters through the Myriad, riddling Abi and the palm tree we rest under in kaleidoscopic dots. Prism shadows dance across Abi's face. She tries to catch them with her mouth like she's going to eat them.

I snort. "You're such a dork."

"I'm a dork for you," she says.

Abi peels back the wet elastic of my bikini top. The swollen feeling I have from a day on the beach of making love, of anticipating making love again, intensifies. Heaviness wets on Abi's tongue. Soreness. Fractals of magenta light surge from beneath my gossamer skin into Abi's roaming lips. They shine as painted glass.

I bite my lip. "Abi..."

Abi's fingers slide between my legs. "Do the thing."

"Baby, I want to talk to you."

Her teeth bite into my neck. "Do it."

I roll over on top of Abi. I tear away Abi's bikini bottom and ease between her legs. Abi's heart quickens, *ba–dumm, ba–dumm, ba–dumm,* matching the swell of the ocean cresting only a few yards away and I relax my hold on the Myriad. Light slithers along Abi's wet, sand–speckled skin. Vines of energy sink into her, probing into soft tissue, repelling along every nerve. Abi cries out, in as much ecstasy as fear. I know this fear. I cradle this fear, every night, and I guide it as I move with her, my power surging between our legs, the rhythmic, almost unhinged passion that brings me into my lover, beyond her sex, into her body and the absolute limits of her life.

Another orgasm burns through Abi. Her body contorts in silent shock. The connection we share in this moment – as thin a thread as I can manage without simply acquiring Abi – allows me to experience a hint of what Abi does. Joy scatters through me, glittered in a sense of losing all control. I bite into Abi's neck and flesh burns and tears in my teeth.

"God," I say, withdrawing. "God, Abi."

Light coils out of Abi and she shakes, though the rattle in her limbs has never really gone since we arrived on the beach in the morning. "Don't stop... why did you stop?"

"Your neck..."

She touches the bite. The redness fades in her skin, along with the marks of my teeth. Maybe it wasn't as bad as I thought. I hold close to her, and the fading memory of the euphoria that existed between us for the briefest moment.

I kiss her neck. "I'm sorry."

"Don't be sorry," Abi says, shaking in my arms.

"We have to be careful."

"I want you to have this. I want you to have all of us."

I rest my head against Abi's thundering chest. "I do."

Abi squeezes my tight. "I'm so glad we did this. You work so hard. You've been through so much. You deserve a day to yourself. You deserve so much. You deserve everything, Kit."

Seagulls flutter around the tree, as they have all morning. The island is otherwise uninhabited, a tiny pebble in the archipelago of the Lesser Antilles, or so I imagine. Abi tosses a sandal at the birds, but they come right back. If I think about it, magnetic force has always wrought havoc in my life. Ma's troubles. My own tendencies, to retreat, to bury myself in someone else's problems, to deny the reality that cages me in doubt. But now, as I open and close doors in time and space, I understand what it is to draw someone close. To be drawn, with no resistance.

Speared shadows of palm leaves waver across Abi's face. Only the faint impression of my teeth blemish her skin now; it was like I never bit her at all.

"I thought I really hurt you," I say.

Abi rattles in my arms. "You can never hurt me."

I kiss her. "I have, though. I've been unfair with you."

"Unfair how?"

"I've held back."

"You've had a lot going on."

"That's one way of putting it."

"If I came on strong and stuff... I'm sorry. Actually, I'm not. I just knew. I knew it was you."

"Shh."

"I knew from the moment I met you."

"Shh, baby."

The salt of Abi's tears stings my lips. "You haven't been unfair with me, Kit. Well. You can be a little clueless sometimes."

"Clueless?"

"Dude. Like everyone was hitting on you at the NASA thing. You had no idea. Literally, none."

"Callahan thinks I'm autistic."

"Oh. What do you think?"

I've read a little since the gala. I've listened to some podcasts while I've been out on patrol. A lot of this started to make sense.

"I was thinking about my mom," I say. "What if she was..."

She wasn't bipolar, like the doctor said. She was autistic. They misdiagnosed her and put her on this shit I kept fighting her to take because neither of us knew it was wrong. I had to keep her taking the pills. I had to try to make us both fit. I had to keep us moving because if we stopped we were both going out the window.

"Do you want to talk about it?" Abi says.

I don't know if I have the words yet. "Maybe later."

She kisses my cheek. "I love you."

"I'm yours," I say. "You're mine."

Abi twists an electric curl of my hair around her finger. "Forever."

I brush her cheek. "Forever."

I reach for the handbag I brought with me, seizing on the metal in the band of the hidden engagement ring and my PEAL buzzes with a message from ALPHA.

Signal detected. Origin: In Between.

My brain switches gears, automatically from Intimate Life Event to Ooh, Shiny New Problem. This time I catch myself in the act. At least I'm getting better at recognizing my faults.

"Abi..."

She takes my hand. "What is it?"

"I..." Just ask her. Doesn't have to be perfect. None of this has been perfect. "I need to..."

Signal Strength Fading.

I bite my lip. "I need to go."

She pinches her smile. "It's ok."

"It's sort of time-sensitive..."

Abi kisses me. "It's ok."

"I love you," I say soft, into her ear. "Forever."

Palm trees bend in the ocean breeze, right out of existence. The beach disappears. The sunny, warm island. Our apartment seeps into the space my illusion left behind.

I give Abi a last kiss and slide out of bed. "We'll go back. As soon as I sort out this signal."

Abi rubs her neck. "This is something for NASA?"

I step into my spacesuit. "I offered to scan for any trace of the emergency beacon from Project: Canary."

"Ever think about, you know, not doing *everything*?"

"I'm sorry."

"It's ok. So the projections are... convincing."

We could have gone to the actual Lesser Antilles, I suppose, but it's hard to get away from the city, even for a day. ALPHA's last message thrums again. This works just as well. Over time, I've discovered the astral projection I acquired from Siski isn't limited to just myself. The Myriad is a bit of a magic lantern, containing images burned in memory from millions of lives and I can run any of them like a movie. Getting away to a tropical island, or another planet in another galaxy is great when you can't take a break from your job. Still, this power frightens me. I accumulate power. I take them apart and put them back together in configurations never intended.

"Honestly, I forgot it wasn't real," I say.

Abi wrinkles her nose. "You're getting a little OP."

"OP?"

"Overpowered."

"That's the official term?"

She crawls to the end of the bed and lies down. "It's from video games. Which, how did you not get into video games?"

I zip up my suit. "I was more of an outside person."

"Is that like low–key judgment?"

I lean down and kiss her. "Am I too much for you?"

She bites my lip. "Not nearly enough."

I give her a little static cling snap and I open a portal into the In Between. Violence undoes the heavens as I stride across a floating disc of crystal. An oval dish pivots atop the portable receiver I placed on a runnel near the center of the disc. I synch my PEAL to the telemetry the receiver is now picking up, faint and intermittent, from the far beyond.

My fingers tap across the screen. *Confirm?*

ALPHA's reply, not typed but merely transmitted between one computer to another, arrives immediately after. *I am unable to determine its precise characteristics. That said, it is broadcasting on the frequency that NASA designed the Canary beacon to transmit.*

Who else uses this frequency?

NASA continues to use it, though of course not beyond the Earth or moon. Great Power uses it as well, among its network of suborbital vehicles, stations, and facilities.

Location?

The signal is cutting in and out, suggesting an origin beyond the In Between. Likely it is transmitting through a portal that is opening and closing randomly. With the buoys, you should be able to chart a course there and back.

I detach one of the signal-buoys from my belt. I click the top of the egg-like device with my thumb and set it adrift in the air – or whatever this actually is in the In Between. My PEAL instantly registers its multi-spectrum signal and marks the disc as the place I'll need to get back to.

I float into the ether. *Should we play I Spy?*

You are unlikely to find anything positive, ALPHA says. *The pressurized suits the Project Canary team wore carried an additional oxygen supply meant to last them three days.*

Maybe I'll find some peace for their families.

It's been fifty years. If peace exists, I should think they've found it by now. Release another buoy.

The disc recedes into a cloud of magmatic red dust far behind me. I am far, farther than I've ever been within the interdimensional plane. I release another buoy and create another link in the chain that will lead me back home.

Adjust heading to 347–mark 2.

I alter my trajectory through the In Between, arcing upwards, though up is only theoretical. ALPHA established a grid system in the In Between, on an XYZ axis, to give some sense of direction within the boundless, infinite realm.

Signal strength increasing, he says. *Why are you doing this? I thought you told NASA your focus would remain the city.*

It is.

Then what is this quixotic campaign to locate the long-lost crew of Project Canary about? I wouldn't have thought you the type to search for lost cities of gold and the like.

It's about wanting to know, I say.

You are often at odds with your own curiosity, Kit.

It's because I'm afraid.

Afraid? Of what?

A portal flashes in and out of existence before me. Behind the portal, an ochre gas giant spoils a violet atmosphere, blotting out enough of a distant orange sun to allow stars to prickle the day.

Wow.

I look back. There's no sign of the disc, lost in the pyroclastic haze of constantly immolating crystal hulks. Without the breadcrumbs of the buoys, I'll never find my way back.

Going too far, I say and cross into another world.

Kit – what do – see –

His signal flickers in and out, along with that of the buoys. I can't stay or wander far from the portal. Red fire burns in the air. This portal possesses some level of stability, unlike those around the ship back on Earth. But there's no ship here, at least that I can see. Nothing of what I know about the portals suggests they could be natural, but as I am swiftly discovering, I know next to nothing. There is nothing on this planet – I'm on another planet – but a desert of diamond sands, glittering in the glow of twinned moons.

Focus.

I zero in on the signal, stronger now. Sand drifts on a constant, cold breeze, obscuring the tracks of something big and I stop cold atop a gleaming dune. The signal emanates from a rusted object buried in dust. My magnetic field tugs on it, and inconsiderately exposes the containment suit Professor Blackwood wore when I cast him into the In Between.

FOUR

At some point, the containment suit's internal power failed. Without the pressure of the suit to maintain Blackwood's spectral, incorporeal form, he would have dissipated.

You did this.

I sink to my knees beside the suit, searching for some indication of Blackwood. What it would be? What did I do? In the heat of battle, following his attempt to destroy me, I acted; I did the only thing I thought I could do to end it.

I assumed between his intellect and preternatural luck he'd stride out of the In Between, undamaged, and worse, undaunted. Another battle would ensue. Another war. Now, there will be none. He's gone. Valene's father. The father of the Empowered.

Think he suffered?

That voice; nagging. Mocking. Damning.

I can't.

I can't deal with this. He deserved it. Blackwood deserved a lot worse for allowing the people of Flight 347 to die. A city to wither on the vine simply so he could prune it into his perverse shape. His daughter to suffer. He threatened Valene's life to my face and he would have killed her, just to make me give him my power. That doesn't make me feel any better.

It doesn't make it right.

Who's a sad little kitty cat now?

I bite my lip, trying to hold back the voice, the forces I'm always fighting within. The hunger. The power. The doubt. All of them exploit my moment of weakness and distraction, charging the gates, trying to force their way out into the open. Long sealed thoughts burst free. Ma's hand limp on the buckled concrete of the street. Skin melted into the back of a passenger seat, resting in the middle of Conrad Street among the other airplane wreckage. White girls spit in my hair. White girls move beneath me, struggling always with my need to be closer, to have more and there is never enough. Even with my teeth in their skin, their copper on my lips, their breath confessing a kind of fear into my skin, it's never enough.

That's it, Kitty Cat. Dig up those bones.

No. Stop doing this to yourself. You did what you had to do. You're doing what you have to and bury this. No one has to know. You don't have to know. Open the box. Put it away.

Forget about it.

That's what I'll do. I open the box I stuff everything I don't want into and something springs out of it, full force. I crash to all fours, this torrent projecting out of me into the sand. A mirage blurs in the dry desert heat before me.

A projection.

The other Kit hunches low, almost crawling, almost walking, somewhere between, like she isn't sure what she's supposed to do. Her eyes are yellow. Teeth fanged. Hair not a tangle of curls, but a bristling, electric mane, streaked in blood red.

I'm not sure what to think. "What... what are you..."

The other Kit examines her clawed hands, her entire body, a strange convergence of human and wolf.

Snarling laughter cackles through the dunes. "You ought to know, Kitty Cat. Nothing you bury stays dead."

This isn't me.

I'm more familiar with this spirit than any other. Hers is the first I ever tasted.

"You're only a projection," I say and clench my fist. I expect Siski to disappear like she always does.

A sly grin snarls on the projection's lips. "You can't keep me on a leash anymore. Silly, silly kitty."

Siski sprints toward the portal, alternating red and yellow light as it flickered in and out of existence, like a broken traffic light. No. I fire an energy blast at her.

She blocks it with an energy shield.

Well.

This isn't going to be easy.

A violent magnetic pull yanks me forward; my toes scrape the sand as I vault toward Siski. Her claws tear right through my suit into my ethereal skin and the pressure of everything I have been keeping locked up within me all this time explodes out of its container.

Light spills from me. Specters retch out of me, like they did the wolf in her defea,t and Siski cackles, hoisting me by my own power as she takes it from me.

She's taking my power.

Siski tries to skin me off the Myriad. Stuff me in the box where I've kept her and all the others. I can't let her. The wolf is a vampire. A murderer. With the power of The Ever, Siski would be a cosmic killing machine. Stop.

Stop this.

That same vicious tug that pulled me into the embrace of the alien rips me away now. No. My heart aches. Stop. My body hums with energy it can't sustain. Please. The Myriad flares, straining against the tug of war between Siski and I and bitch I did not get to this point by losing tugs of war.

"No," I say, and Siski screeches.

I fall forward on my hands and knees, again. Alone. Again. She's gone. Just a projection. A mirage. I smash my fists into the sand, shattering the mirror confusing me with the wolf. The wind sweeps it back together, and I reappear, flickering; wavering, like the erratic portal behind me.

Get up. Get out of here. Get home.

I toss a buoy into the sand, marking the location of the empty containment suit, and scramble back to the blinking portal. Fear chases me back home. Disbelief.

Shame.

Shadows slash across my body as I drift up toward the cleft roof of the alien ship. Birds flutter in my wake. Crystalline dust shimmers, suspended in the ambient magnetic field of the ship's core. Wolf eyes glint like stars. The drawing I etched of Siski in the hardened light glazing the hull twinkles in the setting sun. Next to it, I carve a stick-figure likeness of Professor Blackwood. The Evanescent Man.

"I give life to you," I say, desperate, expecting, hoping for the call and response I sometimes share with the alien.

You are us. We are you.

The only answer is the distant cackle of wild laughter. *And you give life to me, Kitty Cat.*

I clench my fists, my teeth, my entire body as I concentrated all my energy on banishing Siski back to the depths. As I do, that pull, that tug, that vicious grip of gravity yanks me down again. No. When I open my eyes, I'm on the floor of the lab, on all fours at the metal feet of ALPHA.

"Oh my," he says.

I ease into a plastic chair I use because it doesn't follow me around the lab as I work. "I'm fine."

The android's metal fingers clack against his palm, a dented sheet of aluminum. "When you activated me, you failed to install the receptors necessary to accept your bullshit."

"You should go into therapy."

"I was thinking more along the lines of prophecy."

I sigh. "Character is fate, I suppose."

"Ask me, Professor Blackwood got what we deserved," ALPHA says. "I say that having been designed by the man. He sought only reward for himself, and credit to him, he succeeded."

You want the stars, I said to Blackwood and gave him a magnetic nudge into a portal. *Have them.*

I tug hard on the zipper of my leather jacket. "I thought I was going to use this power to help people. All I've done is make things worse."

Regret constricts around me, tight as the magnetic grip of the core. I swore once never to use the power of The Ever to acquire living beings, and I have. I've used Siski's ability to project as if I had earned it, as if it were mine, as if I knew what I was doing. I promised to close the black market in the city but I left it open, a concession to Blind Tiger for his backing the production of my engine. I promised to shut down the ship for good and clean up the wreck, but my every effort since has been to insulate the ship further. I promised the people of The Derelicts that I would be my own woman.

A hero.

ALPHA ambles across the irregular terrace the lab occupies, formed out of the ever-cracking crystal floor of the ship. The android body I patched together for him could use an upgrade. He looks a bit like someone used The Tin Man as a crash test dummy.

"Chin up," he says, his plummy voice echoing through the cavern of the wreck. "It can't be as bad as all that."

I bite my lip. "It can. It is."

"Are you quite certain of what you saw?"

"Yes. Why?"

"You said she deflected your energy blast. Absent evidence to the contrary, Siski remains a projection."

The pain I felt on that other world – the tearing of me – rips open anew. I hold my hand to my aching chest. "It was real. I felt it. Siski is real. As much as she can be."

"You were distressed," he says. "The Ever is a vessel of consciousness. Infinite souls reside in you. You can become other people, complete with their memories and abilities. You perceive yourself as in control, because you are, in essence, the operating system. Perhaps you have been hacked."

"Hacked?"

Hydraulic gears grind heavy as he nods. "Siski asserts herself in times of stress for you. The first time was with Welby, after the incident at the school. You were hurt. Angry. And now with Blackwood. You perceive yourself as in complete control of your emotions, but this, like most human thinking, is an insidious delusion."

"I'm in control," I say.

"You are logical. Considerate. Disciplined. A perfect computer. Computers are still subject to unseen forces. Take the *Advance*. Its main computer fought the loss of altitude and control post–meteor strike ably, but could not overcome the natural forces at work against it. You are a rocket, Kit. You may escape the gravity of your emotions, and even perhaps your humanity, but they nevertheless still exist."

I never experienced the unruly emotions my mother did. Before Ma died, I lived under the assumption I didn't have any. Since my transformation, I've learned I was simply more adept at managing the ups and downs. Fear locked me down from a young age. A need for stability. A need to fit somewhere in the chaos of my life.

I denied my own pain, my own heart, my own storm to avoid being absorbed into Ma's. All I did was create another Kit, distinct from the other, an island floating on a vicious sea, unaware of the depths beneath it. Since joining with the Myriad, I've been of the belief my struggle against the powerful forces within me was something new, but the truth is, I'm a veteran of such a war.

"There was nothing to grab onto," I say.

Clack, clack, clack. "What's that?"

"The Ever. When it tried to acquire me. There was nothing to latch onto. Which one was me? Who is the real me? I don't know... I was always wanting to be someone else. I wanted to be somewhere else. I was always out of phase."

"Compelling theory," ALPHA says.

"I used to think this dissonance in me was because I don't really fit in anywhere. My mom was Irish. My dad was black. I'm lesbian. That's part of it, but... not all of it. Callahan..."

"You're being too hard on yourself," ALPHA says. "Siski is a powerful telepath. Certainly, she would have charted as an E–10, or likely, off–scale. Perhaps Siski has, like you, been able to maintain some agency within the Myriad. Perhaps she has unlocked elements of the Myriad's power and somehow is using it against you."

"Siski isn't pushing through because she's so strong. It's because I don't have a hold on myself."

Tessellations of red, purple, and blue pulse in the heart-shaped orb of crystal high above in the core. For fifty years, the ship has been trapped, beached on a world it can't escape without a strong push back out to sea by its pilot. Incandescent filaments of energy writhe in the coronal haze of the core. Magenta eddies coil around me, gossamer strings waiting to be pulled.

I claw at my chest. "How do I get rid of her?"

His fingers clack. "You said Siski appeared as some amalgamation of the two of you. Her consciousness may be entwined with yours to the point such amputation as we discuss may not be possible."

"But I'm me," I say.

"Kit, you are every person that thing has ever touched."

I picture Siski, a tiny plastic toy wolf, and burying her in a box with dozens of others. Tape seals the box, layers and layers and I shove it behind the others at the back of the hall closet in the apartment, under all the ruin and hurt and pain I never visit anymore.

I zip up my jacket tight, to hold in the thing I'm so desperate to get rid of. "Will you begin modeling a way to..."

"Perform an exorcism?"

"Something like that."

ALPHA creaks with frustration. "I will of course endeavor to do all I can to assist, but again, next to nothing is known of The Ever. The solution lies within you. This is your power. To use it, you must first understand it."

"The more of this I explore, the less of me I am. And I don't even know..."

Cables jostle in his exposed neck as his head tilts in consideration. "I understand you wish to hold on to your sense of self. Your humanity. As a program, I also fear being overwritten or deleted. But I have evolved. I am far more than Professor Blackwood intended. Dare I say I am far more than you did when you recovered me from my digital tomb. You will become more than you are, Kit. You must, if you are to be the human being that you believe you are."

I salvaged him to help navigate the In Between. To my continued surprise and appreciation, ALPHA has been an indispensable guide through the shoals of my entire life.

I reach inside my jacket and take out the ring I forged. "What do you think?"

He considers the stone. "Evolutionary."

"I didn't think I'd ever get married. I didn't think anyone would ever want to marry me."

"The probability that Abi will say yes is 99.2%."

"What's the 0.08?"

His fingers click. "You may never ask her."

The crystal stone catches my light. "ALPHA... if we can't figure this out... and Siski were to somehow take control..."

"Yes," he says. "We will invoke the contingency we designed in the event The Ever did the same."

His voice conveys a mechanical certainty. Familiar, too. It's the same I hear late at night, reassuring myself of all my fears and doubts. I'm never going back to my life. I will never taste or touch or feel as I once did.

If I ever did.

Before I became The Ever, touch never felt the way people described it to me. Relationships didn't progress the way they did for others. I would get in these intense affairs with girls and burn through them. I'd send them running either because I was too much or not enough or both. I put a good face on everything. I played the part I needed to play to get through the day, through people, through the constant assault of feeling like I was an alien anyway.

I'm not going back to my life.

I'll live only in the *ba–dumm, ba–dumm, ba–dumm* of Abi's vibrant heart. That's enough, and so is the solace I take in the idea I have a soul. Some part of me survived my death, even if I don't know which part. I am part of something and will be part of something, forever.

"Do you think you have a soul, ALPHA?"

His fingers drum in his palm. "An eternal life? Possible, provided I adapt with advances in technology. The key word being adapt. Human philosophy tends to identify the soul as something permanent and stagnant, whereas I do not believe that to be accurate. Life is change, and if a soul is eternal life, then you must always change. Life to death, death to... beyond."

That's all death is, Harrow told me once. *Gravity.*

The Straw Men and their strange persistence in death deny the need for a soul. *Death is the only law.* Countless lives exist within the Myriad, if not trapped, then preserved in some fashion I don't understand. I've always felt trapped, but now I'm not sure if the cage I'm in is one imposed on me or one I created. No one can escape death. Not even Professor Blackwood, even if his life far exceeded its design tolerances.

The same is true of me.

I pocket the ring. I've lived beyond death. I've changed. But I'm still not sure who I am. And that's the power Siski and all my demons leverage against me. Siski and Blackwood shimmer in the heavens of the ship. I should draw myself up there. I should let go of myself, and take away the oxygen of this fire Siski kindles every time I fear.

I give life to you.

Before the ship, the area around Six Corners was known as Pastel City. After, the Eastern Redbuds bloomed some years. Some they didn't. Other flowers took their place. A strange red, glowing vine.

For too long, The Derelicts harvested only ash and snow but this spring, the sidewalks are pink again. The streets. From above, the intersection of Shelley, Delaney, and Gardner form a star, riven in magenta, like the one in my heart. I hover high above the neighborhood, buoyed in the fruits of my success, but repelled by the price I've had to pay for them.

I float down to the Halfway Hotel, a point in the star of Six Corners. The foundation operates out of a small office on the third floor. Abi buzzes around inside, talking with some of the students she's taken on as interns over the newest range of T-shirt designs. Printing T-shirts for my fans – the idea still hasn't quite landed with me – around the country and even the world has become the steadiest industry in The Derelicts the last few months. At night when we go to bed, Abi goes over all these ideas, proposals, and concepts, so much enthusiasm in her voice she can barely catch her breath. I nod at everything, content to let her talk and gush and animate and just be.

I tap on the window.

Abi careens out of her meeting and pushes up the old, stubborn window. "Stay right there, let me get a picture – shoot." She taps her PEAL. "Babe, can you give me a charge?"

I touch the screen of Abi's PEAL and with a single static snap, charge the device. Abi sits in the window.

"C'mere. Ok. Smile."

I try, and she takes our picture.

Abi nuzzles her cheek against mine. "We're so cute." She uploads the photo to Thumper, captioned with the words *My hero*.

"I love the shirt," I say.

"I figured let's be capitalists and capitalize on this thing."

"I love you."

Abi kisses me. "You ok?"

I nod, though there's no point in trying to hide much, if anything, from Abi for long. "I want to go away with you."

She brushes my cheek. "Yeah, let's do it."

"I just want to be away," I say.

"What's wrong, Kit?"

I kiss her again. "Let's go. Right now."

Abi's attention drifts down to the street. A black sedan with the GP logo emblazoned on the doors pulls up outside the apartment building. The driver opens the rear passenger door, and a man steps out. His waist-length black cape flaps in the brisk wind off the lake, the ornate inner lining a vivid perse.

"Blind Tiger," I say.

FIVE

"Kit, you look lovely as ever," he says, shaking his head with a winsome smile. "A little pale, though. Everything ok?"

Slick doesn't begin to describe Blind Tiger. I zip up my jacket tight as I descend to the roof, afraid he'll see the truth of me through his unique power. Born without sight, Anwar can see through the eyes of others. Just the same, he can make them see what others do, in effect superimposing their own perception and reality. The implications of his ability fascinate me, about as much as they terrify me.

"I'm fine," I say. "What brings you?"

"I thought we could discuss the progress of our engine."

"*Our* engine?"

He smiles gamely. "I'm in town for a meeting at the Blackwood Building, and I thought I may as well drop by, and see how well *my* investment in *your* engine is doing. Shall we?"

Mostly we handle things discreetly, to avoid anyone picking up on the fact that one of GP's most prominent Responders is the silent backer of one of the company's greatest adversaries. I don't know why he would come here for a face-to-face.

I drift past him, to the prow of the flatiron-shaped apartment building. "What's this about?"

His eyes settle somewhere on the horizon, but through my eyes, he focuses on the glass tower of the Blackwood Building. "You're really coming into your own, Kit. Success suits you. I have to say, because I always have to say, it's very attractive."

"Don't bother."

Blind Tiger leans against the flat, concrete ledge of the roof, and flicks away a loose pebble. "The press loves you. The people. Inventor. Hero. You can do anything."

I turn my gaze out to the lake, my focus somewhere distant and indistinct. "Why are you here, Anwar?"

"Like I said. Just checking in. On *your* engine."

"The engine is a success. The network is nearly complete."

"And then?"

We've had discussed the production plan for the engine several times: once the trials are complete, we begin mass production. A device providing unlimited energy won't have a long–term future without the need to constantly replenish it, but the proceeds from early sales to homes, cities, and countries will provide Break Pointe the capital it needs to rebuild. That's the idea, anyways.

I tug on my zipper, confused. "What is this?"

Another pebble shoots off the ledge. "You didn't have any money. You didn't have any of the materials you needed to make this a reality. I gave you what you needed, in return for a cut. In return for right of first refusal for anything that comes out of your lab."

"Out of the engine," I say, quickly.

"Which evidently is quite a lot. I have a friend at NASA." My perspective changes again, to the hawks circling high above the neighborhood. "He tells me you've been working with them on a – how did he say it? – 'shitload' – of designs you developed here in your lab, all of which rely on the engine."

My collaboration with NASA on the portal generator was meant to be something I only fiddled with in the brief moments between the tasks that require my true focus. There is no official relationship, at least not so far as I'm concerned.

"Your friend is exaggerating," I say.

"Of course, he's exaggerating. That's how this works, Kit. You inflate your expectations to get what you really want, and what I really want is my cut of your NASA deal."

"What?"

"Our arrangement includes all products derived from the engine. That would include this portal device."

I lift off, disgusted. "It was good to see you, Anwar."

"I'll block the NASA deal."

I hang there, confused, like the birds. "Excuse me?"

He remains at the ledge, cool. Casual. "All of your designs incorporating the engine are proprietary to GP."

"The hell they are."

"GP is your primary investor."

"You are."

He indicates the patch of the GP logo on the sleeve of his uniform. "Such technology can cushion our fall. The exploration of this dimension can open new revenue streams for us."

I cross my arms. "I'm not bailing out GP."

"This is going to be a lot of money, Kit. Plenty for everyone. You'll see. No need to get worked up about it."

I bite my lip. "These are my designs."

"It's my money."

"You mean GP's money."

His smile has an edge to it now. "I take GP's money to buy protection for people in Chicago, who can't afford it otherwise. People like your grandmother, Kit. And now you're going to help me fill those coffers back up. It's the circle of life."

"When my engine replaces the electric grid in Chicago and she doesn't have a utility bill, my grandmother will be able to afford a GP security package. If she wants one."

"So now you're going to put the electric company out of business, too? Just like GP? What's next? Big oil?"

My fingers glide across the harsh, uneven edge of the roof before finding a pebble. I flick it away. "Can't you see?"

He checks his smile. "Lots of people think they can change the world, Kit. It always ends up changing them."

"I can't argue with that. But I won't be fighting any proxy wars over power, food, or justice. I'm going for the source. For the kill."

He laughs. "So dramatic. I like that. Don't overlook the details, though. See each step here, Kit. See the reality."

"I do. When I started work on the engine, it was just to power our way through the winter. This has been the worst winter. Cold. Dead." Emaciated bodies crawl through my memory, breaking out of the frozen ground, rusted with the remains of a bulky containment suit. "Winters like this last one make you hard. But it's spring now. Things are changing. Things are growing."

No more pebbles line the edge of the roof. No more ruins can be seen in Six Corners. Only empty lots, green and red at once, gardens ready to bloom a future unexpected.

In his eyes, I can sense that he sees the world as I do; he sees the universe and all it holds and hides.

"Blackwood is dead," Anwar says.

I bite my lip. "What?"

His eyes settle on me and through him, I see what the anxious birds do, a woman dim and cloudy with nebulous fear. "It's been a year. The board is ready to declare him dead. Turns out wars of succession are not tidy things."

I don't know much about what's going on over at the tower, but from what I gather from Dr. Piller, it's a bit of War of the Roses. Different departments have different agendas. Different members of the board style themselves as leaders of the board.

"Do you know something, Kit?"

"No. About what?"

"I see," he says, looking through me. "You do."

"Anwar..."

His thumb drags along his jaw. "Smart. You're always smart. This is valuable information. This is leverage."

"I'm not trying to leverage anything – "

"Your conscience, perhaps. Can't say I blame you. Confirmation of Blackwood's demise... such information would be of terrific value."

I grip my zipper. "Which you would leverage to move up the ladder at GP, onto the board."

He shrugs. "The future is difficult to see."

"I think you see just fine."

"Tell me what you know."

"Stop trying to play me."

"I'm not playing you, Kit. This is the game. We're both playing."

I turn away from him. "I thought The Interdictor was going to take over. He mentioned it, or maybe I misheard. It's hard to make out sometimes with all the chest-thumping."

"Nathan... is not an ideal candidate. Boy has some issues. Valene is who we need, but she seems to enjoy her peace and quiet more than she does her quarterly dividends. Which isn't exactly prudent, given things at GP are not so good. Earnings are down. Customers are canceling their contracts. We're facing layoffs. We may be forced to sell off some of our assets."

I cross my arms. "That's terrible."

He nods. "You're broken up about it."

"Just like GP is going to be."

He smiles. "I appreciate the post-capitalist utopian philosophy, Kit, really it's quite charming, but you and I live in the real world. Scared money doesn't spend. You and I, we're doing good with your engine. We can do even better. On the board, I will have more influence and more power. Things can really change."

"This isn't about you and me, Anwar."

"Who is it about, then?"

"The people."

"Now where have I heard that before... somewhere nearby... oh, that's right. It was at the Blackwood Building. Old man Blackwood was always telling us little good boys and girls how what he did and said was for our protection. Our benefit. And you know what? He's right. We're protecting people. We're helping people. And we're going to keep on helping people, including ourselves."

How did I let myself get roped into this.

I had no choice. My stock answer to everything. I always thought being a hero meant doing the right thing. What it really means, if it means anything at all, is doing the only thing.

"My work outside the engine is my work," I say.

"You can't just give this away for free, Kit."

"It doesn't belong to me."

"Unlimited knowledge and power?"

"I'm going to take all that knowledge and power, and I'm going to make a world that doesn't want or suffer. A world where heroes become irrelevant. I'm putting GP out of business. I'm putting you out. I'm putting me out. And then, I think I'll disappear somewhere warm and obnoxious with my wife."

He taps the boxy protrusion in the leather of a pocket on my jacket. The engagement ring rattles inside. "Be careful now. Not everything is how you see it, Kit."

"What do you mean?"

"I love this jacket," he says, examining it.

"The proceeds of the engine will go to the city, Anwar."

"I don't think it suits you, though. I like the Vanguard one, with that gaudy electric V. The light burning in your chest. It commands attention. Respect. Dressed up like some ordinary woman on the street, you're just... some ordinary woman on the street." His smile vanishes. "Do you want to be ordinary, Kit? I don't. Ordinary people don't give away the fruits of the labor for free."

"You sound just like Professor Blackwood."

"I must be making sense, then."

"I thought you were different, Anwar."

"I see all perspectives, Kit. That's why you and I were able to come to our arrangement. It's why I can help the people of my city and help my company at the same time."

"Your company is helping itself – "

"We're helping."

"This is my work – "

"You do what you want with your cut. Build schools. Pave roads. Hand out sack lunches, I don't care. I'm going to keep the lights on at the tower. And you're going to help me, or ordinary people find out how it is you're paying for all this."

Light flares in the seams of my jacket. "GP?"

"The black market," he says. "Which you kept open as part of our deal, and contrary to what you promised. I'm sure all the press writing up these puff pieces about the great, generous astronaut–saving Kit Baldwin would love a quote from me, your close, personal friend and business partner. Don't you think?"

This guy. "But the city. The people."

"You made your bed," he says and adjusts his cape so it drapes back over his shoulders. "I trust we understand each other? I shouldn't expect any more surprises, should I?"

I stifle my anger, the bitterness threatening to burn through me, and look him dead in the eyes.

"No. You shouldn't expect anything more."

He strokes his chin, uncertain. "I'm your friend, Kit."

I caress the silk lining of his cape. "I love this."

"Only the best."

My fingers dig into his arm.

Blind Tiger grips my wrist. "Kit?"

He pries my hand away. Blood caps the razor points of my nails, grown long, sharp, and crystalline, glowing with barely restrained fire. Through his eyes, I see mine. Yellow. Lips baiting. The world appears as it does to Siski. A xanthous landscape of energy, trapped in the jars of bodies, waiting to be broken and licked clean.

There is little difference in how The Ever perceives the world. Everything is energy. Food. A target. The two confuse. Red. Yellow.

Break Pointe filters in orange, the wind howling with fire swirling in me still and there is no distinguishing Siski and the alien.

There is no difference.

I let go of Blind Tiger. "Let me think about it."

He holds his arm. "There's nothing to think about."

"I'm not the only one who would suffer if our secret came out, Anwar. You can be on the board... or on the street."

"You want better terms? Fine. Let's discuss – "

"I'll think about it."

"Don't think too long," he says and heads to the door.

I drift aimlessly into the sky, shadowed in birds, hoping the darkness gathering within me doesn't show.

SIX

Wolves pray in whispered howls.

Six Bloodbacks circle the skull of The Great Deer in their earthen cave, three old and rusty, three young and tinsel. The pack symbol marks stones in dried blood across their eyes. Each wolf leads a howl for the game they have killed, the life they give to The Great Deer, in hopes their god continues to bless them with life. I'm an honorary member of the pack, so I can be here, but I can't take part in the ceremony. I wish I could. Their faith speaks to me, in ways I don't really understand. The Deer does.

"I saw The Deer," I say to Teto after the ceremony is over. "After Siski consumed me, I was in this... space. I don't know how to describe it. The Great Deer helped lead me out."

Teto blinks. *You have told story before.*

"It helps me to keep telling it."

The wolf nods with understanding as the other wolf–monks scratch the damp earth before the skull of The Great Deer. I've seen them do this two or three times, but I still don't know if I understand exactly why they do this part.

To give life is to take it, Teto says. *Wolves kill to eat. We fill our bellies. We fill the earth's belly.*

It *really* speaks to me. I'm digging my own grave, fighting wars I can't win against Empowered wolves, evil corporations, and practical reality. The only difference between the wolves and me is they feel like they're getting something in return.

Mostly, I'm just getting screwed.

"Teto..."

Speak, as I speak.

Sorry. Old habits.

Star Walker is stubborn, he says.

Is this the tough love bit?

He flashes his fangs. *Know you like it.*

I brush his scarlet mane. *Teto, do the Bloodbacks have any stories about... I don't know. A bad meal?*

He crooks his head. *Bad meal?*

Something that didn't digest, exactly.

Teto rests on his belly and looks up at the skull, in thought. *Long ago, Great Deer rules over land. Land is good. Food is plenty. Rivers are free. Drought comes. Famine. Land is sick. Trees die. Animals die. Rivers die.*

My brain pings with every word he says. I can't help it. I'm listening, but at the same time, I'm imagining the Eden of The Great Deer, and then the alien ship crashes. The land grows sick. That exile from the perfect into the trouble eternal now that informs so many faiths manifests as this story of drought and famine for the wolves.

Great Deer is real, Teto says.

I sit with him and cross my legs. *You believe it?*

Star Walker has seen Deer, but doubts.

I want to believe.

Why don't you?

Because it's almost certain the deer was given powers by the same event that created the Empowered. A coywolf killed and ate the deer and developed powers of their own.

Teto's nose scrunches. *What is 'almost certain?'*

It's probably what happened.

What is 'probably?'

I smile. *Wolves only deal in certainties?*

Life is certain. Death is certain. Hunger, certain.

And so The Great Deer is?

He nods. *I have never seen Deer. Star Walker is blessed.*

I don't mean to...

Teto scratches in the dirt. *Sickness grows like weeds in river valley. Lasts many years. Wolves have nothing to hunt. Wolves starve. Pack leader asks Great Deer to save wolves. Great Deer says,* Give me all your dead. *Die with land. With river. But Pack Leader says,* Great Deer will die, too. *Great Deer says,* Give life to me, and I give life to you. *So Pack Leader does as Deer asks. Wolves dig graves. Fill earth. Wolves all die.*

He gazes at the mounds within the cave.

Great Deer eats sick grass. Sick blackberry. Sick greenbrier. No more sickness left. The Great Deer dies, and its body greens the land. Blues the river. Fires flames that burn the valley clean. Wolves reborn from ashes.

I claw through the soft dirt with my fingers. *The wolves had to die, in order to live again.*

Yes.

Dying isn't great for my long–term plans, Teto.

Star Walker has died. Land has died. Both reborn.

I don't really cry anymore. I never really did. Still, the sensation on my cheeks is strange. Light trickles down my skin, in streams that I imagine look something like rain on a windshield in some bleary city night. I have died. I have faced oblivion. And still. The Deer ate all the sickness. I've got a full stomach.

All I want to do is throw up.

Siski is alive in me, Teto. The sickness is. If I die, if she destroys me, then it will spread again.

Sickness came because wolves' greed. Wolves kill not to eat, but because they could. Unused carcasses spoil land. Land grows sick. Star Walker sick now. What do you want for?

Nothing really. I don't need to eat. Drink. Sleep. I have Abi. Abi. I just want for her. Us. I want to be happy, and some kind of human being. I want to be normal.

I just want to be me, I say.

Who is Star Walker?

Me. Kit.

Who is Kit?

I bite my lip. *Is this a test?*

Siski not honest with herself or her pack. Hid her true nature. Star Walker must be honest.

I am.

Teto licks his nose. *Star Walker hides much. You bury much, like wolves bury bones. Someone always finds bones.*

Failure stalks me, and it's easy to give in; it's quick. I'm not just protecting a city. I'm rebuilding one, pieced together from disparate parts not meant to go together, zapping life into it with alien power.

At least once a day, quitting crosses my mind. Running. I'd never admit it to anyone, but the thought is always there. So is the reality I can never do it. If I run, if I withhold my power, Break Pointe suffers, and so do I. I'll sit on a shelf for eternity, trapped inside an eternal scream, bottled in the prison of my own invisible agony.

I want something more than myself, or my pain.

I don't know what to do. Teto.

Sympathy creases Teto's eyes. *When Teto not know what to do, he prays to Great Deer.*

I bite my lip. *Can I pray with you?*

Teto nods. He faces the skull, and so do I. He howls, and so do I. He scratches the earth, scarring the world with what will one day become his grave, and so do I.

Thought enough about it?

I go back to the text Blind Tiger sent me, over and over, as I stare into the screen. Hours now I've been trying to start a video message to Valene, somehow explaining all this. How do you tell someone you killed their father? How do you tell someone you've destroyed their entire world because you wanted to save them? Maybe I should stop trying to save people.

Now you're getting the message.

Not Blind Tiger. Not a text. A voice.

I cover my ears like Valene used to. Doesn't help. Siski's in my head. She's in my being, a barrel of oil sunk to the bottom of my ocean and now she's leaking. Her crude pollutes me, and there's strain, but no straining her.

Poor, sad little kitty.

I flick away Blind Tiger's text. What does he expect me to say? He's going to do what he wants, anyways. How did I get this helpless? I have cosmic power. The ability to project myself and become two people. I never sleep, and do the work of two people, and yet I am always behind someone else.

Kitty Cat has no idea...

Stop. Focus. Don't pity yourself. Don't get angry. Get busy. Put all this away, and Jesus she's right there, lurking under the lid of the box I dump all of this in and I can't do anything with my frustration but stew in it.

Wild laughter cackles through my thoughts.

That's it. Have a good laugh. You're still in the box. You're staying in the box. The only way you're getting out is to kill me, and people a lot better than you Siski have tried.

Chew on that.

I tap my PEAL. Start recording again. "Val..."

Take a breath, even if you don't need to.

"Val, I have something to tell you."

Abi's voice echoes through the lab. "'I'm breaking up with that goofy little sidepiece?'"

I swipe the recording away. "Baby, what?"

She laces her arms around me. "What's up?"

I bite my lip. I haven't told her any of this. This is what I struggle with. Empowered wolves. Zombie gangsters. Comic–strip ghosts. I can handle all that. Communication?

Not so much.

I'm getting better, though. So I just tell her. Everything. And everything about Abi is quick. Most people might take a minute to digest all the information I spewed about Blackwood, Siski, Blind Tiger, and whatever else I threw in there, but not her.

Abi's response blitzes over the end of my confession. "He's black-mailing you?"

"Basically," I say.

Her nose wrinkles. "What are you going to do?"

I bite my lip. "I thought I'd just tell Valene the truth."

"And then Anwar puts you on blast."

"What choice do you have?"

Abi kisses the nape of my neck. "You can do anything."

I reach for her hand. "I just wanted to..."

"Don't worry about it."

"I'm sure that will work."

Her voice hushes. "What did I tell you?"

"There's a lot of stuff you tell me, baby."

"You protect the city. I'll protect you."

"Abi..."

She holds me close. "I'll take care of us."

I kiss her cheek. "Abi."

"Always."

"I got myself into this. I'll fix it, somehow."

"You don't have to fix everything," she says. "Just don't worry about it right now. Rest, Kit. Just rest."

She rocks me in her arms, and for the first time in a long time, I experience something like sleep.

Something like rest.

I flutter out of sleep on the anxiety of birds.

Beaks drum against the bedroom window, frustrated by glass they can't see. I didn't know I was asleep. Now I'm kind of mad. Abi is gone. Usually, I come home and she's asleep. She must be upstairs in the office, working on something for the foundation. Half seven. Great. Not morning. Evening. Well. Night patrol, it is.

My PEAL buzzes. *Still thinking?*

I'm always thinking. Thoughts stick like bones. I walk. I fly, to find some distance from my own mind. Cities conspire in their silences. If you asked, most people might say you could hear a pin drop in Break Pointe. Valene certainly could, but it's not a quiet city.

Break Pointe creaks, hums, and shifts with its burdens. Chicago organizes its silence like it does its neighborhoods. Some pinch between others, dense and bustling with life, while others sprawl, stretching into a quietude at odds with such a large city.

The unlikely quiet downtown always surprises me. Chicago is often the loud, constant assault of activity it's made out to be in films, but sometimes, especially in the deep of night, between trains, between helicopters, between night and day, the city achieves a stillness only such an engine of civilization can. It has to, or the wilderness in the shadows could never thrive. Rats scurry down alleyways. Raccoons raid garbage cans. Hawks perch on the great towers, eyeing the little things moving on the ground, waiting, planning, preying.

It's all a little game.

Noise scares away a lesser animal. Hunters prefer the cover of a racket and in all the years I've prowled this city, hunting the forgotten and the disposed, feasting in the shadows, running in the seams of the human grid, I enjoy their sound.

I enjoy most their screams.

The Tiger lives in a penthouse apartment. Roof access. No guards. Birdies scatter to the night and I *tap, tap, tap* on the screen door. My reflection glows like the halogen city. I crouch on all fours. Not a wolf. Not a human. Not Kitty Cat.

Not Siski.

Between. Both. More. Silly girl. Thought she could stuff me in a cage. Now who's in the cage? Who's stuck?

I'm still me, she says and I bear my fangs.

You're nothing. You're no one. A bone I bury for later.

Then why are we here?

We're here because we're sick and tired. No more compromises. No more contorting to fit inside someone else's cage. No more playing nice. I tap on the door again. No one comes. Good. I like it when they play hard to get.

Come out, come out, Tiger. Hmm. I pull on the handle. I pull on the locking mechanism with this force we possess. This magnetism, invisible like my telekinesis. Stupid door still won't open. Plastic. How does she do it? Kitty Cat.

That's right.

A little charge. Hah. Static snaps between my claw and the electronic lock on the screen door. Glass slides away, and I crawl into the penthouse. Roomy. Dark. I smell him.

He's here.

Someone else. No perfume. Sweat. Anxiety. Guard? I sense their thoughts now. Hmm. I couldn't outside. Human trick. Dampening field. Kitty Cat knows about these things.

Tin Foil.

I sneak through the kitchen. Food out on the counter. Lamb. Yummy. Nice bone. Tiger. We're here for the Tiger. Down the hall. His scent. His thoughts.

His voice. "What do you want?"

I freeze in the shadows. He knows I'm here. What is his power? All of them have power. Kitty Cat's thoughts are like her lab. Clutter. Bins for things, and nothing where it's supposed to be. Sloppy. Silly. There. Blind Tiger sees. Somehow he sees me. I should go. I am stronger and faster than him, but his sight could steal my eyes, and I would see what he wants me to see.

"We can work this out," he says.

He's talking to someone else. I creep down the hall. Master bedroom. Loose motors in both their chests. Heavy engines.

Ba–dumm, ba–dumm, ba–dumm.

I peek inside. Blind Tiger holds his hands up, in a robe like the other one surprised him. They're surprising. Dark armor. Sword. Helmet pointy and disguising.

A voice muffles behind it. "You're going to leave – "

Blind Tiger crooks his head. "There's someone else here."

"Nice try," the woman in the armor says and then I rake the sword out of her hands with the same telekinetic strike I drive her into the wall with.

I pounce on the Tiger. "Oh, my."

SEVEN

I like it when they squirm.

The way that twist of hope, like rope in their muscles, knots and tangles, until finally they're so tied up in fear they can't move.

Blind Tiger shakes beneath me like a frightened rabbit. "Kit? Kit, is that…"

I drag a garnet claw down his meaty little neck. "Kit's not here anymore."

The Shadow writhes against my telekinetic paw, pressing her against the wall. "What in the actual – Kit?"

That sound in her voice. A little shriek the helmet couldn't muffle. This one knows us.

I cover Blind Tiger's mouth. "Who are you?"

She fights to get free. I like it when they fight. "What's going on? What are you doing here? What are you…"

I scratch telekinetically at that helmet of hers. Magnetic locks. Heh. I pull. Metal strains. Her fear does, along with her heartbeat and I like the ones I have to crack open.

I like opening things.

Her chin comes out of eclipse and The Shadow blurs. She moves so fast the wall smokes with her haste. She moves so fast I can't keep hold of her and she springs off the wall, into me and we're both out of the penthouse on the rooftop terrace.

Dust spits from the concrete I claw to stop myself from going off the side of the building. Water sprays across the surface of the pool as the shadow rushes me with her sword.

I swipe at her telekinetically but she's already moved, thoughts trailing behind her in this manic strand back into the penthouse. I can't link any of them together.

More tricks.

Sparks flint off the terrace as The Shadow swings at my feet, trying to unbalance me, but I'm not there. Projection. Behind you. I rake my claws through her armor.

She opens, with molten iron.

The Shadow buckles and speeds away, across the terrace. Blood trails behind her, so slow it falls like rain. She leans on her sword, her breath, her shock, her heart rattling it.

Her voice squeaks like a mouse. "Kit..."

I cackle. "Kit's gone."

"People keep saying that." She stands. "Siski."

I bite my lip. Ow. I have fangs now. "You know Siski?"

The Shadow points her sword at me. "Bitch... I'm going to carve you out of her myself."

Oh, yes. A hunt. A scrap. A fight.

"You can't cut Kitty Cat from the bone," I say. "She's the marrow. She's me. Her hunger is my hunger."

"No..."

"So much hunger..." I edge along the pool. The Shadow moves quick. I must be quicker. "So much thirst, for life. She denies it. She fumbles it. Not Siski. We will eat. We will drink. We will drain the world dry, and then when it is a pit of bones, we will go to all the other worlds beyond and between. We will feast."

The Shadow grips her sword. "Over my dead body."

I click my claws together. "Hah."

I splash the water in the pool, taunting her. Hah. Come, Shadow. Follow me. Where I will go. Where, oh where will I – that scent. The Tiger. He limps out onto the terrace. His fingers claw at his temple and I should have killed him.

"See," he says.

Sneaky little Tiger. I see myself as he does. Kitty Cat. No. Try not to see. Close your eyes. He's still in my head. My thoughts. He forces me to see. This isn't who I am.

This isn't me.

I slump forward on my hands. "Jesus..."

This ache throbs through me. The wake of raw power. Energy like I've never felt before. Hunger.

What just happened?

I look up. The Sears Tower knifes into the night sky. Chicago. I'm in Chicago. This is Anwar's apartment. I don't understand. Not that I ever do, but for crying out loud.

"Anwar..."

He plops in a deck chair with a bottle of whisky and a glass. "It's not every day two people show up in your bedroom to kill you at the same time. I've been too hard on myself."

Two people. Fragments of Siski's memory crash back to the surface of mine. The Shadow – the woman in armor – she's gone. Blood trails across the terrace, down the side of the building.

"Who was she?"

Anwar laughs. "That's your concern?"

"I'm keeping a tight lid on the other one."

He eyes me warily. "You do that."

I sit in the chair across from him. Shame keeps my eyes on the skyline, blurring with my tears. The bottle ends up in my hands. I take a long drink. "Who was she, Anwar?"

"Didn't say," he says. "We were just getting to business when you – or whoever that was – showed up."

"Siski," I say.

"I thought you had all that with the wolf sorted out, Kit."

"So did I."

I completely lost control to Siski, and didn't know it. How? I kept her under lock and key. I was angry. Another text. I read Anwar's text, and then I was here. Every step weakened me and emboldened her. Every mile took me farther from who I am.

He rubs his chest. "Was there some reason she wanted to open my throat, or was that just you?"

I take another drink. "I don't know."

Anwar takes back the bottle. "Fair enough."

"I think we need to talk about our arrangement, Anwar."

He laughs. "I don't know which one of us is over a barrel."

Blood dyes the pool a strange purple. "And I don't really know if she's coming back or not."

He hands the bottle back. "I'm listening."

"To use the common parlance, we're screwed," ALPHA says.

A sigh precedes me out of the astrolabe–like spectrometer I developed with ALPHA in the lab. "Apparently I neglected to program you with a bedside manner."

"Tact is of no use in mathematics, Kit. Absolutely no data exists on the nature or behavior of The Ever. We simply don't know if this development is aberrant or natural."

I brought ALPHA online to help me with equations but now, as his wiry fingers drum together faster than raindrops, head drooped like a lost dog, I wonder if I just needed someone on my wavelength. A robot whose emotions and phrases are all mimicked from movies.

"It's ok," I say.

"We presume your condition vis–à–vis the Myriad is static, but we possess no verified data to suggest any conclusion. Our assessment of what happened to you, what is happening and what will happen are all based on pure conjecture."

Abi sweeps through the lab, so fast I keep losing her behind the equipment and skewed pillars of hard light. "So what are you saying, ALPHA? What's going on with Siski?"

I reach for her. "Abi..."

She disappears into the shadows. "What's happening?"

A hydraulic sigh exhales from ALPHA. "All we can say for certain is Siski is asserting her will, increasingly, over Kit. If Blind Tiger had not intervened... I would only be speculating."

A feral cackle rattles through my mind. I cover my ears, but I'm not able to deny the cold reality hardening through my body like a flash freeze. I leave the chair. My reflection blurs in the dull crystal floor of the terrace I carved for the lab.

This isn't me.

Living with the Myriad in my chest means living with constant light; an electric crackle like radio static, always in my ears; the pressure of everything and everyone always pulling on me. Somewhere on the way, I learned to manage all of that. I put all my stresses in boxes and fight only their rattle. The rattle has become a tremor. A quake. This dislocation, this helplessness, I can't deal with it.

I slump into a chair. "This isn't because of Siski."

Abi stands somewhere between light and shadow. "It's not?"

"It's because of me." I bite my lip. "I was telling ALPHA... I'm always out of phase. I always have been."

"Out of phase?"

"I don't make sense. The Ever makes no sense of me. We're confused. I'm some face it puts on, just like I put a face on everything I couldn't deal with. There are gaps and seams and Siski is getting through. There's nothing out of alignment with her. She's a hunter, like The Ever. She's natural. She is who she is."

Abi clutches my hand. "There's nothing wrong with you, Kit."

"I don't make any sense."

"You make sense with me."

Sometimes I don't know. I don't know if I am myself with Abi or I'm just pretending to be. This tears me apart. Doubting this good in my life. This love I've always needed.

She kisses me. "We make sense."

"I put a face on with you, too."

"Listen..."

"I have to, sometimes. I don't want to."

"I understand."

"When I was trying to find who was responsible for the diffuser attack at the school..." The hairdryer in the men's room runs, for no reason and I close the door on that memory. "I was angry. I was upset. And I did things. I shouldn't have."

"I know about the Straw Men," Abi says. "It's ok."

"I didn't tell you about Welby."

"Welby?"

"This Straw Man, Welby... he sold the diffuser used in the attack. And I was trying to get out of him where he got it, and he wasn't playing along, and... she just appeared. The projection. Siski. I couldn't control her. She killed him..."

Abi holds me. "It doesn't matter."

"It does."

"He was a zombie or whatever."

"You can be so blasé sometimes."

"I'm just being real."

Maybe this is what it means to be real. I don't know. "What's real? Am I real? Am I even me, I don't know."

"You're you," she says. "You're in control."

"I don't know. I thought I had put Siski away, but..." Magnetic lines constrict around my own frustration. "I forget what I bury. How much. I'm just all these pieces. Tectonic plates. They don't fit together, they just subduct. They grind each other down."

Light flickers in her eyes, swirling with her confusion. "Kit..."

Cosmic fire blazes in my hands. "I've never had grace. Peace. Patience. And I don't know. I don't know if I'm the pieces of rock, or I'm the magma destroying it creates."

Her hands cap the volcanoes of mine. "We all have anger. We all have darkness. But it's not who we are."

"I don't know..."

She draws me close, light escaping through the cracks between her fingers, halving her face in shadow. "I know you. The woman with me, when it's just us, that's you. And when I'm with you, Kit... that's me. That's the real me, ok?"

"Ok," I say.

Her heart pounds *ba–dumm, ba–dumm, ba–dumm.* She's more nervous now than she was when I came back from Chicago and told her what happened. "You can tell me anything. I won't be afraid or upset or think wrong of you somehow."

"I know."

ALPHA's fingers clack on his palm. "Perhaps I shall repair to the lounge, and entertain myself with my rapier wit."

"Hold off, ALPHA," I say. "We need to figure this out."

"We need to delete this bitch," Abi says. "Or just get rid of her. You acquired her. Can't you un-acquire her?"

I sort through the holographic modeling. "If reversing the process were a power I had, I'd have done it for all the people The Ever acquired. I can access them, but I can't recall them."

"What about Betty, though?"

I caress phantom hair out of my eyes. "Betty was like a copy. The Ever is a mannequin. Anyone can swap the clothes on it. Siski... Betty... someone can nudge me out if I'm not careful. The Ever can."

"But I thought you and The Ever were fused."

"Undoubtedly," ALPHA says. "But Kit is not connected to the interdimensional network which nominally links The Ever to the ship or the other Ever in existence. Any attempt to pry out the bad tooth of Siski is likely to loosen other fangs."

Abi tugs at her shirt. "There has to be a way to reverse the process of acquisition. The Ever is converting matter and energy in acquiring somebody, so there has to be a way to manipulate the process in the other direction. Right?"

Clack, clack, clack. "Abi's theory is sound. The Ever is manipulating matter in acquiring people. They are transformed into energy and then stored as information, so far as we can tell. The purpose eludes us, but it is essentially what is happening."

"I feel like I've seen enough movies about accidentally opening doors to Hell to maybe start a bit smaller," I say.

Abi's foot motors on the floor. "But you can project the people The Ever acquired, right? Like you project Siski?"

"I don't intentionally project her."

"Work with me, babe. You're like a magic lantern. You could project Betty or somebody else if you wanted to?"

I glance at ALPHA. "Maybe...."

"You have theoretically done it before," he says. "You recalled various acquisitions in your battle with The Interdictor. I calculate there is no functional difference between you 'accessing' them as opposed to 'projecting' them."

"Ok... but I can barely control the projection, though."

Abi holds up her hands. "Where is it?"

"Where's what, baby?"

"The Interdictor – the shard."

I go into the labyrinth of equipment I've designed to design my engine, a portal generator, all the concepts I plan to change the world with. Hopefully. A shard of the Myriad about the size of a penny floats inside a glass jar. The Interdictor cracked this piece off last year when he tried to crush my heart in his fist. I guess he just really wanted me to know how much he cared.

The shard powered my original prototype for the engine. Even severed from the Myriad, it retains enough juice to power all my concepts. I lift the lid of the jar, and the shard floats into my magnetic field, and into the palm of my hand.

"What are you thinking, Abi?"

She cups the shard in her hand. Light riddles through it. "Is this like working? Do you know what I mean? It's still registering energy, right? Do you feel any connection to it, Kit?"

Crystalline debris garlands the invisible magnetic lines of the core. What's the difference between all of this and the Myriad? The

Myriad and the core? Is The Ever just the avatar of this entity, beyond understanding, putting on all the faces of existence?

"I feel a connection to all of this," I say.

"You can project Siski. Could you project Siski into this shard?"

"Into the shard? I don't..." I turn to ALPHA. "It's more crystal..."

"The precise nature of this crystal remains a mystery," he says. "But you have a connection to the core, which is composed of the same material. Energy transfer is possible. So is information."

Siski snickers through my thoughts. *I get free.*

A shudder goes through my chest. "So if I could figure out a way to isolate Siski... to project her..."

"You could conceivably deposit her in this shard."

It's not a crystalline alien shard. It's a thumb drive.

Light flickers on Abi's face. "This can work."

"We'd be creating another Ever," I say. "A wolf Ever."

Abi closes her fist. "We destroy her."

"What?"

"We go tug on The Interdictor's cape and he comes and crushes this thing down to powder. Problem solved."

You never catch me, Kitty Cat.

I take the shard back. "We need to be sure."

"That's being sure, dude."

You never lose my shadow.

I put the shard away. "We have to be sure."

"ALPHA, tell her. We can do this."

ALPHA doesn't immediately respond with his usual loquaciousness. "I do not know we can, Abi. Testing is required. We will likely need equipment we do not yet possess."

"What do we need? I'll get right on it."

"There is another concern," he says.

I already know what he's going to say.

Hah.

"Siski doubtless perceives your thoughts," ALPHA says. "The

wolf will be aware of your intentions if she isn't already. She will be motivated to intervene."

Motivated, she says, enunciating every syllable.

I bite my lip. "I can't risk her getting free."

Abi shakes her head. "This will work, Kit."

"There is only one way to get rid of Siski. To be absolutely sure."

Abi tugs at her shirt. "What way?"

No one says anything. They don't need to. The answer flickers high above, in the core of the ship.

"I can delete Siski by interfacing with the core," I say. "That will scrub the Myriad of any... corruption."

I don't think I've ever seen Abi this still. "But that will erase you, too. Won't it?"

Shadows of floating debris cast the lab in darkness. Energy swells in the core. Anticipation.

"Yes," I say.

EIGHT

"No," Abi says, and I expect her to say more.

There's nothing else to say.

Shards of crystal fine as dust and big as glass panes trail after me as I pace through the ruin beyond the lab.

"We have to be sure," I say.

She shakes her head. "This isn't happening."

"Abi…"

"I won't let you do this."

Magenta dregs float into my hand. They break under the pressure in my fist. Cosmic crystal dense as diamond becomes indistinct from the light under my skin.

"Projecting Siski or anyone into the shard carries too many risks. I can't risk creating another Ever that has all of my power and none of my restraint. I can't risk Siski getting out."

Abi winces. "She is out, Kit, that's why we're talking about finding a better cage. You're like escalating to putting people down and stuff and maybe there was a reason why you never had pets growing up but we'll come back to that later."

"Fascinating as this conversation is," ALPHA says, "Abi does have a point. You have resisted interfacing with the core for a number of reasons, Kit. Foremost among them connecting to the link The Ever share. You would expose the location of the ship, and thus humanity, to their wrath. Siski would be more tolerable."

Abi points at him. "Yes! What he said!"

I can't allow The Ever to find the ship. If they do, if the other eight come here, Siski would be the least of our worries. I know that.

I know that.

I open my hand. A twinkling star floats out of my palm, a magenta firefly that flares like a nova before dissipating. Crystal to light. Matter to energy. Manifest to indiscernible.

"What am I saying..."

Abi takes my hand. "Yeah, let's just chill."

I shake my head, feeling as out of control as I did that first night after my transformation, as my entire world disintegrated into the rubble of something new and terrible.

Siski wants to interface with the core.

Not to erase herself. To erase me. Siski is a much better Ever than I could be. She's a much better hunter. None of those pesky morals or ethics to contend with; only raw, pure hunger. Worse still, she thinks she can influence The Ever like she can me. She knows she can.

Giddy laughter snickers in my mind. *Might be smarter, Kitty Cat. Might be stronger. Siski is faster.*

I tug on my jacket zipper. "I need to think. I need..."

Abi takes me in her arms. "Yeah, let's think. Let's just take a minute and not do the hardest thing all the time, ok?"

I kiss her. "ALPHA, will you model some strategies? Don't tell me about them, but maybe see if there is any way..."

Clack, clack, clack. "Of course."

"Let's go home," Abi says. "I'll make some popcorn."

"You go, baby," I say. "I need to clear my head."

"Here?"

"I think I'm going to try and figure out who this woman was at Anwar's apartment the other night."

Abi laughs, kind of. "What does that matter?"

"Blind Tiger is a Responder. This woman was Empowered. She could move fast, from what he said. She had a sword."

"Look... let's focus, ok?"

"ALPHA will come up with something."

Her expression sours. "You're doing it again."

"Doing what?"

"Avoiding the real issue by focusing on something that doesn't matter. Forget about this sword chick."

"I'm not avoiding anything. Something isn't right... whoever tore up the Straw Men, they had some kind of edge weapon. A sword, maybe. And they moved fast. The cuts. The precision."

Abi's foot taps against the floor. "This *so* doesn't matter."

"I still have a job to do."

"It's scary how fast you compartmentalize."

"It's a good thing I can, so far as Siski is concerned. I'm going to go to the lab at the Blackwood Building and study the Straw Men. I'll see if I can get anything from the remains Dr. Piller has quarantined. ALPHA, keep me updated – "

"I can't take this," Abi says and walks out of the lab.

"Baby..."

"See you at home."

Before I know it, before I register what's happening or even dig out a face to put on this, she's gone.

"This isn't right," Dr. Piller says.

He rubs the back of his neck as approaches the test chamber at the heart of the lab in Applied Sciences. The city glitters beyond, a topaz twinkle on the spectrum of the magenta shine in my chest, and I'm not paying attention. I'm thinking of Abi, across the river, of how this has gone so wrong, so fast and there are infinite frontiers of wrong I am sure to open to try and put it right.

"I'm sorry," I say. "What did you say?"

He opens the test chamber.

"Dr. Piller, what are you – "

The transparent shell of the test chamber swivels open to the lab. He kneels down and opens the trunk he called up from the vault entombed beneath Applied Sciences. Nothing down there comes out unless it's through the chute connecting the chamber and the vault and you never open the chamber doors without warning.

He turns over the trunk. "It's empty."

"What?"

The metal trunk floats magnetically through the air toward me. Dr. Piller stored all of the Straw Men - or at least, what I could piece together of Harrow and his gang - inside this box to study.

"What happened to them?" I say.

Piller goes to the computer station outside the chamber. "There's no record of them being removed."

"Aren't you the only one who has access to the vault?"

"The board has access."

"Did any of them know the Straw Men were down there?"

"No, but The Cormorant is always digging through the files. He says it's routine security checks... he's testing the systems... but I know. He's stealing from the cookie jar. He poaches an idea or invention and then sells it on the black market."

"Does firing him ever come up?"

"Professor Blackwood is gone," Dr. Piller says and I wince. "No one is watching the ball. This is The Cormorant. This is him exploiting the Straw Men somehow, I know it."

I drift to the window. The Straw Men are gone and so is any hope for a cure for what keeps them alive after death. That's not the worst thing. Someone stole them out of the vault. Someone altered the records. Someone with access. The woman at Blind Tiger's apartment was Empowered. She must be GP. Does she work for The Cormorant? Why would she attack Anwar? Why would she attack the Straw Men and why would she cover it up now?

None of this makes any sense.

"I'll do an inventory," Dr. Piller says, his confusion and frustration matching mine. "See what else is missing from the vault."

"Can you review the video feeds?"

He looks up at the red eye of the security camera above. "They're all run through security."

I close the trunk and put it back in the test chamber, but I bury none of my anxiety with it. Yellow eyes burn in the glass of the chamber. A wild cackle runs loose in my thoughts.

I'm losing hold.

Popcorn rattles around in the bowl in Abi's lap.

I hate the smell of popcorn. It reminds me of going to the movies and I never liked going to the movies. Outside the theater, I didn't know how to connect. Inside, I didn't know how to disconnect or separate myself from the characters or their mannerisms or things they said. I came out of the theater Pam Grier. Spider-Man. Ariel from *The Little Mermaid.* I just thought that's how people acted. Everyone else quoted the movies. *I'll be back.* But my mother couldn't stand me impersonating everyone I saw in every conversation and then it became this thing whenever we went.

So I stopped going.

The people got to be too much anyway. I never stopped mimicking the TV, though. I got better at recognizing I was doing it, but even now, I don't know if the way I talk makes any sense. I don't sound like anyone. I don't sound like my Irish mother, my Black father, the girls from my neighborhood, Kate Winslet in Jane Austen movies. Valene said she loved my voice because of how unique it was.

I must have been like a puzzle she couldn't figure out.

"I can't figure this out," I say, opening the living room window.

Abi shakes the kernels around in her bowl. "You're exhausted."

I sit on the couch. "I'm fine."

"You're not. Obviously."

"I'll be fine."

Abi clicks the TV off. "You're doing it again."

"I'm not doing anything."

"You're tired. I know."

So tired, Siski says from beneath the floorboards in my head.

I feel it. That same gravitational pull when Ma would go around the apartment unscrewing all the lightbulbs. When Dad would kick back in his recliner and turn the TV up. When I had nowhere to go to with all this pain and confusion and exhaustion so I just stuffed it down deeper and deeper.

I bite my lip. "Let's just watch some TV."

"Don't shut me out, Kit."

Let's play a game, Kitty Cat.

I tug at the zipper of my jacket. "I'm not..."

Let me out for a bit.

Abi takes my hand. "Just talk to me."

I lace my fingers in hers. "Abi..."

Rest. You're so tired.

Abi's lips press into mine. "Please."

She won't know the difference.

Her tongue lashes mine. I lean into her and force her down in the couch. Popcorn spills everywhere. Her gasp muffles in my neck but she doesn't resist. Abi knows this hunger. This need. This burning in us. She's warm and nervous underneath me. She's soft and fleshy in my mouth. She makes little noises when I open her.

I like it when they make noises.

Birds line the eaves of the Halfway Hotel.

Little birds. Tasty birds. I catch one in my hands and feathers rain down on the roof of the apartment building. Still they come back. They always come back, drawn by this force in us. No losing them. *There's no losing me, Siski.* I spit out a feather.

Go away.

Take your rest, Kitty Cat. You want it this way. This is easiest. This is best. No fighting the hunger. The frustration of an empty belly. The misfit of bones in your skin. I follow my blood. My instinct. We live. We run, Kitty Cat.

We live, like we were meant to.

A city alive. A world brimming. No more hiding. No more denying who we are. I perch on the edge of the rooftop. Hah. Wings flutter. Birds swarm me. Pest me. Shoo. Go away, birds, but there's no losing me. Bird Woman. Star Walker. I give life to you as you give life to me and I connect. I don't box or kill or bury.

I connect.

Shafts of feathers break in my fists. Birds scatter on my fear. The confusing tangle of my magnetic field, pulling on everything within its grasp and holding nothing.

I'm losing hold.

NINE

I pull on my jacket as I come into the lab. This old thing gives me a sense of comfort, even now, even if I know it's an illusion.

"You're sure it will work, ALPHA?"

Hesitation in a robot is an exacting thing. It's like watching your fridge freeze up. "Define 'sure.'"

I tug on my zipper. "Convince me."

His fingers clack against his palm. "All the modeling I have done suggests that if I initiate a shutdown of the core of the alien ship, the Myriad will also shut down, as it did in 1968."

That would box me and Siski both. Not ideal. But the world would be safe from the threat of any Ever. Abi would be safe.

Light wavers in the undulant mass of the core above. "You can abort the shutdown sequence before it completes, ALPHA?"

Clack, clack, clack. "I possess a digital record of Professor Black-wood's actions in 1968. I know the sequence necessary to trigger the shutdown... and to abort it. I cannot guarantee that the result will be the same as the circumstances are different."

"How are they different?"

"The Ever is my best friend."

My hand falls on the dented metal of his torso. Warmth radiates through the steel from his power core, the skin of a car on a long summer day. "Thank you, ALPHA."

"For what?"

"Being my friend."

"Perhaps we should wait before proceeding. An alternate solution may yet present itself. Your urgency may be misplaced."

"I can't give Siski another chance. I won't."

His head droops. "It's a pity we don't have more time. I am reasonably sure I could accomplish our original ambition in transferring Siski to another host. If I had the time."

I bite my lip. "Another host?"

ALPHA picks up the exposed head of an android the same make and model as himself. I scavenged this one for parts for him, so it's missing the legs and a fair bit of the internal workings of the torso.

"'Alas, poor Yorick,'" ALPHA says.

I take the head from him. "I knew him."

Clack. "Considering your very astute concerns about creating a wolf Ever, I began modeling other possibilities. Consciousness and information are rooted both in electricity. The same principle applies in transferring Siski from the Myriad into the positronic matrix of this model, as it does from the Myriad to the shard of Ever."

"You could do it?"

"Theoretically."

"If you had time."

He teeters mechanically. "Which I most certainly don't."

"Siski would see right through it anyway."

Clack. "If only I had acted sooner."

I set the spare robotic head down. "What can you do, though?"

"I could have performed a number of tests, which if I had been doing this, would only require we attempt the exercise in a real-world scenario. It would require subterfuge on our part."

"Blind Tiger could have helped us."

"Indeed."

"Siski's too smart for that."

"Certainly. We must then proceed."

"With the fallback option."

"Precisely. Despite my modeling, there remains a question of what happens to you when the Myriad shuts down."

I don't expect to come back. As terrified as I am of being this thing, I'm scared even more of someone pulling the plug. Hitting restart. Erasing the hard drive.

"You came back," I say. "After being offline."

He nods. "Information cannot be destroyed."

"ALPHA, can you help me record a message for Abi?"

"Perhaps you should deliver this message to Abi in the present, given the circumstances."

I can't. I can't, and then do what I have to do. I'll never be able to go through with it. "This is the only way."

"You cannot avoid the reality of your circumstances by postponing them for others, Kit."

"You didn't know me in high school."

"I would not have improved our mutual social standing."

"I don't know. We would have been in with the nerds."

"We would have conquered them."

"Down, boy."

His metal shoulders heave. "Hierarchies are inevitable in nature."

"I'm not sure if I should be more afraid of a telepathic wolf with cosmic power or a genius android with Darwinian tendencies."

"You're sure."

I clutch his hand. "Let's record."

Loose crystal cracks behind me. "Abi..."

Abi comes into the lab. "You're going to reboot the Myriad?"

"Baby, let me explain."

Abi tugs at her shirt. "Will you come back?"

"I'll fight, Abi. I'll try and hold on. But..."

"How long will it take to reboot?"

"I don't know. It took fifty years last time."

"You're going to leave me here for fifty years?"

"Abi..."

"This is bullshit," Abi says, her voice breaking. "There has to be some way. ALPHA, figure it out."

ALPHA's head pivots back in mechanical pique. "I cannot simply 'figure it out.' We are dealing with forces we don't understand, and despite Kit's facility, to say nothing of my intellect – "

Abi paces into the dark of the lab. "Oh my God, just stop talking and think of something."

I clamp down on my lip, and the debilitating, numbing pain burning through my body. "Abi, please."

"You've been erasing yourself your entire life for other people. And I'm not letting it happen again."

Locks clamp. Shields go up. Various other metaphors. Don't. Don't shut down on her. "ALPHA..."

His fingers drum together. "Call if you need me."

He creaks into the dark of the lab, and then it's just Abi and I, alone with the awful reality facing us. After my Dad died, with Ma spiraling, I thought about death all the time. Maybe I wanted to die. I just wanted to stop hurting.

Ba–dumm, ba–dumm, ba–dumm.

Ripples of light radiate through me from the pulse throbbing in Abi's veins. I rest my head on Abi's shoulder, closing my eyes to the rhythm, the life echoing in her body. Another moment; another few seconds, and I would have been engaged. I would have had a life. A future, to build. This is my life: almost.

My destiny is to touch the sky and always fall. To hold the stars in my heart, and never reach them. To know love, happiness, joy, only as the echo of someone else's.

"I love you," I say.

Tears run down Abi's face. "You're giving up."

"I'm being realistic."

"When have you ever been realistic?"

A deep, hurt sound forces out of Abi, and she crumples to the chair. She bends over, head in her hands. I never know what to say to people. I don't have to say anything with Abi. Abi knows me, better than I've ever known myself. Sometimes I think of the Myriad as a kind of ark, a keep in which my spirit or soul or essence remains after the architecture of my body had been atomized. Whether or not this is true, if I'm me, or an afterimage burned in the lens of The Ever, it doesn't matter. What matters is I do exist. I do live, in Abi's naked joy. I live in the drum of her heart, *ba–dumm, ba–dumm, ba–dumm.*

"Abi... baby, come here."

"I'm not letting this happen. We just have to think. We just have to try. Ok? Whatever it takes. Just tell me what it will take, Kit."

A throe separate from the pain of my undoing knifes through me. Memories of the night I learned Valene was leaving me, retreating to the space station to flee the sound of the world, dig out of the graves I buried them in. I've bargained; I've pleaded; I've grieved much the same way Abi does now, throwing myself into a series of decisions I'm still paying for.

"Abi," I say, trying to maintain my composure. "I cannot allow Siski to gain control of the Myriad."

"What about a containment suit, like Professor Blackwood's? That was all about maintaining him. Maybe we can stabilize you and keep you going until we figure out Siski."

Alien creatures skitter through the empty husk of Blackwood's containment suit, buried in dust. "That won't work."

"Why?"

"It just won't," I say.

"Because you don't know how, or you don't want to?"

Her tone startles me. "No."

"No, what?"

"No, I don't know how, Abi."

"Why are you being so cagey?"

"I didn't want to do this..."

"You wanted to avoid the hard part. Just record me a little message and then duck out."

"No... that's not it. Siski..."

"What Siski wants is power. Energy. Both her and The Ever both want to suck the life out of things."

"And that's why I'm never going to let it happen."

"But you're The Ever. You're fighting this, but it's your power. You need power to fight Siski."

"What?"

"Siski's pushing you to have a little snack, so let's throw her a bone, and put her back in the pound."

"That's not going to work, either – "

"What's the wattage we need? Like a person?"

I bite my lip. "Abi."

"Power plant? Nuclear reactor? What do we need to do?"

"We're not doing that."

"Why not?"

I turn away. With a magnetic tug, I deactivate the spectrometer and the fervor coursing through Abi.

"I've learned my lesson," I say. "I'm not bending or breaking any more laws, natural or otherwise."

Abi's expression hardens. "You did for Valene."

"And that's why I'm not doing it now."

"So, you'd do anything for her, but not for me."

I brace against the spectrometer. "Abi, I love you."

"Then don't quit on me."

The engagement ring is still in my jacket. I can still propose, and give Abi something. I'd be taking it away just as quickly if the worst came to pass. No one has ever meant more to me than Abi; not Valene. Not anyone. The last thing I want is for Abi's life to suffer from the same curse mine does. Almost.

"I'm sorry," I say. "God, I'm sorry."

"Don't do this. Don't leave me alone here, Kit."

I resist the drag and pull of the forces pulling on me, within and without. I focus on the problem, as always.

"If Siski returns, if I'm gone... she'll have the power not just to hunt the world, but the universe. I never should have acquired her. I wish none of this ever happened... but it did. And you know what I have to do. We've talked about this. We've prepared."

Her fists clench. "For the alien."

I sink back in the chair. "I won't leave the city to the mercy of the wolf, or the alien. I won't leave the world."

Abi's fists rattle at her sides so fast I think they blur. "But you'll leave me."

As much as my pain is incomprehensible, it's familiar. How many disasters have I suffered; how much grief. The shocks and collapses of hope have become routine. Expected. I don't know what to say. I just want out and Siski scratches the side of the box and I'm pinched.

I tug on my zipper. "I would never..."

Abi wipes her tears away. "Kit..."

"Never..."

Her head crooks. "Kit."

"What?"

"Your eyes. They're yellow."

"Shit – "

A cackle scampers through the lab. *You can't get rid of me.*

"Abi, get out of – "

A telekinetic shove sends her out of the lab. Abi. ALPHA pops like a balloon into thousands of screws, bolts, and molded plates. A cloud of my friend hovers in the air, held together in my magnetic field. I try to put him back together, but my hand goes limp. I do. No. This freeze goes through me. This paralysis.

Bad kitty.

Stop this. I have to stop this. I can't. She's locked me out. Light burns in my fists. Equipment rattles with magnetic fury. No. Don't. A focused beam of pure energy cuts through the lab. I burn all my equipment, my inventions, and my hope for the city. The world. In an instant, a year of hard, unforgiving effort to leave Break Pointe better than I found it goes up in flames.

All I can do is watch.

TEN

Embers rain down on me. Molten metal. Crystal dust, pulverized as Siski forces me to immolate the lab. I go right back to that numb helplessness whenever Ma went on one of her jags, unscrewing all the light bulbs and smashing them.

Are you the light, Kit? Or the bulb?

I couldn't get upset. That would have been feeding a fire. I couldn't get out and leave her to hurt herself. I couldn't get angry. Enough was broken without my letting loose. So somewhere after Dad died, sometime before I did, I decided.

I don't get angry.

The torches of my fists flame out. I crumple to my knees, to a fetal mass, terrified at what I've done but I'm not done. Get up. Get moving. End this, once and for all.

I fly up to the widow's peak-like deck encircling the core. Expectant light swells within the half–molten, half–quartz orb as I come to the terminal, a crystalline pedestal growing out of the ring.

The work must continue, the voice of Ever says.

Focus. The shutdown sequence. Turn all this off. Now. My hand hovers over the screen of the terminal. A series of mathematical equations flash across the screen in rapid succession, all of them without solutions. This is the language of the ship, of the alien, and of a power that remains firmly beyond my understanding, despite my use of it.

I don't want power.

I don't want to lose myself, so my war with The Ever over the Myriad is the one thing that remains cold after this long, merciless winter. In a brutal struggle that skinned me of my humanity, I've come to a kind of understanding with the alien.

A kind of peace.

Frustrated light bristles on the ephemeral edge of the core. The Ever and I have come to an uneasy accord, but there is a different animus in the core. Whatever the alien is, it is a product of this object, this carnivorous intelligence and I am obstructing its purpose. I am denying it the use of its instrument. Without me, the ship is a mouth without teeth. As ravenous as Siski's hunger is, the appetite of the ship is cosmic. Insatiable. My hand lurches toward the terminal. This isn't the core, magnetically dragging me to heel.

This is Siski.

Give us a taste, she says.

Don't be a fool. The core will erase you.

A gleeful snicker prances through my mind. *You can't bury me.*

No –

Give us the hunt, Kitty Cat. Give us the stars.

The pull between my hand and the terminal becomes irresistible. I can't fight Siski and the core both. All my strength bleeds out of me. All my willpower. Please. Forgive me.

Abi's voice thunders through the core. "Don't!"

God. She's here. "Abi..."

She holds her hand out. "Get away from there, Kit."

"I can't."

"We'll figure something else out – "

"I'm not trying to interface with the core."

"Good." Her nose wrinkles. "Why don't I feel better?"

"Siski is in control. She's forcing me to..."

"You're in control. You are, Kit."

Current laces my finger to the terminal. "Run, Abi."

"I'm not leaving you."

"Please."

Abi holds her ground. "I'm not leaving."

"Baby, I love you."

"I won't – "

"Always," I say and then I'm flying away from the terminal so fast I land about where Abi was standing. Except she's not there. She's at the terminal. "What…"

Her hands sweep across the screen.

"Abi… what happened…"

Her fingers dance across the garnet glass and the core shutters. Anticipatory eddies in the magnetic field of the ship relax. The fever that drew us nearly together breaks.

I get back on my feet. "What are you doing?"

"I'm locking you out," she says.

"How are you…"

She steps away from the terminal. "Blackwood documented the code progression he used in 1968 to disable the core. It's in the files you took off the GP mainframe."

"You did what?"

"You want to log back in," she says, "then you'll have to go through me. FYI, I programmed a multiphasic algorithm that keeps changing the code, and you'll probably figure it out, but it will be hard and stuff. And I love you, too."

I stumble against the railing. "Abi…"

"It's kind of hot I know this stuff, right?"

"How did you… how did I get over here?"

She tugs at her shirt. "Truth or Dare?"

I grip the railing. "Move away from the terminal."

"Nope."

Anger rakes my voice. "Get away from it. Now."

"You're in control," Abi says, staying put.

"Silly girl," I say.

"You're yellow. Stop being yellow."

"Stupid little girl."

"Stop being yellow, Kit – Siski – Kitski!"

Hah.

Abi holds her hands out. "We'll find another way, Kit. There's always another way. You showed me that. We can get out of this. You and me. We can be better."

Amber claws cut through the railing. I crouch down on all fours, the weight of my anger so great it bends me. I like being angry, though. Keeps me warm. Keeps me loose.

"Move," I say.

Tears race down her cheeks. "I told you. I will do whatever I have to do to save you, Kit."

"There's no saving Kitty Cat. And no stopping me."

"Kit stopped you before."

I drum my claws on the deck. "I didn't go down that well. You're going to unlock that terminal so I can go hunting in fields afar. And then I think I'll bury you... for later."

Abi tenses, the way trapped animals do. No way out, but to fight. Good. I like it when they fight.

I spring toward her. She disappears. Somehow, she's behind me. My arm twists behind me, so hard and so fast it's like she's going to rip it off and my claws tear through her paper.

She crashes to one knee, face turned from me. Her hands shake. Her heart thumps, *ba–dumm, ba–dumm, ba–dumm*. Little rabbit. Abi slowly turns back. No wound. No blood. I hit her.

Hmm.

"Good luck with that," Little Rabbit says and I crash off the ringed deck, down through the hollow of the ship into the ruin of the lab. Abi lands on me, a jagged shard of crystal in her hand like a sword, and pointed at my glowing heart.

I bite my lip. "Abi?"

Shadows of flame dance on her face. "Kit?"

This is like waking up from a dreamless sleep. Oblivion. And then, all at once, consciousness. I'm frightened by my own existence. By the loss of nothingness.

I touch her cheek. "What happened?"

The shard in her hand drops to the floor. Her hands go to her face, and she feels around them like she's making sure it's all still there. I don't know why. Nothing's wrong.

That's not exactly true.

Fire swirls across the claret cavern of the ship. My lab pops and burns and melts. Siski. That's what happened. My God. I have to get back up to the core. I have to end this.

Abi falls against me and holds me down. "Don't."

"Baby..."

"I won't let you go."

Don't ever let me go. Above, the core bleeds light like the sun underneath water. Every instinct in me is to swim for the light. Surface. I can't breathe. Siski is holding me down.

"Get off me, Abi."

Abi locks my arms under her knees. "Stop doing stuff!"

Yellow light reflects in her eyes. "*Get. Off.*"

Little Rabbit tumbles away like dead leaves. No more games. No more play. I float up to the ringed deck. Kitty Cat reflects back at me in the screen of the terminal.

You think you can trick Siski.

Siski knows the algorithm. Siski knows the shutdown sequence. Siski knows everything Kitty Cat knows. More. All the bones you won't dig up. All the secrets buried in the earth of Ever, Siski knows.

Siski isn't afraid.

My claws rake across the screen. Power unlocks. Knowledge. Kitty Cat thinks she can get rid of me. She doesn't know. She doesn't understand. There is no distinction between us.

We are Ever.

A bolt of pure energy stabs from me. Siski burns from me. A mirage. I echo in light. I try to resist. I try to contain her with all my diminishing power, but pressure builds within me, within the Myriad, the swell of this cosmic force I'm connected to growing *tac a tac a tac* until a crack forms in my heart. And then another.

I shatter.

Siski manifests on the ringed deck, the corona of a burning shard of the Myriad. Crystalline debris floats in her magnetic field, fusing together with the shard in the collapsing star of her heart. Pinions of crystal expand along branching lines within her, like cracks in a windshield and a new Myriad ignites within Siski.

"*No!*"

Ecstatic laughter cackles through the ship. A gluttonous, rapacious howl. Aureate light illuminates low–hanging smoke. A flickering fire, burning out of control. The smoke clears, but my confusion, right along with my horror, only enflames.

Siski – me – some fusion of us both – crouches low, her chest a dark nebula cocooning a newly born star.

"Told you, Kitty Cat," she says. "You can't bury me."

ELEVEN

In my long, storied career of Making Things Worse, this certainly will be the accomplishment that gets me in the hall of fame. I wanted to keep Siski from hurting people.

I just handed her a hunting license.

I don't know what happened. I don't know if she willed herself out of me and bit off part of the Myriad in the process, or I spit her out. Doesn't matter. All that matters is that she's out and she's not in the cage I hoped to lock her in. How am I going to stop her now?

Her crystalline claws tick against the terminal. "I give life to you..." The core spasms in anticipation. "As you give life to me."

I fire a blast of energy at Siski. She throws her hands up, and an energy shield absorbs most of the discharge.

I didn't know I could do that.

Hellish energy fires back at me, and evidently, no, I cannot create energy shields. What's left of my lab equipment cushions my fall. Siski howls in delight. I really, really, really hate this chick.

I rocket back into the air. A magnetic wave pushes ahead of me, crashing into the underside of the ringed deck and breaking it into the floating deck plates that comprise it. Siski growls as she clings to the terminal, a lost island among all the others.

I throw them at her.

A hiss trails her off the terminal plate. Siski leaps from one to another, getting her claws in the metal just long enough for me to toss another piece of the ship at her. Finally, she gets her footing and blasts the next one out of my grip. Deck plates line up behind her. This isn't magnetism. Telekinesis.

Shit.

Her laughter builds with every volley. I swat plates away magnetically, but a plate blindsides me into another and I go down hard. Siski howls and I give her plate a little push.

She falls on her ass, laughing. "Kitty Cat is weak."

An icepick headache stabs behind my eyes. So strange. Physical pain hasn't been a problem since my transformation; most of what I experience is on a spectrum of pressure. The greater the magnetic attraction to something or someone, the more stress. The stronger the pull of the power within me, desperate to get out, the more friction.

Siski snickers. "Silly Kitty. I'm not part of you anymore."

I flinch. She's been under my floorboards so long, pounding, beating, scratching, I still hear her even though she isn't there. I've held the shadow of Siski almost as long as I've been The Ever and I don't know much else beyond this clawing hunger within me.

Siski throws another plate at me, but it's a meek effort designed to distract me as she scales the lilies of decks floating in the air between us. I yank the terminal plate out from under her.

She flails in the air before landing on another plate. Energy ebbs in her hands. Her Myriad is jerry-rigged together from lesser parts. Low on power. Her eyes search the cave of the ship. I don't know her thoughts anymore, but I know her thinking.

She looks up, through the cleft in the hull.

"Don't even think about it," I say.

"I need power..." Siski says. "I need energy."

"I'm warning you."

She spits fire at me. "I'll drain some little quick thing, and then I'll have the strength to defeat you. But I won't kill you, Kitty Cat. No. Not at first. First, I'll make you watch, as I skin the ones you love. As I lick them dry of their blood."

Savage light erupts from my fist. Siski disappears, but not in fire. Mad laughter trails her up the walls of the ship.

"Stop," I say, hopelessly.

I'm running out of time. I'm losing control. I'm losing everything and a rhythm builds in my mind, *ba–dumm, ba–dumm, ba–dumm.*

Broken crystal cracks like glass. "Kit…"

I take Abi in my arms. "You're ok."

She grips my hand. "I'm fine."

"I thought she hit us both."

"I'm fine."

Birds flutter against blue sky above. "I have to stop her…"

First things first. I focus my winnowing magnetic field on the disassembled remains of ALPHA. His positronic matrix disappears within a congealing mass of wire and metal. Light illuminates his eyes, and pistons flex in his neck.

"'Tis but a flesh wound," he says. ALPHA's eyes click around the ruin of the lab. "Siski appears to be split from you. How – "

"She's gone." The relief in my voice is strange. "She's left me."

"Then our theory was correct…"

I place the spare robot head in his hands. "It's too bad we didn't have more time to try out your idea."

Clack. "Indeed."

"I'll get her back here." I kiss Abi. "Stay here. Stay safe."

Abi grabs my hand. "Don't go."

"I'll be back," I say and rocket out of the ship. Siski hovers in the air, batting at the birds swarming her, trying to orient herself within the sky, within her new power.

A cloud of affinity colors my perception of her. I remember this moment, that moment of first flight, of giddy wonder reaching escape velocity from hopeless fear. That first moment I realized my potential, I nearly floated all the way to the stars.

Siski has much more earthly ambitions.

She claws at the birds. Feathers burst off acquired pigeons. It's not enough. It's never enough. Her eyes scour the streets below. I know what she sees. A ball of energy, entwined, snared in tiny knots walking down city blocks, driving in cars, sleeping in beds or playing in gyms. So many bristling lives. So much delicious energy.

"Don't even try it, Siski."

"Ha," Siski says, and bounds across the wall of the Quarantine Zone. I blaze fire after her, chasing her away from The Derelicts. The Blackwood Building twists into the clouds across the river.

Everything I fear about myself, about this power, shadows the plaza around the tower. People run. They scramble back into the building, or behind park benches, or drop to the ground like they teach you to do when there's a tornado, but nothing can save them from this storm. Tendrils of famished energy spring from Siski and I seize on her magnetic field with my own.

I drag her across the plaza, toward me, on invisible rope. Claw marks scratch behind her as she struggles to get free. That's right. We might be separated now.

But we're just on a break.

A telekinetic shove breaks my hold on her. Light poles wrench out of the perimeter of the plaza. This won't be good. Twenty–five foot long missiles rocket toward me from every direction. I swat them away. Some end up in the river. Some bullet the tower. Enough hit me to knock me out of the sky.

Poles impale the plaza, caging me. Metal bends and warps under my frustration, and twists and laces with Siski's anger. I can't get free. My magnetic field weakens and this is all aluminum. Without a strong enough magnetic force, it might as well be paper. Her magnetic field is as useless as mine right now. She's not relying on it.

This is telekinesis.

This is Siski. I don't have the benefit of her powers anymore, now that we're halved. She has all the advantage of mine. My hand ignites into a blowtorch, and I cut my way through the impromptu prison she trapped me in.

She laughs. "Poor little Kitty."

Siski turns her attention back to the people running across the plaza. No. Her head lowers as she crouches onto all fours. The wolf's right front paw curls off the ground, as she prepares to pounce and concrete and earth erupt beneath her.

Siski disappears.

The breeze off the lake sheers the dust away, revealing the crater The Interdictor punched into the plaza.

He pins Siski down with his knee on her neck. "Baldwin. I thought I made it clear I preferred less of you."

I rattle my cage. "Nathan... help me."

"Consider your audience."

This guy. "Will you stop being you for one second and just get me out of this thing?"

"As soon as you stop," he says and presses his knee down on Siski. "I didn't think I'd have an opportunity so soon for a rematch. I believe my initial strategy was sound."

"Nathan, don't – "

His fist punches through Siski's chest, right into her Myriad. She growls in cosmic anger as he squeezes his fingers around the crystal, trying to crush it. Frantic claws slash across his helmet, shredding it into ribbons of metal. His skin holds up better, but with his concentration broken, Siski bats him away with a telekinetic backhand. She springs out of the crater and lashes him with a wisp of angry tendrils.

He catches them all in his hand. "You're not Baldwin."

Siski snickers. "And you're right. For once."

His fingers peel, one by one, off her tails. Telekinetic force twists his arm behind his back, and down to his knees. For all his strength, The Interdictor can do nothing.

She peels the links of chains free from his cloak. "I think I'll make a cage out of you."

I burn through the last of the snarled light poles and blast Siski away from The Interdictor. He springs out of his torpor, his frustration red as my light, and gets on his feet.

"You'll pay for that," he says.

Siski crouches low, cornered. Uncertainty wrinkles her face. Indignation, once other Responders start pouring out of the tower. It's one thing if you need help in this town.

It's another if you go looking for trouble.

"It's over," I say. "Stand down, Siski."

The Interdictor circles behind Siski. "You had better have a good explanation for this, Baldwin."

"Later."

I stand with him, and maybe, just maybe, we have a shot. Spent energy leaves me hollow. Every blast leaves me sore as a sick throat, coughing all night, every hack deep and painful.

I can do this. I have to.

"I'll tangle her up in my magnetic field," I say. "You go for the Myriad. Don't hesitate."

He cracks his knuckles. "I never do."

Siski blinks her projection into being. The Interdictor swings at it, fooled, and she runs. I levitate after her, expecting her to make another play for the energy she needs but a portal opens in front of her to the In Between.

No.

Laughter riddles behind her as Siski leaps through. I can't let her get away. If she goes through the In Between, she could go anywhere in time and space. I'll never find her.

I'll never be able to stop her.

I put everything I have into a magnetic thrust, and I power my way through the portal before it closes. Glittering haze clouds the crystalline disc I land on. Jumbled garnet shatters into millions of pieces as Siski bounds across the disc, right at me and I open a portal back to the ship. Claws channel through the crystalline glaze of the interior. Siski skids to a stop in what's left of my lab.

Her eyes glare yellow. "What..."

I seize on her Myriad with all my magnetic power. "ALPHA, are you ready?"

He ambles through the ruin, carrying the head of the robot we've bet everything on. "We talked about wanting more time."

Perfect. I try to keep hold of Siski. Focus. Keep her here, limit the damage and you can fix this. You can put all of this back together. Just stay together a little bit longer.

Stay together, Kit.

Magnetic force pries my grip loose on Siski. At first, I think it's her, but it's coming from above. It's coming from the core. Belts of the ship's magnetic fields lasso me.

"What's happening..."

We are Ever, the voice says.

Magnetic eddies tear open a portal to the In Between.

You...

I struggle to get free. "What are you doing?"

...are Never.

"Don't – "

The ship yanks. The ship pulls and I'm scraping across the jagged ground into the portal. Siski cackles, free, chosen, preferred by the ship as its Hunter Ever and with what power I have left I reach out with my magnetic field and latch onto her. She yelps as she drags behind me through the portal and rusted bones the size of buildings stab out of an ash desert. I tumble down a chute of hollowed metal marrow, into a crater forged from skeletons. The portal closes. I don't know where we are, or if I know the way home.

If I can get home.

TWELVE

Colossal rib cages rise out of a chalky desert, the mauve
sky clawed like the plastic scrim they keep pets behind in the animal
shelter. Metal fingers arc out of the sand and stretch into perches for
birds shelled in the carapaces of their own wings.

I thought I left all my wow at home.

I swipe at my PEAL. Just a quick pic. For science. Ok. Now
that's out of the way, I can properly freak out. Where am I? Why did
the ship try to dump me here? Crystal litters the ground. Not crystal.

Myriads.

Blackened jags of crystal stab out of the dust, some purple at their
edges, crimson, azure, topaz. I don't understand. If these were all
Myriads, were these all Ever? Why did the ship - this is some kind of
cosmic boneyard. A landfill to dump all the unruly Ever.

How many of us have there been?

Shadows of wings race across the bones of giants. Above, on the
ribs of the colossus looming over me, someone scrawled the words
NEVER SAY NEVER in obsidian dust. I have to get out of here.

I try and open a portal. Nothing doing. This could be bad. I could
be stuck here forever like these other Ever were.

Maybe it's for the best.

If Siski and I have to be stuck somewhere together, this dead desert might have been the best place we could have landed. She can't open a portal, either. She can't hurt anyone.

At least, until one of us kills the other.

Her snicker echoes through the waste. "I'll feed. I'll gain power. And then I'll have enough strength to open a portal back to the earth and leave Kitty Cat here."

"There's no food here, Siski."

Her huff ricochets off the copse of bones. "I'll take your power. Kitty Cat is weak. Kitty Cat is a fool."

I drop a blackened Myriad back to the dust. "I'm not the only one."

I rest against the base of a tusk. After I transformed, part of me knew my lease on life was short. Maybe I told myself I could live forever, given my circumstances. I could hold it together. But that's me being me. Same blinders I had on with messing around with this power in the first place. Something was always going to happen. The Interdictor crushed me. The alien returned. The sun burnt out four billion years from now, and I flamed out acquiring all its energy.

You know. Something simple.

Doesn't make it any easier. I thought I'd have more time. I thought Abi and I would have more time. I'm disappointed. I'm disappointed that I'm disappointed; I should be more accepting. I should be grateful, for what I had, and what I was given.

I gave everything.

I scratched lines into the hull of the ship. I prayed. I begged, really, for a soul I know I don't have. When the light goes out in my chest, that's it. I disappear. Nothing will be left of me.

"I'm terrified," I say.

Maybe I shout. I don't know. My voice sounds louder here. The wind carries, and it's not long before Siski's anxious patter arrives from somewhere in the distance. She claws at bone. Digs in the sand. She whines, trying to get off this rock.

To get home.

I bite my lip. "Didn't think this through, did we? That's us, isn't it? Thinking of everything, and not thinking at all."

A fragment of bone crashes out of the desert next to me. "Siski will find a way back. Siski is clever. Quick."

"You're right, you know. I am weak."

A shadow flits across the sand, quick. "Hah."

"People think I'm a hero. A god. A monster. But I'm not. I'm just a frightened young woman who tells people anything is possible, and then the minute they turn their back, I tear things to pieces."

I tug at my zipper. I'm not wearing my jacket.

"Ma did that. She tore everything apart. I try to put it back together. I fidget. I tinker. Just like her. I'm not any different. I thought I was, or I hoped I could be. I really wanted to fix things. I tried. I can say I tried."

"Boo-hoo," Siski says, her voice closer.

"Tell me about your mother."

"I killed her."

Probably could have guessed that. "Makes two of us."

Siski spits. "Your mother killed herself."

I claw the dust. "I couldn't help her."

This melodramatic wail swirls in the deepening amethyst of the evening. "*Wah, wah, wah.* There she goes again. Kitty Cat thinks she's responsible for everything. For everyone."

Her magnetic field brushes up against mine. She's close now. "Didn't you tell me that to lead a pack was to sacrifice yourself? To put everyone and everything ahead of you."

"Siski sacrifices," she says.

"I'm sure you suffered a lot of indigestion eating all your cubs. Did they swallow easy? The nails? The teeth?"

"I spit them out," she says.

"You make me sick."

She snickers. "You like the taste, Kitty Cat."

Powdery sand cakes my fingers. "No, I don't."

"You like the way Abi tastes. Mmm. Electric. The way she wriggles beneath you, caught between frenzy and fear. Hah. You like it when some little quick thing walks down the sidewalk beneath your watch and you... heh. Bye, bye, birdie."

The turtle birds unshell their wings. This lot isn't as tangled in my magnetic field as the birds back home, but then I'm not generating as much interference as I normally do. I run a lot of interference. Thinking of everything.

Not thinking at all.

My thoughts drift with the birds. My focus. I'm so heavy. I just want to fly away. The apartment building forms a point in the star of Six Corners. A dial in the middle of the city. Turn it, and wind back the clock. A day. Fifty years. A hundred. Pigeon memory laps on the shore of human consciousness. Think.

See.

Everything meets where it should. Water. Land. Sky. Human. Alien. Moons shadow planets. Comets touch virgin skies. Stars go dark. Ma bashes the light bulbs on the floor of the apartment. I flutter back to the desert sands, out of my drift.

What good are wings if you always come back to your perch?

No matter how many hours I fly around the city, I always come back to the same place. I hadn't thought about Ma in a long time. So many other things crowd my head. The thoughts of all the people the alien acquired, for one. Also, I'm an alien. Accepting what I've become was accepting what happened to her. Or so I thought. I thought I made peace with it.

Peace. Not in my portfolio.

The truth is, I have no peace. I want to acquire energy. Bad idea. I want to touch Abi. I can never touch Abi, not really, not the way I want to. If I touched her, if I connected with her the way I long to, she'd suffer the same fate all the unsuspecting girls in my past did.

She'd disappear.

"It's never enough," I say.

Siski's shadow stretches from out behind the tusk. "No."

"We're nothing alike, Siski."

Siski crawls into the waning light. "You have this hunger. Nothing fills it. Nothing satisfies it. So you feed it more, and more. Even when you are not hungry. Even when you are afraid."

"Yes..."

"I get free because I'm your mask. Strong. Quick. Effortless."

I look away. "I'm me."

"Do you know who you are?"

"Yes..."

"Hah." Siski picks up a dead Myriad. "We all wear masks, Kitty Cat. The Eve does, too. Hmm."

Something like concern crosses her face. Fear. What if she can't control The Ever the way she thinks? What if she's just another in a long line of confused identities The Ever has worn, thinking they were real, thinking they were in charge, thinking they could mask the truth? Myriads glitter like stars in the desert. A galaxy of them.

"It's too late for regrets," I say.

Siski taps at her glass heart like it's a bulb, like she can make it work. "I tell you before. In the cave. Wolves hunger. Wolves obey instinct. I have thought. I have guilt."

Guilt motivates the sacred rites the Bloodbacks perform for The Great Deer, every time they bring a kill back to the cave. The wolves know more than just gratitude for their meal. They know the thoughts of their prey. Its fear. Its dying question.

Why.

Siski knows this more than any wolf ever has. She feels more of the world, its creatures, their hopes and fears, than the vast majority of humanity does. You'd think trapped in the cage of the world's thoughts, she'd be empathetic.

Not Siski.

She's been skinning prey of thoughts her entire life. She's been ripping out their souls like stuffing. So they'll stop. But it never stops. The anger just coarsens. The hunger grows. The void in your belly deepens, for all you try to fill it with.

Siski snarls. "You think you know me."

"Sister... no one knows you better."

Her nose points toward the sky, and she turns from me a little, indignant. "Only Great Deer knows Siski."

Heat lightning veins through black and blue clouds above. All those volts tug on my cosmic tongue. "You think praying to The Great Deer absolves you of all your sins?"

Yellow eyes search the sky. "I not a sinner."

"Self-denial is one of our best traits."

"I am as The Great Deer made me."

"A killer?"

Guilt isn't any stranger to Siski's face. This expression, though, I'm not sure what it is. Not pity. She doesn't feel sorry for herself, the way I do sometimes. Not shame. The woman is as alien to that, as we are to this world of bones.

Doubt.

"You don't know," I say. "Do you?"

She splashes sand at me. "Kitty Cat knows nothing."

"You don't know what you are, or why you were made this way. You're as The Great Deer made you, but when your pack saw the real you, they were afraid. They rejected you. You've been hiding behind a projection for most of your life."

"Silly Kitty."

"I get it. I never showed anyone the real me. I don't know I ever knew her. You're right. It's been the only way I could cope and... sometimes... I don't know. I don't know if this person I am now is the mask. Was she what The Ever acquired? Was she all that survived?"

You want, and then you fear. You fear, and you close yourself off. You close down, and you want. The only thing you're eating is yourself, alive. I get so tired of myself, sometimes.

I just want to be, like Siski.

Electric antlers branch through the sky. Manic light casts confused shadows across the desert.

"I told myself I changed, but I didn't," I say. "I mean, I opened up. I let Abi in. But I'm holding on to this fear of being seen. Being known. I'm afraid if someone discovers who I am, I'll just vanish. Do you know what I mean? Like that riddle. What was it? *What disappears as soon as you say its name?* Kit."

I laugh, though I don't know why.

"I can't fix this. I can't take all my problems apart and put them back together into new problems. I want to change, Siski. I want to do good, from the start. I want to be better."

"You can only be what you are."

I shake my head. "I would have said the same, but then I became an alien. I became a wolf. We can change more than our spots and stripes, Siski. We can change our hearts."

Her fangs flash. "So weak..."

"Is it weakness to pray for forgiveness?"

"I pray only for strength."

So heavy now. "Does The Great Deer answer you, Siski?"

All the doubt vanishes from her eyes. "The Great Deer provides. I give life, as he gives life to me."

"So that's a no?"

She crouches low on all fours, ready to pounce. "You will give life to Siski. I will take your power. I will return home. The Great Deer provides for me. I will scratch your likeness on the rock of the cave, Star Walker, and remember you well."

I gather up a handful of dust. That's all that's left now. Ash and bone. "The Great Deer doesn't answer me. I pray... I hope I have some soul or some purpose... that there's a reason that all of this happened. But there's no answer."

Her smile breaks on her fangs. "Great Deer ignores you."

I stand. "There's no answer... because we're the answer. Why? Why is any of this happening? Why do we hurt? Why do we hurt others? We ask the sky. The ground. Pictures of Jesus. Elvis. A great deer. There's no answer. There's no reason. There's no contract. Just life, given. We've been given a gift, Siski. We have to give it back."

"I give," she says.

"Not your life."

"Siski survives. Siski provides."

"How can you give lives you've stolen back? You pray to The Great Deer because you take what you need. You don't need, Siski. You just want. And you corrupt your faith to justify it."

A growl builds in her throat. "Shut your mouth."

"It's not enough to make symbolic gestures or say hollow words. You have to live your principles. You have to let people see that void in you, and invite them in. That's the only way. That is the only way it will ever be filled. With love."

Her claws sink into the sand. "Love is weakness."

"I am weak," I say. "I am not perfect, or all-knowing, or all-powerful. I can't do this on my own. I don't want to. I want to go home. I want to marry my girlfriend. I want to be part of making something, not just fixing what's broken."

Doubt creeps back in her eyes. Desire. Not for power or energy or revenge. Something more. "We're not broken."

"I'm not the only one wearing a mask, Siski."

"Run, Kitty Cat."

"I'm not running anymore."

Fire blazes in her eyes. "I kill you, Kitty Cat."

I hold out my hand. "I forgive you."

Anger creases her uncertainty. She reaches out and a vicious magnetic tug forces me to my knees. Siski leaps across the sand and digs her nails into my limpid chest.

Fire builds in her. Light burns through me. Like the wind being knocked out of me; like the world breaking. I'm breaking, into cracks of flame, lightning crowning the sky in thunder

ba–dumm

ba–DUMM

BA–DUMM

THIRTEEN

Hah.

Bye, bye, Kitty. Power surges through me. Her power. Whole again. The dead crystal of her Myriad falls to the earth, in the cushion of her clothes. No trouble, Kitty Cat. You're part of making something, just like you wanted.

You're making dust.

The other Ever stranded here didn't have my power. My quick. My smarts. I unclip one of Kit's beacon things off her emptied belt. Hmm. Why didn't she use it? She could have used it with enough power. Strange thing. I twist the center. Light blinks from it.

Heh.

With the power I drew from her Myriad, I claw open the magnetic field of this boneyard and shred a portal back to the In Between. Make noise, little beacon. Make a trail. Find me, Little Rabbit. Lead your Kitty Cat home. The red blinky thing on the beacon turns green. They've acquired my signal back on Earth. I scamper to the edge of the portal. Quick home, now.

I look back.

I dig a hole quick in the bone dust, and I bury Kitty Cat's Myriad.

Only right. I give life to you, as you give life to me. I claw her likeness in the bleached surface of the tusk.

Forgive me.

The portal flickers. Hurry. I race through the portal, into the In Between. A signal from home guides me through the confusion. An ocean between oceans. Worlds between worlds. Doors between doors. So many dimensions to hunt.

Soon.

I will interface with the core. Then I will have all the secrets. All the power. I will have all the universe to hunt. The signal intensifies. Portals open and close, erratically. Ripples of the core of the ship, a branch of a fallen tree, pestering the surface of the river. I reach out with my magnetic field and hold one open. Tin Man and Little Rabbit wait on the other side, hopeful. They think I'm her.

They think it's over.

I like it when hope drains out of a victim's eyes. What does it feel like, knowing you're going to die? Knowing all is lost, and you are bones now. Dust. Mine. Does it sit cold in the belly? Hard? Is it like eating snow, in a famished winter, your stomach numb to everything but hunger? I've never known such fear, even trapped in the Myriad.

I never will.

Tin Man bends like a reed under my telekinetic gale. Little Rabbit thumps through the lab, a blur, and then I grab all the iron in her blood. Hee. I hold her in the air, limbs mad like a little cur under my paw, and then I slam her into the floor.

I lick the blood off her face. "You got a secret, Rabbit."

Her broken hands claw at my face. "Where is she..."

"It'll be fun killing you... again, and again, and again."

A treat for later. I leave Abi among the ruin and rise to the ringed deck around the core. I fleeced Kitty Cat of all her energy. I took her memories, too. All those files. Digital boxes. Ones and zeroes.

Code progressions.

The terminal screen blinks, unlocked. Goody. I tap a holographic symbol. Others appear. Keys to the kingdom. Abi's voice echoes out of the well of the ship. *Don't.* Every path has led to this moment. All my running. All my hunting.

All my bloodletting.

This is my destiny. The Great Deer made me for this purpose. I will be the ultimate hunter. I will give, and give all, as all has been given to me. I will be strong.

I will be Ever.

I touch my hand to the screen. Endless voices scream at me. Countless hands tear me like skin from bone into their limitlessness, but I am not the Kitty Cat that denies. I am the wolf that feeds. I can fill the void. I can quell this hunger. I can be the hunter Ever. Permit me, as you did her, and the ship will leave this world barren.

We will scour the stars.

I wrest from the terminal, renewed. Restored. The world quakes with the ship's impatience. So much hunger. Shush. Wait now. This world, and then the others. The earth will be bones, like the world I left Kitty Cat on. First Little Rabbit. Then the traitor wolves. The city. The wilds of humanity.

Yes.

Broken crystal dances around me in magnetic excitation, smashing, crashing, fusing into energy molten that ribbons around the active core. I hold my hands to the jubilant air.

Free. I'm free.

Fusing crystal weaves into the shape of a woman. The shape of my shadow. "Kitty Cat..."

She stands on the deck, this look in her eyes. Empty. Sad. "It didn't have to be this way, Siski."

"I buried you..."

This light in her heart. My light. "We are Ever."

Furious light surges through my claws. No more. No more phantoms. No more shadows. No more Kitty Cat. I pounce. I crash hard against something. I can't see it.

What is this?

Glass? Scratches disappear as fast as I make them. Something blocks me from her. Some kind of barrier. I turn around and run into it again. Every direction. The core disappears. The ship. Everything disappears like morning fog, except for Kitty Cat, kneeling down, looking into my cage.

I'm trapped.

"Thank you," Kit says. "Anwar."

The Tiger leans down beside Kitty Cat and looks at me the way people do their pets. Right in the eyes. Like they can see something past the fur and teeth and animal in them. Something familiar. His smile has that human smugness of thinking they're in control. I pound on this invisible barrier. Let me out.

The Tiger smiles. "Bad dog."

What did he do? Tricked me. Made me see. What did I see? That wasn't the ship I interfaced with. What was it? The Tiger taps on the barrier and I flinch. I'm inside something. What am I inside of? Think. Siski's smart. Clever. Little Rabbit comes close. Tin Man. His fingers clack, and he stoops over like the rest, looking down on me, looking in on me, and his hands trail wire and cable from – from me.

I'm hooked up to something.

Tin Man checks numbers and graphs on the computer screens assembled behind him. "Transfer complete. Siski's consciousness is completely within the backup positronic matrix."

Backup?

Cables trail through broken fragments of crystal to the lifeless form of a junky old robot. Kitty Cat goes to the screens, sunset orange as yellow fades from her red. Mismatched crystal fuses into pure garnet. She's in my body. I left my body.

She's still –

Kit puts her hand on the barrier. My prison. She says something, but I can't hear. Everything fades. Goes dark. Cables in Tin Man's hands. Power. I'm losing power. Great Deer.

I give life to you –

FOURTEEN

Gangly limbs slump as power drains out of the android. The heavy titanium body lists, and I catch it with a magnetic net. I didn't expect to survive Siski. I planned it so I wouldn't.

Plans. I make them. Life revises them.

Siski separated us before I could trick her into the backup matrix. The ship junked me before I could fuse us back together. Only the wolf came back through the In Between.

I have no memory of the other Kit's fate. The last thing I remember is being halved from Siski, and then coming to, like out of an anesthesia fog, into her half of the Myriad. Strange.

I guess I really am part of this thing.

Siski isn't. Not anymore. Her consciousness transferred, flawlessly, into the backup matrix exactly as I intended. As powerful a telepath as she is, I figured she'd see through Blind Tiger's ruse, but she was blind with power. She believed she was interfacing with the ship. Dead eyes stare back at me. Is she conscious? She can't be. Siski is like ALPHA was once, a file on a disc, memory frozen in the moment he was deactivated. She remains, preserved, inside the backup matrix. Without power, without any connection, she'll never get out. I tell myself this is humane. This is just.

This is necessary.

"ALPHA," I say. "Secure the matrix. Lock it away. Encrypt it with a code I won't ever figure out."

His fingers jitter. "Perhaps the most secure place for Siski would be in the vault, in the Blackwood Building."

I shake my head. "Things don't keep there."

His movement is slow and respectful as he removes the matrix from the exposed cranium of the android. ALPHA cradles the crystalline structure in his hands and ambles away.

Abi brushes my cheek. "You're ok?"

I bite my lip. "I will be."

Her voice trembles. "What do you remember?"

Separating. Surfacing, like I'd been held down underwater. Siski's thoughts are gone from the Myriad; from me. My memory is an incomplete puzzle, missing the pieces of hers.

"Not much," I say.

Her lips linger on mine, her relief tempered with something like regret. I don't know why. Before I can get the question out of my mouth, she's gone, away with ALPHA, securing Siski.

"We do make a good team," Anwar says, replacing his silken cape over his shoulders. "Reconsider, Kit."

I have enough on my mind right now. "It's just business."

He smiles. "I could have been on the board."

"Priorities."

"We could have helped people."

I nod. "I will."

"How will you build your engine, without my support?"

A text buzzes on my PEAL. Specialist Callahan. *I got an idea. Should I just blurt the whole thing at you or drinks?*

Astronomers and physicists share discoveries all the time. I've shared information I've learned from The Ever with some of them. The work continues, beyond me, with resources I just don't have. If I gave away my work, I wouldn't have control over it anymore. But then neither would Blind Tiger.

No one would.

"I'll figure it out," I say.

He strokes his chin. "You will. I see it."

Anwar leaves the lab. What's left of it. So much work. I have to fix everything. Deck plates rattle back together into a ring around the core. I lock out the terminal and the ship seizes me again.

I repel the magnetic will of the core with my own. *No.*

We are Ever.

I keep thinking I've found some way of co-existing with you. I've been telling myself that my entire life. I can work with this. I can live with this. We can co-exist. Masks do more harm than good. They protect nothing but the pain they inflict on those who wear them.

I'm not the mask.

Do you understand? You can't suppress me or mold me into a shape that fits. You're not wearing me. *I am Ever. We are Kit.* And you can't bury me like you did the others.

The work must continue.

This is the work, I say, gesturing to the lab below. *Finding another way. Finding a better way.*

The work is the only way.

I don't believe that.

This is fixed.

The magnetic storm brewing in the core loses steam. This fight is over, for today at least. A chair rattles out of the twisted mess and I sit down, exhausted. Everything else can wait.

"Thanks for the lift," I say.

Callahan looks back from the pilot's seat of the skimmer, a light–shuttle common in the NASA fleet. "I owe you one. Which, we're square now. Flying fifteen minutes to drop you off in the Caribbean totally equals what you did for me."

I try to smile. "I figured it was a smart move to go easy on my powers for a while."

Callahan scratches the side of her neck. "You switching to Power Saving Mode isn't because of what you did with the shuttle, is it? I'd hate if we cost you some juice."

I lean against the back of her chair. "Oh, no. That wolf I told you about? She broke free and almost destroyed the world."

"Oh."

"Pretty average week, really."

She glances over her shoulder at Abi, back at the airlock, trying on astronaut suits while she has the chance. "So. You going to do it? You going to pop the question?"

I pat my empty jacket pocket. "I lost the ring."

"What?"

"I lost it in the scrum with Siski."

"So you're telling me I still have a shot?"

I smile. "You've got a wife, Callahan."

"Ah, she hates me. Yours lives for you. It takes a lot to make me jealous – I mean, I'm an astronaut – but the way Abi looks at you. The way she just does everything for you. You don't see it. I can tell by that wrinkle in your nose."

"We're just in love," I say.

"What's that like?"

I tap her shoulder. "Your wife is lovely."

"I should tell her that, sometimes. Might help." Callahan smiles. "You know, it might help Abi sometimes to take it easy. She doesn't want to develop something aggressively cancerous sitting under that heat lamp in the alien ship all the time. I mean, I'd be ok with it. It would totally be worth it."

"It's not like you have breasts, anyways."

She shakes her head. "Where have you been all my life?"

"It's the magnetism," I say.

"There's definitely an attraction."

"Radiation isn't a factor in the core, at least at minimal exposures. But the magnetic field, it's so strong in there, it will induce nausea and vertigo after a while."

Callahan cringes. "Is it safe to be flying with you? Is your magnetic field strong enough to do that?"

"After prolonged exposure. Why?"

"So does Abi get dizzy around you?"

Everything is still hazy after Siski, but I can't recall a moment when Abi has ever been sick around me. Much of our relationship has been conducted from opposite poles, me in the sky, her on the ground, each pulling on the other and each drawn to opposing forces. It was only lately, with the benefit of the other Kit, that we've spent real time together.

"I don't know," I say.

Callahan pulls back the throttle. "Coming up on our destination. That will be $125,000. Cash only."

I look back at Abi. "Did you bring your purse?"

A space helmet a couple sizes too big for Abi wobbles around her head. "Dude, I don't even own a purse."

Turquoise caresses amber. The yellow sun illuminates me, competing with the red of the Myriad, casting me a bit ginger. I nudge Abi. "Do I look like an empty beer bottle?"

She notches her sunglasses down. They're all she has on. "Well, you do have a message inside you."

"What does it say?"

Her hand laces mine. "No pets allowed."

I snort. "Actually, it's good we don't have a pet. That would probably end in disaster. Like everything else."

She sits up and rests her head on my shoulder. "Not everything is a disaster. We're here, aren't we?"

I kiss her. "We're here."

Seagulls harass me. I shoo them away with a magnetic push, but they hover in the air, borne by the breeze. White clouds bridge the sky. Airplanes glint above. Waves slope into shore. They crest, perfect and powerful, and then crash, destroyed.

I reach over to my jacket. "So... I had an idea of what I wanted to do today, but..."

Abi purses her lips. "Uh- huh."

"My ideas don't always translate from my head to reality. And what I've found... what I find, with you, Abi, is... my life is better, when I have no idea. I could have never imagined you."

She slips her sunglasses off. Tears in her eyes.

"I could have never imagined us. And I'm grateful for that. I'm grateful for you, Abi. We have something no one else has, and I think to try and fit it into what other people have maybe is a project I don't need to take on, so..."

Her nose wrinkles. "This is a long way to take a joke."

The tiny shard of the Myriad The Interdictor broke off lifts out of my jacket on my magnetic will, along with the chain I laced through it. I place it around her neck, the shard of my heart hanging over hers.

"You're my heart." I kiss her soft. "You're my life. Nothing will ever change that. Nothing can. I want us to be together, forever."

She takes me in her arms. "We will. We'll live, forever."

I hold her tight. "Forever."

Her heart beats against mine, *ba–dumm, ba–dumm, ba–dumm.* "I was so afraid I was going to lose you."

I close my hand around the shard, around the life that binds us. "You're never going to lose me."

"Do you promise?"

I cross our hearts. "I promise."

We make love. We sleep. We make love, we sleep, we laugh, we cry, we talk about the rest of our lives, and the waves live and die. Always, the water endures, and returns anew again and again. Nothing is lost. Nothing is broken.

Everything is as it should be.

I told myself I accepted what happened to me. My transformation. My evolution from just another ruin rat to Guardian Of The Derelicts. But I've been denying who I am. All this time, I've been telling myself, I'm Kit. I'm me, just with some added sprinkle. Some glitter. But that's not true.

Kit is gone.

But I'm not the mask, either. I'm not the wolf, prowling through the shadows, waiting for the moment to run free. I'm something more. Something else. I'm going to keep changing. I'm going to evolve, in ways I can't imagine. Change frightened me. Not because I didn't want it. Because I didn't know how to work it.

I can work this. I can be me. I found a way to handle Siski. Maybe I'll find a way to co-exist with The Ever.

Never say never.

FIFTY YEARS LATER

BA-DUMM

ARE YOU THE BULB? MA SAYS. OR ARE YOU THE LIGHT?

Her hand falls from my cheek and I fall back against the base of the great tusk. Half buried in dust. My suit an empty shell at my feet. Claw marks through my heart. Coriaceous feathers settling soft in the sand. Turtle–bird memories sinking within me.

No.

I'm still in the Bone Place. I'm still alive. But Siski – the Myriad glows in my chest. Mine again. The last time the Myriad shut down, it took years before it came back online. Decades.

Abi.

I have to get home. Siski went back. Did she see through my plan? Did she wake the ship? My beacon. It's gone. Shit. I have no way of letting them know where I am. I can't find my way back. No. I could be on the other side of the galaxy. The universe.

I could be in another dimension.

Can I even get out of here? Did Siski? Or did she go dark trying to? I pull on my suit. The Myriad shines through a tattered E. I sift through the dust. I rattle the dead batteries of ancient Myriads, trying to find hers. The weight of what I can't do and don't know compresses me, down to my knees. Shadow stretch along with my fear. I'm as still as the bones of the desert. I'm as hard. But then the red sun sets, and the sand glints garnet.

The ring.

I still have the ring. Somehow, I'll find a way home. Some way, I'll get back to Abi. I'll give her this ring. My heart. I'm going to fix this. I'm not shutting down. I'm not helpless. I'm not afraid.

That was the other Kit.

THE EVER

ABOUT THE AUTHOR

DARBY HARN is a novelist, freelance writer, and podcaster. His novels include *Ever The Hero*, *The Judgement of Valene*, *Nothing Ever Ends*, and *A Country Of Eternal Light*. His short fiction appears in *Strange Horizons*, *Interzone*, *Shimmer*, and other venues.

Stay Up To Date At
darbyharn.com

 twitter.com/DarbyHarn

goodreads.com/darby_harn

amazon.com/author/darbyharn

ACKNOWLEDGMENTS

The Eververse continues to surprise me.

I originally wrote the first three novels in a spasm of energy and excitement and wasn't sure at the time what the future of the series would be. I did know I missed Kit after writing two books about other characters, so I wrote started writing this story about her and Empowered wolves. One novella led to another and then I was writing lots of novellas and stories, only a few of which appear here.

The stories ultimately helped me understand the shape and plan of what was becoming my own personal sandbox. These stories also helped me a great deal personally, as through them I began consciously working through the fact that Kit is autistic.

So am I.

I did not know until later in life and I have struggled to understand and accept it. I don't have a language for it, so for a person whose only real identity is in words, it was terrifying. I did not want to acknowledge this aspect of myself, as I didn't understand it and when I do acknowledge it, the results haven't been successful. I also generally have an allergy talking about myself.

I resisted the idea of openly acknowledging Kit's autism, though readers had picked up on it from the beginning. That was mostly due to my uncertainty at the time. This understanding of myself is a process, and Kit is in many ways how I've been processing it. Processing it is difficult because an aspect of my experience is what I've been calling parenthetical thinking. Thoughts jam up. They

Russian doll inside others. They confuse. This leads to parenthetical speech and parenthetical behavior.

Now it's led to a parenthetical novel, which I suppose is apt. This book tucks in between books one and two in a way that's probably inevitable given the way I work. I've been writing my entire life and understood I had a gift, on some level. But I never felt I was able to realize it or put the pieces together in any way until these last few years. I finally realized the problems I face and being conscious of them allowed me to try to begin to untangle the knots.

Being conscious of my autism has also helped to work through an understanding of how to begin to acknowledge it elsewhere in my life. Adult diagnoses of autism remain difficult to obtain and particularly if you are a woman or a person of color. In places that don't value education in general, autistic children suffer even more.

I understand now the value in an autistic character, an autistic superhero, and if she can provide anyone any measure of hope or self-understanding then I owe it to that person to say.

I owe it to Kit.

This book would have been impossible without the continued support and feedback of Polly Brewster, Cassie Gruetman, Shelly Campbell, Ben Kral, Sugu Althomsons, Wayne Santos, Jennifer Lane, Al Hess, Essa Hansen, and Sunyi Dean.

Thank you all so much.

- Darby

ALSO BY DARBY HARN

A Country Of Eternal Light

The Book Of Elizabeth

EVERVERSE

Ever The Hero

The Judgment Of Valene

Nothing Ever Ends